A Dec Wee Man

By

George Donald

CHAPTER ONE

I cannot say with any certainty when I decided to do the things that I did, but I know that the first murder I committed was a split-second decision, not something that had been lingering in my head for a while. I mean, it's not as if I go around *planning* to murder people, you know what I mean.

Of course, like most people that commit such a rash and spontaneous act, I didn't think about what I was doing at the time or even consider as I later did that I should have maybe have made him suffer first and put him through the agony that he had inflicted on my old pal Scooby.

Then after I killed him the worrying part of my concern was that I'm not a young man anymore and not only was I surprised that I murdered him, but I had to be very careful not to get caught by his mates. After all, I'm not a hard man and it's not as if I'm at an age that I can mix it with the young people that peddle that kind of nonsense, the drugs I mean that he was probably involved in.

Besides, I definitely did not want to get myself caught and arrested by the polis. Aye, hands up here and to be honest, yes, I did it, but let me tell you, I'm not sorry and because of that I'd still like to remain free and out of the jail.

The only thing is, how am I going to go about it, staying free I mean?

Oh, I suppose that you will be wondering what I'm on about, so I'm thinking that this is a good time to explain exactly who I am and what I did. I'm not an educated man, so if I just tell you the story in my own words, then you can do me a wee favour and have a bit of patience and tolerance with me and then maybe you'll understand what I'm talking about, eh?

Right then, I'll start at the beginning with my name and tell you a wee bit about myself.

I'm James McGrath or as I'm better known here in Pollok where I live, Jimmy McGrath, no middle name. My old Ma didn't think I needed one. When I was a wee boy my Da who was called Robert or Bobby to his pals and he called me 'the wee barra'. That's a kind of Glasgow saying that parents sometimes call the youngest wean in the family.

I came fourth in my lot. Fifth really, if you want to count the baby that didn't make it out of the maternity. I've an older brother Eddie who was the firstborn and I did have two big sisters. The baby boy that died came after my big sister Liz, who was a right good looking lassie, so that meant he would have been the middle wean if he'd lived. So far I've outlived my older brother and poor Liz who passed away when she was just forty-five years of age. The other older sister, Sara, well she moved to New Zealand with her man when she was just nineteen and not long after both my folks died, her letters just sort of stopped coming so I've no idea what she's doing these days.

Anyway, we'll get back to the story and me.

Right, by way of description, let me say that I'm a couple of months short of my sixtieth birthday, about five feet five inches tall in my stocking soles, thin as a whippet and what thinning grey hair I have left is plastered down with Brylcreem. I'm always clean-shaven and proud to say I still have all my own teeth though they're maybe not as bright as they once were. In these days of casual dress, I don't usually wear a tie unless it's something special or maybe on the odd occasion when I'm going to Mass, but by habit I always wear a clean shirt and I iron my trousers with a razor sharp crease. I've never been a man to wear denims or anything like that.

I've lived most of my life in the same mid-terraced house in Hapland Road where I live now. It was my parent's home when they got married and it's the house that I grew up in.

I remember my childhood as being a happy one. I was no different to any other young lad growing up in Pollok and if you don't know the place, it's a large sprawling council estate on the south side of Glasgow. Physically among my pals, I was usually the weedy one of the bunch that I hung around with and to be honest, I didn't grow that much more either.

My teenage years were spent with my mates at the dancing and in the pubs and that's where I learned that four or five pints definitely weren't the best aphrodisiac to attract the women. Not that I was particularly successful with the girls anyway and I never quite understood what Jeannie, the lass who became my wife, saw in me. When my father died, my new wife Jean and I moved in to be with my mother to see her through the first few months. I say Jean, but that was what we joked was her Sunday name, but I always called her Jeannie.

To be honest, moving in with my Ma wasn't too much of a hardship after moving away from the wee, damp-ridden pokey one bedroom flat we had in Langlands Road down in Govan; a single-end they were called in those days. The tenement building was demolished in the late seventies; part of what the council called the 'Govan Regeneration'. I'm shaking my head when I tell you this because I still hear people from Govan talk about 'community in the tenements' and the 'fine big Victorian rooms'. Short memories some folk have, forgetting about the chilling dampness, the communal toilet on the half-landing shared by three families, the open rat infested middens round the back courts and the lack of central heating that meant in the freezing winter, one tenant sniffed and the whole close caught the flu.

Jeannie and I had only been married for just over a year and we were just getting to really know each other. Ours had been what used to be called a shotgun wedding, meaning she was pregnant, so it was off to Martha Street with my folks and her best pal as bridesmaid. My best man was my pal Scooby, but I'll tell you about him in a wee while. Jeannie's bridesmaid was a work pal. Her folks didn't attend because being strict Catholic, they were ashamed their daughter got pregnant out of wedlock. She was awfully upset about that, but I'm pleased to tell you my mother God bless her, treated Jeannie like her own daughter and with my old Da, they made the whole day about her. Different times in those days.

There was no fancy reception for us two newlyweds; no, it was just high tea for six at the big hotel in George Square next to Queen Street railway station, but for the life of me I can't recall what it was called in those days.

We had been courting for about two years and planning to get married, but the pregnancy just happened and if the truth be told it was bloody carelessness on my part. The sad thing was our wee baby was never born for Jeannie aborted in her sixth month and the doctors at the Southern General said she couldn't have any weans after that because of the damage done to her womb during the operation to save her life.

I never told her and God forgive me; if I had been asked to decide, well, my Jeannie meant more to me than the baby. I don't know if that makes me a bad person, but I couldn't have lived without my wife.

Anyway, it's said and done now so there's no need to rake over the coals about it, eh?

The doctors kept her in for a couple of days because of the bleeding and when she got out of the maternity ward I brought her back to the flat in Govan. While she rested for a few weeks to recover her strength, I went back to my job with the Corpy or to give it its proper name, the Corporation of the City of Glasgow, but these days it's called the Glasgow District Council. In those days I was working as a binman out of the depot in Helen Street. I know what you're thinking, that it wasn't the most glamourous of jobs, but it kept body and soul together and besides as my old Da used to say, every job brings its own dignity.

Jeannie too was working with the Corpy as a typist so all in all we were doing okay with our two wages.

We had met at the dancing in Sauchiehall Street. Back then the name had been changed to Tiffany's to give it a wee bit of glamour, but everybody still called it the Locarno. I'm laughing when I tell you this because it's been a long time since I've been to the dancing. I'm sure I heard a few years back that they closed the place as a dancehall and turned it into one of them swanky casino's.

Gambling? That's a mugs game as far as I'm concerned.

Sorry, I'm rambling a wee bit, aren't I?

Anyway, back to what I was telling you.

So there I am working away on the bin lorries and Jeannie recuperating at home when I get word that my Da, wee Bobby McGrath had keeled over at his job in Fairfield's Shipyards in Govan. Well, it's a bit like I was saying earlier. It was *known* as Fairfield's, but a couple of years earlier had become the Upper Clyde Shipbuilders. My Da had worked there as a riveter all his life when suddenly without any kind of warning, he keels over with this hell of a pain in his chest.

Dead before the ambulance arrives.

So there's me, twenty-two at the time and newly married, arranging my Da's funeral because my older brother Eddie and his family is in Australia. Him and his wife had packed up years earlier and travelled out there on the ten pound passage and hadn't been home since. Between you and me though? No sad loss as far as I'm concerned and Australia was welcome to him.

I used to get the occasional letter, but they were few and far between and usually it was him telling me what a great guy he is and how much money he was making. The last letter that arrived from him was almost six years ago and informed me that Eddie and his missus had divorced and he'd re-married, but then I got a letter from his new wife, whose name I don't even recall, to inform me that Eddie died shortly after the honeymoon.

Honestly, it was like reading about a stranger and to my embarrassment, I wasn't that overly concerned. Jeannie nagged at me that I should reply to the letter, but to my shame I never did. Anyway, back to the story about my Da. Well, the neighbours told me later my mother Mary collapsed when the polis turned up at the door to tell her my Da had died at his work.

Physically, she wasn't a strong woman my Ma. Loving and faithful to my Da, yes, but if I'm honest with you, a wee timid woman who lived for her husband and her two sons and two daughters and hardly stepped over the door except to go to Mass or to clean the chapel. I *say* her two sons. I did what I could for her, but that rotten bastard Eddie, forgive my language, he never even sent Mass Cards for my Da or Ma's funeral services or replied to the letters I sent telling him they had died so you'll maybe understand why I wasn't overly concerned about *him* turning his toes up. My big sister Liz was a good help at that time, but I'll tell you more about Liz in a minute. My other sister, Sara, rot her soul; she's a right piece of work, she is. When Da died, she sent a letter from New Zealand asking if Da had life insurance and if there was to be a payout, would it be split four ways.

I didn't reply to *that* letter either.

Honestly, some people.

In the days that followed my Da's death, it was obvious my Ma wasn't going to cope on her own and well, the house in Hapland Road was just too big for her on her own. The house is mid-terraced with three bedrooms so it kind of made sense when me and Jeannie

offered to move in with my Ma. My sister Liz was happy enough
with the arrangement because in truth it meant she didn't have to
keep running across the city to Pollok to check on our old Ma. Liz
had a flat in the west end of Glasgow over by Byres Road that I only
ever visited once when she needed a built-in wardrobe dismantled. It
was a huge place with three bedrooms and though she worked in an
office in the city centre, I always suspected that her wage wasn't *that*
good that she could afford a flat that size in such an affluent area.
What she did let slip once was that she had a gentleman friend. I
think if I'm being honest, she was a kept woman and I'm guessing
that the guy was probably married, though I never met him. Besides,
Liz never interfered in our lives so I didn't think it right to interfere
in hers.

Sadly, when the cancer took her I never saw or heard of her
gentleman friend visiting the hospital and she was gone in just a few,
short weeks. Awful it was, seeing her waste away so quickly like
that.

Ma, Jeannie and I were the only relatives that attended the funeral,
though there were a number of family friends and people from Liz's
work that included some men, so her gentleman friend might have
been any one of them.

I never did find out, but among the floral tributes that day was a
large one bouquet with a card that I kept and still have somewhere in
a drawer up the stairs, because it had written upon it, 'To The One I
Truly Love.'

I'm pleased to say that Ma and Jeannie got on well. Jeannie's folks
lived in Skye, because that's where she was from, so she didn't have
any family living locally in Glasgow and my mother, having lost Liz
and with Sara so far away, kind of adopted Jeannie as her own.

So like I said, it made sense for us to move in with Ma and anyway,
the flat we rented in Crossloan Road down in Govan was a shithole
and because it was privately rented, the landlord charged us an arm
and a leg for it. We were on the Corpy's housing list, but if you're
old enough to remember what it was like in those days trying to get a
Corporation house or a tenement flat, it was pure murder and really,
you needed to know a councillor or have the money for a back-
hander to get moved up the list.

So the week after my old Da is laid to rest in St Convals Cemetery
outside Barrhead, Jeannie and I packed what meagre belongings we

had and at my mother's insistence, we moved into the biggest of the three bedrooms at Hapland Road.

"I'm on my own now, son," I remember her telling me. "It's not as if I need the space now your Da's away to Heaven."

Like I told you, a strict, practising Catholic was my Ma and I think that's another reason she was so fond of Jeannie, because like her my wife followed the Faith and every Sunday or Feast day, dragged me with her to Mass along the road at St Convals chapel.

To my shame, now that I'm on my own I have kind of fell away from attending the church and maybe that's not a bad thing because what I've did will likely *not* be forgiven by God. I still call myself a Catholic, but like a lot of folk, I've questioned my Faith through the years and nowadays I think I'm more agnostic, than Catholic.

That said though I still occasionally go and bend the knee at St Convals; kind of keeping my options open, if you will.

I'm getting a wee bit ahead of myself here, so where was I?

Oh, aye, right then.

The week after my Da's funeral service, Jeannie and I arrived at Hapland Road with three suitcases, a half dozen boxes of ornaments and dishes and a free standing mirror that Jeannie had got as a bargain at the Glasgow Barra's.

Oh, and we were skint too because the last of our money went on the final rent payment.

Now, in those days I wasn't driving and everything we had was brought there in my best mate Scooby's wee Austin van, or to give Scooby his Sunday name, Michael Toner.

Don't ask me when we started calling him Scooby, but as far back as Missus McKinley's class at Damshot Primary School, that's how he was known and even his wife Alice calls him by that name.

A good guy is Scooby, though sometimes partial to more than just a few halves down at Howden's Pub in Paisley Road West and then he becomes a drunken, maudlin wreck and the worst singer of IRA songs in Glasgow. When he was younger, those republican songs got Scooby into more fights than Mohammed Ali ever had, though if memory serves me correctly, Scooby's yet to win one of his.

Saying that, him and his missus Alice and their three weans, young Michael, Charles or wee Chic as he's called and Shona, the apple of her Da's eye, have been good friends to me through the years and been there for me, not just for the loss of my folks, but also during the terrible months when Jeannie faded from my life.

I think it's fair to say if I hadn't their support…well, let's just say I'm so very glad I did.

So, I'm taking a deep breath here and continuing my story; there's me and Jeannie now living with my Ma in Hapland Road and to be fair, I didn't expect that things would go as smoothly as they did. For the short life that she had left, my Ma continued to be the housewife she always had been and it meant that when Jeannie and I arrived home from work there was always a hot meal on the table and sandwiches made that night for our lunch break the next day at work.

Of course, Jeannie did her fair share of the housework and the cleaning while I attended to the front and back gardens and cleaning the windows and suchlike. All in all it wasn't a bad set-up, for my mother also recognised that Jeannie and I needed our wee bit of privacy so Ma settled herself into the small room that was the furthest away from the big room.

What she couldn't hear, she couldn't blush at and one of the first things I did with my next wage was replace the mattress for the old one fairly kicked up a racket when Jeannie and me were making a right good go at it, if you get my meaning.

As the winter months drew close that year, it became obvious to Jeannie and me that my Ma wasn't herself and after much persuasion, I finally got her down to the doctor's surgery at the roundabout on Braidcraft Road. We had a bit of a laugh when we had to re-register her there because she had never attended for anything, preferring to treat herself with what she called her own medicines. Nowadays I think folks call it homeopathic medicine or as my Jeannie used to call it, homicidal witchcraft.

Anyway, the doctor gave her a prescription for some ailment and for the life of me now, I can't think what that ailment was. Jeannie used to tell me my memory and listening skills was a man thing; in one ear and out the other.

Now to let you understand, I left school at fifteen and like I told you at the start of my story, I'm not an educated man, but it seemed obvious to me that my Ma just missed my Da dreadfully. After his death, I think that she just gave up and when she died nine months after him, I'm of the opinion it was of a broken heart, but they're not going to put that on a death certificate, are they? Yes, I know, for a wee while she had a lease of life looking after Jeannie and me, but that soon faded.

She really did miss my Da.

Fortunately, one of the precautions my Ma insisted on taking in the months before her death was one rainy day she made me take her in a taxi to the Corporation housing office up at the Barrhead roundabout and she signed her house over to me. Of course, the wee lassie that we spoke with tried to bully my Ma, telling her that it just wasn't on, that there was all sorts of regulations and that I needed to be on the list for such and such a time. I forget how long it was supposed to be, but none of that mattered to my Ma.

Do you remember me telling you what a wee timid woman she was? Well, by God, you should have seen her *that* day.

"Listen hen," I recall her poking a finger at the lassie, "my man's died and I'm a widow woman now. My son and his wife are caring for me in a house too big for one woman. I'm doing the Corpy a favour by sharing my home with them. Besides that, he's earning a wage and will be paying the rent for God knows how long because with the pittance the Government give us widows, I can't afford it on my pension. So, it's only right that it's my Jimmy's name on the rent book, understand?"

The lassie just shook her head, my Ma and I signed some forms and that was me now the Corporation tenant of my own home. Sad to say and it still brings a lump to my throat because my dear wee Ma was only with Jeannie and me for another three months before she passed away and joined my Da in the plot at St Convals Cemetery, up in Barrhead.

Well, as the years passed, Jeannie and I settled into our life here in Pollok, getting on with our neighbours and minding our own business.

I stayed with the Corpy or the Council as they are now for another few years and then an opening arose within the education department and I moved from being a binman to working as a school janitor's assistant at Bellarmine Secondary School in Priesthill. The money was a wee bit better and as it was a big school, there was three janitors employed there, me being the junior man working with Pete McGuire who was the boss and Donnie McKay, Pete's charge hand, but who was a right sleekit wee bastard; excuse my French again.

Pete was a good boss and divvied the workload fairly between us. The problem was McKay was a lazy bugger and I always thought him to be a bit of a pervert, the way he would watch the young lassies and take every opportunity to talk to them. He used to hang about outside the girls toilets and give out fags and I think the only reason that Pete didn't report him was that McKay had a wife and a young family and Pete was worried that if McKay lost his job, it would be his wife and weans that would suffer.

Pete was a good man, but not so good at confrontation and when he *should* have put the foot down with McKay, he backed away.

I tried to avoid working with McKay and if I'm being honest, it irked me that Pete and I would sometimes end up covering for the sod, making sure that work that *he* was supposed to have completed was in fact, done.

As it happened McKay tried it on with one of the cleaners, a young lassie that was a bit dolly dimple. She went home that night and told her mother about McKay touching her under her overalls. What I later heard was the mother complained to the headmaster who in turn told Pete. Cutting a long story short, Pete had no option but to inform his district supervisor of the complaint against McKay who was then given the choice; be sacked or accept a move to another post. Talk about the council looking after one of their own.

The last I heard about him he was operating a grass-cutting machine somewhere over in one of the big parks in the north side of the city.

I tell you this though, no sad loss that bugger and if it had been me, I'd have reported him to the polis at Brockburn Road, bleeding pervert that he probably still is.

As it happened, McKay's removal from Bellarmine and Pete's pending retirement put me into what they call pole position to take over the running of the janitorial duties at the school. Pete was kind enough to give me a really good reference and though there was a bit of an interview, it was more or less inferred that the job was mine. Or so I had thought.

As it turned out, there was an interview process and to be honest, I've never been very good at those sorts of things. Jeannie was very supportive and ironed my suit and cut my hair the night before the interview with the district supervisor, but it didn't matter; I made a real hash of it.

The guy that got the job was called Dennis Morrison and had come over from a school in the north of the city. I heard a whisper that his uncle was a local councillor, but maybe I'm just looking for an excuse for my own failure because to be fair to him, Dennis wasn't bad at the job and turned out to be a good gaffer.

It was round about that time that I got into reading books. Like I told you earlier, I had left school at fifteen and I wasn't really a reader, but Jeannie introduced me to our local library up at the Braidcraft Roundabout and I used to visit there with her. I was right into the cowboy stories, Louis L'Amour and Zane Grey and writers like that and I liked some of the war stories too.

Then of course, there were the pictures. Jeannie and me would go to the movies every Friday night down at the Mosspark Picture House, but the old cinema was tore down about nineteen seventy-three or four and they built an employment centre there.

Our favourite actor was 'The Duke', big John Wayne and I don't think we ever missed any of his films. Nowadays you can buy his films on DVD for a few pounds in the shops. Aye, he was definitely our favourite though we did like James Stewart as well.

Anyway, moving on and I hope that I'm not boring you with this story.

So, like I told you Dennis got the top job, but they made me the charge hand and took on an apprentice as the third janny, a lad called Willie Ross.

We worked well as a team for a couple of years then my big break came. The district supervisor popped in one day and took me aside to explain that I hadn't previously been ready to take charge of the janitorial duties in a big school, but asked if I would be interested in running my own school, a primary next to Leithland Avenue.

Would I?

I was that excited I think I could hardly speak. The supervisor told me that the janny was retiring and they wanted a young man in there, somebody who lived locally for call-outs and was prepared to stay at the school for a good few years. I'd be working on my own, he told me and not part of a team, but I don't think I let him finish because I was nodding my head and pumping his hand up and down and thanking him.

Well, you're talking about a brisk, five minute walk from my house in Hapland Road to the school so that also meant no travelling expenses, another wee saving towards the motor car that I was hankering after.

"Oh, aye," I had grinned like an idiot. "I'm your man, sir," I told the supervisor.

I was dead excited when I went to meet the old janny and the headmistress Missus Benson the next day and again I was wearing my neatly pressed suit.

The school itself wasn't new, built round about the early sixties, but I was in my element. For the first time in my life I was to be my own boss.

Well, other than running after Miss Benson I mean and let me tell you from the outset, she was a right old fashioned headmistress. A dyed in the wool spinster, Miss Benson had one of them sarcastic tongues that could rip the paint from the wall and if she took a dislike to you; well, that was your goose well and truly cooked.

One thing that stood out about her though was she had a face like a well skelped arse. I mean, she wasn't just rosy cheeked; it looked like she'd dipped her coupon into a pan of hot fat. Oh aye, It was pretty obvious to me from the outset that Miss Benson liked her wee dram or should I say, her half bottle for breakfast, lunch and dinner. As for her vocabulary, she used words that I'd never heard of and it seemed to me she took delight in bullying her staff. The teachers lived in fear of her while the other school staff, the cleaners and the dinner ladies; well, they just kept out of her way.

I remember one young lassie started there as a trainee teacher and heavens, did she give that wee lass a hard time. My God, at one point I thought I would have to call an ambulance, for the poor soul fainted dead away in front of her class when old Benson gave her a right tongue-lashing. I was in the corridor outside the classroom and heard it all and you know what? It was because Miss Benson was annoyed that the kids didn't get to their feet quick enough when she entered the room.

Aye, a real harridan was Miss Benson.

Anyway, I started working at the school the next week and I have to tell you that Miss Benson aside, it was the happiest time of my working life. Not only was I in sole charge of the school maintenance, supervising the cleaners and running the lads football team, but there was a fair wee bit of overtime when I was supposed to be off duty because often the school opened at night for parent meetings, PTA fundraising dances and sometimes adult education classes. And of course I also got callout pay when the police chased the weans off the roof or the very occasional burglary when the local neds would break in to vandalise the classrooms or steal what they could. It was because of this type of callout I got to know some of the local polis and to be fair, some of them were all right and sometimes during the day would drop by to speak with the kids about road safety or just drop by for a cuppa in my janny's wee room. One of them was a really nice young lad, Craig Wallace. Craig had been a policeman for just over eight years and was married with a wee girl and a baby son. He and I hit it off right away and he'd often pop in either with a neighbour, as he called his partner or on his own and sometimes bring a packet of digestive. Occasionally if he was on during the weekend, he'd stop by the house and always brought a cake or a bar of Cadbury's dark chocolate for Jeannie, her favourite.

I like Craig, but if I'm being very honest he's a bit of a bum and a worse gossip than an old woman. He's a got a story for every occasion and sometimes I wonder if half of them aren't made up and sometimes I think he just says the first thing that comes into his head. That aside though he's not a bad lad, though a wee bit full of himself. I'm sure you'll have known people like him.

Through the years that I was the school janny, I must have seen thousands of weans pass through the school and like all weans are, most were a bit cheeky but not really bad. Well, like I said, most of them anyway.

I once heard it said that children grow up and reflect their parents. If the father's a bully, the son will be too. Now I don't know if that's true of *all* children, but one of the kids who was in primary five when I started work there, certainly seemed to prove that saying to be right enough.

That wee boy was called Neil McMillan and if you've got the time and I'm not boring you, I'll tell you more about him as I go on.

CHAPTER TWO

So, how did I become a man intent on murder you might ask and particularly because from what I've told you so far you might be of the opinion that I seem to be a fairly decent sort of man.

I had just turned fifty-six when I lost my Jeannie.

I don't want to go on too long about what happened because to be frank, it still hurts being without her and the time of her illness was the worst of my life.

It had started about eighteen months earlier.

Jeannie hadn't been feeling too well and then coughed up a bit of blood. Eventually at my insistence and let me tell you, it was some terrible argument we had, she went to the doctor's surgery down at the roundabout; the same one my parents attended when they were alive.

Doctor Gillespie is a nice man. Whippet thin and bald, he smokes like a chimney and used to joke that if he didn't get through two packs of twenty a day, his lungs would burst from his body to look for their tobacco fix.

That first time Jeannie visited him he took some blood for analysis and told her to phone down the next week for the result of the test.

As it happened, four days later he phoned Jeannie at the house, a Tuesday it was and told her that the following day she was to get herself down to the Southern General Hospital down in Govan, that the results had come back and there was 'some concern' is what he called it.

Miss Benson wasn't too happy at me taking a day off work, but there was no way that I would let Jeannie go by herself, worried like we both were.

So, there's me and Jeannie in the consultants room and he's telling her that she needs to be admitted for more tests. I can't remember exactly what he said; all I do remember is Jeannie holding my hand and squeezing it so tightly I thought the bones would break.

She had some grip did my lass.

Now I know a lot of folk complain about the NHS and how badly run it is, but let me tell you this; Jeannie was admitted the next morning and they kept her for three days, pushing all sorts of needles into her. It fair broke my heart that she had to undergo this and each evening I visited, she looked paler and more drawn than I had ever seen her before.

I'm not ashamed to admit it but, aye, I was frightened.

The day she was discharged the consultant requested we visit him in his office.

"The news is very grave, Missus McGrath," he began and slowly took off his glasses to stare at her. "In fact, it's the worst of the worst, I'm afraid."

My heart was in my mouth and I remember that as I listened to him, my knees began shaking and even though it was Jeannie's diagnosis he was telling us about, it was she who comforted me.

"No more than three months," he had said.

He was a kind man, the consultant and of course had offered all sorts of therapies, treatments and medicines, but in the end admitted that none of them would have saved her. I know I'm making him sound blunt and matter of fact, but he was very honest with us and told us that though the medicines and therapies might prolong Jeannie's life, they would involve the necessity of her admission to hospital and pain and extreme discomfort.

"No," she had shaken her head and quietly told him. "If I'm to die then it will be in my own home with my husband and friends tending me."

I had never been as proud of my wife as I was at the moment. If courage needed a name, then that name was Jeannie McGrath.

Try as I might I don't recall how we got home that day, whether we took the bus or a taxi. The rest of the day just seemed to slip by and all I remember is sitting in the living room and Jeannie in the kitchen asking if I wanted peas or beans with my fish and chips.

It's stupid the wee things you remember, isn't it, when the important things just don't come to mind.

From the minute we returned from the hospital to the minute she died, we lived each day as though it was our first meeting.

Curiously, though I've maybe painted a black picture of her, I have to admit that Miss Benson surprised me, taking me into her office and sitting me down. Now like I told you, she was a hard, bullying woman and I'm certain the words kindness and compassion weren't in her vocabulary and yes, I'm shaking my head when I admit this; I didn't really like her. However, though I don't know how she had heard about Jeannie being at the hospital and told me that any time I needed to take off wouldn't go through the book. She also told me that if I needed to slip away during the day to tend to Jeannie she would turn a blind eye just so long as I was there at the end of the day to lock the place up and open up each morning.

How did the rest of the school hear about Jeannie? Well, if you work in a school or an office or a place like that there's what I think is called the grapevine and somehow or other Jeannie's condition slipped out. Before I knew it, the teaching staff, cleaners, lollipop women and dining staff were all shaking their heads, patting me on the shoulder or rubbing my back and quietly telling me how sorry they were for me and Jeannie.

To be honest, their kindness was overwhelming and sometimes I had to lock my room door to have a wee greet to myself.

That Friday, the day after Jeannie had received the awful news, I was called into the primary seven classroom where the kids had taken a collection and bought Jeannie a big bunch of flowers.

I was that choked it took me all my time not to burst into tears and I could only nod and mumble my thanks.

Jeannie beat the consultant's prediction of three months by two weeks and one Saturday morning, when Scooby's wife Alice was sitting with her, she quietly slipped away.

To my everlasting regret, I wasn't there with her for she had insisted that I went to my school where the lads' football team were playing in a district cup semi-final against a Nitshill team.

We won and it was when I was congratulating the excited boys that I saw Scooby walking across the pitch towards me, his face pale and my heart stopped because right away, I knew.

I was lost without her.

She was everything to me.

The funeral was conducted by the Parish Priest, Father Stephen Reilly, a nice young man, tall and fair haired with glasses.

I have to admit I was a bit blinkered when I walked behind her coffin into the church and biting my lip to stem the tears, could only see the pallbearers that were six of the local St Vincent De Paul people.

Scooby later told me that the place was packed out with people standing in the porch because they couldn't get a seat.

It was a tribute to a fine woman, he had said and surprised me for I hadn't realised how well known in the parish she had been.

Father Stephen spoke of Jeannie as a friend to many and to him in particular, getting a laugh from the congregation when he recounted his arrival at the parish three years previously when she would bully him and make him attend the wee social nights in the church hall beside chapel. He grinned and shook his head when he told us how Jeannie would persuade the parish women, her cronies he called them with a smile, to get him up for the dancing and in particular, the Slosh.

The service seemed to fly by and the next thing I know is I'm at the graveside in St Conval's cemetery, Scooby holding me by one arm and Alice gripping my other hand, my legs are shaking and I'm watching as my beloved Jeannie is lowered into my parents plot.

I don't remember much about the wake back in the church hall because Scooby and Alice plied me with bevy and I have to tell you, at that time I wasn't much of a drinker.

I should say that before then I had been partial to a wee dram or a can of Tennants now and then, but I never have smoked because that's what killed my sister Liz.

Anyway, the memory of that time is a bit hazy, but thankfully the council gave me bereavement leave and arranged that a temporary janitor took over my duties. A week after the funeral, my district supervisor visited me at home. Over a cup of tea he told me to take as long as I needed, that Miss Benson had informed him that while she would meantime 'suffer' a temporary janitor, her words not his he had smiled at me, she had curtly told him that, "…the school will await the return of Mister McGrath at whatever time he chooses." Honestly, that woman just continued to surprise me.

As it turned out, I was off for a little over five weeks and when I returned it was just in time to see Miss Benson retire and replaced by a younger woman, Missus McNee. I was pleased that I was able to wish Miss Benson farewell and best wishes though felt a bit of a fraud because as I said, I wasn't her biggest fan.

I heard a few stories about her, after she retired. Some said that she took the lump sum the council awarded her and with her pension supposedly legged it to Spain with a man. To be honest, I found that a bit hard to believe. Others apparently heard that her drinking habits caught up with her and she could be found wandering round the pubs in the east end of the city, out her face with the bevy. Knowing she liked more than a dram, I found that a bit more believable. The best story of the lot though, was that Miss Benson took vows and joined a convent.

Now that would have been strange for as I recalled, she was a Baptist.

But you know yourself how these stories just seem to grow arms and legs. What *is* true is that I never heard of her again.

Anyway that's me, who I am and how I arrived at the man I am today, so when all's said and done let me tell you about the time when the trouble began.

It was just a few weeks after Jeannie had taken ill that we and I should say that by 'we' I mean the residents in Hapland Road, began to hear young hooligans shouting and swearing and by the sound of it, getting up to all sorts of shenanigans in the park opposite the houses.

Maybe I should explain. In front of my house in Hapland Road there is a large green area, an expanse of grass that slowly rises from the road way to about ten feet above the road height. We call it the park though it's really just a huge field that has never been developed by the council. There used to be a lot more trees there, but the council in its wisdom had them cut down though there is still a small forest of trees in the centre of the field. Since the council introduced the by-law forbidding people to drink alcohol in public, I heard the wee forest has become a hiding place for the local alcoholics who go and sit there with their cheap wine.

In the summer it was a great place for the weans to play and in winter, covered with snow, the kids used to come from miles away to sled in it and roll up their snowmen.

It was also a nice outlook from the houses rather than looking out onto other houses.

But then recently the neds moved in.

It was one Saturday evening I heard the effing and blinding going on and went up to the front bedroom window because it overlooks the field, to see what was causing the racket.

There must have been more than a dozen of them. They had set a fire about thirty yards into the field and were sitting about drinking and carrying on.

I wouldn't have minded if they had cut the noise down, but it was intolerable and as I said, their language was beyond the pale.

I phoned Pollok police office and the lassie that answered said the beat men were responding to a number of calls about the disorder, is what she called it.

I went back up to the front bedroom window and with the light out, stood back in the darkness of the room, watching to see what would happen. Sure enough a polis car came creeping along the road, but the neds were fly to it and screaming abuse as the two cops got out of the car, started to run away across the field. One stopped and threw a bottle that smashed on the road near to the policewoman that was driving the polis car. The cops went up onto the field, but I knew that in the darkness and carrying all that equipment they have to wear these days, there was no way they would catch the gang.

That was the first night and though to be honest, they weren't there every night, the whole road was on edge because we just didn't know when the gang would arrive to cause trouble up in the field.

The next morning I took a walk up the field to where the neds had been sitting. The place was a disaster with a huge burned area in the grass where they had set the fire and dozens of empty bottle of cheap wine, cider and beer cans lying about.

They returned two nights later and again set a fire and danced about it with their bevy.

Again I phoned the polis and again, they sent one car. It was like a pantomime as I watched the two cops, both men this time, run up the hill and try to catch the cheeky buggers, but of course they never did. That set a trend and over the week, more and more hooligans came from all over to light fires and get drunk. Their numbers grew and one night I'm guessing there might have been about thirty up there and not all lads, because I could clearly hear some lassies voices too. If you asked me I would have described them as a horde.

But it didn't stop there.

I think it was about a fortnight after they started their carry-on that the bottles began to rain down on the road outside the row of houses where I live.

With my neighbours, I went to my front door to see what was happening and it was like a line of Apaches on the hill; the sods had lined up and were screaming abuse at us and offering to fight with us. They weren't hard to see because the street lighting round our way is pretty good and was renewed just a few years ago.

Big Billy King, who's built like the proverbial brick shit-house and who lives three doors along from me had to be held back by his wife. Billy is in his late forties I think and works in demolitions and is a hard man in the real sense of the word. I've no doubt that had he mixed it with the gang some of them would have been hurt, but there was no way he could take on what looked like about twenty of them and that twenty also included half a dozen young women.

Honestly, they were as bad as the lads and their language was outrageous. There was one young lassie in particular that stood out from among the crowd. My God, but she fairly went her dinger, so she did. A tall, fat lassie with short blonde hair that was too blonde to be natural and I think it must have been dyed. She was wearing a bright yellow tracksuit and screaming all sorts of abuse, threatening to have a 'square go' with all or any of us. She actually stood in front of the rest of her pals and was using not just the F word, but the C word too and you know, that's a word I don't even like hearing from men, let alone a young woman.

Heavens above, it was awful.

Fair play to the polis; within five minutes they did show up, but it was the usual beat men encumbered with all their equipment while the young teenagers and some in their twenties I think, just laughed and run off.

The worse thing was it was distressing for my Jeannie and she was frantic in case I went out to challenge them.

Me, challenge them? Let me right off that I'm not a hero, not by any means. I was never a fighter, not even at school and I'd rather walk away then get involved in fisticuffs. Some might call it cowardice, I don't know. It's just that I've never felt that strongly about anything that would make me want to fight or hurt another man or woman. Well, I used to feel that way, but like I said at the outset of this story; things have changed.

CHAPTER THREE

So, that's me back working at the school, but after losing Jeannie my heart just wasn't in it anymore.

Like I told you earlier, I had never been a heavy drinker. I also have to admit that to my shame I had taken to buying a wee half bottle of whisky that I would finish nightly after my dinner.

My pal Scooby and his wife Alice, who had both been a source of strength throughout Jeannie's illness, confessed they were a little worried about me and would pop by every second or third evening to see that I was doing okay. Now, Scooby and Alice were not averse to taking a wee bucket themselves, but usually restricted their heavy bevy sessions to the weekend and most Friday or Saturday's would find them at the social night in the church hall next to the chapel. There had always been an active social committee in the hall and most weekends there was the line dancing or a ceilidh or something going on. During the week there would be the bingo or some kind of meeting; the AA or the slimming club.

It was about six weeks after I laid Jeannie to rest that I finally gave in and said I would meet Scooby and Alice at the club for the line dancing, for an hour or two.

I'm shaking my head with embarrassment as I tell you this because before I went, I finished a half bottle and fuelled by the whisky, had a wee glow in my cheeks before I made my way there. It was only a five minute walk along the road and still light, but as I walked along I could see that already some of the gang of neds were skulking about up on the hill, their heads and faces covered by the hoods of their tracksuit tops.

I can't explain it, but I was kind of relieved that I reached the hall without any nonsense shouted at me by the gang. In the hall, I was surprised by the number of people who greeted me and a wee bit humbled by the attention I was getting.

Now, to let you understand, I'm not saying that people all knew *me* and that they all liked *me*. I was astute enough to know that most of them had some affection for Jeannie and because of that affection, had a lot of sympathy for me.

As you'll probably know if you regularly attend church hall functions, it's quite a mature crowd and it's mainly members of the congregation, their neighbours and friends who attend these nights. Scooby and Alice were already there with some of their own neighbours from Lochar Crescent and greeting me just inside the door, Alice led me to their table.

It wasn't a bad evening and I had been seated for about thirty seconds when a half of whisky and pint of Tennants was set down on the table in front of me.

Of course I was already buoyed up with the half bottle I'd drunk earlier and the wee four piece band was in full swing with half the women already up on the floor and in the middle of the Slosh.

I have to admit I was having a nice time and saw Father Stephen with a pint in his hand and doing the rounds, laughing as he resisted a couple of old biddies who were trying to pull him onto the floor.

I can't say for certain, but I think it was about ten o'clock when a brick came crashing through one of the upper windows of the hall and bounced off the head of one of the dancing women before it skittered along the floor and struck a second woman on her ankle.

The first injured woman collapsed in a bloody heap while the second woman fell down screaming.

The broken window had showered people at a table below it with fragments of glass and in the confusion and the screams of more women, some men run to the front door to try and catch who had thrown the brick.

I regret I hardly got my bum off my seat because by this time the whisky was taking its toll and I couldn't trust myself to stand.

Scooby shrugged off Alice's restraining hand and joined the men who had run to the door and then he come back to the table a few minutes later, blazing mad.

"It's they wee shites that bevy up on the hill," he snarled. "They're up there the now, challenging us to come out and fight! There must be about a two dozen of them!"

By this time the lights had all been turned on and there was pandemonium in the hall. Father Stephen was trying to calm everyone down and calling out that somebody should phone the police and for an ambulance.

I could see a throng of people standing over the woman that had been hit on the head with the brick and I heard somebody say, "It looks bad."

I remember thinking to myself how bright her blood looked on the dance floor and I could hear somebody shouting for fresh, clean towels from behind the bar.

I could vaguely make out through the crowd a man whose face was vaguely familiar to me, knelt down holding the injured woman's hand and I guessed he was the husband. A lady standing beside him was covering the prone woman with a blanket that had been fetched from somewhere.

Still there was a lot of confusion with some women crying and men cursing, then apologising when they saw Father Stephen wagging a finger at them.

Of course it was the drink that had fuelled people's emotions and I could almost feel the tension in the hall.

I'm sitting there, pretty befuddled with the drink and several minutes pass before I heard the sirens of the ambulance and the police.

How did *I* feel?

To be honest, I didn't really feel anything.

Maybe it's because I was a little tipsy or maybe I just didn't care.

Maybe it was too soon after Jeannie's death and my emotions were still in turmoil.

Father Stephen was moving among the crowd and suggesting that if we had nothing to tell the police then we should all make our way home, but then raised his hand for quiet. When the hubbub died down, he said, "Listen to me, there are some stupid people out there who have wantonly thrown a brick and injured two of our friends. There is a likelihood if the police have not chased them off they might still be hanging about. Please go home in groups and take care and I'll see you all at Mass tomorrow. God Bless."

After that, he knelt down to comfort the woman who had been hit on the ankle while a couple of paramedics attended to the woman struck on the head while her man still knelt beside her, holding her hand. It looked to me like he was crying.

Scooby and Alice walked me home and came in for a late night cuppa. Looking out of my front living room window I could see torches flashing up on the hill where the polis were searching for the thugs, but there was no doubt they were now long gone.

Like I told you earlier, I wasn't really one for going to church and truth be told, the next morning between my hangover and my parched throat, I wasn't worth a button, but decided anyway that I'd go to the eleven o'clock Mass.

The church was crowded and it's only my opinion mind you, but I think a lot of people were there to hear what had happened the night before in the hall.

I sat near the back, but with the loudspeaker system it was easy to hear Father Stephen when he was on the pulpit.

I remember he mentioned the two women that had been hurt. The lady who had been hit on the head, a Missus Laurie was in the Neurological Ward at the Southern General Hospital down in Govan and apparently her condition was what he called 'giving cause for concern.' The other lady, I forget her name, had been treated for a badly bruised ankle and after being X-rayed at the hospital, was allowed home.

Father Stephen requested prayers be said for Missus Laurie and her family and also told the congregation that at the conclusion of the Mass, CID officers would be outside the church to ask if anybody had any information about the people who had caused the disorder or the person who had thrown the brick.

I didn't go for communion because like I said, these days I wasn't a regular visitor to the chapel.

On the way out I saw Scooby and Alice and gave them a wave.

Four men in suits and holding clipboards that I supposed were detectives were speaking with some people outside the main doors, but I didn't have anything to tell them so after a few words with Scooby and Alice, I just went home.

I spent most of that day watching the television and when the night drew in, I stood for a wee while at the bedroom window upstairs, watching the field.

The neds didn't come that night and though I'm only guessing, I think it's likely because they guessed if they had shown their faces there was probably a squad of polis waiting for them.

It didn't last though and nearly a week later, a Friday I think it was, they were back, shouting and swearing as if nothing had happened. I don't remember if the polis came that night, but because of the noise I had taken to sleeping in the back room; the room my old Ma had used when Jeannie and I moved in with her.

It was a couple of days later when Scooby dropped by one night for a wee half and a can of lager and he told me that the woman who had been hit, Missus Laurie was still in hospital and wasn't out of the woods yet. He said that the word from Father Stephen was that there is some likelihood that she won't fully recover, that the blow to her head had caused massive brain trauma. Scooby told me that Father Stephen, who I think is the nicest man that God ever took into the priesthood, is going off his head in the pulpit at each morning Mass, telling people not to put up with the gangs nonsense and reminding the congregation if they had any information they should tell the police.

I remember going down to get some shopping to the Co-operative at the Braidcraft roundabout and listening to some people in the queue for the till talking about the brick throwing incident and hearing that the police hadn't arrested anyone yet.

It was a woman in the queue whispering to her pal when I heard her say a name I recognised. I remember she said, "It was one of his gang; the guy that does the drugs. You know, him that has they two big dogs and lives in one of them newish semi's in Dormanside Road. That young guy, Neil McMillan he's called."

On the way back up the road with my shopping, I wondered if the woman meant the wee toe rag who had been a pupil at my school.

I hadn't given any thought to McMillan since he had left Leithland Primary about eleven or twelve years previously and went on to the secondary school, Crookston Castle I think it was.

Crookston Castle is a really good school, but like most schools in those days and I include my own school days, it was subject to all sorts of budget cuts. It wasn't anyone's fault; it was just the way of things back then so the teaching staff had to concentrate on the pupils that were interested in being at school and ignore the ones that couldn't be bothered.

Now, Dormanside Road had been a bit of a place in its day, going from a lovely tenement area with friendly neighbours to a real shabby road where it seemed the council had taken to dumping all the junkies and troublemakers from other housing estates throughout the city. I suppose it was a bit like putting all the bad apples in one barrel, if you like. Though it's relatively close to where I live, I don't make a point of going down there but I understand that there has been quite a lot of development in the recent past. In the last few years though, Dormanside Road has had a lot of council and housing association money ploughed into it. Most of the houses are now privately owned and of course there is still a lot of decent people live there. But I also heard that these decent folk are being overwhelmed and in some circumstances, terrorised by the antics of the very few who use the back gardens like rubbish dumps, neglect the front gardens and generally don't care about the area in which they live. I mean, why should these unruly types be bothered for after all it is the

DSS that is paying their rent and working men like me that is paying the money in taxes for their Giro's, so they have no respect for where they live or the people who live round about them. I had also heard, mainly from Scooby of course, that the druggies had moved in and there was a lot of money lending going on too.

I'm not really laughing when I tell you this, the days were that if you didn't own an uncontrollable Alsatian dog, you wouldn't get a house in Dormanside Road. As I said though, the area has come up quite a bit from what it used to be, but there is still the social element living there that don't care about anyone or their own environment and it's this type of tenant that was being moved into some of the council properties there. Heaven help the decent people who have bought their houses and have to live among these scummies.

I'm shaking my head when I think about him; Neil McMillan.

If it *is* the same guy, then the wee lad I knew had been a bully, picking on the pupils in the junior classes. Unless my memory is faulty, I think there was a few times he had been hauled up in front of Miss Benson for stealing the dinner money off some other weans. I didn't know anything about his parents, but one of the cleaners in the school lived in the same road and again if memory serves me correctly, I remember her telling me and the other cleaners that McMillan's father was a drunk and always being lifted at the weekends by the polis for beating the mother.

I know you'll think I'm mad, but I used to feel sorry for the wee lad; I mean, being brought up in that kind of environment.

So, I wondered as I turned into my garden gate, if the Neil McMillan mentioned by the woman in the Co-op the same wee lad who had attended Leithland Primary.

Well, as you might have guessed by now, I was drinking far more than I ought to have been and to be honest, I shouldn't have been drinking at all; at least, not while I was still working.

It got to the point when I was having a wee nip first thing in the morning before I went to open up the school, another couple of wee nips during the day and polishing off a half bottle or more and a couple of cans of lager before I went to bed at night.

Though he later regretted it, Scooby wasn't any help either.

The bugger used to drop in to me with a carry-out because he knew if he took the drink home Alice would first lambast him and then pour it down the sink. Fly bugger that he is he also knew I wouldn't dub him in to his wife, so the two of us would get rattled and then he'd leave to wind his way home.

The thing is Scooby could hold his bevy a lot better than me, so half the time he didn't seem at all fazed while I was a slobbering wreck.

I should have mentioned that by this time, the new headmistress had started at the school and though she was pleasant enough, unlike Miss Benson there was some things to which she didn't turn a blind eye.

Anyway, it came to a head one day when I had a surprise visit from my district supervisor. Like I said, he was a decent enough man and sitting me down in my wee room, told me that there had been some concerns.

For 'concerns', I presumed 'complaints' and started to bluster, but he held up his hand and told me that he had been backed into a corner. The new headmistress had phoned him and said that unless I was moved to another school, she would make a formal complaint about my drinking on duty and that, he had told me, would in turn require me to be suspended and maybe at the worst, sacked.

"You've been drinking today, haven't you Jimmy?" he quietly asked me.

Well, I could hardly deny it and simply nodded.

In the end, I was caught and no matter what I said or what excuse I might have made, I had to put my hands up to it.

What bloody annoyed me was the headmistress never once challenged me herself. If she had even indicated that I must stop, I swear to God, I would have.

Aye, Miss Benson was a hard taskmaster and like her or not, she wouldn't have missed me and would have been honest enough to bawl me out and that would have been the end of the matter.

Anyway, like I said I'm caught so that was that.

Being the school janny meant everything to me; that and the weans and the lads in my football team.

Since I had lost Jeannie…

Sorry, I had to stop there for a wee minute. To be honest I got a wee bit emotional just thinking about it.

Anyway, the supervisor did me a huge favour and instead of formally suspending or disciplining me, he told me that my previously exemplary record counted for a lot and got me to sign a paper that requested I be granted early retirement. In the end I left with a council pension and a small gratuity that straight away I put into the bank account.

So that's me then. Nearing my sixtieth birthday, no job, no wife, no trade skills and frankly, unemployable.

The first few days were difficult for I was still getting up at the same time to head to work. Worse, I was drinking even more in the evening then one night, making my way upstairs to bed, I took a tumble and fell backwards.

I think it was about three in the morning when I came to, lying on my back at the bottom of the stairs and my God, did I ache.

I lay there in the darkness, too afraid to move because I worried that I might have broken something, but after about…I don't know, two or three minutes maybe, I started to move first my arms, then my legs and finally with one hand on the banister, pulled myself up onto my feet.

To my shame, I'd peed myself.

I sat heavily back down onto the stairs and began to cry. Not soft, tearful cries, but real, deep wailing.

No, I wasn't crying because I'd peed myself. No, I was crying because I'd lost my Jeannie, lost my job and worse of all, lost my dignity.

I'd turned into the very epitome of the man I despised.

I had become a man who had given in to despair; a man who had turned to drink rather than face reality.

I took a deep breath and turned to go into the bathroom to shower. Tomorrow, I decided, I was going to sit down and look at my life anew.

That sounded like a great plan, didn't it?

Of course, I was kidding myself.

I got out of bed, went down stairs to the kitchen and reaching for the half bottle in the top cupboard, I told myself this was the last. No more after this mouthful, I promised myself. Do you know I had the cork off and the bottle to my lips and had actually started to swallow some whisky when with a shudder, I stopped.

What the hell am I doing, I wondered?

But stupidity won and I decided one wee nip wouldn't do me any harm and took a mouthful, smacking my lips together in satisfaction as the whisky settled into my stomach.

Aye, so much for my tearful decision the night before, eh?

To be fair to myself, I did sit down and spend some time thinking about what I was doing, but that's not what decided me against the drink.

No, what decided me was the news I received later than night.

I had just made my dinner, mince and tatties with Brussels sprouts if you're interested, when the phone went.

Now, my usual teatime routine is I'd make the dinner, put the plate onto a tray and with the very occasional can of lager or on most occasions a glass of diluting juice, sit down in front of the television in time for the STV six o'clock news.

I'm a wee bit annoyed and wondering who the in the name of heaven is phoning at this time of the evening.

As soon as I pick up the phone I can hear crying.

It's Alice Toner.

"Jimmy," she's sobbing in my ear, "it's Scooby."

Of course, the dinner gets abandoned and even though I still had my wee black coloured Ford Escort parked in the road outside the house, I hardly used it these days, mostly because I reasoned that I was usually over the drink driving limit. However, I hadn't had a tipple since the whisky that morning so I jumped into the car and rushed round to their house in Lochar Crescent that was literally just two minutes driving time in the motor.

I got there to find their son Charles's car and an ambulance already parked outside their mid-terraced house.

Inside, in the lounge, Alice sat watching while the two ambulance crew were tending to Scooby, sitting in his favourite armchair and whose face and shirt was covered in blood. Before I could ask what had happened, Charles took me by the arm and led me into the kitchen.

"Uncle Jimmy," he started and let me explain. Scooby and I had been pals for so long his kids grew up calling me uncle.

"My Da was coming home from the bookies when he got jumped in Linthaugh Road. Three of the bastards," he snarled, "that gave him a right kicking. Rifled his pockets and took his money and his watch."

I knew the watch, a silver watch with a large ornate face on a silver bracelet that a couple of years earlier, Scooby had bought in Spain. He used to boast he got it for a song and it was worth a lot more than he paid for it.

"Do you know who they are? The guys that attacked him, I mean?" I asked.

Charles shook his head. He lives with his wife in a flat in the west end of the city these days and apart from visiting his parents, he hasn't lived in Pollok for almost ten years.

"My Da was in no position to fight them off anyway," he sighed. "It's not just his age, he's had a good drink and likely was staggering home from the pub, making his way across the green bridge from Kinnell Crescent when they attacked him."

"Have you called the police?"

"Aye, they were here for a few minutes and have left to look for the bastards," he spat out. "They said they'd be back to speak to my Da when the ambulance people have finished with him."

"Shouldn't he be going to the hospital?"

"That's what the ambulance crew suggested, but you know my Da, Uncle Jimmy," Charles shook his head. "He says he's fine and wants to go out hunting for the three of them. Stupid old bugger," he shook his head again and I could see in his eyes how angry he was, but whether at his Da or the neds I wasn't certain, though probably both.

I heard a commotion at the front door and we both turned to see Jimmy's daughter Shona rush into the lounge.

"Oh, Da," she cried out and pushed past the ambulance crew to give her father a hug.

Shona was the apple of Scooby's eye. A natural blonde with model looks, she works on the perfume counter of Frasers in Buchannan Street.

Alice rose from her chair and taking her by the shoulders, persuaded her daughter into letting the ambulance crew finish what they were doing and then led her into the kitchen where we stood.

"Uncle Jimmy," she threw her arms round my neck and sobbed into my shoulder.

I have to admit, Shona was a favourite of Jeannie and me too.

The next twenty minutes were spent talking quietly while in the kitchen while the ambulance crew did their thing. During that time the polis came back and one was young Craig Wallace who gave me a nod when he saw me.

The ambulance crew left, but not before they had a word with Charles and again they suggested his Da should go to the casualty at the Southern General Hospital for a head X-ray.

Charles said he'd try to persuade Scooby to go, but we knew what his answer to that would be, don't we?

I watched young Craig take a statement from Scooby, but then shaking his head, he joined us in the kitchen while his partner went out the back door with Charles for a smoke.

Shona went into the lounge to sit with and hold her Da's hand.

"There's no much he can tell us, Missus Toner," Craig said. "As you can see for yourself, he's had a wee drink and all he can say is that there were three of them, that they were young and once they'd pulled him down to the ground it was just a blur from then on."

Craig sighed and returned his notebook to a pouch on his belt.

"As it's a robbery, the CID will want a word with your husband, but I'll tell them to wait till tomorrow. To be honest, I don't think they'll get much sense out of him tonight."

Alice offered the two young cops a cup of tea or coffee, but they had to get on, Craig said.

"It's that mob who are causing all the trouble round here in the past wee while," he sighed. "They know the streets and where to run at the back of the houses better than we do and as soon as they see us approach, they're off."

"But you know who they are," I ventured.

"Oh aye, Jimmy," he nodded. "But it's the same old story. Knowing something and proving something are two different things."

Alice screwed her eyes as she asked, "So, you have an idea who it was that attacked my man then?"

I watched Craig hesitating before he replied, "I've a good idea, Missus Toner, but like I was saying to Jimmy here; knowing or suspecting and proving are two different things. Frankly, it could be any three of a dozen. The problem is that they're all part and parcel of the same team."

"Is it anything to do with that bastard Neil McMillan that lives over in Dormanside Road?" she snapped at him. "You know, him that runs the young team and does the drugs."

My eyes narrowed, for that was the second time in a short while that I had heard McMillan's name mentioned, but of course I didn't say anything.

Again I watched Craig hesitate and he tactfully replied, "Let's just say that the person to whom you are referring has an undue influence in some of the young people in this area, Missus Toner. Though I can't say with any certainty if he knows or is aware of who assaulted and robbed your husband, my guess is that somewhere along the line Mister McMillan will be privy to that information. Will he tell us?" he shook his head.

"To use an old Glasgow analogy, Mister McMillan wouldn't piss on the polis if we were on fire."

"So, there's nothing you can do about my man getting beaten and robbed?" she said, her voice full of scorn.

I saw Craig draw himself up to his full height of six feet as he replied, "Missus Toner. Nothing would give me greater pleasure than visiting Mister McMillan and introducing him to this here," he replied, stroking at the metal baton strapped to his belt, "but as the law stands, without a witness I've nothing to go on. Maybe when the CID visit your husband tomorrow morning he might be able to recall some detail, but in the meantime…" he shrugged and opened his hands in futility.

Needless to say, Alice wasn't happy with the young cops answer and turned away in a huff. Me, I merely shook my head because like Craig had said, I realised that he couldn't do anything without the evidence to back it up.

I stayed on for another hour and had a cuppa with Alice, Charles and Shona while Scooby snored loudly in his armchair.

So much for the ambulance man's advice about not letting him sleep. The ambulance crew had bandaged his wounded face as best they could, but tomorrow he was going to be one sorry man. His eyes were already ballooning, his lips puffy and the crew had reckoned he might have at least one or maybe even a couple of broken ribs.

However, his absolute refusal to be taken to the casualty annoyed Alice who even though he was unconscious through drink, continued to remind me during that hour what a bloody idiot she was married to.

I drove home at a more sedate pace and it was just after I left the house in Lochar Crescent and was turning into Hapland Road from Linthaugh Road that I saw the crowd of about a dozen teenagers standing at the phone box, drinking and jumping about the road. I tried not to stare as I passed them by, but they started shouting and jeering at me and I startled when I heard what sounded like a can bounced off the roof of my car.

I gripped the wheel a little tighter and resisted the urge to speed up to get away from them.

Then I thought to myself, this isn't right; what am I worried about? I'm the one that's lawfully driving in my car on the road. They are the ones that are drinking in the street when they shouldn't be. They are the ones breaking the law, not me.

Why should I be afraid?

I stopped the car outside my house and stared at my hands. I was gripping the steering wheel so tightly my knuckles were white.

Later that night after I had reheated my dinner in the microwave and just as I was doing the dishes in the sink, I heard them.

They were back up the hill, carrying on as usual with their shouting and screaming.

I didn't take a drink that night because I was still angry with what had happened to my old pal Scooby.

I went to bed and when I got up in the morning and opened the curtains in the living room, I thought I was imagining it.

Still wearing my dressing gown and my slippers, I nipped out to my car.

My heart sank.

The front windscreen was smashed and on the passenger seat there was a half brick lying among the shards of glass.

CHAPTER FOUR.

It was a young policewoman who came to the door about an hour after I'd phoned.

She was pleasant enough, but when she thought I wasn't looking, I caught her glancing at her watch. I was a bit peeved because obviously she thought I was wasting her time, making a complaint about my broken windscreen.

"Right," she snapped her notebook closed and stood up from my couch, "I'll be off then."

"What, you're not going to make some inquiries, hen? Maybe ask my neighbours if they'd seen anything?" I asked her.

"Look, Mister McGrath," she shook her head, "we both know it's that crowd that hang about up in the field there. They're just a bunch of wild teenagers…"

"Teenagers that every night is causing bother round here," I snapped back at here.

"Aye, that might be so, but without witnesses I'm sorry, there's not that much I can do for you."

"And you don't think there might *be* a witness next door or somewhere along the street? Is it not worth even chapping a couple of doors?" I asked a wee bit angrier than I meant to sound.

She stared for a few seconds at me as if I was mad to ask and simply said, "You know as well as I do, Mister McGrath, that even if one of your neighbours did see something, they are not going to give me a statement that might mean they'll be identified in court to these buggers, are they? People are just too frightened to put their head above the parapet these days."

I was shaking my head in frustration when she continued, "I'll submit a crime report and I'll phone you the crime number for your insurance, Mister McGrath."

"What about the brick, hen; can you not get fingerprints or some of that DNA stuff or something off it?"

She smiled at me like I was an idiot and told me that no, there was nothing she could get from the brick.

"Stick it in your garden rockery or something," she called over her shoulder to me while she walked along my garden path towards her Panda car.

Bloody cheek!

I stood watching her drive away and wondered.

If the polis can't protect people round here, who will?

I was never one for computers so used the trusty old phone book to get my insurance company to arrange for a windscreen replacement company to come and sort the car.

Though he was later attending that afternoon than I'd been promised, the young guy was civil enough and chatted away while I stood watching him.

I must say I was really surprised how quick he was; the bits of the broken window was out and the new one in within half an hour, but he did warn me that I'd likely be picking up slivers of glass from the front seat upholstery and carpets for weeks to come. Though of course the insurance was paying for it, I was so pleased that I bunged the lad a tenner for his trouble.

"You'll not remember me, Mister McGrath," he said while he was collecting up his tools.

I stared at him. "Sorry son, do I know you?"

He grinned and said "Maybe about a dozen years ago. Peter Young's my name. I was in Miss McDade's class at Leithland. You were the school janny."

I smiled, but neither the face nor the name was familiar to me.

"There's been that many kids passed through the gates during the time I was there," I shook my head.

"So, you're not working today then?"

"No, I'm retired," I admitted with a huge sigh.

"Well, after running after snotty nosed kids for all those years you likely deserve it," he smiled and pulled open the van door.

"Are you living here now, in Pollok I mean?" I asked him.

He turned towards me and shook his head. "No, not anymore I'm not. My folks moved out of Dormanside Road about a couple of years ago to a lower cottage flat in Croftfoot. If you ask me, from what I hear of the place now, they got out just in time. I'm still with them at the minute till my girlfriend and I can get the money together for a mortgage."

"Dormanside Road," I slowly repeated as I shook my head. "If you're passing by there you'll see some changes, Peter."

"Aye, I've a pal still lives there. He tells me that nutter Neil McMillan," then stopped and stared at me. "Do you remember him, Mister McGrath? He was in my class too. A right bad wee sod, so he was. Word from my pal is that McMillan hasn't changed any, apart from getting a lot bigger. Apparently he's in a ground flat in one of the council mid-terraced cottage flats that were recently built there. My pal says McMillan keeps a couple of vicious Alsatian dogs as guard dogs because of the stolen gear and drugs he has in the house and reckons it is McMillan who's running the gang that is causing all the bother round here the now."

He stared quizzically at me. "The half brick through your window; do you think that's who did it, McMillan's gang?"

I slowly nodded. "More than likely it was, son. They come here at night and sit up in the field there getting drunk and I hear, smoking the dope. I run past them yesterday evening while they were hanging about the phone box just opposite St Convals and they gave me the evil eye. Likely they know my car and," I nodded to the Escort, "that is their way of telling me not to stare at them."

He shook his head and climbing into the van, rolled down the window.

"My advice Mister McGrath is keep out of their way. McMillan was a real nasty wee boy, even through secondary school and I can only assume that he's turned into an even nastier man. Good luck to you, now."

I waved him away and turned to go back inside, but my mind was reeling.

I stopped on the garden path and glanced at my front living room window.

My stomach lurched and maybe it was because I didn't have a drink the night before or maybe it was just my age, but for some reason a cold shiver run down my spine.

For the first time in my life I felt really, really vulnerable.

I was having a cuppa and decided to phone Alice to ask how Scooby was faring.

We had a lengthy conversation and it was obvious that she had got a real fright and that she'd worried that Scooby might have been killed.

"The worst thing is, Jimmy," she said to me, "is that drunk as he was, Scooby heard them laughing when they were giving him a kicking."

The phone went quiet and I heard a sob as Alice started to cry and I offered to go round and sit with her, but she said her daughter Shona had stayed the night and was there tending to both her mother and her father.

Good kids, the Toner's weans and their parents are lucky to have them.

I know that you'll think I'm either mad or just a stupid old fool, but coming back into the house after speaking with the young windscreen guy Peter, I had made a decision.

I needed to protect myself.

It had occurred to me that if these thugs, for that's what they were, if they came to my door, how could I defend myself?

Now, before you raise your eyebrows and think I'm off my head, let me explain. I grew up in Glasgow in the sixties and it was common practise for young guys and even some women, to carry a weapon or sorts. I mean, it wasn't the razor gangs of the fifties or anything like that, but there was an adolescent belief that whenever you were out of the house, you were vulnerable to being attacked and so needed something to defend yourself with.

A flick knife was the favoured weapon in those days and no doubt the Glasgow polis has a fair selection lying in their museum up in the Candleriggs from the mugs that got caught carrying them.

As for me, like I said earlier I've never been a fighter and on a number of occasions I took to my heels or hid to avoid facing up to some of the gangs that roamed the housing estates in those days. I like to think I was just being sensible rather than cowardly.

But in those days I *was* able to take to my heels. Not like today when I'm nearing pension age, unfit and worn down by life. But it worries me that I might have to defend myself in my own home.

Look, I'm not stupid; daft perhaps, but not stupid. I know fine well I can't defend myself against a fit, young teenager anymore than I can keep them out of my home if they decide to come in, but one thing I knew, one thing I had decided. This was *my home* and I wasn't going to let any…any …*bastard* come in and walk all over it!

Inwardly seething at something that hadn't even happened I boiled the kettle and made a cup of tea while I thought about it. Whatever I did arm myself with would have to be something simple; something that I could keep handy behind the front door if the need to use it ever arose.

I poured the water into a mug, added milk then stirred in my two spoonfuls of sugar.

Sitting at the kitchen table, I made the first real decision.

No more bevy; I need to give up the booze.

With a shudder, I remembered how Scooby had looked after he was worked over and I realised that it was by good fortune or the grace of God that he hadn't been killed. Like the ambulance man had told Alice, it was fortunate that Scooby was so drunk the alcohol had almost anaesthetised him and that's why he hadn't felt the blows as much as perhaps he might of, had he been sober.

But like young Craig the polis had also said, the drink had impaired his reactions and that's also why he was easy pickings for the thugs that attacked him.

Sitting there, nursing my tea in both hands, my blood curled when I remembered what Scooby had told his son Charles.

They laughed while they kicked him.

Aye, that made my mind up and reaching up to the kitchen cupboard for what was left in the bottle, I poured it down the sink.

Now don't get me wrong, I was tempted to have a wee swallow before I got rid of it, but my mind was made up.

I think that was one of my better decisions and hope that if she were alive today, my Jeannie would have been proud of me.

So I'm standing there, both hands on the lip of the sink and I'm thinking to myself. How will I go about getting myself some sort of weapon?

I took a deep breath and in the privacy of my own kitchen, I grinned with embarrassment at my foolishness. Was I really considering arming myself with a weapon? Was I that frightened of what these people might do to me?

But still, the thought persisted.

What kind of weapon would I need?

I decided that probably the best kind was one that I made myself.

Now, I've always been a kind of handy man and working as a janitor, I often had to make small repairs in the school, so I like to think I know my way around the basic tools.

As you now know, I live in a mid-terraced house and that means I have a back garden. It's not a huge garden and I do like keeping it neat and tidy and pottering about in my wee tool shed at the bottom of the lawn. As a school janny I had a variety of tools that I used to keep the school grounds clean and that included rakes, shovels, spades and things like that. Now, when these things wore out or got broken I had to indent for replacements and as was often the case the old tools were still useable. If anybody looked into my shed they would find some of the old and used tools there and that also included a couple of yard brooms.

These yard brooms the council issued their janitors were heavy duty ones with stiff bristles, but more importantly for my need they had thick wooden handles.

It was the handle that I needed and five minutes later in the tool shed, I've got a handle in my workbench vice and with a small wood saw, lopped off the top fifteen inches.

I weighed the cut-off in my hand and it felt good and solid.

I secured the cut-off in the vice and with my electric drill I punctured a hole through one end and passed a small piece of thin, black coloured, nylon rope through it, tying it off to make a loop that I could attach to my wrist. I then used black coloured PVC tape and wound it round the bottom to make a non-slip grip.

With the rope round my right wrist I hefted my new baton in my hand and drawing my arm back, had a practise swing in the shed, but forgot how narrow the bloody place was and brought down a shelf full of jars of screws and nails.

Bloody idiot I am.

The wood was strong, but I still felt as though there was something lacking, that the baton needed that wee bit extra punch behind it. What I needed now was to ensure that if I had the need to hit someone with it, it would hurt. I mean, what's the point of hitting someone if you're *not* going to hurt them, eh? Besides, I'm not a strong man and if I swung it at someone, it would need some weight behind it to do any damage.

It was as I gathered up the fallen jars I stared at one jar that was full of one inch screws.

I got a handful of the screws out of the jar and again securing the baton in the vice, began to insert the screws into the top of the rounded head of the baton till there was a mass of them that covered all round the top six inches. All of the screw heads were flush with the wood and as I worked at it I could almost feel the weight of my homemade baton slightly increased.

There now, I waved the studded baton about and grinned like a happy wean. If that doesn't stop one of these buggers, nothing will.

It was when I got back into the house I wondered; why is it that I would go out and leave this behind the door and be defenceless when

I should really be taking it with me? After all, what's to stop them if they decide to have a go at me in the street?

By now you'll have guessed.

I was getting just a little paranoid.

Well, paranoid or not though, it didn't stop me thinking.

Upstairs, I searched through the chest of drawers in the middle room and I dug out a pair of my old janitor trousers that had been issued by the council.

Now, I used to get my annual uniform issue that among other things like shirts and jackets also included two pairs of trousers. In the last couple of years, the council had bought all the surplus stock from the police whose new uniform was cargo pants and polo shirts.

As far as the council was concerned, they got a good deal because the surplus police trousers were heavy serge and came cheap, albeit the pairs that I was issued had to be taken up to accommodate me being a short-arse. Curiously though, for my purpose the former police trousers had something that I used to laugh at.

But I wasn't laughing now.

The right hand pocket of the police trousers had an extra pocket sewn in where the cops used to carry their old wooden batons, so guess what fitted in there nicely?

Trying on the trousers, I slipped the baton into the pocket and to my relief it fitted nicely. A wee bit heavier than I thought, but of course that was because of all the screws I had inserted into the end of it.

I spent a good ten minutes practising pulling the baton from my pocket and at the end of it, felt a bit more confident about going out.

Thinking that I could do with a wee bit more practise and because it was quiet round the back of the house, I sneaked out to the shed again and fetched a six feet length of four by two plank of wood that I placed across my back fence.

With a quick glance around to ensure nobody was watching me from an overlooking window, I raised the baton above my head and brought it sharply down onto the length of wood.

Did the bloody thing not bounce back up and nearly clobber me on the head?

Feeling a wee bit foolish, I secured the length of wood a bit better and this time with a firm whack, brought it down onto the wood.

Bugger me, but the plank almost snapped in half.

I was a bit taken aback and thought if I hit anyone with this I might do some real damage. Now admittedly, I'm like most men around my age and have my own Jiminy Cricket sitting on my shoulder as a conscience, but then I thought of my pal Scooby, an all round good guy who never did anyone any harm and what the gang of thugs did to him.

I shook my head.

If I need to hit anyone with this I told myself, then it stands to reason that they must deserve to be hit.

Strutting around the house I was really self-conscious about having the baton stuck down the inside leg of the ex-police trousers and thought that anybody looking at me might think I was walking a bit odd. The real test would be if I was outside in public. That's when the idea came to me.

I checked the fridge and sure enough, I needed milk anyway so decided to take a walk down to the Co-operative in Braidcraft Terrace at the roundabout to see how it felt, carrying the baton with me.

Locking the front door behind me, I could feel the weight of the baton in the inside pocket and stared walking as normally as I could. Now, maybe I've already mentioned this. I'm a just an ordinary wee man, my once dark hair is thinning and going grey and I'm only five feet five inches tall; don't ask me what that is in metric because I never could get the hang of that stuff. Anyway, it was soon apparent to me that the length of the baton made me seem to be a wee bit stiff legged so I stopped and seeing that there was nobody on the pavement and nobody at their windows, I hooked the nylon cord of the baton up and tucked it into the belt of my trousers. I was wearing an anorak, an old maroon one Jeannie had bought me years ago so the strap that I had attached to the baton couldn't be seen under the anorak.

To get to the Co-op at the roundabout I could walk either way from my house along Hapland Road to the roundabout, but the quickest way is if I turn right when I leave the house and walk towards the Braidcraft Road.

If I'm really honest with you, I didn't want to walk the other way because that way would have taken me past St Convals Church and I was a bit worried that the neds might be hanging about at the telephone box that is on the pavement opposite the church. I tried to persuade myself that I wanted to avoid a confrontation till I got used to my newly made baton, but the truth is I was a little frightened about meeting them.

There, I've admitted it.

I was scared.

Anyway, it took me just over five stomach wrenching minutes to get to the Co-operative and by that time it was starting to get a bit dark. The big security guy they have there in the store was standing just inside the front door and gave me a wee nod when I went in, but I could see that his attention was taken by a young, tall skinny guy who was, I dunno, maybe about nineteen. The skinny guy was carrying a six pack of Tennants held in one arm and a bottle of cheap wine in the other hand. The security guy must be over six feet tall with long, greasy hair tied back in a ponytail. He's not so much heavy-set as fat and every time I've seen him he's standing at the door either picking his nose, reading one of the magazines off the rack or looking like he's ready to bolt at the first sign of trouble.

I kept my head down, grabbed a basket from the stack and went to the fridge and collected a one-litre carton of semi-skinned, then went to pay at the checkout till.

The guy with the drink stepped in front of me and I took a step back to avoid colliding with him. He didn't pay me any attention, but muttered something I didn't catch and whatever he said caused the young lassie at the till to be red-faced. That's when I heard the young guy say, "What, no tick for an old pal, Gina? I mean, Neil might not like that, eh?"

The security guy must have heard him too for he walked over and asked the lassie, "All right there, Gina?"

The skinny guy, a right cheeky bugger and sounding as though he already had been drinking, didn't even turn his head when he said to the security man, "What if she's not, big man? What are you going to do about it?"

The security man didn't even have the bottle to reply, but I saw him turn pale. Then he stepped back when the young guy laid the wine on the counter and lifted his hand as if beckoning the security man to what they call 'come ahead' and by that I mean fight.

My eyes opened wide because that's when I saw it.

When he'd lifted his hand, the young guy's tracksuit sleeve slipped back and I could see he was wearing Scooby's watch on his wrist. Now, you might think wait a minute here. How did I know it was definitely Scooby's watch for after all a lot of watches these days are very similar in appearance, aren't they?

But trust me here. I knew it was Scooby's watch and the reason I was so positive is that a couple of months previously, Scooby had been drunk and caught a bus up the road. When he was getting off at the Corkerhill Road bus stop, he missed his footing and taking a tumble from the platform, he went his length on the pavement. Typical of Scooby, he didn't really hurt himself other than a couple of grazed knees, but his arm had clattered off the ground and he lost a link from the bracelet just at the watch face. I remember him telling me that he was so fond of that watch he was going to put it into a jewellers shop to get mended, but he never did.

Aye, there was no doubt about it. The skinny guy was wearing Scooby's watch.

I was that taken aback that I almost blurted out that he was wearing a stolen watch, but I bit my tongue.

Was I nervous?

No, I was bloody terrified.

Anyway as I was saying, the security guy backed off and the skinny guy pulled some coins from his pocket and without checking the amount, threw them onto the counter and started to walk out with the six cans under one arm and the wine in his other hand.

The lassie, Gina he had called her, was clearly not going to argue with him and shuffled the money into her hand then put it into the till.

I can't say for certain, but I don't think the money the skinny guy paid was the full amount, but it seemed obvious to me that the lassie and the security man were just glad to see the back of him.

I could see the lassie was upset and tight-lipped she tried to smile at me as I handed over my pound coin, but she kept glancing nervously at the door and I think she was worried the guy might come back. She rung the milk up and I waved the penny change to the Yorkhill Children's Charity can on the counter. That's me; a right philanthropist, eh?

Turning away, I put the milk into a plastic carrier bag I had brought with me.

These days it costs five pence for a plastic bag so I always carry one in my jacket pocket.

I couldn't explain it, but my knees were a bit shaky. I think it was because seeing Scooby's watch on that skinny guy was so unexpected.

I tried to walk as casually as I could out of the front door and nodded again to the security man, but he either ignored me or more likely was too intent on going to have a word with the lassie behind the counter. Anyway, I don't think he even noticed me leaving the store. Now you might be asking yourself why I didn't say something to the skinny guy, why I didn't challenge him there in the shop and ask him why he was wearing my best pal's stolen watch.

I'm kind of shrugging here when I tell you this because yes, the truth is I was too frightened to say anything to him. Aye, there's no other way to describe it. The skinny guy was younger than me, taller and a wee bit frightening.

I mean, let's face it. If somebody the size of the security guy wasn't going to challenge him about short-changing the store for a carry-out and let's not forget; that's his job, then I'm hardly likely to say to him, 'Hey pal, why are you wearing my pal's watch that was stolen when three thugs beat and robbed him?'

Anyway, I'm in the dark outside the store and I see the skinny guy walking about ten yards in front of me towards the roundabout. The direction he was taking seemed to indicate to me that he was heading towards the dual carriageway to cross in the general direction of Linthaugh Road.

He wasn't really hard to miss because not only was he wearing a lime green coloured tracksuit top and a white skip cap that was turned back to front, but he had a wee stagger on him as well and I realised my guess was probably correct; he must have been drinking before he went to the store.

Again you might be thinking why I haven't asked the security man to phone the police and inform them about Scooby's stolen wristwatch.

You know, I've asked myself that a dozen times since. I mean, if I owned one of they fancy mobile phones I suppose I could have done it myself. Believe it or not, the curious thing was it never occurred to me to call the polis.

What I did do and this will surprise you, was I followed him, keeping the ten yards between him and me all the way.

At the dual carriageway on the Corkerhill Road, I hesitated and watched as he didn't even hesitate, but just strolled across at the pedestrian crossing. Lucky for him there wasn't any traffic. Almost in an arrogant manner he crossed over the road into the centre reservation then again crossed over and started walking in Linthaugh Terrace and alongside where the pensioner's wee flats are.

He stopped once and my heart in my mouth, so did I, but all he did was shuffle the pack of beer against his chest to adjust his grip and then with the bottle of wine in the other hand, started slowly walking again.

Not once did he turn around or glance behind him and that got me thinking; what would I have done if he *had* turned around?

I know this might sound really strange, but without realising why, I was getting angrier and angrier and had already convinced myself that the skinny guy was one of the three sods who had attacked and robbed Scooby.

One of the three thugs who had without mercy or any thought for his safety, beaten and nearly killed my best pal.

Again, without realising it I was walking as quietly as I could and had drawn closer to him and was now walking just a few paces behind him.

Don't ask me to explain it, for I can't.

All I know is that one minute I'm transferring the plastic bag with the milk to my left hand and reaching into the pocket for the baton that's suddenly in my right hand and I'm raising it up above my head.

It's funny, but time just seemed to slow down.

I didn't even have the sense to look around to see if there was anyone else walking nearby or even if there was any cars passing. You know, there might have been, but I just can't say.

I was kind of… I don't know what you'd call it. Fixated, perhaps, so you might say I was fixated on the back of this guy's head. He didn't even turn around when I brought my arm down and battered him on the back of his head with the baton.

In the films, the guy that's hit on the head usually goes unconscious and the hero moves on, but in real life it doesn't seem to happen that way.

The skinny guy dropped the beer and the wine bottle that smashed onto the pavement and I instinctively took a step back as the wine splashed all over the pavement. His skip hat began to turn a dark colour as he dropped to his knees and his arms fell to his sides, but the funny thing is, his hat stayed on.

He said something that sounded like, "What the fuck…" and started to slowly raise his arms towards his head. He was starting to turn around to see who or what had attacked him, but by this time my blood was up and so was the baton. I took a step forward and again I whacked it as hard as I could, this time right on his crown. His body just seemed to go kind of limp and he pitched face downwards to the ground without another word.

I stared at him and that's when I saw the dark stuff seeping out from under his head and from under the cap. I couldn't see the colour because of the darkness, but I knew it was his blood.

I could hardly breathe and then it occurred to me that someone might have seen me.

I turned my head back and forth to see if anyone was watching me, but there didn't seem to be anybody around.

Did I think about calling an ambulance or the polis?

Not bloody likely!

I stepped round him and my hands were shaking.

I had the good sense to shove the baton into the plastic bag alongside the milk and began to quickly walk away.

CHAPTER FIVE

It took me a few minutes to get back to the house, retracing the route I had walked to get to the Co-operative. I figured it was safer than maybe passing the telephone box where the skinny guy's mates were probably waiting for him coming back with the carry-out. It was getting even darker and I don't recall seeing or passing anyone in the road and the only traffic was a bus travelling on Braidcraft Road towards the roundabout.

But then a cold hand gripped at my heart; I might not have seen anyone, but did anyone see me?

Of that I'm not certain, but dear God, I hoped not.

I was shaking like a leaf when I got home and drew the living room curtains tight. In the kitchen I upturned and emptied the carrier bag into the sink and watched as the plastic milk carton and the baton tumbled out and rattled into the steel basin. The baton was stained with the skinny guy's blood and some of it had transferred onto the outside of the milk carton and onto the inside of the plastic bag. I emptied the milk down the drain. I mean, it doesn't matter that the blood was on the *outside* of the carton; would you drink it after the carton has had blood spilled on it? I run the cold water tap for a couple of minutes until the baton, the milk carton and the plastic bag looked like they were clean of the blood then the carton and the carrier bag went into the waste bin under the sink.

My hands were shaking and I made fists to stop them, but I couldn't stop my body shaking and I felt physically sick.

I stumbled to the bathroom in the hallway and kneeling down, threw up in the pan.

When I finished retching, I sat with my back to the wall and that's when I noticed that I was still wearing my anorak and that there were spots on it. Like I told you earlier, the anorak was maroon coloured, but I was in no doubt that the spots were blood. I almost tore the jacket off and checked the polis trousers, but because of their dark colour I wasn't sure if they had bloods spots or not. That didn't matter; they were going into the washing machine with the anorak. I thought I'd better throw my shoes and socks in as well.

First I get into my pyjamas and dressing gown then the next ten minutes was spent setting the washing machine to a hot wash and scrubbing the baton with a nail brush. When I'm satisfied that the baton looks clean of the blood, I decide that the tape had better come off the handle because if that CSI programme I watch on tele is correct, then it's likely there might be a blood reside on the tape. Screwing the tape into a sticky bundle, that goes into the bin too.

That done, I then hide the baton at the back of the cupboard under the sink behind the plastic bottles of bleach and detergents.

Finally, I'm as satisfied as I can be that there is nothing that has any blood spots.

I know, I know; we've all watched the CSI programmes on the television and how the forensic experts can get all sort of evidence from clothes and stuff, even though they've been washed and it set me thinking.

Would it be wiser if I got rid of the baton and the anorak and the trousers?

It's about forty minutes later and I've stopped shaking at last. If ever I wished I had a dram, it was then, but I settled for two Paracetamol and a mug of tea.

I sat in front of the fireplace with the tea, thinking again of what I had done and half expecting the polis to come steaming through my door to arrest me.

How badly had I hurt the skinny guy, I wondered?

Was it possible…I almost dropped the mug at the thought; was it possible that I had killed him?

No, I convinced myself. I know I hit him hard, but I couldn't have *killed* him. No. I mean, that would be murder, wouldn't it?

Did I do the right thing, was the question I asked myself.

Should I have just followed him to find out where he was going then got to a phone and called the polis?

But then I remembered about the watch; Scooby's watch.

The guy was still wearing it. I had forgotten to take it off him.

But that was a good thing, wasn't it? I mean, I'm thinking to myself, how would I explain to Scooby the manner in which I'd got his watch back. It would mean telling someone else what I'd done.

No, it was the correct thing that I didn't touch the watch.

I started to shake and I thought that I wasn't going to be able to breathe.

I remembered when I was a janitor that some years previously I had to take part in a mandatory first aid course and on the course the instructor taught us something about hyperventilating and how it could be brought on by different things, things like stress.

Well, let me tell you if battering a guy over the head with a screw-laden, wooden baton doesn't cause a man my age some stress, then nothing will.

Anyway, I knew then I was hyperventilating. I forced myself to breathe slowly and stumbled into the kitchen where in a drawer I found a paper bag. I began to breathe into the bag and after a minute, my breathing slowed down.

Honestly, I felt as weak as a newborn kitten; as if I'd done three rounds with Mohammed Ali.

I returned to the living room and sat heavily down into my armchair. Like I told you before, I'm not a particularly religious man, but I said a silent prayer that no one had seen me batter the skinny guy and that the police wouldn't come crashing through the door.

Did I say a prayer for the guy I had attacked?
Curiously, I didn't care about him and God forgive me, I still don't care.

I don't remember falling asleep.
I'm shaking my head and thinking what a stupid thing to say. I mean, who *remembers* falling asleep?
What I do know is I'm wakening up with a crick in my neck and wondering why I am still sitting in the armchair with the light on wearing my pyjamas and dressing gown.
I can see its daylight because the sun is streaming through a crack in the curtains at the window. I feel stiff and my back aches and my mouth is as dry as if I'd been chewing my day old socks.
The clock on top of the fireplace says it's a little before eight o'clock so I force myself to stand upright, no mean feat after a night in the chair I can tell you, and make my way into the kitchen in time to switch on the radio and catch the hourly news.
I listen with my heart in my mouth as the newscaster reports the first item; a story about a bus crash in the north end of the city that left two people dead and then there it is; the second news item that reports the discovery of a man's body in Linthaugh Terrace in the Pollok area of the city.
I can hardly breathe.
He's dead?
I shake my head because I had already known in my heart that I had killed him and that after the two times I had battered him on the head with the baton, I just knew that nobody could have survived blows like that.
As I listen to the radio I think I hardly drew a breath and then my hands are shaking and I switch the radio off.
I need to think, need to work out what might happen if the police come calling at my door, what I should say.
I boil the kettle and sit down in the kitchen chair, my mind in turmoil and my legs almost unable to support me.
The report had not given much information, but isn't that the way of it; isn't that what usually happens in these type of things? The polis put out a statement that it is a suspicious death and they are investigating and looking for witnesses.
Dear God, I'm thinking. What have I done?

The kettle switches itself off and I get up, suddenly tired and weary even though I've slept soundly. My hands have stopped shaking and to be honest, in my mind I've almost resigned myself to getting caught. I pour the boiled water into the teapot. I was never one for brewing a teabag in a mug.

The word I daren't use is now foremost in my mind for I've committed the capital crime; murder.

The skinny guy was murdered and it was me; I am the murderer.

My mind is a riot of thoughts and as I sit back down at the kitchen table with the mug, I glance over to the washing machine. The cycle had obviously completed some hours previously and the anorak, trousers and one of my shoes are crumpled and pressed against the glass like accusers, reminding me of what I have done.

I stood and opened the door and fetched them out. They have been well wrung and were more damp than sodden.

We used to have an old style drying pulley on the kitchen ceiling, but Jeannie had wanted it gone in favour of a rotary dryer out in the back garden.

No way was I putting these things out there, I'm thinking and instead took them through the living room and upstairs to the bedrooms and hung the anorak and the trousers over the radiators. The shoes were old anyway and well past their best, so they went into the bin at the back door.

It was when I was closing the back door that I remembered.

When he had been at the till, the skinny guy had called the lassie behind the till Gina and he said something like, "Neil might not like it." Well, something that sounded like that.

There was that name again.

Neil.

Was he talking about the guy called Neil McMillan and if he was, did that make the skinny guy one of the gang that was causing all the bother round here?

I had already convinced myself that the skinny guy was one of the three that mugged Scooby and the young cop Craig Wallace had more or less inferred they were part of the team that was being led by Neil McMillan.

I mean, I didn't have to be a detective to put the pieces together.

I tried to work it out in my head and then with the mug of tea went through to have a seat in the living room.

In the very recent past I had heard Neil McMillan's name crop up a couple of times and now this mention of 'Neil.'

The skinny guy, oh all right then, I suppose if you want to be *correct* about it, the guy that I've killed. If I'm right and Neil *is* Neil McMillan, then the dead guy was a pal or working for this Neil.

And what was it that the young guy Peter who repaired my car windscreen had told me. He had said something about Neil McMillan living in Dormanside Road and keeping stolen gear and drugs in his house.

I'm sitting back now and believe it or not, I'm nodding my head because you know something, say or think what you like, but I was beginning to feel a wee bit better about killing the skinny guy.

I've worked all my days and never been in trouble in my life. I've paid my dues, obeyed the law and never been any bother to anyone. I've never claimed from the social and always tried to be a good and decent man.

So why then should I feel guilty?

I mean, I'm not pretending to be any kind of expert, but the skinny guy just seemed to me to be one of them parasites who sponges off everybody else. If you have lived in a council housing estate, you'll have been among that type of person all your life, seen them hanging about outside the shops, the pub or the bookies, waiting to tap money off someone they know will be too frightened to refuse them. If you had been there in the Co-operative, seen the arrogance of the skinny guy, you would know exactly what I'm talking about.

That and let's not forget, he was wearing Scooby's watch.

Am I trying to justify or excuse what I did? I'm not certain, but the more thought I give it, the less guilty I feel; so there.

My only problem now is will the polis come to the house and arrest me? Will somebody tell them that I did it?

I'm shivering a wee bit, but it's not because I'm cold.

If I'm honest, it's because I'm scared shitless.

I know I have to eat something so I check the fridge and end up making myself scrambled eggs with toast and smothering it in tomato sauce. Jeannie used to turn her nose up at the tomato sauce. She liked the mustard, herself.

Washed down with another big mug of tea, I'm feeling a wee bit better and decide to have myself a shower before the hourly news bulletin again.

I've got the SKY package on the television and that has the SKY and BBC twenty-four hour news programmes, but they don't report the local Glasgow news unless it's really something big, so I'm guessing a murder in Pollok won't really make the news. I'm going to have to wait for the six o'clock news from STV before I get any more details.

Well, not unless the police come chapping at my door, I mean.

So that's how my day goes; me sitting at the television, nervous and listening to the hourly radio broadcasts, but there is no new update and the news broadcaster just tells the same story over and over.

You can imagine my mind is still reeling and when about half past two that afternoon, the phone rings, I nearly keeked in my pants.

"Hello?"

"Aye, Jimmy. It's Alice here," she almost whispers into my ear.

"Alice, is Scooby okay hen?"

"Aye, Jimmy, he's fine. Just his usual moaning faced self," she tells me and then adds, "but the police have been to the house. Can you come round?"

I caught my breath and my mouth is suddenly dry. "The police, you say? What did they want?"

"Listen, just come round to the house and I'll explain when you're here," she replies and then says cheerio and hangs up.

Well, that sets my hands shaking again and I slowly put the phone down. Was it a trap, I'm wondering? Are the polis at Scooby's, waiting to arrest me there?

I'm shaking my head and thinking, don't be bloody stupid McGrath. If the police wanted you, they would have come to the door.

I grab my old janny's anorak that's hanging on the stand at the door that I use when I'm out cutting the grass at the front garden and decide to take the car. I'm locking the front door and wondering why Alice's voice sounded so hushed. Is it because the police are still there?

It occurs briefly to me that maybe I shouldn't go, but what excuse would I have for not going, so almost in resignation I get into the car and start to drive towards Scooby's house in Lochar Crescent.

A minute or two later I'm passing St Convals church and as I slow down for the junction of Hapland Road and Linthaugh Road, about a hundred yards away to my right I can see a police caravan parked on the road at the junction of Linthaugh Road and Linthaugh Terrace. I'm staring at the caravan and see two uniformed cops standing outside talking, one with what looks like a clipboard in his hand. I'm a bit taken aback and still staring for what, I don't know, a minute perhaps when I hear a car horn beeping behind me. Well, honestly, I nearly jumped out of my skin and glancing in the rear view mirror I see a car behind me and the woman driver is angry and waving that I move.

I get such a fright do I not go and stall the Escort?

I wave an apology, re-start the engine and turn left into Linthaugh then drive the short distance towards Lochar Crescent.

Driving slowly into Lochar I look for police cars parked there, but the space outside Scooby's house is empty, though his daughter Shona's wee blue coloured Nissan Note is parked in the driveway. I didn't realise it, but I'm breathing like a hundred yard sprinter and actually have to force myself to stop shaking.

Taking a deep breath, I get out of the car, lock it and make my way up the path to Scooby's house.

"Uncle Jimmy," Shona pulls open the front door and gives me a peck on the cheek before ushering me into the lounge.

Alice and Scooby are sitting in opposite armchairs with a wee low table between them and the remains of mugs of tea and a plate of toast on the table.

"Come away in, Jimmy," Alice rises and also gives me a peck on the cheek. "Have you had your breakfast yet?"

That's just like Alice, always fussing over me and forever thinking since my Jeannie passed that I can't look after myself.

"Aye, I'm fine hen," I tell her as I sit down on the couch while at my back Shona goes to the kitchen to put the kettle on anyway.

"Good to see you old pal," Scooby is wearing pyjamas under his dressing gown, but manages a grin and I can see that he's still is a lot of discomfort. His face is some mess, both eyes swollen and turning a yellowish black and blue. His lips are so puffy they resemble a blow-up rubber ring that you find in the swimming pools.

My God, Alice was right enough I'm thinking; he's lucky to be alive. His speech sounds slurred and I'm guessing he must be half doped with pain killers. When he sits down in the armchair, I see him wincing and remember then that the paramedic guy said there might be broken ribs.

You can imagine how nervous I am so I turn to Alice and ask her, "You said the police were here. Was it because of what happened to Scooby?"

"Aye, sort of," she grimaces. "Did you hear about the murder last night near to the Braidcraft roundabout?"

I'd already decided I would admit to hearing about the murder on the radio, but not anything else and I nodded. "Aye, it said something on the radio about a body being discovered?"

"Well, the CID was here this morning with his watch," she nodded towards Scooby. "Said they found it on the dead guy and asked if it was the same watch that had been stolen off Scooby."

"And was it?"

"Oh aye, it's Scooby's watch right enough," she nodded to me. "They had the description from the crime report they took and you know that watch, Jimmy. It's a big, ugly thing and pretty easy to identify. The polis that took the crime report, he was the one that suggested it might be the same watch."

I recalled the young cop Craig and his partner being at the house when I arrived and wondered if it was him that had found the body. "The watch was on the dead guy?" I feigned surprise. "How did he get it?"

"Here you go, Uncle Jimmy," Shona walked through from the kitchen and handing me a mug of tea, placed a plate of toast covered in butter and jam on the wee table beside the couch. "That'll put some hairs on your chest," she grinned as she pulled up a small footstool and sat down between her father and me.

"Thanks hen," I smiled at her and patted at her shoulder with my free hand, then again asked Alice, "The watch. How did the dead guy get it then?"

Alice shook her head. "The CID didn't tell us *that* much, but they did say that they suspected the guy that had the watch, the dead guy I mean; he might have been one of the three that attacked my man. Then," she shakes her head again and bitterly adds, "they had the *bloody* cheek to ask where Scooby and me where last night?"

I'm stunned. "You mean, they thought that maybe it was you or Scooby that…"

"Killed the guy, aye," she finishes for me.

"You can't be serious Alice!"

She sighs and I can see she's upset, so upset that Shona rises and sitting on the arm of the chair, puts her arm round her mother's shoulders to comfort her.

Scooby sits silently watching and I know he must be feeling angry at not just being attacked and robbed, but at the polis coming round to infer it was him or Alice that committed the murder.

I'm sitting there thinking that maybe I should go and confess to the police, tell them it was me, that my lifelong pal and his wife know nothing about what happened, but coward that I am, I sit and say nothing.

Then Shona pipes up and quietly says, "They had to ask, Uncle Jimmy. I think it was obvious that neither my Da nor my Mum had anything to do with the guy's murder. In fact," she smiles, "they even asked where I was last night, but of course the three of us were here all night looking after my Da. Then they wanted to know about where Charles was, but he was away home and his wife will be able to tell them that too." She smiled again and said, "Then they asked about our Michael…"

Alice interrupts and with her own grin, says, "I just told them good luck with that. He's on holiday in Tenerife with his wife and two weans."

Shona rubbed at her mother's shoulders and continued, "No, they weren't seriously thinking we had anything to do with the murder. I mean, we didn't even know who the guy was before today so how would we know he had my Da's watch?"

"Did the police name the dead guy, then?"

"Oh aye, he was some guy called Alex Paterson that lived in Kempsthorn Road. The detective said he was nineteen and the polis knew him because he hung about in the gang that is causing all the trouble round the Pollok area and though we're not supposed to know this, they let it slip he was well known as a junkie."

I work hard at keeping my face straight, but suddenly I feel as though a weight is lifting from my shoulders.

For the first time that day, I smile and tell Shona, "This toast is lovely, hen. Thanks."

CHAPTER SIX

I stayed on visiting with Scooby and Alice for about another hour then turning down the invitation from Alice to stay for dinner, I made an excuse I'd the house to tidy and a washing to put on and took my leave of them.

Getting into the car, I turned and waved cheerio and drove onto Linthaugh Road.

Now, I could have went straight home, but thought I'd take a wee turn past the police caravan, just to do my nosey and see what was going on.

As I approached the caravan, I didn't see anyone standing outside and guessed whoever was manning it must be inside.

What I did see though as I passed by was three of the tracksuit brigade hanging about on the pavement outside and a young man who was wearing a suit. Two were young guys, maybe in their late teens or early twenties and wearing the skip caps they all wear these days and as usual, back to front.

Honestly, do they no realise how stupid they look?

The third one stood there was a young lassie, maybe about the same age. She was wearing a tracksuit too, but no hat and her light coloured hair was cropped almost like one of they seventies skinheads.

The girl was standing looking down at a couple of bunches of flowers somebody had left on the pavement at the verge while the two lad were speaking with the suited guy who looked like he was writing something in a notepad in his hand.

None of them turned to watch me as I drove past them and that's when I saw two or three Rangers scarves and at least one Celtic scarf tied to the nearby railings.

I did a quick U-turn on the roundabout and headed back up Braidcraft Road before turning into Hapland Road.

Stopping the car outside my house, I got out and had a quick glance up at the field, but it was still only the early afternoon so I couldn't see anyone there.

I wasn't really fibbing about putting a washing on. I only use the machine every other day now and unless I'm doing towels or bed sheets, it's never really full. However, on the way home in the car I had thought again about the police and their forensics and didn't think it would do any harm to put another wash through the machine and that would likely get rid of any trace of blood that might still be stuck in the pipes.

While I'm thinking about it, it might not be a bad idea once I've did the wash to run the machine on empty, but with a good dollop of bleach in it.

Aye, I'm nodding to myself, that's what I'll do.

An hour later, the washing is in the basket and I'm hanging it outside on the rotary dryer and the machine is running on a bleach wash cycle.

"Catching the good weather there, Jimmy?" said a voice behind me.

I turned and I kid you not, I almost fainted. I got the bloody shock of my life for in the common close between me and my next door neighbour stood young Craig the polis with his female partner standing behind him.

My legs almost turned to jelly while I just stood with a couple of wooden pegs in my gob, a wet vest in my hands and staring at him like an idiot.

I could see his face change and he said, "You all right, old yin?"

I spat out the pegs and in a faltering voice says to him, "Aye, fine, Craig. Sorry, you gave me a wee bit of a fright there. My mind was elsewhere."

He smiles and holding up a hand tells me, "Mhari and me were just popping by to see if you had the kettle on, but if you're busy…"

"No, no," I drop the vest into the wash basket and wave him to come down the stairs from the close. "Come away in and I'll stick the kettle on."

I turn to go up the back stairs to the kitchen door and Craig sticks his thumb over his shoulder and says, "This is Mhari. She started with us a month ago and I'm just showing her round the area."

"Hi Jimmy, pleased to meet you," the young lassie waves a hand to me and follows Craig and me into the kitchen.

I settle them in the living room and return to the kitchen to stick the kettle on to boil, but let me tell you; my stomach's churning and I'm working hard at keeping my bum cheeks together.

God, I got such a *bloody* fright when I saw the uniforms at the back close.

My hands are shaking a wee bit as I put three mugs, sugar bowl, spoon and milk jug onto the tray and fetch a packet of Tunnocks caramel wafers, Jeannie's favourite, from the wall cupboard. I glance through the door, but they can't see me taking a big, deep breath and forcing a smile, return back to the living room.

"Here, let me," the young lassie gets up from her chair and taking the tray from me she places it down onto the wee coffee table.

She's taken her cap off and heavens, but she's a cracker right enough. Taller than me and before you say it, I know that it doesn't take much to be taller than me. Jet black hair pinned up, bright red lipstick and fresh complexion. The stab proof vest, bulky belt and uniform she was wearing didn't hide the fact she was a slim, good looking young woman.

"Milk and sugar, Jimmy?" she asks me.

"Aye, hen, milk and two please," I tell her.

She doesn't ask Craig so I'm guessing I'm not the first place they've shared a cuppa.

I tear open the packet of biscuits and shake them out onto a wee tea plate before offering them. Craig takes one, but the lassie doesn't.

"My figure," she explains with a smile, but I get a bigger smile when I tell her that is something I don't think she has to worry about.

Don't ask me why and I know this sounds crazy, but I find myself blushing.

Isn't it amazing that even the heart of an old widower like me can still race at the sight of a pretty young woman.

"So what's new?" I ask, concentrating on keeping my face straight and praying that they are not here to ask me where I was last night when the guy Alex Paterson was murdered because maybe I haven't mentioned this before, but I'm a terrible liar. You see, being married all those years to Jeannie, I never had any reason to tell lies. Besides, I remember my old Ma telling me when I was a wee boy that to be a good liar, you needed to have an even better memory. That kind of stuck with me through the years.

"Just staying clear of the office for the minute, Jimmy," Craig shrugs. "You probably heard that there was a murder last night over in Linthaugh Terrace. The CID and the murder squad have more or less taken over the office, so the sergeant told us to get our arses out and to stay out. We've only to go in for our piece break or if we have an arrest."

"The murder, yes," I slowly say and nod, trying hard that they don't see my throat tightening and forcing my shaking knees together. "I heard about it this morning on the news on the radio. Then a wee while ago, my pal Scooby's wife, you know, the guy that got mugged; his wife Alice phoned to say the CID had visited them. I took a wee turn round there and they told me that the CID had found Scooby's watch."

"Aye, the watch," Craig solemnly nodded as he chewed thoughtfully at his chocolate biscuit. "It was on the dead guy's wrist. Mhari and I recognised it from the description Mister Toner's wife gave us."

"Oh," I poke a finger at them in turn, "was it you two that found the body, then?"

"No, that was the nightshift cops," he replies, "but at the morning meeting when we started at seven, the sergeant read out the deceased's name and description of what he was wearing and we put two and two together, didn't we?" he turns to Mhari with a grin.

I'm watching him staring at her and right away, married with kids or not I can see he's smitten with her.

No wonder I thought. She's a right cracker, is Mhari.

She leans forward in her seat, her mug held tightly in both her hands and her eyes are bright with excitement as she tells me, "My first murder, Jimmy."

Aye, mine too hen, I silently think to myself.

"Did you hear who the dead guy is, Jimmy?"

"Eh, Alice mentioned a name, but it doesn't mean anything to me."

Craig turns to Mhari and say, "Jimmy was a school janitor at Leithland for a number of years," he explains to her then says to me, "You must know a load of the young people round here, Jimmy."

"Some of the names and the faces are still familiar," I sigh, "but you know what it's like, Craig. Weans grow up and while I remember them as ten or eleven year olds, most of them are now adults." I shrug my shoulders and add, "Occasionally I'll pass some of them in the street and they'll say, 'Hello Mister McGrath, do you remember me?' and I'll kid on I do, but to be honest," I shake my head, "there was far too many for me to remember them all from the years I worked there."

My nerves are on edge and I see that I've got their interest and I'm wondering if maybe young Craig is fishing for something, so I decide to go on and try to steer the discussion away from any talk about the murder.

"I don't know if you're aware, but I had one of your colleagues down here yesterday," then tell them about finding the brick through my windscreen.

"The young lassie that took the report, I didn't get her name, but she wasn't…" I hesitate but then think, bugger it and I tell them. "She wasn't the friendliest police person I've spoken to. I mean, she wasn't *rude* or anything, but…"

"Was she a wee red headed policewoman with big tits?" Craig asks me and flinches when Mhari uses her elbow to dig him in the ribs.

"Eh, aye, that sounds like her," I nod to him, but I'm a wee bit embarrassed at his description. I know it probably sounds silly in this day and age, but I've never been comfortable talking about women's attributes when there's women present. Oh, I *suppose* it's all right when it's just lads together, but like I said, it's a different age now.

Craig doesn't seem to notice I'm blushing for him and shakes his head as he scowls. "Pauline Martin. A lazy cow if ever there was one. A big chest and a bigger hit for herself," he adds. "I'm guessing that when she was taking the report she made it seem like she was doing you a favour?"

I nod as though I'm a bit self-conscious, telling him.

His eyes narrow and he asks, "Tell me this, Jimmy. Did she chap any of your neighbour's doors to try and find a witness or anything?"

I shake my head and taking a deep breath, I diplomatically reply, "Not to my knowledge, no."

He shakes his head again and finishing his tea, stands and says to me, "Thanks for that, Jimmy. I'm sorry that your windscreen got broken. I'm guessing it was that crowd that hang about up in the field. Do you have any idea why they picked on your car?"

"None at all," and this time it's me shaking my head. It didn't seem worth it, telling him I thought it was because I gave them the evil eye when I drove past them.

"Right, has Martin phoned you down the crime number for your insurance yet?"

"Not yet," I shake my head again.

"Lazy wee bitch," he quietly mumbles and says, "I'll see it gets done today, Jimmy."

He puts his cap on his head and I walk him and Mhari to the front door where I see their panda car parked behind my Escort.

I'm thinking that's the end of the discussion about the murdered Paterson when Craig turns and says to me, "Keep it to yourself, Jimmy, but the dead guy, Alex Paterson. He was a junkie and working for a drug dealer that lives in Dormanside Road called Neil McMillan. Does that name mean anything to you?"

I thought fast. Aside from the time I overhead it spoken at the Co-operative, the name had been mentioned twice to me; once by Alice and again by the young windscreen guy, so hoping this isn't some sort of trick by Craig to catch me out I look thoughtful and reply, "Did he not attend Leithland? The name sounds familiar."

Craig smiles and says, "Aye, I think he did. Well, you've got a right good reputation round this area as a decent man, Jimmy, so if anyone should happen to mention anything to you about the murder or what McMillan's up to, bear me in mind for a quiet word."

I nod and bidding them cheerio, close the door behind them.

After I lock it I lean with my forehead against the door, catching my breath and knowing that my heart is beating against the drum of my chest like Ringo Star on speed.

So that was it, then. I've read enough detective stories to realise that Craig was trying to impress the good looking your police woman Mhari. He's brought her in for a cuppa and an introduction and now he's likely telling her in their panda car that I'm one of his street sources.

I'm grinning like an idiot again and pull open the door to go out and finish hanging my washing.

In a way I'm pleased at Craig's visit for if nothing else, I've learned for definite that Paterson *was* one of Neil McMillan's drug dealing gang and that eases my conscience that little bit more.

I make my dinner at the usual time and I'm sitting with it on the tray, ready for the STV six o'clock news to start after the adverts.

The first report is the bus crash over in the Great Western Road area that claimed the lives of two young people, poor souls that they are.

The second report is the murder of Alex Paterson and I sit there, watching with bated breath.

They show a photo of a smiling young teenager and I see the face of the young man I killed. He's shaven headed and leering widely with teeth like tombstones or I should say those teeth he has left and small diamond stud earrings in both lobes. The photo looks to have been taken abroad because he looks tanned. The report cuts away to a press conference and introduces the man in charge of the investigation, Detective Chief Inspector John McManus who is a florid faced man with bulbous eyes and dark hair slicked back. Sitting beside him is a woman in civilian clothes and a thin faced, unshaven man with greasy looking, collar length fair hair and a hung dog look whose face is vaguely familiar.

McManus introduces the man as George Paterson, the father of the deceased and I'm wracking my brains trying to recall where I've seen him before.

As I listen, McManus describes the murder as a brutal attack upon a defenceless young man, cut down in the prime of his life.

McManus then admits that the police require the assistance of the public to solve this dastardly murder...aye, honest; I'm not joking. That's what he calls it, a 'dastardly murder.'

Then he kind of ruins it by admitting that Paterson was known to the police and was fighting a drug and drink addiction. I'm thinking he's stating this because likely the news reporters will be making their own inquiries in the area about the dead guy and then it hits me who the suited guy talking to the two young neds where I killed Paterson must have been. He was probably a reporter, too.

So, I'm unconsciously shaking my head as I think about it. A young man cut down in the prime of his life? I think most sensible people and certainly the ones living around here would read into that as 'junkie drunken thug with court convictions.'

The scene cut away to show where Paterson had been murdered and bunches of flowers lying heaped on the pavement in Linthaugh Terrace.

Do I feel guilty watching all this?

Do I heck.

I finish my dinner and switch over to watch an episode of 'Come Dine With Me,' but it still niggles me because I'm certain that I've seen Paterson's father's face before.

They came back that night, howling like rabid dogs over in the field. I kind of half hoped that the murder of one of their own might have curtailed their nonsense, but it seems not.

Do I phone the polis? No, I don't for really, what's the *bloody* use. Instead, I make myself a cup of hot cocoa and again go to bed in the back bedroom.

CHAPTER SEVEN

I wake up early the next day and after my toilet, go and open the curtains in the living room to a bright morning. My first thought is for my wee car, but it looks to be all right. It's a Saturday, but when you're retired the days just seem to run together and half the time I have to remind myself what day it actually is.

I'm standing there staring out and I'm thinking again like a victim. These people, regardless of what age they are, are oppressing me so much that I'm hoping they ignore me.

The more thought I give it, the angrier I'm becoming. I'm breathing hard because I'm so *bloody* annoyed at my own feeling of helplessness.

I shrug and make my way into the kitchen for my breakfast and thinking that I'll take a walk down to see how Scooby is doing today.

Then I remember the bins are due to be emptied this morning so breakfast will need to wait for a couple of minutes. Funny day for the bins to be emptied I know, but I still catch the odd snippet of what the council is up to and I heard the union got an agreement with the council and it gives the bin men a wee chance at some overtime. Still wearing my dressing gown, I hump the big, plastic bin up the stairs and through the common close, along my garden path and leave it on the pavement to be emptied.

That's when I see it.

In the house that's three doors along from me lives Mary Baxter. Old Missus Baxter must be in her late eighties now. When I was a wee lad growing up in this house she was a young woman living there with her husband and weans. I sometimes see her in the street, though these days she's a bit wandered and the social work have carers coming in the mornings and evening to make sure she gets her meals and get her washed, dressed and suchlike. I remember she had four children, but two are dead and I don't know anything about the other two other than from what I heard when Jeannie was alive, that they seldom visit their mother.

When she was alive, Jeannie was good to old Mary and mainly because she knew the old woman's children didn't bother with her. I say children, but if memory serves me correctly, they're both men and they must be in their late fifties or early sixties; about my age or even older than me by now.

I mean, I can't say for any certainty, but I think that none of the kids liked their father and because of that they all kind of took off at an early age and just didn't keep in touch with their mother. Mind you, he's been dead for God knows how man years, so really there isn't any excuse for them not visiting their mother, is there?

Anyway, as I'm standing there I see old Mary being escorted to an ambulance and a police car parked behind it. The cop that's standing by the panda is the polis woman that took the report for my windscreen, the lassie that Craig called Pauline something.

She was writing in her notebook and to be honest, my curiosity got the better of me, particularly because I saw some other neighbours standing watching.

I walked over and stood next to Billy King who was wearing a Rangers tracksuit and lives through the wall from old Mary.

"What's going on, Billy?" I ask him.

"What, did you not hear that?" he nodded towards Mary's house.

I turn and to see what he is talking about. Mary's front window is boarded over with a huge sheet of plywood that doesn't quite cover the whole window and I can see that the window has been smashed.

"Happened about two this morning," Billy tells me. "That mob up on the hill again. Mary's that far gone these days she couldn't have known what she was doing, but anyway, she went out to challenge them about the noise and they were shouting and screaming at the old biddy. I phoned for the polis, but it was the bloody usual. As soon as the panda arrives with its blue lights on, they scarper and they're away back over the hill, but not before they lobbed a brick through Mary's window," he shakes his head then almost spat out, "Bastards!"

That turned the policewoman's head and she scowled at Billy, but he just stared back at her as if challenging her to say something and she turned away again to write in her notebook.

Billy turns to stare curiously at me. "Did you really not hear the commotion?"

"No," I shake my head. "I sleep in the back room these days," but I'm too embarrassed to tell him why.

"Where is Mary going?" I ask him.

Like me, Billy knows that Mary's family don't really bother about her. His wife Irene, just as my Jeannie used to do, will occasionally drop in every other day to visit the old woman or take her in milk and bread.

"The ambulance guy says he's been instructed to take her to a council home in the meantime. Says that Mary's social worker will visit her there to determine if she's fit to live by herself," Billy tells me.

Old Mary sees us standing watching and waves at us like she's the Queen or excited about going away for a holiday. We wave back as the ambulance man closes the back door and then they drive off.

The policewoman is still standing there and I'm about to go over to her and be a bit cheeky and ask when she's going to phone down my crime number, but without as much as a second glance at us all standing there, she jumps into her police car and drives away.

I'm tempted to ask Billy if the policewoman chapped his door for a statement, but to be honest, I can't be bothered because I think I already know the answer to that one.

Seems Craig was right about her.

Back in the house I go about my usual routine of breakfast, shower and getting dressed in that order.

Curious isn't it that I'm not thinking too much about the murder. I mean, all day yesterday I couldn't get it out of my mind, but here I am this morning thinking more about my cereal and what I'll wear today rather than battering the life out of a young guy.

Ah well, maybe that's just the way of it.

I suppose when I think about it, yesterday's visit from Craig the polis and his partner kind of settled my nerves a bit.

So I'm in the shower and I'm thinking that I'll pop down to the shops and buy a couple of newspapers and read what the story is about the murder. Don't get me wrong here. It's not as if I want to revel in what I've done. No, it's more what I like to think of as research; try and discover what the polis intend doing about catching the murderer who is, by the way, me.

Why am I smiling when I think of that?

Am I so without conscience that I really don't care about the dead guy?

Aye, I suppose as far as *he's* concerned, I am.

My thoughts turn to wee Mary Baxter. What happened to her is absolutely shocking and I grit my teeth at the animals who subjected her to such terror. To live your whole life and then be treated by these thugs like that? The poor wee soul must have been half frightened to death, but then again, Mary's mind is almost that far gone she probably didn't realise half of what was going on.

The window though. That must have been terrifying when the brick came through it.

I'm shaking my head at the senseless morons who did it and wondering if they have granny's or elderly relatives.

Probably that drunk or drugged up they didn't care or even give a thought about what they were doing.

So there I am, standing in the shower, soaking wet and angry again. My imagination starts running riot and I'm imagining what I would do to the evil sods if I had the opportunity, how I would hurt them. Torture them even and none of that biblical turn the other cheek nonsense.

I shake my head because the sad truth is that no matter what I'd like to do to them, the reality is that I'm just a wee guy turning sixty, not very fit and not very strong and I've never hurt another person in my life.

Well, apart from murdering one of them, that is.

I'm grinning now as an evil thought enters my head.

I've killed one of them, so who's to say I can't kill another one?

Dressed now in my old baggy trousers and a clean polo shirt, I stick on my training shoes and wearing the old gardening jacket, stuff a carrier bag into the pocket and head down to the shops.

I thought about wearing the police trousers and taking the baton with me, but it's the middle of the day, the sun's shining and maybe I'm a wee bit cocky, but I feel safe in daylight. Besides, that polis on the television, the detective in charge said that there would be an increased police presence in the area, though obviously he didn't mean last night when the bastards chucked the brick through wee Mary's window.

I was about what, maybe around a hundred yards I think from the church when I saw two of them hanging about the telephone box. I didn't want any confrontation and crossed the road to the other pavement, keeping my eyes front but a wee wary eye on them too. That's when I saw the third guy walking towards them and being handed something by one of the other two. The third guy then walked quickly away towards Linthaugh Road and by this time, I'm only about fifty yards from the telephone box though it's on the other side of the road.

The first two guys were watching me and I'm thinking; they all seem to be wearing the same clothes these days. Track suit tops, skip hats turned back to front and jeans or tracksuit trousers.

I could feel their eyes boring into me as I'm passing by the church gates then I heard a voice shout, "Jimmy!"

I turned and there's the parish priest Father Stephen waving to me from the front steps of St Convals.

I didn't realise that I'd been holding my breath or how nervous I was. In fact, my mouth was as dry as a Welshman's humour. If they two guys had challenged me…anyway, I'm just relieved they didn't get the chance.

"Thought that was you," he puts out his hand to shake mine. "Have you time for a wee cup of tea?"

"Eh, thanks Father, but I was just on my way to collect the paper," I reply, but he won't hear me saying no and before I know it he's leading me by the elbow round the side of the church to the presbytery and into the reception area.

"Bide here a minute Jimmy and I'll fetch the teapot out," he winks at me and he's away through the door to the kitchen before I can say no.

He's gone a couple of minutes and I'm thinking there's bound to be an ulterior motive for a priest hijacking me when I'm passing by the church when he comes back with a tray on which is a teapot, two cups and saucers and a plate of digestive biscuits.

To be honest, I'm a retired man so it's not as if I'm in a hurry to go anywhere fast.

He's pouring the tea when the ulterior motive raises its head.

"Now that you're a retired man, Jimmy," he begins and that's when my heart sinks because I can guess what's coming, "and with all that experience you gained as a janitor. You know, keeping the school grounds neat and tidy and that, have you given any thought to maybe volunteering to do a wee bit of work here at the church grounds? I mean just to keep your hand in like; mowing, weeding, that sort of thing?"

I'm staring at him and thinking that Father Stephen is a right good and kind man, but he's chancing his arm thinking that I'm going to take on a job like the church grounds. It's a hell of a big place, if you see what I mean.

"Look father," I put the cup and saucer down and raise my hands apologetically, "I appreciate that you think enough of me that I might do a good job…"

"Of course you would, Jimmy. You're very decent man and highly thought of in the parish," he interrupts me. "My, it was only the other day I was speaking to some of the parishioners who were singing your praises, Jimmy."

Did I say he was a right good and kind man? Conman more like. Anyway, cutting a long story short, two cups of tea and three digestive biscuits later I'm agreeing to come round twice a week to tend the grounds.

I didn't know then how handy that wee job would become.

Father Stephen walks with me to the church gates and I have a glance over at the telephone box. The two guys are still there and watching us though they're pretending they're not.

"What are they all about?" I ask him without actually pointing towards them.

"They're always hanging about there. That's them selling their dope, Jimmy," he tells me.

Honestly, at first I thought he was kidding me on and I am absolutely aghast that right opposite the Catholic Church there is two guys dealing drugs.

"Have you not told the polis, Father?"

"Oh, I've told them right enough. I even suggested that if they want to hide here in the church grounds and jump out and catch the buggers they are very welcome, but the Superintendent at Pollok tells me that they want to catch bigger fish and very soon, though how soon I don't know. They're intending mounting an operation, he tells me that will *ensnare* the guy supplying the drugs, not those two wee shites over there."

It's a bit unusual hearing a priest using language like that, but I agree with his sentiments.

They are a pair of wee shites.

I make quick decision and chancing my arm, I ask, "Have you heard anything about the murder, Father?"

He shrugs and replies, "Only what I've heard on the TV and the radio, but likely at Mass on Sunday the rumour mill will be working overtime. Will I see you there at the eleven o'clock Mass tomorrow, Jimmy? You know you'll be very welcome."

I kind of grin sheepishly at him and half shrug, but I don't say aye or no.

So there I am, standing there with Father Stephen and you'll remember that I was brought up Catholic, though for a long time I've never really been attending Mass when a cold shiver creeps up my spine. I suddenly had a tremendous feeling of guilt, what they call 'Catholic Guilt' and believe it or not I have to stop myself from confessing to the Father that *I'm* the man who murdered Alex Paterson!

Crazy, isn't it? I'm actually considering telling this young man what I've done.

But I can't, can I? I mean, it's pretty well known that priests cannot divulge what they hear in the confessional and even though I know that if I tell him what I've done, it will put one hell of a burden on him. He'll know I'm a murderer and try to persuade me to give myself up to the police and remind me that I won't be forgiven till I do that.

The thing is, I'm not really bothered about forgiveness because the more I think about it, the more I'm convinced Alex Paterson deserved what I did to him.

So there it is God, deal with that, I'm thinking to myself.

"So, you're away for the papers?" says Father Stephen and startles me because I was that wrapped up in my thoughts.

I'm smiling at him and nod cheerio as he turns to walk back to the presbytery.

I start walking back down towards the church gates and out into Hapland Road towards Linthaugh Road and all the while I'm keeping my eyes on the pavement in front of me. Suddenly one of them across the road, a fat bugger wearing a vertically striped red and white football shirt and yes, you've guessed; a skip hat that's worn back to front, shouts to me, "Get a new window for your car yet, did you wee man?" and they both laugh.

I'm so angry that I want to cross the road and throttle them both, but what I want and what I'm capable of are two different things.

My pride's hurt and my face is crimson because they know they're on safe ground. I'm just a wee, ordinary guy that can't take on one of them in a fistfight, let alone two of them.

But I've seen their faces mind you and they are faces I'll not forget in a hurry.

It was a different security man and now there is a young man behind the till when I go into the Co-operative. I lift a wire basket and moving along the aisles, collect three daily, local newspapers, but didn't bother trying to read the headlines in the shop. No, that can wait till I got home. I collected another litre of milk, a loaf of bread, a meat pie from the frozen section and a packet of that instant potato that can be made in the microwave. As a wee treat, I bought myself two jam doughnuts for my late night cup of tea while I watch the television that night.

The two women in front of me at the till must have known each other and while I wait behind them I hear the older woman talking about the murder.

"Aye, I heard it was a drugs thing," she was saying. "The woman along the road from me told me her man's nephew is in the polis and he heard that the dead guy owed a lot of money for drugs. My God, you never know the next," she shook her head. Collecting her change, she nodded cheerio to the other woman and left the shop. Her pal lifted her basket onto the counter and that's when I saw it and my blood froze.

I might have seen it before, but I've never really taken any notice of it, but there it is, mounted on the wall above the cigarette shelves behind the till.

A security camera that had a wee, red light that winked at me as I watched it.

Oh dear God. I'm thinking if the CID come in and find out that there's a security camera in the shop here they'll backtrack Alex Paterson's movements before he was killed and they'll see me standing in the queue behind him. Then they'll speak to the security man and the girl, Gina I think her name is, and they two will tell them, 'Oh aye, that wee man bought milk and left the shop right behind the dead guy.'

"Hello there? Mister, are you wanting served or not?"

It's the guy behind the till and he's speaking to me. I dump my basket onto the counter and he's shaking his head as he lifts my shopping from the basket and runs the bar codes through the machine. He's probably thinking that I'm either drunk or just another dopey old guy. I stuff the shopping into a plastic bag and my hands are shaking again. That will likely confirm what he thinks; that I'm drunk and I've got the DT's.

"Sorry, I was miles away," I'm smiling at him, but he just sighs and tells me the bill. I hand him a ten pound note and get my change. I'm walking from the store past the security man, but he's smoothing back his gelled hair and ignoring me because of the young lassie with the short skirt walking past the door who's taken his attention. That's me got a new worry now. I must be recorded on the shops CCTV. Oh God, how will I explain that? It won't take an expert to work out that if I've left the shop straight after Paterson, my route home must pass by him as he's getting killed and the CID will easily work out that either *I'm* the murderer or I watched him *getting* murdered.

God, I stop and take a deep breath.

Just when I thought I couldn't be connected to the murder.

I take a detour and walk to Hapland Road from the other side, past the doctor's surgery. The police caravan is still parked across the road and I can see three, maybe four detectives I think they are, standing outside. A couple are holding clipboards and two are smoking. They look like they're having a laugh and one, a woman, she starts doing a wee jig on the pavement. Probably celebrating the overtime she's getting for working a Saturday and just as well there isn't any reporters hanging about.

So much for the grim faced detectives that I keep hearing about on the tele.

I get into the house and I never used to bother about locking my front door behind me when I was in the house, but since the trouble started, I keep the front and the back doors both locked. Sign of the times, I tell myself.

The mail's been delivered, but it's the usual rubbish that comes through the door. To be honest, other than utility bills I don't get personal mail.

I head into the kitchen and empty the carrier bag. The newspapers go onto the kitchen table while I boil the kettle for a cuppa and that done I begin flicking through the first paper for the story of the murder. There isn't that much more reported than what the radio or television has already told me and so I move onto the second paper and that's much the same.

The kettle whistles and I brew the tea.

The third newspaper, the 'Glasgow News' has almost the same report and I'm starting to think that all three reports could have been written by the same reporter when I see something a wee bit different.

According to the 'Glasgow News' report, an unnamed police source that I take to mean the reporter probably made the 'police source' up, is apparently quoted as saying that Alex Paterson was currently on bail for several drug charges and a serious assault charge. There aren't any other details about the charges, but what it did was again made me feel that bit better for killing him.

I'm sitting there, sipping at my tea and treating myself to one of the doughnuts when I remember the two who shouted at me earlier on. The wee fat guy laughing about breaking my windscreen made me angry enough to…well, you can probably guess. Of course I'm in no doubt it was him that did it or at least he was there when it was done, but the worrying thing is that he recognised me as the man that owns the car.

I'm leaning with my elbows on the kitchen table and wondering to myself; if he recognises me, do they have something else planned for me?

Then I remember what Father Stephen said about them always hanging about there at the telephone box, selling their drugs.

If that's true and he meant the wee fat guy with the striped top then I'm smiling, because that means I know where to find him first.

CHAPTER EIGHT

I know you'll laugh at this, but I'm thinking of getting myself a disguise.

Do you remember me telling you how I got into reading books, the cowboy stories and the war stories? Well, I sat and sipped at my tea and gave this a lot of thought.

You already know I'm not a young man and I'm not a fighter either, but one thing I learned when I was reading books was the heroes in the war books always use the element of surprise. Another thing I remember reading about was that attack is the best form of defence. I can't recall where I read these things or who wrote them, but you'll know yourself if you're into reading books that sometimes these wee things stick in your head.

The meat pie is cooking in the oven and I'm sitting here at the table, working out a plan in my head.

So, here's what I'm thinking.

I'll put on the police trousers with the baton in the pocket and wear something dark on top. The old maroon anorak too and I've got a navy coloured woollen Tammy in my sock drawer upstairs. I'll wear that as well. I'll get my old working boots out of the cupboard and last of all, now don't laugh here; I'll rub some boot polish onto my face.

I'll park the Escort round in Dormanside Road, maybe about fifty yards away and that means it will be just out of sight of the telephone box.

What I'm thinking of doing is pretending to be a customer for the drugs, like I saw that guy today and I'll stagger up and then batter the two of them with the baton. If I'm quick enough they'll not know what hit them. If I manage to deck them both, I'll run round to the car and leave the lights off as I drive away.

Sounds simple, doesn't it?

I'm shaking my head. Aye, it does sound simple enough, but will I have the bottle to do it and particularly, if the detective on the television was telling the truth about there being extra police on the street, I might be taking one heck of a chance. Curiously though, I don't believe him and I think he's just trying to reassure us, the public.

You'll be thinking that I'm mad or maybe a bit stupid

Aye, I suppose I am, but why am I even considering this? Well, frankly I think once the CID cotton on to the CCTV recording in the Co-operative, they'll be round here chapping on my door and that will be me. Handcuffed, taken away and goodnight Vienna. But if I *am* going to get taken away then I will prefer to be taken as a man, not a mouse because you know what they say, it's better to be hung as a sheep than as a lamb.

The thing is that wee fat sod leering at me today was the final straw and I'm still blazing angry at him. Funny though, angry as I am at him, I'm just as angry at myself because I didn't have the bottle to challenge him. It's a bit hard to explain; it's just that when he and the other moron ridiculed me, it made me feel like a right coward so this might be my only chance to redeem myself.

If it doesn't work out, so be it, but like something else I once read; it's better to try and fail than fail to try.

I don't know where *that* comes from either, but it's not a bad saying, is it?

I'm thinking that a wee drink to bolster me might be in order, but I've poured away the last of the whisky so that's knocked on the head.

The kitchen clock's telling me that the pie is ready, so I microwave my mashed tatties and open a can of peas. I'm hungry enough to eat a monkey dipped in fat and when I'm finished my dinner in front of the television, I wash up the dishes and make myself a cuppa.

My nerves are on edge and I'm thinking of all sorts of reasons not to go through with my plan.

The time crawls by and by now it's dark outside. Glancing through the upstairs front window, I can't see any of the gang up in the field. To pass the time I give Scooby a wee phone and I'm pleased to hear that he's feeling a bit better and is able to talk a lot easier, now that his lips are not so swollen. I'm on the phone for about half an hour and because it's Saturday, he tells me he's disappointed that he's not able to attend the night in the social club. He's tried to persuade Alice to go, but she won't go without him.

Their daughter Shona went home this morning, but made him promise if Alice needs a hand with him, Scooby is to phone her and she'll pop back. That's just like Shona; a right good daughter and I know why they are both so proud of her.

Their son Charles visited last night and told them he had phoned his brother Michael, who is still abroad and told him about their father being mugged.

Scooby is annoyed at Charles because he didn't want Michael worrying and his holiday being ruined.

I ask if the CID have been back, but he tells me that he hasn't heard from them since they visited him, the morning after the murder.

We chewed the fat for a wee while, talking about this and that and football. If you're from the city you will know there is a religious divide in Glasgow; if you're a Catholic you support Celtic and if you're Protestant, then it's Rangers. It's daft, I know and I shake my head when I think of the men and women I know who support Celtic because they associate Celtic with Catholicism, just as other side support the Gers because they think of them as a Protestant team. Scooby's wife Alice is a wee bit like that. She thinks that God is on Celtic's side because they're the Catholics. I'm very fond of Alice but really, how stupid is that? Me, I gave up following football when I married Jeannie who coming from Skye thought the whole religious thing was silly and divisive.

A wise woman was my wife.

I'm pleased that Scooby is feeling better and even more pleased that almost in a whisper, he told me that he's happy the guy that did that to him is dead. I know he'll probably feel a bit guilty thinking like that, but he'll never know how much that makes me feel even a wee bit better about what I did.

Now, I'm not saying it was right or trying to justify what I did as an excuse for the attack on Scooby. I mean, yes I saw the watch and the red mist come down. Anything I did after that, it's down to my conscience.

What I'm thinking of doing tonight?

Well, that's something I intend doing just for me.

The night's fairly drawing in and outside it's as dark as a coalman's arse. I know, I know, I shouldn't be saying things like that, but I've a hard time trying to keep up with what they call political correctness. It used to annoy me when I was working, management telling me what I could say and what I couldn't say. Wee things like it was wrong to call women 'hen' or the Chinese takeaway shop the 'Chinky.' I mean, these are words I've used all my life and I've never intended to offend anyone with them. I mean there are more offensive things happening today than using silly words like that.

Try asking my old neighbour Missus Baxter what's the more offensive; calling her 'hen' or chucking a brick through her window? I know, I'm kind of old fashioned and I'm what the young ones today call a dinosaur.

Well, if being a dinosaur means being polite, courteous, trying to live a decent life and not causing anyone any harm, then I'm a dinosaur.

Well, and I'm kind of sheepishly grinning here, not causing anyone any harm doesn't include murdering a drug-dealing scummy or intending to batter a cheeky fat guy.

It sounds like I'm talking for the sake of talking, that I'm trying to stave off getting myself ready to go out and do what I intend.

But no more stalling. I take a deep breath and fetch the police trousers and anorak from the radiators upstairs and change into the trousers and a navy coloured polo shirt. I rummage through the sock drawer and find my old, woollen Tammy that Jeannie knitted for me all those winters ago.

From the hall cupboard I fetch my heavy working boots and that's me nearly ready.

From under the sink I reach in behind the detergents and grab the baton. It feels reassuringly heavy in my hand as I slip it into the baton pocket in the trousers.

From the old wooden box I grab a tin of black polish and take it into the bathroom. I'm a bit self-conscious as I dip my forefinger into it and smear it onto my face. I'm grinning like an idiot and looking at myself in the mirror, I burst out laughing, but it's a nervous laugh. Taking a deep breath, I stare at my reflection and wonder; do I really have the bottle for this?

Then I remember what the fat guy shouted and I'm angry; angry with myself for doubting that I *can* do this.

I grab the Escort keys from the wall hook in the hallway and opening the front door, I peek out, but the street is quiet and I can't see anybody walking or any cars coming down the road.

I sneak out and locking the door behind me, keep my head down as I walk quickly to the car.

Right away I realise that short-arse that I am, I can't drive properly with the baton stuck down the trousers of my leg so I take it out and hide it beneath the passenger seat. Then I think oh, oh, because I haven't thought what I might say if the polis were to stop me and see my Al Jolson face.

I'm not daft enough to drive straight down Hapland Road to the telephone box, but instead I take a circular route by going the other way towards the Braidcraft Road. I'm on the side road that is parallel to the dual carriageway and when I'm driving towards the roundabout I see the police caravan is still parked across the road there, but I don't see anybody hanging about it.

I have to admit, the sight of the caravan gives me cause to wonder what the hell I'm doing.

I cruise past the police caravan, but I still don't see anybody there and it looks like the interior lights are out so I'm guessing there's nobody inside.

When I turn into Linthaugh Road I drive slowly past the junction of Hapland Road and there's two figures standing near to the telephone box. The street lights are on and I see one is wearing the striped red and white shirt; the fat guy. Even straining my eyes and believe me, even at my age I've still got sharp eyesight, I can't be certain if the other guy is the same guy I saw earlier.

I stop out of sight on Linthaugh Road and take a deep breath.

This is it; make or break time.

I don't see anybody walking in the street and only one car coming on the other side of the road that passes by without stopping.

That's when I realise I have been holding my breath.

I take another deep breath and snatch the baton from under the passenger seat and stepping out of the car, get a fright when the interior light comes on. Bugger, I should have thought about that and shut the door again, then shove the switch to off.

I open the door and this time step out of the car and put the baton into the pocket of my trousers.

I decide to leave the car unlocked and hope it won't get nicked when I'm away, but I know that I'll be in a hurry when I'm coming back and I don't want to waste time trying to unlock the driver's door.

I close the door quietly and I'm surprised at how calm I feel, because my hands are not shaking anymore.

I glance about me and still there is nobody walking in the street and as I turn, that's when I hear the faint sound of music. I had forgotten that tonight being Saturday the church social club across the road from the telephone box is holding a wee dance night. I can see that under the bright light above the front door of the club there are a few figures standing together, likely out for a smoke because they're not permitted to smoke inside. I'm guessing that the bright light will probably dazzle them and besides, with a wee drink in them they won't be paying attention to what's happening in the darkness across the road.

I walked towards the telephone box and now it's just forty yards away. I pretend to stagger a wee bit and keep my head down, but even though my guts are twisting and I'm that tense I think every nerve in my body is quivering like a guitar string, I'm determined to do this.

I force my mouth closed because I'm worried that my teeth will chatter.

That's when I see that the two guys together at the telephone box are standing with their backs to me, watching the hall across the road.

I quicken my pace and then stop still. The fat guy has turned side-on to me and the dirty sod is openly peeing against the telephone box! I can't believe that he's so arrogant that he's whipped out his wee man and urinating. Has he no dignity, the dirty fat git!

That does it. Before I know it I've the baton in my hand and I'm beside him with the baton raised. He's that concentrated on peeing a design on the side of the telephone box, he hasn't heard or seen me coming.

I bring my baton down squarely on his skip cap and let me tell you, all the indignities of my past, the 'yes sir, no sir, three bags full sir' that I've endured in my life, the disappointments in my jobs, the turning the other cheek, the sneering as I walked past the fat guy. All these things went into that one blow and it was the hardest blow I think I've ever struck.

He collapsed like a bag of coal and just as I'm delivering a second blow, his mate turned towards me.

Now, I'm about to panic because I'm thinking I'm going to be in a fight for my life, but to my surprise, the guy just stares wide-eyed at me. I can only imagine what he's seeing and what I *think* he saw was a darkly clothed maniac with a big stick laying into the fat guy.

That's probably why he starts to scream like a wee girl and took off at a run without looking back.

Me, I took off at a run in the *other* direction towards the car.

In the car, I throw the baton down onto the rubber mat on the passenger floor and grab the keys from my pocket. My hands are shaking and it takes me a few seconds to shove the ignition key in and start the engine. Then I stall the bloody thing and have to start it again and all the time I'm praying to a God I no longer believe in that He helps me get this *bloody* car started!

I take off faster than I intended and travel for about a hundred yards before I remember to switch on the lights.

All I can think about is that I need to get home, get out of these clothes, get my face scrubbed and dear God, how I wish right now there was a half bottle waiting for me.

A few heart-stopping minutes later, that's me in the house now and I'm in the kitchen, tearing off my jacket. I'm checking it for signs of blood and though I can't see anything, I throw it into the washing machine anyway and the same goes for the trousers and the woollen Tammy. Curiously, the baton doesn't seem to have any blood on it either, but that doesn't mean I won't give it a good scrub anyway. My boots look okay and I'm not getting rid of them like I did with the shoes, so later tonight I'll set about them with the polishing brushes.

I start giggling like a wee wean because there's me standing in the kitchen in my polo shirt, underpants and my socks and looking like a refugee from the Black and White Minstrel Show from the nineteen-sixties. If Jeannie could see me now she'd have a fit.

In the bathroom, instead of a wash I decide to have a shower and I don't know if you've ever had boot polish on your face, but have you any idea how difficult it is to scrub the bleeding stuff off? Finally, I'm washed and dried and in my pyjamas and dressing gown, I make my way through to the kitchen and you guessed it, stick the kettle on.

While it's boiling I'm wondering about the fat guy. I know that I gave him one hell of a bang on the head with the baton when I hit him the first time, though maybe not so hard with the second blow, but even so I'm thinking I might have cracked his skull. Certainly, I wasn't intending killing him or anything, but yes; I did want to hurt him.

I'm not that bothered how badly hurt he might be, though. Maybe I'm becoming…what do you call it; immune to my actions, but I don't care. Live by the sword, die by the sword. Isn't that some sort of quote from the bible and in fact if memory serves correctly, I think it was the big man Himself who said it.

With my mug of tea I make my way upstairs to the front room and in the darkness, peer out the window. I don't hear any noise but there is a faint blue hue on the rise of the grassy hill and I'm wondering what it is when it hits me; it's the glare from the blue polis lights on top of the cars that have arrived at the telephone box.

CHAPTER NINE

I'm up early this morning and downstairs in my pyjamas in time to switch on the radio for the eight o'clock news. The first item is about the second murder; murder?

'...and police are appealing for anyone who might have information,' droned on the reporter.

That stopped me in my tracks, I can tell you. The reporter continued that the deceased had been discovered badly injured then conveyed to the casualty at the Southern General Hospital, but succumbed to his injuries a short time later. I sat as still as a statue, taking it in as the news went on about some ferry sinking somewhere abroad, but to be honest, I wasn't listening anymore.

I sat heavily down onto the couch. I was that taken aback I spilled some of the tea into my lap. It was boiling hot and I jumped up in fright, holding the soaked pyjamas away from my crotch before the tea seeped through my trousers and burned my willie.

Murder?

Bugger me.

I'm shaking my head and go to fetch a dishcloth from the kitchen; the wee fat guy must have died.

Died? No, I've obviously hit him too hard, a lot harder than I thought and I've killed him. That bloody baton I've made must be a lot heavier than I anticipated and with me bringing it down with my weight behind it.

Oh, dear God, I didn't really expect this, I'm thinking to myself.

I'm at a loss to understand what I'm doing. Honestly. I've now killed two young men and I should be wringing my hands in despair and holding my head in shame.

Funny though, I feel a wee bit funny. Not funny 'ha ha'. Just…well, it's difficult to describe. You see I'm not *really* that bothered for I've convinced myself now that the two of them deserved what they got. What I have to do is protect myself because bad guys or not, the polis will be hell bent on finding out who killed the two toe-rags. Oh, and don't think I've forgotten about the recording from the security camera in the Co-op. That's in the forefront of my mind and yes; I expect that anytime soon I'll be getting a visit from the polis. So what precautions should I take?

In bed last night I thought about cutting up the baton, but instead I'll steep it in bleach just in case there is some blood residue on it and stow it again under the sink. I'm taking these precautions because I watch them forensic programmes on tele and a great source of information they are too.

If the polis search the house and find the baton, I can always explain it away by saying that because of the almost nightly disorder in the field outside my front door that the police *don't* seem capable of dealing with, I keep it handy in case my house gets burgled.

I'll give the washing machine a rinse with bleach too and I've already hung the clothes over the radiators to dry. I'm confident they will be fine and stand up to any examination the polis make.

Then it occurs to me, something I might have missed; the rubber mat that's on the floor of the car. When I threw the baton down after battering the fat guy on the head, it might have…what do they call it again? Yeah, it might have transferred some blood to the mat.

I hurry upstairs and jump into trousers and a shirt and then nip out to the Escort. It's Sunday morning so the street's quiet while I collect the rubber mat and bring it inside. That goes into the washing machine too and I set it for a woollen wash. I mean, a hot wash would melt the rubber wouldn't it? See, I'm not *that* daft.

Almost with relief my mind's ticked off one more problem and for the life of me I can't think of any other problem that might arise; at least not at this time.

One thing that concerns me though and it's got nothing to do with the police.

Do you think maybe I'm starting to enjoy this?

What I'm doing, I mean?

I've showered and changed into fresh clothes and for the second Sunday in a row I've decided to attend eleven o'clock Mass.

Not that I need any forgiveness or anything. Let's face it; I think I'm a bit past that now.

No, I want to know what the craic is and there's nowhere better for gossip than from the folk who attend Mass.

Before I leave though I give Alice and Scooby a phone call, just on the odd chance they might be going too and I can suggest meeting them at the church gate.

There's no reply so I'm guessing they must be on their way.

There's a fine drizzle coming down now so I fetch the wee pop-up brolly from the cupboard under the stairs and locking the front door, that's me on my way.

I'm going to walk. I think the less I'm seen in the car in the next few days, the better.

It takes no more than a few minutes to walk to the church, but as I get closer I can see uniformed police officers standing beside a white tent that's been set up on the pavement and there's a police panda car and a couple of vans. There's blue and white tape surrounding the grassy area at the back of the telephone box that's stretched around the tent and it's tied to a lamppost and a nearby garden fence with a couple of uniformed cops standing guard at each end of the tape.

It's like something off the television and don't ask me why, but it take me all my time to resist the urge to giggle at the murder scene. Am I going off my head or what?

There's dozens of people all heading towards the church gate and into St Convals and despite the drizzle, I can see that they're all walking slowly, turning their heads to watch the police and the people in white overalls that are working at the telephone box.

I know from watching the programmes on the TV that they will be the forensic people.

I'm hunched under my umbrella yet I still get the feeling that they know it was me and that it's some kind of trap.

I'm nervous again but I do my best to ignore the police and I walk quickly to the church gate.

A few people I know by name and others by sight nod to me as I go through the gate, but I'm keeping my eyes fixed on the big wooden doors at the top of the incline in front of me.

I hear people muttering and shaking their heads and listening to comments like, "Bad business," and "Right outside the chapel, too." One wee woman makes the sign of the cross and stopping beside me, she turns to stare at the telephone box and I hear her say to her man, "God forgive me, but he was a bad wee shite, that Calum Black. He fair broke his mother's heart, so he did."

Calum Black.

That's the first time I've heard the fat guy's name mentioned. I'm walking through the wooden doors and I dip my fingers into the wee bowl on the wall that contains the holy water and make the sign of the cross.

Calum Black. Alex Paterson.

The names of the two young men that I've killed. No, not killed…murdered.

I push through the doors from the porch area into the nave and hesitate as I stare at the altar at the other end.

One of the pass-keepers hands me this morning's order of service, but my eyes are fixed on the huge crucifix suspended above the altar with the body of Christ staring back at me.

I move to the right and walk up the outside aisle. The church is almost full and on the other side I spot Scooby and Alice sitting. He's not hard to spot and looks like a Sikh with the white bandage wrapped around his head.

I shuffle into a pew and almost immediately, the congregation stands as Father Stephen and the altar servers walk from the sacristy towards the altar.

The choir in the loft above the porch burst into a hymn and the church is filled with sound.

I kind of half listen to what is going on, stand when everyone else stands and kneel when everyone else kneels because to be honest, my mind is elsewhere.

I'm starting to think what the *heck* am I doing here after I've just murdered two young men?

Ah well, here's as good a place as anywhere I suppose.

Father Stephen is up on the pulpit and he's asking for prayers for the recently departed and in the names of the parishioners that he reads out, he includes Alex Paterson and now Calum Black.

"These young men might not have been members of this congregation," he's telling us, "but let us not forget that they were taken from their loved ones before they had the opportunity to experience life."

Maybe it was my surroundings or maybe I was feeling a little remorseful at the priest's sermon or maybe even the Catholic guilt is kicking in again; I'm not really certain what it is, but then to my surprise I hear somebody behind me snort as if unconsciously agreeing with me that the two of them were bad sods.

Father Stephen, leaning with both forearms on the pulpit, then admits that both young men were known to be troublemakers, but asks the congregation to forgive Paterson and Black for their sins against the community and reminds us that in death they will face a higher court.

Somehow I feel that the priest is agreeing with me; that the two buggers will be no sad loss to society, though of course he's restrained by his dog-collar from telling us what a right pair of shit's they both really were.

Before he finishes his sermon, he tells us that again the CID will be outside the main doors and that anyone who has any information regarding the two murders might consider speaking with the detectives.

Aye right, I'm thinking.

Needless to say I don't take communion and as the Mass draws to a close with a final hymn, I can hear the people standing at the back start to shuffle out of the church doors. I'm guessing that likely they will want to have a look at the detectives who are waiting outside and as the hymn finishes, I genuflect and make my way with the crowd outside.

I'm keeping an eye open for Scooby and Alice and give them a wee wave to let them know I've seen them and nod that I'll meet them on the path outside the main doors.

In the courtyard outside the main doors there are half a dozen detectives with clipboards speaking to people and I'd be lying if I didn't admit I was desperately keen to know what people were telling them. I suppose I was just relieved that nobody was pointing a finger towards me and screaming, "That's him, that's the murderer!"

"Two Sunday's in a row, Jimmy," I see Alice smiling at me. "You'll be joining the priesthood next."

"Let him alone, you," Scooby is holding on to her arm for support, an aluminium walking stick in his other hand.

"How are you?" I ask him.

"Each day's a winner," he grins at me. "My knee is still giving me gyp, but old Doctor Gillespie popped in yesterday morning and says once the swelling is gone if there is any more pain, he'll organise an x-ray."

"At least the swelling on his face is gone, interrupts Alice.

"Is it? I didn't notice," I kid him on.

She nods towards the detectives. "That's some business there, isn't it? Another murder I hear."

"I heard a woman going into Mass saying the guy was called Calum Black," I lower my voice and confide to them.

Scooby's eyes narrow and he nods to Alice before saying, "That will be Alex Black's boy right enough then. They live over in Dormanside. You'll know Alex," he then says to me. "Never worked a day in his life, but a right bevy man. Sports a scar on his left cheek and used to boast that he was the hardest man in Pollok before he got a kicking a few years back, up in Nitshill somewhere. Drinks down at the halfway on Paisley Road West and word is he's done time for thieving, drug dealing and giving his wife bleaching's. The boy that's dead, I think he was the oldest son and from what Alice was telling me, he must have taken after his Da because he was into the drugs too."

I'm staring at him and my face must have registered my surprise, for Alice then explains, "I was down at the shops early this morning for the rolls and the newspapers."

"And you learned all that from a visit to the shops?"

"Oh aye," she sniffs. "It's surprising what you hear down there."

I slowly shake my head because when it comes to gossiping in Pollok, nothing surprises me.

"What about you being attacked," I ask him. "Has the CID been back to see you yet?"

He shakes his head and replies, "No, but they did say when they visited the last time that if they had any new information they'd come and see me, but nothing yet."

We stand for another five or so minutes while a wee crowd forms round about the detectives and I'm wondering who's really being interviewed; the public or the police. I glance now and then towards the area that is cordoned off round the telephone box.

"Jimmy," Alice pokes me with her finger. "You're not listening. Do you want to come round for your dinner this afternoon? It'll be steak pie and pudding, but you're very welcome. Say about half past four?"

"Oh, aye, that'll be grand," I nod and then take my leave of them. The congregation is starting to disperse and I think I'm away, but before I get to the gate my arm's grabbed and I die a thousand deaths.

It's Father Stephen, not the CID.

"Jimmy, I'm glad I caught you there," he smiles at me. He's a wee bit out of breath as though he might have been chasing me. He glances up to the cloud filled sky and says, "That wee matter we discussed. If the weather improves, how are you fixed for Tuesday morning?"

To be honest, Father Stephen's request had completely slipped my mind. I mean, I've had a lot going on, as you well know.

"Aye, no problem Father," I tell him. "I'll be by about nine if that's okay."

We agree nine o'clock and with a slap on my back and telling me what a decent man I am, he turns away to speak with someone else and I'm heading out the gate.

I'm tempted to turn and look back at what's happening at the telephone box, but convince myself that would be stupid. All it would take was a nosey detective to wonder why the wee man with the brolly was paying so much attention to their crime scene and right now, all I want to do is get home.

If you don't know Hapland Road, let me explain. It starts at Linthaugh Road and is nearly half a mile long in a wide, gentle curve that ends when it meets Braidcraft Road. It's not *really* a road, more a crescent. Facing onto Hapland Road for most of its length is the field that I've been telling you about. The reason I'm explaining this now is there's me walking home from the church when round the curve, as it were, I see a police car parked right outside my house. I get such a fright that I almost stopped dead.

My throat tightens and I swallow with some difficulty, but continue to walk towards the house and through the drizzling rain I can see two figures sitting in the front of the panda car.

It did occur to me to run away, but let's face it. Where the hell would I run to?

My first thought is that *finally*, the CID has watched the recording from the security camera in the Co-op and I'm wondering; who gave them my name and address?

I take a deep breath and decide to brazen it out.

I get closer to the house and I'm peering through the rain splattered windscreen when the driver's door open and young Craig Wallace pops out.

"Jimmy," he calls and waves to me, "thought that was you."

The young good looking lassie cop, I forget her name, gets out of the passenger door and gives me a broad smile.

I'm thinking to myself; they're awfully cheerful for polis that is here to arrest me.

I'm fumbling in my pocket for my keys when they join me on the path to the front door and stand behind me.

"Are you okay, Mister McGrath?" the lassie asks me.

I remember now. Mhari, that's her name.

"Eh, I'm fine hen. Just the old arthritis playing up," I tell her.

I don't really have arthritis. I'm just trying for a sympathy vote before they arrest me.

The door springs open and I step inside. Normally I'd shake the umbrella out before I go through the door, but that seems a bit pointless now that I'm getting the jail.

"So, Jimmy," I hear Craig behind me. "Been down to the pineapple?"

We're still stood in my narrow hallway and I turn as the lassie is giving her partner a weird look.

"Pineapple," he repeats and then with a resigned look, tells her, "The chapel."

"Oh," she grins and looks a wee bit sheepish.

I'm wondering. Is this some sort of game they're playing with me and should I even bother taking my coat off.

"So," Craig rubs his hands together, "what's the chance of a cuppa then?"

So I do have time to take my coat off and I hang it to dry on the hook.

I'm grinning like an idiot, but inside my stomach is churning as I make my way through to the kitchen to put the kettle on.

They both take off their caps and they're sitting themselves down in the living room because obviously they realise that I'm not going to take off. I mean, at my age I couldn't run faster than a snotty nose.

"Did you see the mob outside the chapel at the telephone box, Jimmy?" Craig calls through the open door.

"Aye, I did," I call back and then for a brief second, I'm wondering. Maybe they're not here for me. Maybe they really *are* just in for a cuppa.

I'm still finding it difficult to swallow and honest, I am really, really nervous.

The kettle's boiled and the tea's brewing. I make up a tray with the three mugs, sugar and milk and plate of digestive that I carry through and lay down onto the wee low table.

"Rotten day out there," the lassie Mhari smiles at me and sits forward to milk three cups.

I'm so bloody nervous I can only nod my head.

"You sure you're all right there, Jimmy?" It's Craig who asks me this time.

I take a deep breath and reply, "Aye, just surprised at what's been happening."

"The murder," he nods.

Now, you might recall when him and the lassie where in for a wee visit that last time, I got the feeling that Craig was trying to impress her with his knowledge. You know, her being one of them rookies, I mean.

So I fetch the teapot from the kitchen and while the lassie pours, I sit down and I'm taking a mouthful to calm my nerves when Craig says, "The CID think it might be a serial killer."

Honestly, I nearly spat my tea all over the carpet.

A serial killer?

Bloody hell, I'm a serial killer!

I wish I could see myself because my face must have been a picture.

Craig puts on a serious face and tells us, "I was talking with a mate in the CID. He says that the two of them that's been murdered, Paterson and now this lowlife Calum Black belonged to the same gang that's run by the drug dealer Neil McMillan that lives over in Dormanside."

Lowlife, he calls the fat guy and I'm thinking that Craig must be right into the American police programmes.

I'm that taken aback at being called a serial killer I've almost completely forgotten about the recording that is worrying me witless. I glance at Mhari and it's easy to see the young lassie is very impressed by her neighbours inside information.

"So," I hesitantly ask, "who do the CID think this killer is then?" Craig, happy to be holding court now, sits back and taking a deep breath, replies, "Well, according to my source…" his detective mate's now a source, I'm thinking, "…there was two guys attacked last night; the one that got murdered and the one that got away."

I didn't attack two guys I'm almost telling him, but bite my tongue. "The guy that was with Black, the guy that got away," he continues, "said the killer was a big man." He extends his arms as though describing a muscular build, "About six feet tall and dressed all in black. He thinks he was a black guy, like one of them big Jamaicans that are in the gangs in London," he adds, nodding his head.

So, now I'm supposed to be six feet tall with wide shoulders and I'm a black man? Seems that boot polish worked even better that I thought it might.

I'm unconsciously shaking my head at the description Craig is giving us.

Apparently enthralled, it's Mhari that asks, "What is the motive for the killings? Did your source tell you?"

"Drugs," he wisely nods, as though disclosing a huge secret to Mhari and me. "It seems there is a drug war going on here in Pollok."

She takes a deep breath, her hand over her mouth and it seems to me, obviously excited at being involved in what Craig is now describing as something that sounds like a Hollywood movie.

I'm as excited as Mhari as we listen to Craig drone on, but at the back of my mind I'm still worried about the CCTV security recording. Should I ask him about it in a kind of roundabout way, I'm wondering. I decide to go for it.

"The first young man that was killed, Craig…"

"Alex Paterson," he nods. "What about him?"

"Do you know what the story there is at all?"

He takes a deep breath and slowly lets it back out and I'm realising that he likes the role of storyteller.

"As far as my source knows, Paterson was down at the shops getting himself some bevy; you know, the Co-operative at the roundabout. Lager and wine I think it was."

I'm nodding that I understand then frighten the life out of myself when I almost make a mistake and agree with him, but suddenly remember I'm not supposed to know any of this.

"Anyway, he leaves the shop and is crossing the road to Linthaugh Terrace where he gets battered on the back of the head."

I pretend to be puzzled and I ask him, "Surely there must have been somebody about at that time of the night."

I see him stare at me and I'm wondering if I've made a mistake in suggesting I know what time it happened, so I quickly add, "I mean, if the shop is still open. Was there not other customers there?"

He relaxes and I unconsciously breathe a sigh of relief because I seem to have satisfied the question he was about to ask.

"There *might* have been other customers, but nobody's come forward."

To my surprise, it's Mhari that asks, "What about the staff in the shop? Didn't they see anything?"

Craig shakes his head and pursing his lips, he replies, "As far as I know, they've been interviewed, but they don't know anything other than Paterson was in the shop and a wee bit aggressive toward the lassie behind the counter. He's been in there before causing bother so he was well known to the staff and the security that they employ there, as a troublemaker."

I'm anxious to ask about the security camera, but I don't know how to bring the subject up when Mhari asks, "If that's the case and these's previously been problems in the shop then isn't there CCTV at the counter because...I mean, I worked part-time during my University years in a supermarket and most of them these days have cameras watching the counter to ensure the staff doesn't steal the money from the tills."

Here it is then, I'm about to learn that the CID have seized the recording for that night when Craig sighs and says, "Aye, there is a security camera, but apparently the DVD player has been broken for months and it's not recording anything."

Honestly, I was stunned then it hit me. I could have jumped up from my chair and punched the air, I'm that relieved. I haven't been caught on camera after all!

All I have to worry about now is if the girl, Gina is her name and the security man remember my face and that I was standing behind Paterson when he got served.

"Sorry, Jimmy," Craig stands up and reaches for his cap from the floor beside him. "Mhari and I better go."

"Thanks for the tea Mister McGrath," the lassie smiles at me.

"Jimmy," I tell her with a huge grin. "Call me Jimmy, hen."

I see them to the door and my heart's beating like a drum, but at least I don't have the shakes.

Watching them drive off I close the door and head to the living room to clear away the cups and tea things.

In the kitchen I wash up and sit down to think over what my next move will be.

Should I avoid visiting the Co-operative in case the checkout girl Gina or the security man remember me or should I brazen it and if they say anything, pretend I don't have a clue what they're on about?

I shake my head and make my decision. There's no need to take a chance and risk them identifying me as the wee guy who stood behind Paterson when he bought his carry-out minutes before he was killed.

No, in future I'll get my shopping elsewhere.

The door's chapped and I'm wondering who it is as I hurry to open it.

It's my neighbour, Billy King and he's looking a bit agitated.

"Jimmy," he breathlessly asks me. "Can I have a wee word?"

Before I get the chance to answer, he's through the door and standing in my hallway.

"What's up, Billy?"

He's licking his lips and yes, he's definitely nervous.

"Have you not heard? It's the CID. They've started their door to door inquiries about they two bastards that got themselves murdered," he tells me.

I nearly laugh out loud because I'm thinking; I can't imagine that Paterson and Black went out of their way to get themselves killed.

"So Billy, you'll have nothing to worry about," I try to reassure him in the full knowledge that it was me that killed the two buggers.

"It's not that," he bites at his lower lip. "You know that I'm in the demolition game, don't you?"

I nod.

"Well, the thing is Jimmy, if the police turn my house, they'll find…" he hesitates.

"Find what?"

"Well, sometimes when we're demolishing buildings, we get a wee opportunity for bits and pieces, you know?"

I don't really know, but I nod anyway.

"It's just that I don't have a garden shed and I was wondering…"

"If you can hide your stuff in my shed," I finish for him.

"If that's okay with you, wee man," he's almost pleading with me. "It will just be till they've, what they call it, conducted their inquiries."

I slowly let out a breath and think, if they're going to arrest me for murder, what's some knocked off stuff?

"Aye, all right Billy, but you know they'll not be interested in searching your house. It will just be to speak with you and the missus; maybe get a statement from you, nothing else."

See, I've learned something from watching all those detective shows on the tele.

Anyway, five minutes later Billy's sneaking along the path at the rear of our terraced houses, carrying two heavy duty plastic carrier bags with God knows what inside and collecting the padlock key from me while I'm stood at the back door.

I consider letting Billy hang onto the key, but I take it back from him. I'm thinking if the worst comes to the worst, I might need my hacksaw to get rid of the baton.

He's not a bad man, Billy; just maybe now and then gives into temptation.

"One I owe you, wee man," he gives me the thumbs up and strolls back to his own house.

As I watch Billy go into his own rear door, it occurs to me that if the CID *is* searching houses, they're bound to search garden sheds as well. That's when I consider leaving the shed unlocked. That way if they do search the shed and find Billy's plastic bags, I can say the shed is always kept unlocked and that I haven't been in it for some time and that somebody must have put the bags there without my knowledge.

But in hindsight, I shake my head because I've got some good tools in there and if by chance they should get stolen, they'd be costly to replace.

It's only when I'm locking the back door I remember that Billy never mentioned when the CID is supposed to be knocking on doors. Now that *would* have been handy to know.

I decide that I had better practise what I am going to say if the CID does turn up at my door. I feel like an idiot, standing in front of the wardrobe mirror in the back room and watching my facial expressions as I put questions to myself.

"What do you know about these murders?" I bark in a strong voice and then feel a little self-conscious about speaking to myself.

My reflection shows a man nearing pension age, but in my minds eye I see a big, hulking brute of a CID officer with a scowling face and piercing eyes poking his finger at me.

"Eh, nothing," I reply to the mirror, adding "only what I've heard on the radio and local gossip."

"What gossip?" I again bark, but stop and think that one through. Maybe I shouldn't bring that up because likely the detectives would want to know who I heard the gossip from. No, I decide, I'll just tell them all I know about the murders is from the TV, the radio and the newspapers. I mean, it's been well reported so they can't trip me up on that.

"Did you know the dead men?" I ask then shake my head. "The names or the photographs in the paper don't mean anything to me, sir."

I think it's a good idea to add 'sir' because I'm thinking maybe a little humility might work; make the detectives that come to interview me think I'm just a harmless old guy.

I take a deep breath, wondering what my next question might be when the doorbell rings.

I can't describe the feeling of doom that settled on me when I heard the chime and it briefly occurred to me that maybe if I don't answer the door, they'll go away.

But I know they will just come back again.

Taking a deep breath and forcing myself to be calm though of course, my stomach's churning I walked down the stairs to the front porch and unlock the door.

I'm not prepared for who is stood there.

A lassie it is. Taller than me by about four inches and slim, very good looking with blonde hair tied back and wearing a charcoal grey business suit with the skirt to just above the knee and carrying a clipboard.

She has a blue, narrow cord thing, a lanyard I think they're called, round her neck with a small laminated card on it that she holds up for me to see.

"Mister McGrath," she smiles at me. "Hello, I'm DC Ella Hopkins from the CID. I was wondering if I might come in and interview you regarding the recent murders that occurred in the area. We're canvassing all the houses along Hapland Road looking for witnesses."

I must have looked stupid, standing there with my mouth gaping, staring at her.

"Mister McGrath?" she says again, her smile now a little uncertain.

So, I'm thinking. Is this the great, hulking brute that's been sent to intimidate me into a confession?

The next thing I know is I'm inviting her in and sneaking a look behind her to see if there's anybody else lurking outside, but other than a couple of neighbours walking past and nosily staring in to see whose visiting me, the road looks empty.

I close the door and turning, almost bump into her.

"Sorry," she gushes at me, "is it all right to just go straight through?"

"Eh, oh, aye," I bluster and raise my hand to indicate she go ahead. She seems to know where she's going and I follow her into the living room and invite her to sit down.

My, but I can't help but notice as she sits down on the couch what a fine pair of pins she's got, this young woman. Still stood there like a gormless chump, I ask if she'd like a coffee or tea, hoping she'll ask for tea because I'm rubbish at making coffee. I always make it too strong or too weak. I never can get it right.

"Oh, no thanks," she beams a smile at me. "If I took a cuppa in every house I visit I'd be peeing for Scotland."

"Oh, right," I reply, but I'm a wee bit taken aback by her forwardness. I sit in the armchair, facing her.

"Mister McGrath," she begins, "as I said we're making door to door inquiries and I have a form that I'd like to complete about you and anyone else who resides here with you…"

I raise my hand and stop her there.

"I'm on my own here, hen. I'm a widower, you see."

"Oh, right," she smiles and there's just a hint of a blush at her cheeks. Most people when they hear you're widowed will say 'sorry', though I never understood why they should be sorry that I'm widowed.

"In that case," she beams at me, "this shouldn't take too long."

She bends her head to busy herself in her folder and I take the opportunity to glance at her legs.

I was always a leg man, myself. My Jeannie, even in her mid-fifties had a fine pair and to be honest, that's what first attracted me to her. Oh, but don't think I ever looked elsewhere. At other women I mean. Oh no, I was a very happily married man, but like most men I didn't mind a wee bit of window shopping now and then. I just never tried to make a purchase, if you see what I mean.

"Right, Mister McGrath," she began with her pen in hand and a form sat on top of her folder. "These questions are designed to elicit details of everyone who lives in the area, where they were at the time of the murders and if they have any relevant information pertaining to the inquiry. Do you understand?"

Now, even though I was smiling at the lassie my hackles were up. She might be using fancy words like 'elicit' and 'pertaining', but I'm not stupid. I mean, I've read a lot of books and even though I left school at fifteen, I like to think my grammar isn't that bad. However, I'm not going to cause an argument or anything because the last thing I need is to bring myself to the attention of the CID, isn't it? So, the simple answer is "Yes, miss, I understand."

"Please," she dazzles me with that big smile again, "call me Ella."

"Aye, well Ella, in that case I'm Jimmy," I smile back at her.

Oh, oh, I'm suddenly thinking. Is this some sort of trap? Lure me into being her friend then hitting me with something like, "Did you kill them two wee shites, Jimmy?"

Do you know, it was just then I realised I was letting my guard down. A pretty face and nice pair of legs and my heads up my bahookey, which if you're from Glasgow you'll know as your rear end, pardon my language.

So there we are; me the murderer and the good looking blonde detective, sitting facing each other in my front room and she's asking me my name, my age and date of birth, what kind of car I drive, where I was on the nights of the murders…at home, of course I tell her…who is it that lives in the houses on either side of my mid-terraced house and did I know anything about the murders of Alex Paterson or Calum Black.

Of course, I give her the answers she expects to hear and do you know, I don't think her heart was in the questioning. As far as she was concerned and mind you, this is just my opinion, she had me sized up at the front door as a wee harmless man.

But then she starts to ask about the gang that was causing all the bother in Hapland Road and I admit I had on one occasion phoned the polis to complain.

She doesn't make any comment about that and I'm suspecting she already knows about my phone call.

"Did you know any of them, the gang I mean?" she asks me.

I shake my head and tell her that even though I had been a local school janny, the children I knew all left the school at aged eleven or twelve and I had no contact with any of them after that, though I admit on the odd occasion now and again some young person would recognise me in the street and say hello.

She didn't seem too interested in that, though.

I also tell her that I was in the social club the night the brick came through the window and hurt the two women. Her face flushes and she seems a wee bit irate at what happened …no, not irate; maybe angry would be a better word and tells me that the woman hit on the head…

"Missus Laurie," I nod.

"Aye, Missus Laurie," she agrees with her own nod. Taking a deep breath, she tells me in a tight voice that the lady is still detained within the Neuro Ward at the Southern and there is now grave concern for her well-being.

Then, before I knew it she is shoving the form she has completed into her folder and snapping it closed, gets to her feet.

"Well, Jimmy, I'm done here and," she winks at me, "I think it's fair to say you're in the clear."

Call me foolhardy, but I was desperate to ask and so I say to her, "Do you, the CID I mean. Do you not have any idea who killed those boys?"

There's a word I know call 'palpable' which means something like intense, so you could say for the next few seconds there was a palpable tension as if she is struggling whether or not to tell me something, to confide in me and remember, like I said I'm thinking that she's already sized me up as a wee, harmless man.

"There is a line of inquiry the boss is following at the minute," she finally confides.

I stare at her and she obviously takes my stare to mean I don't understand for she adds, "The man in charge, Jimmy. The Detective Chief Inspector running the inquiry. He thinks we might have some sort of vigilante running about here."

"Oh," was all I could reply and I slowly nod.

"You understand?"

"Oh aye," I nod again and for good measure, grin at her and say, "I think I know what a vigilante is, Ella."

That's when I got the impression she wants to pat me on the head like some tame wee puppy.

But instead she smiles at me and turns towards the door.

"Right, I'll be off now, Jimmy and it was nice meeting you."

I see her to the front door and watch her or more correctly, her fine pair of legs, walk down the path and out onto the pavement where she turns into the next door neighbour's path, the Campbell's.

I was going to call out that they were away up to the Silverburn Centre for their weekly shopping, but instead just close the door. She'll find out soon enough for herself.

Standing behind my closed door, I let out a huge sigh of relief and I'm grinning for if that was my CID interview, then so far so good. Time I think for another cuppa.

CHAPTER TEN

So, there's me sitting in my front room looking out through the window at the drizzly rain that has just started and thinking if the detective that visited me hasn't got a pop-up brolly in her handbag, Ella whatever her name is, is in for a right soaking.

I'm feeling comfortable relaxed and squirm in my chair, happy in the knowledge that so far no suspicion has been laid at my door; well, at least not yet.

But that's when I think again. Maybe I'm getting just a wee bit too cocky.

I'll give them their due, the polis aren't stupid. They have got to realise that whoever the murderer is must live pretty local so I'm guessing they'll be concentrating all their efforts and their, what you call it, their resources to the people living in the streets round here. No matter what young Craig the polis told me, I know fine well that the CID won't believe that a large, black Jamaican man murdered Alex Paterson and Calum Black. Like me they will have guessed that the other guy who was standing with Paterson at the phone box when I cracked Paterson over the head, the guy that run off, he'll have made up the story to explain why he didn't try to help his pal. The only thing that will confuse the CID is the bit in the guy's story about me having a black face.

Aye, I'm in no doubt that will definitely set them wondering. Anyway, that's me finished getting involved with these bad wee gits. I'm not going to take any more chances and getting myself caught. Sipping at my tea I decide that I'll cut the baton up and get rid of it. No sense in having it lying around just in case for any reason I do become a suspect because remember, I haven't forgotten about the till lassie Gina who works in the Co-operative or the security guard. If they *are* questioned as I'm sure they will be, it might just come back to them that a wee man was standing behind Alex Paterson in the queue the night he was murdered.

No, that's definitely decided me. I've had enough.

Funny that now I've made the decision, I'm feeling a wee bit like Pontius Pilate and that I've washed my hands of the murders.

But then, I didn't know what was to happen later that night.

I think it was about just after two in the morning when I heard the sirens. I got out of bed and grabbing my dressing gown I'm just putting it on when I stumble into the front room. Remember, I'm half asleep, but the horrendous noise and the room flooded with blue light reflected from the two fire engines in the road outside soon woke me, I can tell you.

I drew back the curtains and I even though the window is double glazed and closed, I can hear the shouts of the firemen as they jump out from their engines.

I open the window and looking out I can see that there is a vehicle on fire a couple of doors down. The flames were climbing into the sky and it was an inferno, let me tell you. It was a big Luton vehicle and then I realise it is Billy King's works van that is on fire.

Billy, wearing a Rangers football top and a pair of jogging trousers, is dancing up and down in the road, his hands clutching at his head, pulling at his hair and he's going mental. Even above all the racket that is going on I can clearly hear him shouting and swearing. A couple of cops in uniform look like they are trying to calm him down, but he keeps pushing them away and screaming at them. Billy's wife Irene is in her nightdress and trying to calm him too, but he keeps pushing her away as well.

My God, what the heck happened I'm wondering, but in my heart I already know who has done it; the buggers from the field have torched Billy's van.

I stand there watching and it takes the firemen with their hoses a good ten minutes to put out the fire. Even after the flames have been extinguished they continued to play the water onto the smouldering van. I suppose they are dampening it down in case it re-ignites.

Then I see Billy sitting down on the pavement across the road, his head held in his hands and Irene and one of the cop's is squatting next to him. A fireman walks over and wraps a blanket round Billy's shoulders, but he doesn't seem to even notice.

I hear another siren and an ambulance comes tearing down the road, but the other cop is waving it down and making a cutting noise with her hand across her throat and it must have worked because the ambulances blue light and siren go off. It stops behind one of the fire engines. I watch the cop speak with the ambulance driver, who nods then it drives away and I know then that at least thankfully, nobody is hurt.

I see some of my other neighbours wandering about in their dressing gowns or coats and I wonder whether or not I should go out into the street to join them, but decide that there is enough confusion down there without me adding to it.

Another car arrives and two guys in suits get out who I suppose are detectives. They both speak with the female cop who now is trying to get the neighbours back into their houses. Then I see her point towards Billy and the two detectives walk over to speak with him. The longer I watched the angrier I get.

The van was Billy's livelihood. I remembered him telling me that though he worked in demolitions, you know, knocking down derelict buildings and things like that, he was self-employed by the company whose logo was on the side of the van. Billy, who actually owned the van, was contracted by the company and needed the van to get from site to site. He once showed me inside the van and I was surprised how he'd had it outfitted with all his equipment ranging from the oxy acetylene torches he used to cut through steel girders to crowbars and big sledgehammers. The van was his pride and joy and he kept it neat and tidy with all sorts of wee shelves and cupboards inside to hold his equipment.

I knew there was no use trying to get to sleep now so I went down to the kitchen and brewed myself a cuppa and when it was made, went back up to the front room window. One of the fire engines had gone and though the fire was out, the van is still seeping a lot of smoke. The other fire engine still has its blue light flashing and one fireman is spraying the smoking van with water. I can see that the firemen have dragged two of the oxy acetylene bottles from the van onto the grass across the road and another fireman is spraying the bottles with water. All of the neighbours are now away back into their houses and the only people on the street now is the firemen spraying the bottles or standing having a smoke and the two cops who are sitting in their car with the interior light on.

The CID car is still there so I guess that the detectives are in Billy's house getting their statement from him.

I hadn't realised it, but over an hour has passed since I was woken by the noise.

I finish my tea and get back to my bed and lie awake for a while, but before I know it it's gone eight o'clock and I obviously fell asleep because I waken up still tired and with a raging headache.

In the kitchen, I swallow two Paracetamol then with the glass of water in my hand, make my way back up the stairs to the front window where through the closed curtains, I sneak a glance outside. The road's empty of any people and the fire engine and the polis cars have gone. What's left of the burnt-out van sits outside Billy's house. It's in a right state and burned down to the axle and the tarmac round about it is all scorched. Great puddles of water are all over the place and shiny because it looks like the oil from the van has mixed in with the water. The firemen, I think it must have been, have dragged all the debris across the road from the van and laid it on the grass opposite. The two oxy acetylene bottles lying side by side look like they are the only things that have survived the fire. My nose is killing me and I'm desperate to know what the polis have told Billy, but common sense tells me this isn't the time to go chapping his door. Then an idea hits me. I'll nip down to the shops and gets some rolls and bacon and drop them into Billy and Irene like the good neighbour I want them to think I am. With a bit of luck, I'll get invited in and then find out what the story is.

So that's me now showered and dressed and I'm pleased to see the Paracetamol have kicked in. I get myself down to the shops at the roundabout and into the newsagents next to the Co-op, who does rolls and also groceries. On the way out I pass by the Co-op front door and it's the big fat security guard with the ponytail that's on duty at the door. I almost choked when he turned and saw me, but he didn't give me a second glance and I kept walking, not realising I wasn't breathing till I reached the pedestrian crossing. Standing at the red light, I slowly let my breath out and shake my head at my stupidity.

Why the heck am I taking such a needless chance of getting myself recognised, I wonder?

Before I know it I'm back walking in Hapland Road and approaching Billy's front door. The front room curtains are drawn, but a crack in them lets me see that there is a light on inside.

I walk up the path and then I wonder if this is such a good idea?

I pluck up the courage, but instead of ringing the door bell I knock at the door, half hoping they don't hear me so that I can satisfy myself that I did try.

Almost to my surprise the door is pulled open and its Irene there, still in her nightie but wearing a dressing gown on over the top of it. Her face is chalk-white and she looks shattered.

Now, by way of explanation, Irene King is an inch or two taller than me. A dyed blonde haired woman in her mid-forties, she's a good looking lassie and forever attending one of these keep-fit classes that they run up at the Silverburn Centre. She's always been a sharp dresser and if she's not hurrying to her keep-fit, she's pushing her daughter's twins in their buggy at a speedy rate of knots up the road. A nice woman, I've a lot of time for Irene and she was good to my Jeannie through the illness, bringing in bits of shopping, women's magazines and things like that, but right now it's obvious she's been crying and she looks like she's been dragged backwards through a hedge.

"Sorry, hen, but I thought maybe you might need a wee breakfast after the night you've had," I thrust the plastic bag with the rolls and bacon at her.

"Oh, it's you, Jimmy. Come away in," she nods to me and stands to one side to permit me to pass her. I wait till she closes the door and let her lead me through to the front room.

Billy, still dressed in the Rangers top and the jogging pants, is sitting in the armchair by the fireplace, a small table at the side of him on which stands a half full bottle of whisky and a glass that looks like it needs topped up.

"Jimmy's brought us breakfast, Billy," she tells him then indicating I take a seat, leaves us and walks with the plastic bag through to the kitchen, closing the door behind her.

I've been in their house a couple of times before, but not recently and see that they've recently decorated and the place looks stunningly modern compared to my wee homely house.

"Thanks, Jimmy," slurs Billy and its immediately obvious to me he's half-cut. If you're not from Glasgow, what I'm saying is he's not yet fully pissed, but seems to be getting that way.

I sit down on the couch and wait for him to speak. The last thing I want to do is let on that I'm there for information.

He reaches for the chunky glass on the table then holds it up and squints at it, seeing it's almost empty and reaches for the bottle.

"You'll have a dram," he slurs at me, but I shake my head. "Thanks, but no thanks, Billy. I've taken a wee pledge," I lie to him.

"Wise man, wise man," he repeats as unsteadily he pours three fingers of whisky into the glass and with a thump, returns the bottle to the table.

He sips at the whisky, smacks his lips, slowly exhales then says, "You'll have heard about my van?"

"Aye," I nod to him. "I saw the commotion through the night."

"Bastards!" he bursts out, but doesn't explain who the bastards are.

He takes another sip and peers at me. "The polis thinks it was that lot who sit up on the field," he says at last. "Them that put in wee Mary's window," he snarls, "the dirty bastards!"

The atmosphere in the room is so murderous that I can almost taste his rage.

"But why torch your van?" I slowly ask.

He shakes his head and grins, but it's an evil grin and not at all humorous.

"They, the CID I mean, they think it's because I challenged them that night. Do you remember?"

I do remember. It was shortly after the gang had started their carry-on up in the field. It was the night they had lined up and challenged all the neighbours to a fight. Billy had been intent on setting about them, but Irene had wisely held him back.

"So, the CID thinks it was because of that night?"

"Aye," he nodded, but was prevented from saying anything else when the kitchen door opened and Irene returned carrying a tray with three mugs and a plate of rolls and bacon that wafted through the room.

"I just made coffee, if that's all right Jimmy," she winked at me as she laid the tray down onto another wee side table.

Handing me a plate with a roll and bacon, she said, "If I'm remembering correctly, Jimmy, you take milk and two sugars in your coffee. That's right isn't it?"

"Aye, that's great hen," I reply.

"And coffee for you, Billy King," she orders, then hands him a plate and a mug as she deftly took the glass from his hand.

"Oh, aye right," he nodded. One thing about Billy is that big and rough as he might be he's never to my knowledge said a bad word to his wife.

He's a bit like most men, I suppose; never learned how to breathe through a pillow!

Irene seated herself beside me on the couch, clutching at her mug.

"You're not eating?" I asked her.

"Maybe later, Jimmy," she forced a smile then added, "You'll know about the carry-on with the van?"

"Aye, I was up through the night watching from the window," I admitted, "but I thought it would be silly to come down and add to all the confusion."

"You did the right thing. The place was bedlam with everybody milling about," she sighed. She sipped at her coffee then shook her head and with bitterness, said. "Did Billy tell you about the CID?"

"Eh, just that they suggested it was that team from the field who burned the van because Billy offered them a square go that time."

"Aye, but there's more," and it was obvious to me she was not just angry, but raging.

"The detectives that came in for a statement then asked if the gang that did it thought Billy might be the one that murdered their pals."

I froze, hardly daring to breathe. This I didn't expect to hear.

"Surely not," I stuttered. "I mean, why should they think that Billy…"

She held up her hand to cut me off. "That's not all of it. Then they asked Billy to account for where he was on the nights they two bastards got murdered! When he said he was home with me, they then said that might not be enough of an alibi because I'm his wife and inferred I might be lying to protect him!"

Suddenly I'm swallowing hard. Billy King is a good man and his wife is a good woman. I can't believe that because of me, *he* might be suspected of the murders.

"But they'd need evidence and if they had evidence wouldn't they…"

Again, she cut me off with, "Evidence? They sods don't need evidence, Jimmy! You know what the polis is like. They'll work round what they know or make up something."

A sob broke from her and I gave her a minute to compose herself while Billy, his head down, just stared at the fireplace.

My stomach was revolting against the two bites of the roll I had eaten and I fought to resist the temptation to throw up.

Dear God, I never, ever suspected that this could happen, that my actions would put a decent couple like Billy and Irene at risk.

If at anytime I felt like confessing to the murders, then this was it. But again, somehow, fate intervened.

Taking a deep breath, Irene clasped at my hand and said, "You're a wee decent man Jimmy McGrath and I know you're not a gossip, so I can share this with you." She stopped and took another deep breath.

"Billy has a record for violence. When he was a young man, a teenager really, he got into trouble and run with a gang over in the Gorbals area. He stabbed another gang member and got three years."

She turned to me with tears in her eyes. "But I swear to you, Jimmy. Billy's never been in trouble since he got released from the jail and there's no way, no way on Earth that he would ever commit a murder. Honest."

I gripped her hand that held tightly to mine and replied, "You've no need to persuade me, Irene. I've known you both since you moved here nearly twenty years ago and I know that Billy couldn't have done it."

Tempted though I was to admit how confident I was that Billy hadn't committed the murders, to my shame I didn't say because a wee plan had come to mind.

A plan to ensure Billy King was free from suspicion of the murders of Alex Paterson and Calum Black.

The downside of the plan was that I won't be destroying the baton, as I had intended.

CHAPTER ELEVEN

The rest of that day I spend catching up with cleaning the house and my washing and ironing. Weather wise, it turned out to be a bit of a rotten day anyway with drizzly rain and apart from a wee trip in the car up to the bustling Silverburn Centre to collect some shopping, my day passed without any kind of incident.

I did drive past the police caravan that was still parked at the scene of my first murder where I saw a group of detectives standing in the rain being spoken to by the man I recognised from the TV, the DCI that the detective Ella called the boss. I wish I could remember her second name. Haskins, was it?

Hopkins, I smiled to myself. Her name is Ella Hopkins.

Honestly, I'm at that stage of life I'll need to start writing things down.

After I passed by the incident caravan, I drove into Hapland Road and past St Convals and the telephone box opposite and believe it or not, even though it was a crime scene, there was still two of the buggers hanging about nearby. Granted, there weren't any cops there now, but I was amazed that the sods were still carrying on their drug dealing at the same place. Seems the wheels of commerce continue to turn. Once again I get the evil eye, but I pretend that I don't see them.

So that's me back home, the shopping's lifted from the car to the kitchen and while I'm putting it away, I'm thinking that you'll be curious about my plan to get Billy King off the hook for the two murders.

To be honest, when I give it some serious thought I don't believe for one minute the CID detectives that attended the van being burned really suspect Billy of the murders. However, what they have done is scare the living daylights out of a nice couple and when Irene told me about Billy's prison conviction, the detectives have unwittingly brought to the surface Irene and Billy's fears that his past would be held against him, that somehow he would fit the frame the CID would construct to catch their killer.

If as Irene said the detectives might dismiss Irene's alibi for her husband, then Billy needed an alibi that was rock solid if another murder were to be committed.

Are you starting to catch up with me?

Now, I suppose that like me you'll be inundated with flyers through the door, brochures and leaflets advertising everything from double glazing to take-away restaurants, boiler repairs to estate agencies and every other service that you can imagine. If you're like me, most of these flyers go into the recycle bin without being read. However, it just so happened that on Saturday morning, a load of these flyers came through the door and as usual went straight into the bin, but I remembered that a brightly coloured one had caught my eye.

I collected the leaflet from the bin and flattening it out on the kitchen table, saw that it advertised a newly opened Italian Restaurant down in Paisley Road West.

Now, I'm not an affluent man, but I'm mortgage free these days and my wants are few, so I'm pleased to say I've saved a few bob over the years that sits nicely in my account.

I glanced at the wall clock and reckoned the place would be open. A quick phone call and I've booked a window table for two on the Tuesday night at seven-thirty and quoting the deal that's on the leaflet, I explain that as the meal is a gift for two friends, I'd also like to throw in a bottle of wine and I want to pay the bill now by card.

It takes a few minutes and that's it arranged.

Feeling satisfied with myself, I boil the kettle for a cuppa and begin to prepare my evening meal.

Now, while I'm working here in the kitchen it occurs to me that you might think I'm getting ahead of myself, that I've not thought through what I intend doing.

Well, here's what I *am* thinking.

Like I've already said I watch a lot of the police detective programmes on the television and after a while you get to know the police jargon, some of their methods and things like that. I'm guessing that after they have had their, what you call them, their autopsy's on Alex Paterson and Calum Black, the polis will likely realise that the same weapon was used to kill them both. Now I'm reasoning that if Billy King is having his dinner when another one of them scoundrels gets murdered and the CID discover that it's same weapon that was used to kill Paterson and Black, that surely will alibi Billy King and he'll be in the clear.

Particularly if that alibi is provided by the staff of a certain Italian restaurant down in Paisley Road West.

Simple, you might think.

The only fly in the ointment is that between seven-thirty, tomorrow night and the time Billy gets home with Irene from the restaurant, I have to find myself one of the gang's pals to murder.

It's Tuesday morning and the sky is clear outside. Again it's been a quiet night without any nonsense from the gang up in the field so I'm pleased to say I'm feeling quite brisk and chirpy. I'm in my working gear because though there has been a lot going on I haven't forgotten my promise to Father Stephen about working in the chapel grounds, so after a quick breakfast, I see its eight-thirty and locking the door behind me, I make my way along the garden path and probably out of sheer habit I take my old green canvas shoulder bag with a flask of tea and bottle of water.

Billy King's burned out van lies there like a visible reminder of what I still have to do that night, but hunching my shoulders against the thought, I turn and walk towards the chapel.

It takes me less than five minutes and as I approach, I see some of the parishioners, mostly elderly like myself, leaving the main doors after the early eight o'clock Mass. I nod to a few as I pass them by at the gate and there's Father Stephen, grinning like an ape because he knows fine well that I wouldn't let him down.

"That you ready to start then, Jimmy?" he wisecracks at me and hands me the garage key where the gardening equipment is stored. I return his grin, but I'm taking in the length of the grass that surrounds the church and the weeds growing through the paving stones and I'm thinking that tidying this lot up will take more than one shift. I'll be here all day and likely a few days after as well. With a sigh I take the shed key from him and make my way round to the side of the church where the extra large, brick built garage is located. As soon as I go in the side door it's obvious that Father Stephen and likely the parish priests before him never used the place to garage their cars. I soon realise why. The one window is so dirty I have to switch on the overhead light that thankfully, works. I shake my head because the place is an absolute tip. Dust mites dance in the air and the petrol lawnmower seems to me to be that old the instructions must be in Latin.

A work bench, if that's what you could call it, runs along the length of the wall on the other side of the garage and it's crowded with old, rusting tools, cans and tins of God knows what and there is a real sense of decay in the air. Broken chairs, a wobbly, Formica topped kitchen table and bits of wooden cabinets are stacked to one side and covered with spider webs and mouse droppings.

I take a deep breath because I know that before I can even get working in the garden, I'll have to try and make sense of what's going on in here.

I begin to rummage among what look like Victorian garden tools and start stacking what I might need against the wall at the door. After twenty minutes I turn my attention to the lawnmower and it's obvious that the spark plug needs cleaned and if the empty sound on the tank is anything to go by, it's out of fuel too. I begin to search among the cans on the workbench for some two-stroke petrol and some oil. There must be at least twenty odd bottles and tins there containing everything from weed killer to God alone knows what's in half of them. One of the bottles, an old ginger bottle with the top tightly screwed on catches my eye and lifting it, I wipe the dust from the handwritten label that has a skull and bones drawn on it and read the word 'Paraquat'. Now, if you're uncertain what Paraquat is, let me tell you a wee story. Paraquat is commonly used as a weed killer and can be dangerous if not handled properly. I recall a wee story when I started work as a janny at Bellarmine Secondary, back in the day. My boss Pete McGuire, you might recall me mentioning him, he told a story about a janny at another school, I can't remember where, who apparently spilled some Paraquat on his hands, but didn't wash the Paraquat off. A couple of minutes later does this janny not wipe at his eyes and starts screaming. According to Pete, the guy went blind, but whether it's a true story or one of these urban legends, I can't say for certain. All I know is that it scared me witless and after that I took real care when handling the stuff. But that's not why I mention the Paraquat because when I saw it, I smile for it gave me the smattering of an idea. Cut a long story short, I put the bottle to one side.

I'm back at the workbench, still searching among the tins and bottles. A number of the tins are that old and so rusted the labels have peeled off, so I start sniffing and eventually find what smells like petrol. I can only guess it is two-stroke and fill the machine's tank. There's some oil in another old ginger bottle, so that goes in as well. I'm too canny to start the machine in a confined space and with some difficulty, wheel it outside into the fresh air before I take hold of the rope and give it a tug. Aye, you've guessed. It's not a modern electric starter, but one of the old types with the rope handle that starts it up. So I pull the choke to prime the engine then grab hold of the rope and tug…after tug…after tug, until I'm beginning to think the thing is completely buggered and my shoulder's starting to ache. Then, just when I'm about to deliver a swift kick to the bleeding thing, I give it one more final tug when lo and behold, does the engine not catch and away I go.

I have to admit I'm fair pleased with myself and engaging the gear I give it a bit of throttle and head for the grassy patch beside the main door. I'm thinking if the machine gives out on me I'll at least try to get some of the grass done at the front of the church.

So there I am, working away and over an hour and a half has passed when Father Stephen waves and calls out to me. I throttle down and leave the machine ticking over. Father Stephen is carrying a tray with a mug of tea and a plate with a couple of rolls and sausage. "Thought you might need a wee break there, Jimmy," he grins at me, "so I had the housekeeper rustle this up for you."

Now, I'm not a man that will ever refuse a cup of char, so with the machine still ticking over because I'm worried about stopping it, I take the tray and nod my thanks as he makes his way back to the parish house. I carry the tray to the front steps of the church and start to settle myself down for a seat.

That's when I see them across the road at the telephone box, a young guy wearing a dark coloured jacket and jeans and a heavyset blonde lassie in a bright yellow tracksuit. They're not paying any attention to me, but talking to another young guy who has just arrived. As I watch them, I see the first guy in the dark jacket pass something to the new guy, but then the lassie sees me watching and screams across the road to me, "What the fuck you think you're doing, are you spying on us, you dickhead?"

I'm that taken aback I look away, but I'm conscious the lassie has started walking from the telephone box towards the church gates.

I catch my breath because I just know she's coming for a fight, but before I can even stand up to leg it, Father Stephen is standing behind me and saying, "You all right there, Jimmy?"

There's an edge to his voice and as I half turn, I look up and see that he's staring across the road at the lassie, who has stopped and is standing in the middle of the road and staring at us both. Then she gives us the finger and screams "Fenian bastards!" before turning to walk back to the guy with the dark jacket. The other guy, the customer I suppose he is, is hurrying away down the road towards Linthaugh Road.

My chest feels awfully tight as Father Stephen sits down beside me and still watching across the road, quietly says, "Maybe I'll join you while you have your tea and rolls and we can share some craic, eh, Jimmy?"

I can hardly speak because to tell the truth, I got a real fright. I know she's just a lassie, but she's built like a Sumo wrestler and thin like I am, if she'd came into the church grounds and had a go at me, I didn't fancy my chances, I can tell you.

My mouth is as dry as a two day old sock and I kind of mumble my thanks, I'm that relieved so I am. I force my hand to stop shaking and I take a bite of one of the rolls, but it's like cardboard in my mouth and I slurp some tea to wet my whistle so the bread can go down that wee bit easier.

The lassie and her crony are laughing, but it's not a humourless laugh and they keep giving us glances.

My voice sounds squeaky when I ask Father Stephen, "Can the polis no do something about that pair and the rest of them that hang about there, Father?"

He sighs and shakes his head. "I'm fed up complaining to the Superintendent at Pollok, Jimmy. He keeps giving me the run-around, telling me they've no resources and that those buggers across there," he nods towards them, "are small fry, that it's the bigger fish he's after. Says that if his cops chase them from there, they'll have lost the intelligence, he calls it, of all their customers."

A thought hits me and a cold shiver runs down my spine as I ask, "So, they're watching them the now then? Finding out whose buying the dope from them?"

He shrugs and replies, "To be honest, I've no idea. I thought from what the Superintendent said that he was inferring the police had one of them fancy cameras set up somewhere, but who knows. All I can tell you is that if they *do* have a camera somewhere, it's not here in the church grounds because nobody has asked me for permission to place anything like that in here."

I fight a rising panic and glance up and down the road, but there's nothing that's obviously a camera and I'm realising if there is one, it must be one of those wee miniature things like they use in the spy films.

Father Stephen cuts into my thoughts and says, "If you want my opinion, the Superintendent is giving me a load of baloney. I don't for one minute think there is a camera watching these scoundrels. I think he's told me that just to get me off his back."

That doesn't really make me feel any better, but I nod because I can't really trust myself to speak. I take another mouthful of tea and ask him, "Do you know those two across the street?"

"No, not really, but the girl is there pretty regularly. The size of her and that yellow tracksuit, she's hard to miss," he grins. "The young lad I think is one of the Docherty's sons. The family, if I recall correctly live over in Bonnyholm Avenue somewhere. The family are Catholic, but don't attend here at the church though, so no; I'm not really certain who they are."

"I'm guessing if she's calling us Fenians, she's not a parishioner either," I joke, but I'm not really feeling that humorous.

Father Stephen smiles and then says, "Oh, oh, here's the midmorning shift," and nods at two young lads who are walking towards the lassie and her pal. I watch as all four meet and it's obvious from the finger pointing and bad language that Father Stephen and I are the subject of their conversation. After a few minutes, the lassie and her pal walk off, but not before she remembers to once again give us the finger and callout, "Fenian bastards!"

"What do you mean the midmorning shift?" I turn to him.

He smiles at me and clapping me on the shoulder, stands up. "There are always two of them there from early morning to late at night, dealing their dope, Jimmy. They're like clockwork."

I'm aghast. "And the police know this?"

"Oh aye, they know, but as I said the Superintendent assures me that it's all part of what he calls," he wags the fingers of both hands in the air, "the big picture. Bloody nonsense if you ask me, though."

With that and happy that I'm apparently no longer under any threat of being beaten up by the fat lassie, he nods to me and makes his way back to the parish house.

I finish the tea and the second roll before I resume cutting the grass, my mind reeling from what has happened. At the forefront though is the thought that somewhere on the road, there might be a surveillance camera watching the phone box and the neds hanging about it doing the drug-dealing and if that is the case, I involuntarily shiver, then there must be a recoding of me murdering Calum Black.

The engine began to struggle and then cut out and I realised that either it had run out of petrol or there was a blockage in the line. As it happened, the small tank sounded empty so I used what remained of the petrol and got another forty minutes grass cutting that more or less finished the expansive lawn area.

That left the weeds. I remember a TV programme where the marvellous Joan Hickson playing Miss Marple said something like 'There's no such thing as a weed; it's simply a flower growing in the wrong place.'

Well, let me tell you there's bunches of flowers growing all over the bleeding place. I thought again of the Paraquat in the garage, but remembered I had a use for at least some of it. However, I'm sure if I dilute it enough it should cover some of the area I have to tackle and that's what I do, I use most of the Paraquat, but left about two fingers worth in the bottom of the bottle that will help me with my plan.

So, before I know it it's the middle of the afternoon. I've been that busy with the watering can full of weed killer that I haven't been paying attention to what's been happening across the road, though of course I'm giving plenty of thought to the mad, fat lassie with the yellow tracksuit and you know that feeling you get, the feeling of déjà vu, the feeling that you've met or know somebody from sometime before? It was bothering me that I knew the lassie, but then out of nowhere, it hits me. She was one of the gang that stood on the field the night they challenged me and the neighbours to a fight; the night Billy King's wife Irene had to hold him back. It was the yellow tracksuit and the cropped blonde hair I recalled. I was smiling at myself, pleased that I remembered because there's nothing worse than having something, a name or a face on the tip of your tongue and you just can't quite get there.

Aye, it was her right enough. Bad wee shite that she is, pardon my French.

Father Stephen, a glass of orange squash in his hand walks towards me and is smiling as he's looking around at the grassy areas.

"Heavens above, Jimmy, you've made some difference here, wee man. I can't believe you've achieved all this," he waves his hand about, "in such a short space of time. Well done, sir, well done." He hands me the glass and it's only then I realise how thirsty I am and finish the squash with one huge gulp.

Father Stephen grins at me and asks, "Can I get you some more?" I wipe my mouth with my sleeve and tell him no, that I'm fine.

"I've laid down a load of weed killer, Father and I'll be back in a couple of days to root out the weeds when it's done its job. For now, if you don't mind, I'll just tidy up here and be on my way."

"Aye, of course, Jimmy, but here," and shuffles in his trousers pocket then tries to shove a couple of tenners' into my hand. I back off and wave the money away. "No, you're all right, Father. Tell you what; stand me a pint the next time I'm in the club and we'll call it quits, okay?"

"Aye, if you're sure," he smiles and shakes my hand as he glances at the sky. "I think you just made it there. It looks like it's going to pour down."

Right enough, the clouds are gathering and I can almost smell the rain in the air.

With a cheery wave, he leaves me and carrying the watering can, I head towards the garage for my jacket.

Shrugging into my jacket, I lock the garage doors behind me, but I don't forget to carefully collect and take home with me the ginger bottle with the two fingers of Paraquat.

CHAPTER TWELVE

The kitchen clock tells me it's just gone four o'clock and you'll know my routine by now, for the first thing I do is put the kettle on for a brew.

That done, I start to think about my night and then with the mug of tea in my hand, settle down in my favourite armchair, for I have to consider how I plan to murder another one of the gang tonight.

You might be wondering why I have to kill one of them rather than just maybe bash them over the head with the baton for after all, surely that would give Billy King his alibi. Well, you might be right but the way I see it is that the police forensic experts will need to examine the wound to compare it against the other wounds and if they are going to do that properly, it would be better done on a corpse.

Do you see what I'm getting at here?

Besides, I have my own safety to think about too. I mean, what if I make a complete cod of it and the bugger I pick to club on the head gets the better of me? Even worse, what if he lives and can identify me and the CID come calling at my door?

I shiver because that is just *not* an option.

No, I'll do one more of the sods and that's definitely it. Once Billy's alibi is established, I'm done with it. No more taking chances with my liberty and no more battering these buggers over the head and with a bit of luck, it might even stop them causing bother round here with their carry-on and their drug-dealing.

I'm unconsciously shaking my head as I think about it. Aye, after I've finished with it the polis can do their job and clear the streets themselves. That's why they get paid their fancy wages.

I'm sitting staring at the blank screen of the television when the thought hits me, something that's been bothering me for a wee while now.

It's something that I think I've had in the back of my head, what they psychiatrists call the 'deepest recess of the mind.' See, I do read books, you know.

Anyway, you'll be wondering what I'm on about. Well, here goes. I know you're going to be shocked by this and to be truthful, I can hardly believe myself that I'm even admitting it to me, let alone to you.

I'm taking a deep breath here because what I'm about to tell you is simply… well; let's just say it's unbelievable.

The fact is…I'm starting to enjoy the thought of going out hunting these buggers and hurting them.

There, I've said it.

Now, I know you're not just surprised, but probably upset that me, a guy who people know as a decent wee man, should harbour such thoughts.

But consider this. When you're watching a show on television or reading a book or something like that and one of the characters is a bully or a really bad individual who hurts other people, do you not get a wee thrill, a kick when he or she get their comeuppance? Do you not get a wee burst of adrenalin when the good guy sets about the bad guy? Do you not wish it was you hurting the bad guy?

See? We're not really that much different after all, are we?

Admittedly, I'm not your John Wayne type of character and certainly I don't think of myself as any kind of hero, but the people I've hurt; I know them as the bad guys. Well, at least as far as I'm concerned, they are.

Did they deserve to die? I can't really answer that question other than to tell you again that I didn't deliberately set out to kill them. It's just that when I hit them with the baton, I maybe used much more force than I really intended.

But now they're dead I do know they can't hurt anyone else and the way their lives were apparently going, it seemed to me they were just turning out to be criminals anyway. Potential parasites likely destined to feed off the rest of us, the rest of society.

Now don't get me wrong here. I'm not setting myself up as any kind of judge and jury, but really; apart from their drug-dealing pals and the scummy families they come from, who is *really* going to miss those two?

Okay, okay, I agree. Murder is unacceptable. But here's a thought for you to consider. Let's say for example if Paterson and Black were still alive, they were to find themselves arrested for their drug-dealing and their carry-on and in Paterson's case, mugging my pal Scooby. So, the polis put them before the courts and they get a couple of years inside, but if what I read and hear is correct, they're probably only going to serve less than half that time. So, after being better fed and cared for in the jail than we treat our own pensioners, they're back out and what? Become good citizens? I hardly think so. No, it would be back to their old habits and jailed again on the odd occasion they're caught. In fact, jail to them would just become an occupational hazard. No, I'm beginning to think that I did society a favour here, doing them two in.

I'm sipping at my tea, but realise its gone cold.

I remember my plan for tonight and head towards the bathroom. When I lost my Jeannie, Scooby's wife Alice and her lassie Shona gave me a bit of breathing room then came round a couple of weeks later to help me clear out Jeannie's wardrobe. Alice had told me that she contributed to a Women's Shelter and that Jeannie's clothes would still serve a purpose. Knowing my wife as I did, I could only agree that's what Jeannie would have wanted.

However, while the clothes were now all gone from the house, Alice had no use for the cosmetics that were in the bathroom and strangely reluctant as I was to just dump them in the rubbish bin, I finally had placed in the cabinet under the sink. Among those things I remembered there was a small, clear plastic spray bottle that Jeannie used. If I recall correctly, she would top the bottle up with hair conditioner when she was getting ready for a wee social night at the church.

So I scramble among the bottles and cans and yes, there's the bottle right enough, still half full with liquid.

I feel a lump in my throat and I sit back on the tiled floor with my back to the pan and stare at the wee bottle as thoughts of Jeannie rush through my mind. I'm not ashamed to admit that I have a tear in my eye.

Taking a deep breath I haul myself to my feet and with a sigh, empty the liquid down the sink.

You see, I've got plans for the plastic bottle.

I fetch my canvas bag from the hall cupboard and in the kitchen I put on yellow kitchen gloves and carefully twist the top from the ginger bottle. I set the plastic bottle down into the basin and carefully pour the Paraquat into the plastic bottle till it's half full, pleased that my hands are steady and I don't lose any into the sink. That down, I top the plastic bottle up with water and tightly replace the top. I shake the bottle to dilute the Paraquat and holding the spray downwards towards the plug hole, I practise squeezing it. The fine spray comes out easily enough and I run the cold water tap to rinse the diluted Paraquat away.

The ginger bottle with the remaining dregs of Paraquat I pour down the toilet and flush it before rinsing the bottle out. Tearing the label off, I tear into unidentifiable pieces and also flush it down the toilet. The bottle I dispose of into the council recyclable bin.

That all done, I decide it's time for my supper.

The nights are fair drawing in and it's dark by seven, this night. My supper dishes are washed and put away and I'm dressed in a dark coloured polo shirt and the police trousers with the baton down the inside pocket. I know you'll laugh, but I've still got my slippers on. So that's me, standing in the darkness of the living room, watching from behind the drawn curtain.

Last night, when I went in and told Billy and Irene because I knew they were going through a bad patch with the van being burned and as a wee and very belated token of thanks for Irene's care of Jeannie before she died, I had bought them a meal at the Italian restaurant down in Paisley Road West. The last thing I expected was for Irene to burst into tears. Billy at first was a bit speechless and a wee bit embarrassed, but then insisted I come in and take a dram. I tried to refuse, but Irene had her arms round my neck hugging me and so, in I went and a dram I had. I have to confess I didn't really enjoy it because I felt a bit of a fraud, the real reason of course being that I needed them out of the house and in a public place to get Billy an alibi. However, to be polite I stayed for half an hour or so and now the next night, here I am watching as they get into the taxi and are driven off to the restaurant for their meal, courtesy of yours truly.

I give it five minutes because I'm worried that for some unaccountable reason, they might return home, but at last I'm satisfied and drawing the curtain tightly closed, I switch on the light and settle into the armchair to pull on my heavy boots.

Just like before, my stomachs churning and I'm beginning to regret the large plate of macaroni and cheese I had for my supper. That and being the age I am, my bladder needs emptying for the third time in an hour.

Toilet completed, I fetch my dark jacket from the hall cupboard and shrugging into it, I stuff my navy blue woolly hat into the side pocket. I decided that I won't be bothering with a black face tonight and the reason is this. It's just gone seven thirty and I'm worried that the man in charge of the inquiry *is* telling the truth about the number of extra polis they will have patrolling round this area. I'm going to be taking the car and if for any reason I'm stopped I don't want to be looking like a Halloween character. No, what I'll say is that I'm out for some late night shopping at the Morrisons store in Paisley Road West and that's why I've decided to take some plastic bags with me that I'll leave sitting on the front seat. I make a final check in the mirror and the last thing I do before leaving the house is collect the plastic spray bottle from under the kitchen sink.

That's me ready and locking up, I glance at the field, but it's quiet up there the now so I make my way to the car and get in.

Now, you probably think I'm a bit of an old romantic when I ordered the window table for Billy and Irene in the restaurant, but that's actually part of tonight's plan.

My first act is to drive down Corkerhill Road and then I turn left into Mosspark Drive and head towards Paisley Road West. I've never been to the Italian restaurant, but on their flyer they advertise their location as being opposite the Morrisons store so I turn into the store's car park and before I lock the car up, I pull on my woolly hat so it's down to my eyebrows and over my ears. The car park is busy with shoppers and nobody pays any attention to me. I mean why should they; a wee guy wearing a dark jacket and carrying a folded plastic bag.

I'm standing to cross the busy road at the pedestrian crossing outside the store, but the traffic is pretty heavy at this time of night and I'm impatiently waiting for several minutes. I can see the Italian restaurant in among the row of shops on the north side of the road. I take a deep breath and casually as I can, I walk along the row of shops, most of which are now closed and then I'm passing by the restaurant. With my head down I cast a glance at the table in the window, but I get a shock and my heart misses a beat.

The table's empty.

I almost stop to stare, but force myself to walk quickly on and stop at the corner of Lammermoor Road. I'm physically shaking and wondering…what the heck!

Where are Billy and Irene?

I take a couple of deeps breaths, conscious of the funny look I'm getting from a couple of young women who arm in arm are walking past me.

I cross the road at the pedestrian lights opposite Berryknowes Road and start walking back towards Morrison's car park.

Like I said, at that time of night the traffic is heavy and when I'm opposite the restaurant, I stare across at it and I almost leap for joy. Through the window inside the brightly lit restaurant, I can clearly see Irene walking to a table that's set back from the window. I don't see Billy, but she wouldn't be there herself, would she, so I'm guessing that for whatever reason, they were seated at a different table from the one I asked for.

Buoyed by that, I start walking back to my car and it's only when I'm in the driving seat that I realise I'm shaking with relief.

Well, even though I got a wee scare there, if nothing else part one of my plan is now complete.

All I have to do now is find one of the gang and carry out the rest of the plan.

I drive back towards Pollok through the fine, drizzly rain that's started. You know the type of rain I mean. Heavy enough to require the wipers need switching on, but when you use them they squeak because after one wipe, the rain water has gone. Annoying, isn't it? On the way back I'm retracing my route and ever watchful for the polis, but I don't see any. So much for the extra patrols they promised, eh?

I arrive at the Braidcraft roundabout and I'm taking the turning into Linthaugh Road, but instead of turning into Hapland Road I continue along Linthaugh. The police caravan is still there and there's a light on inside, but nobody is standing near it.

My heart is in my mouth so it is and I have to admit, I'm fairly anxious if this is going to work. I mean, because I see a young teenager walking along the road it doesn't have to mean that it's one of the gang, does it and of course that begs the question; how will I know if it *is* one of the gang?

I'm beginning to think maybe I should have thought this through a lot more than I did.

Before I know it I'm at the old bus terminus at Lyoncross Road and I slow down as I turn into Lyoncross. There's some weans playing football across the road, but they don't give me a second glance as I pass by and suddenly I'm feeling deflated. This is too random, I'm telling myself. I'll never come across one of the gang just wandering about, particularly if it's raining and I start to worry that my brilliant plan for providing Billy with an alibi won't work and no, I'm not bothered about the cost of the meal. To be frank, it's a small price to pay for the good neighbourly care that Irene gave Jeannie in those last few months.

Not that I'm getting desperate or anything, but if I'm honest I'm maybe a wee bit disheartened. That's when I decide that I'll take a turn along Dormanside Road and I'm still amazed at the changes in the place. Where the old tenements used to be are modern, semi-detached and mid-terraced houses that are both privately owned and council rented. It's quite obvious to me that most of the people in Dormanside are trying to make the place nice and many of the gardens have had lavish attention heaped on them. Of course, there are those houses where the occupants or tenants just don't care and these gardens stick out like sore thumbs.

I'm only a couple of hundred yards along the road when I realise that the road is closed off and I can't drive straight through. Bugger it, I think and turn back towards Lyoncross.

It's still drizzling when I get back to the junction of Dormanside and Lyoncross. I'm driving slowly and that's when I see the flash of colour.

It's the bright yellow tracksuit that attracts my attention. About fifty yards away I see the tracksuit to my right crossing Lyoncross Road to my side of the road and I stop the car. Stop it? I was that surprised I stalled it. I turn my head to look down at the engine key and right away, that was a mistake. I turn the key to restart the engine and when I look up, the yellow tracksuit is gone. When I say gone, what I mean is in those brief, few seconds, I've lost sight of the tracksuit. I check my mirror and there are car headlights behind me coming along the road, so I wait till it's passed and see it's a private hire taxi. When it's gone I pull out and drive slowly to where I last saw the tracksuit.

I slowly drive towards the junction opposite the shops in Lyoncross and as I reach it, I see the tracksuit plodding along Barnbeth Road and I realise right away that yes, it's her.

The wee fat lassie with the short dyed blonde hair.

Talk about lucky! I'm thinking maybe I should have put a lottery ticket on tonight.

As I watch her I turn into Barnbeth Road and drive past her and then stop about fifty yards in front of her and pull into the side of the road, judging the distance to be roughly halfway between the lamppost on my side of the road and the lamppost on the other side of the road. I'm thinking that this is about the darkest part of the road and that can only help me. I risk turning my head to glance back towards her and I see she's carrying a plastic bag in her left hand so I suppose she has just been to the shops in Lyoncross. On one side of the road to my right there are mid-terraced houses, but she's walking on the pavement on the other side of the narrow road that borders onto a grassy area that leads into nearby woods.

I make my decision there and then. Gritting my teeth, I glance back and forth along the road, but I don't see anyone walking and there's no cars coming either way.

Switching off the engine, I then pull the lever to unlock the bonnet. Reaching under my seat, I fumble for the plastic spray bottle and grabbing it, shove it into my jacket pocket. Getting out of the car I leave the driver's door open and walk to the front of the car. Without glancing towards her I lift the bonnet and rest it on the metal rod. My mouth is dry and I'm very, very nervous because I'm guessing this lassie has at least about three or four stone on me and she's taller too. As casually as I dare, I pull the baton from my trouser pocket and take the plastic bottle from my jacket pocket.

By now she's about fifteen yards away and still walking without any apparent concern towards the car. When I say walking, maybe I should say waddling because she's got thighs like tree trunks and her shoulders make me think she's either really fat or does weight-lifting. At the same time I'm also thinking I'd better not let her get a punch at me or get close enough to grab me because I don't think I could fight her off.

She's getting closer and if she recognised the car, she certainly wasn't giving any indication.

My heads under the bonnet and I'm gripping the bottle and baton, getting myself ready as I risk a wee look round the side of the bonnet.

I'm conscious that my hands are sweaty and my mouth dry and I sneak a peek at her.

I see that the bag is still in her left hand and she's got a phone in her other hand that's clamped to her ear.

Now, she's no quiet speaker this lassie and I hear her say something like, "Aye, tell him I've got the bevy! For fuck's sake, do I need…"

It's at this point I take a deep breath and step out from under the bonnet to face her.

So there we are; both stood facing each other with the car to my left shielding us from the houses on the other side of the road.

She stops and at first I see she's surprised and puzzled, but then she apparently recognises me for her mouth opens and she's about to say something when I let her have the spray right squarely in her face.

The next few seconds are permanently etched in my mind as I drop the plastic bottle to the pavement.

The bag in her hand dropped to the pavement and there must have been a glass bottle inside for I hear it shatter with a loud smash. The phone fell from her right hand and she is starting to stagger back, clawing at her face with both hands.

Her mouth opens wide and I think she is about to scream, but she never really got the chance because I lift the baton and as hard as I possibly can, I batter her on top of her dyed blonde head.

There is a sudden burst of blood that sprays over me and suddenly she's sinking to her knees, still clutching at her face, tearing at her eyes with her left hand while probably with instinct, her right hand rises to ward off my next blow. Aye right, I think to myself; as if that's going to stop me.

As I'm lifting the baton for another strike at her, all the loathing of her type of bully goes into that blow as I strike her once more, but she had started to turn her head away and I miss her crown and catch a glancing blow to the left side of her fat face.

That blow is a mistake for she bounces across and strikes the side of my car with her bloodied head.

Bugger, I'm thinking. I'll need to wash that off later.

Now she's on the ground and there's a kind of whimpering sound from her, but for good measure, I bend down onto one knee and belt her on the head again and her head quite literally bounces off the tarmac. Aye, I'm thinking, she's not such a hard nut now, is she? I take a breath and belt her on the head one more time for good measure and even in the darkness I see that her eyes are now wide open. She gives a soft sort of sigh, but I'm satisfied I've done her in. That's when I hear the faint voice shouting, "Kyle, Kylie," and realise her phone that's lying near her on the ground is still connected to whoever she has been speaking with.

So that's her name; Kylie. Her mammy must have bee a fan of 'Neighbours.'

I use my hand to push on the side of the car to get myself to my feet and I'm thinking I'd better get the heck out of here.

I shove the baton into my pocket and turn to lift the plastic bottle, but there's an instant panic, because I don't see it where I dropped it on the pavement.

I scramble down onto my knees and to my relief I see it beneath the car. You know that old saying that inanimate objects have a mind of their own, that when you drop something it always rolls to the most awkward place? Well, either the bottle has rolled across the pavement or I've inadvertently kicked it because it's about three feet under the car. On my knees I stretch out but realise I can't quite reach it and have to sprawl my length. That's when I see I'm almost nose to nose with the dead girl, but I'm too busy to worry about that and my fingertips just reach the bottle. With a "Phew," I grab it and I'm back on my feet and with a last look at her, make my way round the car to the driver's door and get in. I force myself to be calm and with a glance in the mirror, see there's nothing coming.

It's only when I start the engine and begin to pull away from the kerb that I notice him.

A wee boy, maybe nine or ten years old who is wearing an oversized Celtic football top and holding a bicycle, is standing in the front gate of the garden across the road, curiously watching me.

I'm that surprised that I stare back, but then quickly turn my head and before I know it, I'm at the T-junction of Barnbeth Road and Meiklerig Crescent. I realise that I haven't switched on the car lights again and decide to do that when I've turned the corner.

Now, I have a wee burst of inspiration and I can't explain why I think of it, but the natural route and quickest way for me to get to my house would be to turn right, then into Templeland Road and follow it into Hapland Road, but some instinct made me turn left to take the long way back to my house. Now, Barnbeth Road is a long, straight road so I also used the indicator when I turned left because I'm thinking if the wee boy is still watching he would see that.

Don't ask me if it was a sound idea, but I'd got a real fright when I saw him there and I can feel my heart pounding in my chest.

A couple of minutes later I'm parking outside my house and fumbling with my keys to get in my door.

Once I'm in, I slam the door behind me and lock it. Switching on the hallway light, I see the dark staining on the front of my jacket and realise it's her blood.

I don't stop but walk straight to the kitchen ripping off my jacket and it's straight into the washing machine. Right there in the kitchen with the blind down, I strip of all my clothes and everything, my underwear, the trousers, polo shirt, socks, boots and even the baton are all shoved into the machine that I set for a hot wash and switch on.

Bare naked and to be honest, a wee bit self conscious, I head for a vigorous shower and then go upstairs and get into clean clothes.

That's when I remember the bottle and the blood splashed on the side of the car.

Now, I've parked outside the house with the driver's side next to the pavement, so the blood staining will be on the passenger side and being dark outside, won't be immediately noticeable on the black coloured car, but I'm so worried about the wee boy seeing me that I want to get the blood washed off right away. That and I've left the plastic bottle lying on the mat on the passenger side, too.

Downstairs, the washing machine makes a heck of a racket on the spin cycle with the baton bouncing off the sides, but that's the least of my worries.

I fill a basin with hot, soapy water and wearing kitchen gloves I grab and a disposable J cloth and go out to the car. First though I make sure nobody is walking along the road before I quickly wipe down the side of the car and retrieve the plastic bottle. In the light from the overhead street lamp, the car seems clean enough, but I'll need to check it again in the morning. The water from the bowl gets chucked onto the grass across the road.

As the crow flies, Barnbeth Road is only about six hundred yards away so as it's a quiet enough night, I hear the faint sound of sirens and I'm guessing that the lassie's body has been discovered.

Once back in the house, I rinse out the basin and I fill the plastic bottle with water a half dozen times and each time empty it down the toilet bowl.

That done I wipe it dry and replace it in the cabinet under the sink. The J cloth gets torn into small shreds and I flush it down the loo. Maybe not my best idea, but I'll worry later if I clog up the drains. Back in the kitchen, you've guessed it; the kettle goes on for a cuppa.

That damned wee boy.

I'm shaking my head and worrying about what he might have seen. I know, I know, it's not the kid's fault that he was there, but it doesn't make me feel any better.

The kettle's boiling away and I'm milking my mug when I realise my hands are slightly shaking. I suppose it's a nervous tension after what I've just done.

For some reason my legs feel as weak as a new born kitten and I sit down on the kitchen chair.

The kettle switch pops off, but I feel too tired to even stand. I'm not certain how long I sit there, a jumble of thoughts going through my head.

God forgive me, but when the thought of the wee boy arises, I'm even considering how I will deal with him when I catch like a huge lump in my throat. Deal with him? Have I become so immune to killing people that I might even consider killing a wee, harmless lad? My God, what kind of monster have I become?

I'm shaking my head to erase such a horrible thought from my mind. No, I'm deciding, I'll give myself up and confess before I will ever, *ever* contemplate harming a poor, wee innocent boy.

That is just *not* an option, I tell myself.

I push myself up from the table and set the kettle to boil again. I'm still on my feet when the doorbell rings and I startle.

They've come, I'm sure. The wee boy has given them the registration number of the Escort and they've come to arrest me.

I know it's no use trying to run because if it's anything like the police shows on the television, there will be cops standing at the back door, but with the blind down, I can't tell. Besides, where would an old guy like me run to?

Wearily I make my way to the front door and to give myself up. Unlocking the door, I'm a little surprised how calm I feel.

The two of them are standing there and I nearly faint with shock.

"Jimmy," says Billy, "are you all right there pal?"

He reaches out as if to take my arm, but I manage a smile and wave him away.

"No, I'm fine Billy. Just a wee bit lightheaded," I lie then add, "It's probably just an age thing."

Irene looks a wee bit uncertain and grabbing Billy's arm, says, "We're just up the road from the restaurant. The meal was fabulous and we thought before we went into the house we'd like to thank you. That was a really nice gesture. You're such a decent wee man, Jimmy McGrath."

I find my voice and manage a weak smile. It occurs to me to ask them in for a cuppa, but to be honest, I'm still a bit surprised it's not the polis and instead I say, "You caught me just on the way to bed, folks."

"Right then," replies Irene, gently tugging at Billy's arm. "You get yourself a good night's sleep, Jimmy and we'll have you into ours for dinner some night. Say, the weekend maybe?"

"That will be grand, aye."

Irene leans forward and to my surprise, kisses me on the cheek.

"Goodnight, Jimmy," she smiles and strokes at my cheek where her lipstick has rubbed off.

"Thanks again, pal," grins Billy and they turn to walk back along my path.

I watch them reach the pavement and wave cheerio before I close the door.

I return to the kitchen, but give up on the idea of a cuppa and instead decide to go to bed.

Upstairs, I walk into the darkness of the back bedroom and pulling aside the curtain, stare over in the general direction of Barnbeth Road. The fine, drizzly rain has ceased and in the night sky I can see a faint, blue light bouncing off the low cloud.

I know right away it's the lights of the police cars that are in attendance at the girl's death.

I close the curtains and head for my own room, content in the certain knowledge that there will be no disturbance tonight from the gang up on the field.

CHAPTER THIRTEEN

Don't ask me to explain, but I sleep soundly and apparently dreamlessly through the night with not even a three am bladder call. Why then do I waken with the mother of all headaches?

I can only guess it is stress, worrying what the day will bring and at what time the polis will come chapping at my door.

First things first, I fetch the washing from the machine and in my dressing gown, I hang it out on the line while I pack the shoes with old newspaper and sit them under the radiator in the kitchen. The baton again goes into the hidey-hole under the sink.

Just like before, I pour bleach into the drum and set it on an empty wash.

Two Paracetamol and a cuppa later, I'm still in my dressing gown and switching on the radio for the eight o'clock news. There's no point in switching on the television because at that time of the morning there's no local news, just the usual doom and gloom from London Parliament and the English sport news.

Dead on eight, the newsreader on Smooth Radio opens with the news that a third body has been discovered in the Pollok area of Glasgow, this time thought to be a young woman. According to the newsreader the police have not issued any details other than the usual appeal for witnesses.

No mention of a dark coloured Ford Escort or the stupid old bugger that was driving it, either.

I don't hear the rest of the bulletin and foregoing breakfast, decide instead to get dressed and walk down to the newsagents at the roundabout for the papers.

Locking the front door behind me I see that the sky is clear and my first thought is the blood staining on the side of the car.

I'm happy that nobody would be suspicious seeing me inspecting my car; not after the damage it suffered when the windscreen was put in.

As it turns out, I have done a better job than I thought for there's no sign of any staining on the passenger side at all. In fact if anything, it looks that little bit cleaner than the rest of the car that makes me think weather permitting I'll maybe give it a wash later today.

I take the longer walk to the roundabout, deciding it's probably better to stay away from the police incident caravan that is still parked in Linthaugh Road. The brisk walk takes a little over five minutes and I nod to a couple of people who live in the road and are making their way to work.

"Something to be said for being retired," I joke with Mary Burns, who lives a dozen houses away and is on her way to work at the Saw Centre. Mary's a nice woman and though she's obviously in a hurry, takes the time to walk with me to the bus stop in Braidcraft Road where she gives me a cheery cheerio, but she obviously hasn't heard about the murder for she doesn't mention it.

The newsagents is unusually crowded and I realise that word about the girl's murder must have got round for without exception, the dozen or so people in the queue are buying at least two newspapers. When I buy my two newspapers and my four rolls, another dozen or so people have joined the queue behind me and there's a steady stream of people coming into the shop as I'm leaving.

I hear the odd mutter about 'that poor wee lassie' and then I hear one woman who is speaking to a man and telling him in a stage whisper, "Aye, Kylie Morrison that lives in Templeland Road. You know, Jinty Morrison's lassie. Not the one with the bairn, her big sister. Kylie's the fat one with the dyed blonde hair."

Kylie Morrison. So that's her name then, I'm thinking.

I'm so anxious to get home and read what the papers are saying that I stop and glance at the 'Glasgow News' front page.

The big headline literally screams out at me.

'Pollok Serial Killer Strikes Again.'

Bleeding heck, that's it confirmed now; I'm a serial killer!

I take a deep breath and that's when I realise I'm standing outside the big window by the Co-operative. When I turn my head and glance in the window, I nearly drop the plastic bag with the rolls because Gina the till lassie is standing behind the counter and staring out of the window at me.

I put my head down and hurry away and I'm thinking; is she staring at me in particular or is she just bored and staring at nothing?

I'm so tempted to turn my head and look back to see if she's left the shop to stare after me and half expecting a scream of "Stop him. He murdered Alex Paterson!" but to my relief, there's nothing.

I'm crossing the road with my heart beating faster than a lottery ticket holder with six numbers and my chest is hurting because I've forgot to breathe.

I'm so shaken that I've haven't realised I'm not retracing my route home, but instead I'm walking past the police incident caravan. Hell!

That's when I hear the voice call out, "Mister McGrath!"

I stop and turn slowly and there she is, wearing a lemon coloured light raincoat, standing at the open door of the caravan and staring curiously at me.

It's the good looking blonde detective with the nice legs and she's with another detective, a big guy and he's staring at me too.

They're both holding clipboards and the woman; God, what's her name again! She starts to walk towards me.

"Mister McGrath," she's still smiling and I can almost feel the handcuffs on my wrists. "I thought it was you. It's nice to see you again. Been to the shops then?"

Holding my rolls and two newspapers in front of me like they're a shield, I'm almost inclined to say is that why you're a detective, but bite my tongue and smile like an absolute dullard because I'm so frightened that I can't get any spit in my mouth.

I nod and I'm grinning like an idiot. I say that because she's staring at me like I am an idiot and by the way, I feel like an idiot too.

"You all right there, Mister McGrath?" she asks, her brow creased as taller than me, she frowns down at me. Her mate, big bruiser that he is, has joined her and reminds her, "Sorry to interrupt, Ella, but we've that interview to conduct?"

Ella. Ella something. DC Ella Hopkins, it comes to me at last.

Almost with relief, I find my voice and manage to squeak out, "Sorry DC Hopkins, I was a wee bit wandered there. Age thing," I grin and nod to her and again fall back on the decrepit old man excuse.

"Aye, right then," she nods at me and smiles tightly in return, but somehow I get the feeling she isn't convinced.

All I need now I'm thinking is Gina from the Co-operative running across the road screaming I'm a murderer.

That's when my bladder reminds me I need to get home and right now or I'll pee myself.

She says cheerio and is walking away when she calls out again to me. I stop and turning, she says out, "It's a dark coloured car you have, Mister McGrath. Is that right?"

There's no sense in lying because I recall she asked me that when she was taking the details down on the form, so I nod and reply, "Aye, a black coloured Escort, hen. Why do you ask?"

I almost choke when I realise, did I actually say that to her? Why do you ask?

Because she probably knows from the wee boy that the bloody *killer* drove a dark coloured car that looked like an Escort, I'm screaming inside.

"Oh," she smiles, "no particular reason. Cheerio," and turns to walk with her partner to a car parked nearby in Linthaugh Terrace.

I'm staring after them and then turn away and my mind is reeling. Bloody liar! No particular reason indeed! She suspects something, I'm sure of it.

And so I hurry all the way home, carrying my four rolls, two newspapers and a full bladder and let me tell you, I'm worrying myself sick.

I just make it to the toilet and it's with relief that I hose down the pan. Honest, I've never before came so close to peeing myself.

Oh my God, I'm staring at my face in the mirror above the sink while I wash my hands; first the wee boy and now that detective Ella knows it's me.

I'm absolutely…and please excuse my French here, shitting myself.

I know now it's just a matter of time before the polis come for me.

I dry my hands and stumble though to the kitchen for, you've guessed it, a cuppa and while I'm waiting for the kettle to boil I help myself to a couple of Paracetamol too.

I've not had any breakfast, but my stomach is churning and I've just no appetite.

When I've poured my tea I sit with the 'Glasgow News' spread out in front on me on the kitchen table. Now, if you're not a regular reader of the 'Glasgow News', let me explain. The headline that is usually described as an 'exclusive' and about some actor or somebody in the public eye dong something they shouldn't be. To be honest it's not so much a newspaper as a gossip rag. Jeannie wouldn't let me buy it when she was alive and the only good thing that can be said about it is that it has quite good local sports coverage on the back pages.

Sipping at my tea, I read about the discovery of a young woman's body in Barnbeth Road and there's the usual police source that names the woman as Kylie Morrison from Templeland Road.

I know that you'll get a laugh at this, but the article quotes a neighbour in Templeland who describes Morrison as a student who was a quiet and modest young woman and who kept herself to herself.

Aye, right, I shake my head, remembering instead the fat blonde cursing and swearing at the top of the field and challenging me and all my neighbours to fight.

This unnamed neighbour then apparently related to the reporter that Morrison lived with her mother Jinty and her younger sister Charlene, aged fifteen and her nephew; Charlene's baby son.

The sister's aged fifteen and she's got a wean? I'm thinking that surely that must be a mistake, but then again these days who knows what young women get up to.

The article then goes on to refer to the two previous murders of Alex Paterson and Calum Black who again according to the neighbour, were known to Morrison.

I smile with relief when I read that the unnamed police source told the reporter that the police are linking Morrison's murder to those of Paterson and Black.

Seems that Billy has his alibi after all, I'm thinking.

At the end of the lengthy article, the paper refers the reader to the Editors Comment on page twelve and turning the pages, I read that the Editor, if indeed it is him that wrote it, lambasts the police for not catching this serial killer and questioning if anyone in the Pollok area is safe from this mad, frenzied killer.

I'm chuckling at this because now I'm not just a serial killer; I'm a 'mad frenzied killer' too.

The other paper I've bought, 'The Herald' is a quality newspaper and as I read it, it seems to be reporting the known facts rather than the gossip of the 'Glasgow News.'

The article by the Herald's reporter is balanced and while it also links the three murders it doesn't resort to the 'Glasgow News' scaremongering nor does it give the polis a hard time, but rather suggests that this latest murder has provided new evidence.

I'm cringing a wee bit as I read this bit, because I'm guessing that somehow the Herald reporter has learned the new evidence is probably the wee boy who saw me and the dark coloured car that DC Hopkins asked me about.

I sit back and stretch my neck that is suddenly aching from poring over the newspapers. My tea has gone lukewarm and because I can't stand cool tea I get up to re-boil the kettle, but my mind is whirling with all sorts of thoughts.

One of the things I'm considering is before the police come for me I get myself a lawyer and go to them. I've heard it said that if someone suspected of a crime confesses before they are arrested it goes in their favour at their trial. But then again, if I own up to three murders, at my age a few years off the thirty I'll likely get won't really make that much difference, will it?

I suppose you're wondering by now, how do I really feel about murdering the lassie, this girl Morrison?

Truthfully, I don't really know how I feel about murdering her. I know I feel guilty about *committing* the murders, but curiously I don't feel any sympathy for any of *them*.

Am I worried about getting arrested?

Don't be stupid! Of course I'm worried about it. I mean, who in their right mind wants to go to jail for three murders?

Then again, who in their right mind *commits* three murders?

So, that begs the question. Am I off my head? Have I taken some sort of mental breakdown that's made me in the frenzied killer the 'Glasgow News' is describing?

I sit down with the fresh cuppa and I wonder about it. Now, don't get me wrong, I'm not a psychiatrist or one of these psychologist types that studies the insane. I'm just an ordinary man.

So what made me commit the murders, I ask myself? What drove me to bash three wee shites over the head with a home-made baton?

I think, in a word it's frustration.

Frustration that the three of them and all their pals think they can do what they want and get away with it. Hurt people and steal with impunity, like they hurt then stole from my pal Scooby. Run amok without conscience among decent, ordinary punters who just want to quietly get on with their lives.

Frustration that though we have the police, they are the very ones that are handcuffed and even though it's likely they know who all the gang members are, the polis can't do anything about them because they have to act within the law, within the rules; rules that these gangsters don't believe apply to *them*.

Frustration that it's the gangsters that is free to roam the streets at all hours of the night while it's ordinary, decent people who have to cower in their homes.

And like I told you before, if they do get caught they don't get punished. No, they get…what is it called again? Oh aye, rehabilitated. That means in the jail they are looked after, get their television, their three squares a day and better medical care and attention than the elderly who have kept their nose clean and abided by the law all their lives before being punted into some crappy nursing home.

And don't get me started on the lawyers and the do-gooders who remind them of their rights; rights that they take for granted even though most of them have never worked or paid taxes or did a single thing to uphold these rights. Oh aye and let's also not forget that the lawyers and the do-gooders will likely make a good living representing these buggers too.

Just thinking about it I've made myself angry and my blood's boiling hotter than the kettle, but worse of all my tea's gone cold again.

CHAPTER FOURTEEN

I've just finished hoovering the front room when the phone goes. I'm a bit old fashioned and don't have a mobile, so any calls I get are on the house phone.

Turns out it is Scooby.

"We haven't seen you for a few days, Jimmy. How you doing?" he asks.

"Aye, fine Scooby. How are you holding up? Your injuries I mean?"

"Not bad, not too bad at all Jimmy and that's half the reason I'm phoning. I was wondering if you might be up for a couple of pints at lunchtime. Not a heavy bevy session or anything, just a couple of jars down at the halfway," he says.

"Eh, aye, why not," I decide. Besides, it will give me the opportunity to ask him if the polis have been back to see him.

I'm actually quite cheered by his phone call and realise I haven't been in touch and felt a wee bit guilty about it.

So that's arranged, but I quite firmly tell him I'll pick him up at twelve midday, that I'm not having him walking to the bus, that I don't need a drink to enjoy myself and I really don't mind driving. On top of that we decide that we'll get something to eat in the pub and I'll get him up the road before three that afternoon because the community nurse is supposed to be coming in to check his wounds.

I finish the housework and take a shower before getting myself ready.

Funny, I'm that busy thinking about my wee outing that I completely forget about the murders and my fear of the polis coming to my door and it's only when I see the shoes sitting under the radiator in the kitchen that I remember.

I shake my head to try and dismiss the thoughts and force the murders from my mind. I realise I haven't had any breakfast and I think, ah well, the rolls will keep till tomorrow. Besides, I'm looking forward to my lunch at the pub with my old pal.

Through the front window I see the panda car draw up behind my Ford Escort and the driver is Craig the polis. The dark haired lassie sitting beside him is his partner, Mhari and holding my breath, I watch them getting out of the car. I see Mhari glancing at my car, but they're both carrying their caps in their hands and I relax a wee bit because I'm almost certain this is a social call.

Forcing a cheery smile to my face, I greet them at the door and invite them through for a cuppa and when I see their faces I'm thinking that there seems to be a wee bit of an atmosphere between them.

"How has your day been?" I force myself to sound cheery as I skip into the kitchen to put the kettle on and organise a tray of biscuits.

"No more than usual," Craig calls through the door as he and Mhari settle themselves into the armchair and the couch. That kind of surprises me because I'm thinking with this latest murder the polis would all have been working flat out. I'm in the kitchen brewing the tea and half listening, but there's no talk between them and I'm wondering if they have fallen out. A couple of minutes later with the tray and three mugs of tea, I pop back through to the front room and say, "I thought with the girl's murder you guys might not have been able to get in for a cuppa?"

Craig grunts and tells me, "The CID and the bloody murder team have no use for us woodentops unless it's standing about protecting their precious crime scenes."

He sounds quite bitter about it and then he adds, "It's us uniform cops that patrol these streets; us that knows who's who, but have they got any use for that? Have they hell."

"Woodentops, what's that?"

"That's what some of the fancy suits call us. Think because they're the CID that they're better than us."

He's pretty irritated and I'm guessing that Mhari, who is sitting not saying a word, has already had her ear bashed by him in the car.

"I didn't know that there was bad feeling between the CID and the uniform officers," I said.

"You don't know the half of it, Jimmy," he replies and reaches for a digestive that he crams into his mouth then excusing himself, he leaves the room to go to the toilet.

I glance at Mhari who leans forward from the couch and whispers to me, "His application for a six month secondment to the CID as an aide has just been knocked back again."

I'm thinking to myself that explains the bad atmosphere, then.

"I didn't know he wanted to be a detective," I whisper back.

She's about to reply when we hear the toilet flush and she sits back and sips at her tea.

I decide to go for it and say to her, "I was reading in the 'Glasgow News' today that we've got a serial killer in Pollok. Is that true?"

"You'd better ask Craig about that, Jimmy," she shakes her head.

"I'm still a brand new probationer, so nobody tells me anything," but it's obvious from her sharp reply that she isn't happy about him.

I'm not daft and I make a poker face, but also realise the lassie has very subtly deflected my question.

Craig pushes open the living room door and sitting back down in the armchair opposite me, asks, "What you up to today, Jimmy?"

"Oh, I'm picking up my mate Scooby; you know, Michael Toner? I'm getting him at midday and taking him for a pub lunch."

"Don't be drinking and driving, now."

"No fear, Craig. I'm not one for breaking the law," I cheerfully lie, thinking it's maybe wise not to mention the three murders.

"Going with Mister Toner to somewhere nice?" Mhari butts in.

"Probably just down to Howden's at the Halfway on the Paisley Road West," I shake my head. "They do a fairly decent, cheap midday lunch. Scooby won't be having anymore than a couple of pints because he's got the community nurse at three o'clock this afternoon," I add.

"How is he doing anyway? Injury wise, I mean," asks Craig.

"I think he's doing okay. I haven't spoken with him for a few days," I admitted, "so I'll catch up with the news this afternoon."

That's when it occurs to me that having learned of Craig's annoyance with the CID, maybe I should press home a few questions.

As though betraying a confidence, I lower my voice and I say, "To be honest, I think him and his family were a wee bit peeved at the CID. When that lad got himself murdered, the lad..." I pretended to forget the name.

"Alex Paterson?" volunteered Craig, now sitting slightly forward and keen to hear the gossip.

"Aye, Alex Paterson," I agreed with a nod of my head. "The CID came back to Scooby and his family demanding to know where they were when Paterson was killed. Scooby and his family felt they were being treated as suspects and they were really upset by it all."

"Bloody CID!" Craig spat out and shook his head.

"To be fair," said Mhari in a quiet voice, "I suppose they were only asking to eliminate the family as suspects."

"Don't kid yourself, hen," Craig turned to her, the venom in his voice surprising me. "They were probably just looking for a quick detection. Most of them couldn't find their own arses unless somebody put their hand on it for them."

A few seconds of embarrassed silence followed that wee outburst before he added, "You know, they've got most of the office at Pollok closed up, running their inquiry. We're trying to police the area and we're not getting a look-in at what's happening. They're telling us hardly anything at all."

"What, you're not getting any information about the murders?" I act surprised.

"Nothing," then he tapped the side of his nose with a forefinger and with a sleekit grin, said, "Only what I'm hearing from certain contacts."

Here we go again, I thought. Craig trying to impress the lassie or, a thought passed through my head; is he trying to impress me?

I put on my most puzzled impression and acting the idiot, which by the way I'm now getting pretty good at, I ask, "So it's not a serial killer like the paper says then?"

"Oh aye, it's the same killer because…"

"No offence Jimmy," butted in Mhari, "but Craig; I don't think we should be talking…"

"For Christ's sake, I'm not saying anything that's not in the newspapers, Mhari!" he snapped at her then turning to me, looked a bit sheepish as he added, "Sorry Jimmy, I know you're a good Catholic. I was out of order there."

"It's okay," I shook my head, but a wee bit taken aback that he thought me a good Catholic.

Mhari, her face chalk white at Craig's rebuke, sits silently and tight-lipped on the couch cradling her mug and staring at the carpet between her feet.

He take a deep breath and pointedly looking at Mhari first, turns towards me and says, "The CID believe it's the same killer that done the three of them, Jimmy. They think the killer lives locally."

I remembered what he had said on a previous visit and I ask him, "Is it still what you said before? It's a drug war that's going on?"

He seems taken aback and it occurs to me he can't recall what he previously told me. Like I told you before, my old Ma used to say you need to have a good memory to be a proficient liar.

However, Craig takes the hint and nodding, replies, "That's what my source says; a drug war."

"Those three young people," I sorrowfully shake my head. "Cut down like that while so young. Who would believe something like this could happen in Pollok?"

"You don't know the half of it, Jimmy," he shakes his head as though inferring the area is a war zone. "You'd be shocked to know what goes on behind closed doors."

"What about people like me," I try to sound anxious. "I mean, I'm not involved in drugs or anything. Is it safe for older people like me to be out on the streets?"

It's Mhari this time who replies. She smiles and says, "If what Craig is saying is correct, Jimmy, then the people who are causing the problems are fighting among themselves. I know that you and your neighbours have had problems with the gang up on the field, but the three that have been murdered; they belong to that gang and…"

She suddenly stopped and blushed and I'm guessing that after trying to prevent Craig from saying too much, she's realised she is almost making the same mistake.

"Well," she shrugs her shoulders, "I'm sure that no matter *what* Craig thinks of the CID," and pointedly ignores him, "they'll get the job done and arrest the killer before anyone else gets hurt."

I hope not, I'm thinking, but smile at her and reply, "That's reassuring anyway. Thanks Mhari."

Craig suddenly stands and lifting his cap has decided that he and Mhari is leaving.

"So, I'm a good Catholic am I?" I smile at him. "What made you say that, Craig?"

He grins and winking at me, replies "You didn't see me the other day did you? Mhari and I drove by St Convals and you were there, sweating away in the sun mowing the grass. I know you're a retired man, Jimmy and you'll not be taking money from Father Stephen so it's reasonable to assume you're doing voluntary work at the church. Only a good Catholic would be doing that," he smiled at his own brilliant insight.

I didn't want to disillusion him that I'd been embarrassed into helping out, so I agreed and for good measure, I sighed as I added, "Aye, you've found me out there, Craig. I'm due back there maybe tomorrow to do the weeding. It's just my way of praising the Lord."

God forgive me for taking His name in vain, but after the crimes I've committed, I'm sure that He'll forgive me that one wee transgression.

I glanced at Mhari who seemed a wee bit embarrassed at my apparent holiness and to be honest, it took all my facial muscles to stop me from bursting out laughing.

Me, a good Catholic?

My Jeannie will be turning in her grave at that one.

I saw them to the door and watched them get into their panda and I'd love to have been a fly on the wall in that car.

It also made me smile as waving them cheerio, it occurred to me maybe it wasn't just a knockback from the CID that had so riled Craig.

Maybe it was a knockback from the lovely young Mhari.

The clock tells me its eleven forty-five, so as I'm ready for my outing I decide to leave a wee bit early to pick up Scooby.

I give the Ford Escort a once over glance and to my relief, I see that there doesn't seem to be any trace of the blood on the passenger side. The short trip to Scooby's house in Lochar Crescent takes just a few minutes and rather than having my old pal rush, I go into the house and at the doorstep, get a big hug from Alice.

"You been looking after yourself, have you?" she chides me with a frown, rubbing with her thumb at the lipstick she's left on my cheek.

"Course I have," I smile at her and realise she's done up to the nines. "You're looking very pretty today, missus. So, where are you off to then?"

"Well, if you two buggers are off out for lunch, so am I. Shona's taking a day off work and fetching me at half twelve for a wee trip into the town."

"Aye, so likely there will be a big dent in the budget this month because she's taking a Visa card with her," says Scooby, walking into the tight wee hallway behind Alice.

He's wearing his favourite old sports jacket and leaning on the aluminium NHS walking stick, but his grin is as wide as the Clyde and he seems perky enough.

"Nice to see you old pal," he continues to grin at me. "I'm ready when you are."

"Right you two, watch yourselves," warns Alice as she stand to one side, but leans forward to peck him on the cheek as he passes her by. I reach forward to help him over the lip of the front door step, but he shrugs me off and tells me he's fine.

"Bring him back relatively sober, Jimmy," she calls out to me. "Remember, he's got the nurse here in the house at three."

I wave in acknowledgement and open the passenger door for Scooby who gets in fairly easily.

So that's us off and turning into Linthaugh Road, I head for the Braidcraft roundabout and I casually ask him, "Any more visits from that mob?" nodding my head towards the police caravan.

"Nothing," he replies with such scorn and bitterness that I almost grin. "Not a word since they tried to accuse me and my family of killing the wee bastard that mugged me."

"Ah well, maybe now that he's dead that's an end of it," I suggest.

"No it's not, Jimmy. Remember, there was another two involved. With a bit of luck they'll end up murdered as well!"

I was that shocked by his outburst I almost snapped my head round to stare at him, but forced myself to face forward and concentrate on the road.

We spent the next couple of minutes in silence and then Scooby says, "I'm sorry, Jimmy. You've known me longer than anyone, even Alice. You know I'm not a bitter man. I've always tried to be a fair and Christian person, but what those bastards did to me that night…" he tails off and shakes his head as the memory seems to disturb him and I hear him clear his throat. "I know the bible teaches that we should turn the other cheek, but not this time. I don't know if this means I'm a bad person, but I'm not sorry that sod Paterson is dead. Not sorry at all and as for his mates; well, if they are not caught they *will* end up killing somebody. I was lucky, Jimmy, very lucky."

He takes a deep breath and I decide not to say anything, just to let him get it off his chest.

"Alice is angry with me. Angry that I won't talk to her about that night, but I know if I tell her how I really feel she'll try to persuade me that it's not right to feel bad about them, that I should forgive them their sins. Well, bollocks to that. I hope the wee bastard suffered when he was murdered."

Not enough I regret, remembering how I bashed Paterson over the head.

"Really, does that make me a bad person?" he asks again as he half turns in his seat towards me.

I shrug and slowly let out my breath and I tell him, "No, Scooby. Like you, I'm no expert, but as I recall the bible does say turn the other cheek or something like that, but it's full of stories of revenge too; so no, I don't think it makes you a bad person. In fact," and here I am, tongue in cheek trying to justify my murder of Paterson, "whoever killed the guy might have saved some other innocent soul from getting hurt."

He turns away and seems to be considering this then playfully slaps me on the arm.

"Good on you, Jimmy. You always know the right thing to say."

I finish the journey asking about Scooby's kids and have decided that I don't want to think about let alone discuss the murders this afternoon. All I want is a wee bit of quiet time with my best pal.

The car park behind Howden's has just a couple of cars parked so there is plenty of space for my Escort. Again, Scooby good-naturedly shrugs off my helping hand and after getting out of the car, we walk together to the pub's front door on Paisley Road West.
It's a nice friendly place is Howden's and though I'm not a regular, anytime I've visited and usually with Scooby, the bar staff have always been cheery and helpful. There's not much of a crowd with just over a half dozen patrons seated at the tables that includes two couples who are eating meals. A couple of guys at the far end of the bar, who already seem to have had more than their fill of bevy, are being a wee bit loud.
While Scooby slowly makes his way to a corner table against the back wall, I go to the bar and after ordering him a pint of Tennants and a soft drink for myself, fetch the drinks and a menu back to the table.
We each decide on what it's known in Glasgow as Catholic steak suppers; fish and chips with beans for me and peas for him and I return to the bar to make the order.
The two guys at the other end of the bar are still noisy and giggling like weans at some joke or other and their language is what my Jeannie used to refer to as fruitful.
The young barmaid, a nice looking wee lassie, with a ring through her nostril and both ears with half a dozen piercings each, smiles and seeing me glance at the two guys, raises her eyebrows.
"I think they've one more drink in them then they're out," she grins at me with perfect neat, brilliant white teeth as she takes my order. As she turns her head I see she has a snake tattoo that starts at the nape of her neck and disappears into the top of her blood red coloured blouse at the shoulder. I never understood the fashion for tattoos or facial jewellery, but then again, I'm a completely different generation and though the lassie's piercings and tattoos look daunting to an old lad like me, she was sparkly and cheery.
The two at the end of the bar are now slapping each other on the back and having a mutual 'what a great guy you are' type of discussion. Not that I'm by any means a heavy or regular drinker

these days, but I know that there's nothing that lowers the inhibitions like alcohol and one drunk's best mate is usually someone who is equally as drunk.

I sneak a glance at the two guys and my blood runs cold for that's when I recognise a face from the television and realise that the guy on the far side of me is George Paterson, Alex Paterson's father. Neither of the two guys is paying any attention to anybody but themselves. I collect my change from the lassie and I'm turning to head back towards the table when I hear one of them, Paterson I'm sure it was, call out, "Hey, doll; move your arse and give us another couple of pints here."

I reach the table and I see that Scooby's face is like fizz and he's watching what's going on at the bar. I turn to follow his gaze and see that the barmaid is facing Paterson and his pal and like Scooby, her face is like fizz too. She's shaking her head and crossing her hands and though I can't make out what she's saying, it's pretty obvious she's telling the pair no more drink. She did say to me that the pair was to get one more drink, but I can only guess that something has been said that made her very angry and now she's refusing them.

The pub has gone quiet and the half dozen or so who are sitting at their tables are now watching what's going on.

Paterson then stands back from the bar and literally screams at her, "Don't you fucking know who I am? I was on the tele! My boy got *murdered*! I'm in fucking mourning here and you, you cow; you're refusing me a drink?"

Scooby hisses to me, "Sit down, Jimmy."

I was unaware I was still on my feet and slowly sink into my seat, but as I'm watching I see the lassie take a step back from the edge of the bar and I realise she's getting herself out of reach of the pair of them. A big black guy wearing a white shirt and an apron round his waist and who I'm guessing is the chef and is wiping his hands on a tea towel, comes out from a door behind the bar and I clearly hear him say, "What's the problem here?"

Paterson steps back from the bar and though his arms are at his side, I see his hands are clenched into fists. He sneers at the big guy and I hear him say, "Who the fuck are you, you black bastard!"

The lassie hurries away to the other side of the bar and I see she's now got a mobile phone in her hand. She looks behind her and then she's talking on the phone.

The chef has his hands raised, his palms outwards to Paterson and his pal and seems to be trying to calm the situation, but Paterson isn't having any of it and now he's got his hands raised as if to fight and he's shouting, "Come ahead if you think you're hard enough!" Now, I'm looking at this skinny, balding man who I'm guessing is about five feet nine tall and probably in his forties, but looks about my age and whose body looks like it's been wasted by drink or drugs or maybe both. On the other side of the bar is this big chef who stands about six feet two, built like an ox and looks like a rugby player and I'm smiling to myself. If the bar hadn't been between Paterson and the chef, I've no doubt who would have been torn in two. Fair play though to the chef, though. He stood there and took the verbal abuse and remained calm, all the while trying to defuse the situation.

The other guy, Paterson's pal, has slunk away and with a stagger is hurriedly making his way to the front door. That's when I hear the barmaid call out to the chef, "Paddy, that's the polis on their way." I'm that engrossed on what's going on that I almost jump when Scooby reaches out to touch my arm and whispers, "That's Geordie Paterson. He's the father of that sod that mugged me."

I don't want to admit I know this and raise my eyebrows to pretend surprise.

It was about then that one of the women who were dining in the pub stood up and shouted to Paterson, "You're a disgrace, speaking to that young man like that. You ought to be ashamed of yourself, so you should."

As a couple of other people called out in support of her I saw the woman's husband who was a good ten years older than me, try to drag her back down onto her seat.

Paterson turned on the woman and began to walk towards her with his fists raised and kicking a chair out of his way. There's only about fifteen feet between Paterson and the couple's table and woman's wee grey haired husband gamely stood to confront Paterson, but skinny though Paterson is it was obvious the older guy wouldn't stand a chance against the drunken lout.

That's when to my horror, Scooby struggled to his feet and shouted, "Hey, you arse! You want to fight somebody, come and see me, you drunken bastard!"

So there's my pal, sixty years of age, recovering from a beating that nearly killed him and standing with one hand on the table and leaning heavily on his NHS stick, offering the drunken and maddened Paterson a square go.

Honest, you couldn't make this up.

I felt my body go limp and I almost collapsed under the table, but to my surprise, I find myself standing upright too.

My knees were shaking and my mouth was as dry as a nun's gusset, but no way was I letting Scooby face this bampot on his own.

He turned and started towards us, but only got a few feet because Paddy the chef, God bless and keep him, leapt over that bar faster than shit melting on a hot shovel. He grabs Paterson from behind by his arms and shoves him face down onto an empty table and all the time he's quietly telling Paterson to behave, to calm down and not to be stupid.

Does Paterson listen, does he heck.

Even with the big guy Paddy using his weight and one large hand to holds Paterson's hands behind his back and using his other hand to press Paterson's head against the table, Paterson's face is turned towards us and he's screaming abuse, but then he stops and stares at Scooby, then screams, "I know you and I'm going to fucking chib you, you bastard! You're the guy that murdered my boy!"

"No, I'm not," smiles Scooby, "because somebody else got there first."

Well, if that isn't enough to set Paterson off again Scooby grins and adds, "Oh and by the way, I heard he squealed like a wee girl when he was getting battered to death."

Just then the door burst open and in come two of Police Scotland's finest. I didn't recognise the cops but boy, was I glad to see them. Quick as a flash they've got Paterson handcuffed and while one struggles to lead the kicking and hysterical Paterson out of the door, the other produces a notebook and speaks to Paddy and the lassie behind the bar.

The cops are away, but I'm still shaking like a leaf and I sit back down as Scooby takes a large swig of his pint. Paddy first speaks quietly to the woman who challenged Paterson and uprights the fallen chair before walking over to Scooby and me and with a friendly smile he says, "Fish, chips and beans for one and peas for the other; is that right?"

Well after that wee incident, the rest of the meal went without a hitch. The barmaid told us, well, actually she went round the tables and told the whole pub, that the polis wouldn't need our statements or anything like that, but the statements from both her and Paddy was enough. That and she handed the polis a CCTV recording of the incident and that's the first I notice the wee cameras above the bar and on the walls. She told us the polis had told her Paterson was being charged with something called a racial breach of the peace and that he was being held over till he appeared at the Sheriff Court the next day.

I am keen to ask if the polis had said anything about Paterson accusing Scooby of murdering his boy, but didn't want to push it and I decide not to raise the issue.

As for Scooby, he was neither up nor down about the whole thing. In fact, he seemed to be delighted that Paterson's father got the pokey and celebrated with another Tennants and a half of a real peaty whisky called Laphroaig.

Once he had supped those, I forbid him any more drink and reminded him I had to get him home by three o'clock for the nurse calling and sure enough, I drop him at his house for two-fifty.

He's keen for me to come in for a cuppa, but I decline the offer and tell him I'll phone him tonight for an update on what the nurse tells him.

With that I head home and less than five minutes later I'm brewing a cuppa. As I sit in the kitchen waiting for the kettle to boil, I reflect on what happened today in the pub.

It's obvious to me that George Paterson seems to be every bit as bad as his son was and it reminds me of a time when I was younger.

Jeannie had just discovered she was pregnant and we had broken the news to my parents.

While my Ma had sat Jeannie down in the front room to comfort her because Jeannie was distraught and worried about telling her folks, my Da had taken me through to the kitchen here to have what he called a man to man chat.

Now remember, I was just about to turn twenty-two and the last thing I wanted to be, or so I thought, was a father so it wasn't just my Jeannie who was in a state of shock.

My Da, God bless him, was a tower of strength. There was no ranting or raving from either him or my Ma, just a quiet support for two young people who were no more than kids themselves.

I remembering him reaching up to the top shelf in the cupboard and fetching down his half bottle of whisky for what he called emergencies only.

Even back then I wasn't much of a drinker and I remember the whisky burned the back of my throat.

But it was what my Da said to me that even today sticks in my mind. He looked me square in the eye and like all we Glaswegians do, used his hands as he spoke. Now you have to remember that he worked all his days in the shipyards. He quietly explained to me that a baby is like a new apprentice and the parent is like a journeyman. Just as through the years the journeyman teaches the apprentice the skills of the trade, it's the parent's duty to teach, care for and succour the baby through the beginning of life to enable the baby to become a responsible and caring individual. If the journeyman and the parent are neglectful in that teaching he told me, the apprentice will fail at his job and the baby will grow up to be an uncaring individual who will have no focus in life, will be without ambition and disdainful of others.

All those years ago and without realising it, my Da described George Paterson and his son Alex.

Would I have made a good father? It is to my sorrow that I never had the opportunity to find out, but in my defence I had the best start in life for I had good and loving parents.

The kettle's whistling away and after my pub lunch there's no need for a full meal tonight so for now, a cuppa will suffice.

CHAPTER FIFTEEN

I awake the following morning feeling fresh and relaxed for I've had a good night's sleep.

If there have been any shenanigans from the gang in the field, I certainly didn't hear it.

As has become my morning custom, I take a quick peek out of the top bedroom window to check on my car, but it seems to be fine and so with my dressing gown wrapped about me I make my way downstairs for breakfast.

I know it does sound strange and believe me, it's no stranger to me that I don't have any recurring nightmares about the three murders I've committed.

If I'm honest with you, I thought that I might have had restless nights, you know, like you read in books or see in the films on TV, but it seems that I'm without conscience.

As Scooby remarked to me yesterday; does that make me a bad person?

Not for the murders I mean, because there's no denying it; I am a bad person for killing the three of them. No, I mean does it make me a bad person for not being regretful?

Do you know, it is times like these I wish I had somebody that I can discuss my feelings or my thoughts with, but let's face it; who can I tell that I've knocked off three scumbags?

Ah well, the complexities of human nature.

So, that's me had breakfast and I'm reminding myself that I told Father Stephen I would do a bit of weeding today. I also mentioned it to Craig the polis so I suppose I had better keep to a routine.

Maybe I should tell you as well that since Billy King has his alibi, I've no intention or any reason to kill anybody else.

Yes, I admit that I still have the baton, but I'll get rid of that tonight. I'll saw it into wee bits and dispose of it in the big rubbish bin.

As for dealing with the gang, I'm not getting involved anymore. It's time I let the polis do their duty regarding the gang. Let the cops hunt them down as they search for their murderer who by the way in case you've forgotten, is me.

I'm dressed in my work clothes and carrying my bag that's got my bottled water and a flask of tea. I ignore the car and walk the short distance to St Convals.

I'm a wee bit nervous in case there is any of the gang hanging about the phone box, but there's nobody there. Funny, that's the first time in a while I haven't seen any of them at the phone box and I'm thinking, is it possible that the polis have done their job? That the gang has been arrested or chased away?

It kind of cheers me up a wee bit that I don't see any of the gang and I turn into the gate at the church and go to the presbytery door, but Father Stephen's not at home, his housekeeper tells me.

"He's away to visit poor Missus Laurie at the hospital," she says, than adds, "You know, the lady that got hit by the brick."

It's obvious she's been crying. "He got a phone call from her family to tell him she's about to fade away and ask him to go and deliver the Last Rites. Poor, poor Missus Laurie," she shakes her head and sniffs. "Such a good, clean living woman she is too and never said a bad word about anyone."

Her hand is shaking as she sobs and gives me the garage door key.

I didn't really know the woman Laurie, other than seeing her at the social nights now and again, but from what I had heard in the church and from Scooby's wife Alice, she was a nice lady who lived with her husband here in Pollok and raised her family of six who had now all left home to get married.

Walking to the garage, I wondered if now that she was dead that meant the assault on her with the brick is murder. If it is then the polis have their hands full, what with trying to catch the sod that threw the brick as well as trying to catch me that killed the other three.

Don't ask me why, but I'm smiling to myself. No, nothing to do with Missus Laurie, it's just the thought of all those detectives looking for a wee guy like me and here's me just about to start weeding the church gardens, good Catholic that I am and *that* makes me chuckle.

Well, I've been here for nearly an hour now and though the Paraquat I'd put down a couple of days ago has made some impact on the weeds I'm on my knees digging between the paving slabs at some of the more obstinate buggers. The black bin bag beside me is almost full and I decide it's time to knock off for a cuppa.

I'm sitting on the steps of the church with my flask supping at my tea. It's funny how your mind works and I start to reflect on what has happened over the last weeks.

I've already decided and accepted that it's just a matter of time before I'm caught.

The police aren't stupid. They must know by now that what the young lad saw when I killed the lassie Morrison must be pretty significant. They'll know it was a wee guy with a black coloured car and if the lad knows his motors, they'll also know it's a Ford Escort. Craig the polis told me that the CID suspect the killer is pretty local, so there can't be many black coloured Escorts in the area these days.

I mean, great car though it is, the Escort is past its sell-by date isn't it and if the detective who came to see me and took my details is worth her salt, she'll remember that it's an Escort I've got.

Then of course if I've learned anything from watching the television programmes about the police they're bound to go over all the statements they've taken and re-interview the witnesses again.

That means the lassie Gina at the Co-operative might just remember seeing me behind Alex Paterson when he was standing in the queue and following him out of the store just before he was killed.

Aye, my goose is cooked right enough, I sigh.

Oh well, if nothing else I'll get these bleeding weeds out before I'm jailed.

I've just thrown the dregs of the tea into the grass when a car turns into the gate and I see it is Father Stephen's old motor.

He gives me a wave then gets out of the car and it's apparent to me that he's not happy.

"How's it going there, Jimmy?"

"Fine, Father, it's fine. I'm just about to take out the last of the weeds and that's the entrance from the gate to the steps more or less finished," I point out what I've done so far.

"Aye, you're making a grand job of it," he nods and then takes a big breath.

"Your housekeeper was telling me you were away to the hospital seeing Missus Laurie."

"Sad day, Jimmy," he claps me on the shoulder and shakes his head and I'm almost sure there's a touch of anger in his voice. "I got there just before she died so at least she has had the Last Rites and now rests with our Father in heaven."

He pauses as if collecting his thoughts and tells me, "Her husband is in some state and so is her family. To their credit, they were all there at the end, even her niece whose one of…"

But then almost as if he has begun to say the wrong thing he takes another deep breath and changes the subject, pointing again to the cleared slabs and smiles.

He half turns towards the gate and glancing across the road says, "I see our friends are not present today."

"No, I was thinking maybe the polis have got off their arse and…oh, pardon me, Father. I mean, maybe they've rounded all the buggers up after all."

"I don't think so, Jimmy," he grins at me. "I was out last night locking the gates and there were two of them across the road, dealing. No," he sighed, "I think maybe they'll be back later in the evening. Perhaps they're keeping a low profile what with the… what is the papers call him or her again? That's it, the frenzied killer who is supposed to be roaming the streets."

Now I know he's kidding, but there's that reference again to me being a frenzied killer.

"Well, I'd better be getting on with this," I say, replacing the wee metal cup on top of the flask and watch as he walks off to the presbytery.

I spend another hour and by that time the weather's closing in and there's the threat of rain in the air. That decides me and I think I've done enough of a shift for that day.

Locking the garage door I return the key to the presbytery, but it's the housekeeper, her eyes red from crying, who takes it from me and tells me Father Stephen is in his room praying.

I nod and make my way down to the gates and that's where I see them.

There are three of them standing across the road, but they're not paying any particular interest in me and seem to be arguing among themselves.

Well, I say arguing, but it's really the biggest of the three with his back to me and who has one of the other two by the throat and pinned against the door of the telephone box.

I'm that taken aback I stop to watch and when the third lad jabs at the big lad with a finger and whispers something, he turns to stare at me.

He might have grown and aged eleven or twelve years, but I still recognise him.

Neil McMillan.

He's staring straight at me and God help me, I'm so surprised I'm rooted to the spot.

Suddenly he releases his grip on the guy he's holding and starts to quickly walk across the road towards me.

Now my first inclination is to run, but I'm that afraid I just stand there like the idiot I am and wait for him. He's a big lad now, is the shaven headed McMillan and the tight black coloured T shirt he's wearing shows off his muscular arms; that and he is almost six feet tall, too.

As he gets closer I can see the tattoos that cover his arms, his neck and even the lobes of his ears are tattooed too. I can almost feel his beady eyes feel boring into my skull.

My stomach lurches and I'm worrying that I might lose control of my bowels.

He's about ten feet from me when his eyes narrow and he slows up, then approaches slowly and stares down at me.

He's so close I can smell the cigarette smoke from him and the fried onions on his breath.

"I know you, don't I?" he whispers to me in a voice that just oozes menace.

I'm so frightened I can hardly speak and wondering where Father Stephen is when I really need him.

Because I seem to have lost the power of speech all I can do is nod.

"You're the janny at Leithland, aren't you?" he cocks his head as he continues to stare down at me.

"I was," I manage to croak, "but I'm retired now. A few years ago," I add and thinking to myself, if I boot him in the balls I might get a head start up the road, but frankly such bravery right now is beyond me. Besides, how would I outrun a fit young guy like him and all I can do is stare back up at him and hope to God somebody, anybody at all, passes by and saves me.

"You never picked me for the football team," he sneers.

My mind's reeling. Never picked him for the football team? What the heck…

"You never thought I was good enough," he sneers again at me and leans even closer so that our noses are almost touching.

I can't stop staring into his eyes and my bum cheeks are tightening against the eruption that threatens me.

"Funny how things turned out, isn't it, janny? Me, running this area and your just a wee, retired janny who turns out to be a nobody, eh? Isn't that right?"

"That's right, eh…"

"Mister McMillan. Call me Mister McMillan," his breath is really fetid and I'm thinking if I don't shite myself, I'll throw up instead.

"Mister…Mister McMillan," I nod to him, hating myself for giving in to his demand.

Suddenly, without any warning, he reaches up and playfully slaps me on the cheek. Not hard enough to hurt me, just enough to humiliate me and cause his two pals across the road to laugh loudly. "You'd better be getting up the road, janny and take my advice. Don't be eyeballing me or my team again. Understand?"

I nod because I don't trust myself to speak and it's as I turn away to walk off I feel his boot up my arse and hear more hysterical laughter from across the road.

My face is burning with shame, but I don't turn round.

I simply walk away up Hapland Road towards my home.

You can't imagine how I feel after that confrontation with Neil McMillan.

I'm home now and my body is shaking with rage, with embarrassment, with a loss of dignity and with emotions of such strength I can't really find the words to describe them.

You won't find it hard to believe that I am so humiliated I sit in my armchair and weep like a wee baby for a full five minutes.

I suppose that there is some people and men in particular who probably think to retain some sense of manly pride I should have fought him or at least tried to, regardless of the beating I would have suffered. It's all very well standing on the sidelines and suggesting that I be brave when you are not in the position I found myself.

I've always known and have always accepted my own limits and my vulnerabilities.

You already know that I'm not a brave man, that I'm not someone who is a fighter.

For starters, I'm not well built or physically strong and in the very few confrontations I have been involved in during my life I've always managed to talk my way out of them, even if it meant capitulating to the other guy.

Aye, I've turned the other cheek, if you must.

It's just who I am.

In my mind, I've never been the heroic type; no, I've always been the guy who watches and admires the hero because courage is not something I've ever known.

I get up and go into the bathroom and wash my face and feel a wee bit better.

It's as I'm staring into the mirror above the wash hand bowl I remember what he said.

I didn't pick him for the football team.

I'm nodding my head because I remember now why that was.

Neil McMillan was a bully at school and he carried that onto the football field, shoving and kicking the lads smaller than him. No, it wasn't his lack of skill that stopped me picking him because regardless of each individual's ability, I always gave the kids a game when I could. Winning or losing wasn't the issue with me; it was being part of the team that I tried to instil in my lads. But where he was concerned, it was his bullying that disgusted me and that's the real reason he was never chosen.

Unfortunately, that now seems to have backfired on me.

Ah well, I smile through trembling lips. If nothing else it seems he at least doesn't suspect me of killing his three pals.

Now, that thought doesn't really make me feel any better so I dry my face and head for the kitchen for…you've guessed it; a nice hot cup of tea,

At least I've stopped shaking, but the humiliation remains with me and my face still is still beetroot red, particularly when I think of the sod kicking my arse. Not that it hurt, but the indignity of it is simply too awful to bear.

I waken with a start and realise that I've dozed off. The clock on the mantelpiece tells me it's almost six o'clock and when I get up to switch on the STV news, I groan because I'm stiff from sitting in the armchair. The room is filled with shadows and a fine patter of rain beats against the window. My tea lies cold and half drunk on the Side table and I guess I must have fallen asleep almost as soon as I sat down.

I'm pulling the curtains closed and switching on the light as the news begins. The murder of the lassie has been dropped to the second item after a disclosure of some wrongdoing or other at the Parliament in Edinburgh. The anchor woman doesn't disclose anything new about the murder, but then turns the report over to their crime reporter who is standing outside Pollok police office on the Brockburn Road. The man in charge of the murders, Detective Chief Inspector McManus is standing there on the pavement outside the police station waiting to be interviewed, but this time I get the impression he isn't really prepared for the interview because he looks really uncomfortable when he's being asked the questions.

He's asked about the newspaper report of a serial killer, but he rebuts the 'Glasgow News' story and simply replies that his team are considering a number of lines of inquiry, whatever the heck that means.

The reporter tries to press him again for information and asks the detective if it is true that Morrison and the others were part of a drug-dealing gang and suggests it might be a drug turf war that is going on.

I'm not quite sure what a turf war is, but I think it's something to do with who controls the area for selling drugs.

Anyway, the detective doesn't even answer that question. He just shakes his head and again looks uncomfortable and repeats his team are carrying out a number of inquiries.

When it's obvious the detective isn't going to be forthcoming, the reporter thanks him for his time and the detective returns to the front door of the police station. The reporter then turns towards the camera and this is what I find really interesting.

He stares at the camera and in a voice dripping with sarcasm, says, "There you have it. DCI McManus, the man in charge of the *three* murder inquiries in the Pollok area, refusing to disclose but the barest details. However, our inquiries with local residents in the area has discovered that the three deceased Alex Paterson, Calum Black and eighteen years old Kylie Morrison were in fact known to each other, that all three were known locally to be drug abusers and members of a group who are alleged to be involved with an unnamed shadowy figure who is the main source in the distribution of illegal drugs here in Pollok. Can it be that the three murdered individuals were targeted by a rival gang and who exactly is the unnamed Jamaican man currently being sought for the murder of Calum Black? The question therefore remains; is this indeed a turf war for control of the Pollok area?"

That said he ended with, "Back to you in the studio."

I think about what the reporter had said about what the detective hadn't said. The reporter inferred the three were involved with distributing drugs and they were all part of the gang run by Neil McMillan, albeit McMillan wasn't named.

I sat watching the rest of the news, but I can't for the live of me tell you what I saw for my mind is reeling.

The reporter had said a Jamaican man.

Oh, that's me I almost smile; the frenzied killer.

But then I think about it. Is it possible that the police *believe* the guy who was standing with Calum Black when I killed him? Can they *believe* that a big black guy was responsible rather than a wee, skinny guy with black boot polish on his face?

My God, I'm shaking my head. Surely they're not *that* stupid and if they do believe it then my God, wonders never cease.

I really don't know what to make of this at all, I really don't.

If nothing else, it takes away from me being Black's killer but, if according to what young Craig the polis told me, the CID believe the same person is responsible for all three murders then how can they be looking for a big Jamaican man for killing Black when the young lad who saw me and my car when I killed Kylie Morrison will obviously have told them it was a skinny wee white man?

I'm befuddled so I am and I'm actually hoping the CID work it out, because I sure as heck can't!

I glance again at the mantelpiece clock and about to rise to make my dinner when the doorbell rings.

I don't usually get callers at this time of the evening. In fact, I don't usually get callers at all these days, so with a little trepidation I switch off the television and make my way to the front door.

Pulling it open, I see there's a vision of loveliness standing there in a light coloured raincoat and shaking the raindrops from her pop-up brolly.

"Hello there again, Mister McGrath, can I come in?" says DC Ella Hopkins and without waiting for a response, she brushes past me.

CHAPTER SIXTEEN

I'm so surprised that not only am I getting another visit from DC Hopkins, but that she just waltzes past me without an invite.

Standing in the small hallway, she turns and I kind of stutter, "Eh, can I take your coat?"

She smiles tightly and bending to put her brolly in the corner behind the front door, she then stands upright and shrugs out of her coat and I see that she's wearing a light blue skirted suit. My, she's not just a cracker in looks, but that lassie has some figure, believe me and I briefly wonder; why am I thinking that when I *should* be wondering what the heck she's doing here at this time of night?

Handing me her damp coat, I hang it on one of the hooks behind the hallway's cupboard door as without a by your leave, she walks on into the front sitting room and stands there, waiting to be invited to sit down I presume.

I point to the couch but she doesn't sit, just sort of glides down onto the couch and crosses her perfectly formed legs.

Bugger it, there's me getting distracted again.

I offer her tea or coffee, but she declines with a shake of her head.

"Just a few more questions if you don't mind, Mister McGrath," she tells me.

On her previous visit she relented to calling me Jimmy, but for some reason it seems I've reverted to 'Mister McGrath' and I'm thinking this can't be a good thing.

With the mood she seems to be in there's no way I'm going to call her Ella. In fact, I make the decision not to call her anything at all.

She scrambles in her folder and pulls out a form, the same one I think that she completed when she was here before.

"You told me that you own a black coloured Ford Escort. Is that the one outside by chance?"

"Aye, that's it. I've had it for," I tap my chin as I try to recall, "I dunno, maybe twelve years now? Great wee car even if it is an older model and it's never given me a bit of bother."

I try to be cheerful, but my nerves are on edge.

The Escort; it's about the Escort.

She rustles the form and then glances up to stare at me. "How often do you drive the car, Mister McGrath?"

There's a tight sharpness about her voice that warns me to be very, very careful what I tell her. I mean, she's not being rude or anything, but let's just say she's not being overly social either, if you see what I mean and though I can't put my finger on it, I get the impression that something's bothering or annoying her.

Hopefully, it's not me.

I swallow hard and take a deep breath as though I'm thinking about her question and then I tell her, "Not very often these days. I drove it yesterday, but most if not all my journey's these days are pretty local. You know, Silverburn shopping centre for the messages or down to Govan for the market where I get my butcher meat."

"When did you last drive the vehicle, Mister McGrath?" she sharply asks.

My brow furrows as I consider if this is a trick question, but then I say, "Yesterday. I drove down to the halfway at Paisley Road West. To Howden's pub with my mate Scooby…I mean, Mister Toner. Michael Toner. He lives in…"

"Lochar Crescent. Yes, I know who Mister Toner is. You took him to the pub, is that correct?"

If she knows this then why is she asking me I wonder and I simply nod she's correct.

"When did you last drive the vehicle prior to yesterday?"

"Eh, I'm not really certain," I extend my hands and shrug my shoulders, pretending I can't remember. "Maybe a few days ago to Silverburn shopping centre? Most of my days seem to run together these days," I try a joke, but she doesn't even crack a smile.

I watch as she makes a note on the form.

"Who else has access to the vehicle? Your permission to drive it I mean."

"Eh, nobody," I reply.

"So, you're the sole key holder for the vehicle, is that correct?"

"Aye, that's correct," I tell her and suddenly decide I've made some kind of mistake, but really, who else could I say uses the vehicle?

"I understand you were in a confrontation yesterday when you were in the pub," she stares at me, almost daring me to deny it.

Now this takes me by surprise and I swallow hard before I reply.

"It wasn't really anything to do with me," I weakly reply. "A guy at the bar was abusing the staff and then my friend Scooby, I mean…"

"Mister Toner," she nods.

"Aye, Mister Toner. He tried to tell the guy to behave and the guy was going to have a go at him…"

"Then you intervened?"

"Eh, no, not me," I shake my head. "The barman did. I think he's the chef in the pub. He was over the bar like a shot and pinned the guy down till the polis, the police I mean, till they arrived and arrested the guy."

"That will be George Paterson, the deceased Alex Paterson's father?"

"Aye, I don't really know the man, but Mister Toner knew him and…"

"I understand Paterson accused your friend, Mister Toner of murdering Paterson's son. Is that correct?"

"Eh, aye, he did say that," I blurt out and I'm starting to get a wee bit annoyed by her attitude. "But that's a piece of nonsense. Scooby's walking with a stick after the beating he took and…"

"And you don't believe Mister Toner is physically capable of murder, Mister McGrath?"

"Physically capable or not, Scooby wouldn't kill anyone!" I burst out.

"Well, how about a family member or friend killing someone on his behalf then?" She smoothly asks me.

I'm stunned to silence. Is she trying to trick me into confessing?

"Look, I don't know what you're getting at here," I vigorously shake my head and wave my hands across my chest. "I've known Michael Toner most of my life and I know his family as well as I knew my own. He would never, ever condone anything like what you're suggesting. Never," I angrily tell her.

She doesn't immediately reply, but just stares at me for a few seconds and then says, "I understand you had your own confrontation earlier today, Mister McGrath."

I can feel my blood chill because I know exactly what she's talking about and I can also guess how she knows what occurred.

However, I decide to get her to tell me what she knows and I say, "What are you talking about?"

Again she doesn't immediately answer, but then says, "This morning, you were working in the churchyard at St Convals and after you finished the work, when you were leaving you were confronted by a local man, Neil McMillan. Isn't that correct, Mister McGrath?"

"How do you know that?" I ask and I can almost feel the blood drain from my face.

"Isn't that correct?" she repeats.

"Yes," I hear myself answer and I'm now almost certain that Father Stephen's theory of a hidden CCTV camera is correct. If it is, then that might be a real problem for me.

"I understand the confrontation didn't go well for you, Mister McGrath," she softly says and I can almost hear the sympathy in her voice.

Now my face is burning red when I remember the slap and the kick on my arse.

"No, it didn't go well for me," I quietly admit it and it takes me all my time to even speak because of the shame that returns.

"Why did he slap you, Mister McGrath?"

I hesitate and then decide that telling the truth won't give away anything.

"He, McMillan I mean. He remembered I was the janny…the janitor, I mean, at his primary school. He was angry because I didn't include him in the school football team."

I can see from her eyes she wasn't expecting *that* answer and her brow furrows.

"What, you mean because he wasn't… sorry," she slowly shakes her head, "because you didn't select him for the school football team? That's why he slapped you?"

I couldn't trust myself to speak and nod.

"My God, that must have been, what, years ago when he was at the primary."

I swallow hard and tell her, "I think about eleven or twelve years, yes."

She slowly lets her breath out through her pursed, soft red painted lips and says, "Is that the *only* reason why he confronted you, Mister McGrath?"

I pretend surprise and say, "Yes, well, that's what he told me and it's the only thing that I can think of."

My mind is working overtime here now and then I recall something else he said and mindful that the place might also be bugged, I add, "He also warned me about eyeballing his team. I think he meant…"

"That's okay, Mister McGrath," she holds her hand up, "I can guess what he meant by that. But you can think of no other reason why he would pick on you today?"

"No, none at all," I shake my head. "I mean, other than when he was a pupil at Leithland Primary, I haven't had any contact with him since he left to attend the secondary school." I shrug and then tell her, "I never picked him for the team because he was a bully and always picking on the smaller and younger kids. He recognised me as the janny that he obviously didn't like when he was at the school and decided to have a wee bit of fun with me. You obviously know the size of him." I try to sound outraged and I ask her, "How can I at my age and build stand up against a man his size?"

She slowly nods, but continues to stare at me.

If nothing else I'm grateful she doesn't mention the kick on the arse and at least is leaving me with some dignity for you can't imagine what it's like, having to admit to another person and a young woman at that, that you're a coward.

"Aye, you're right of course. He is a bigger man than yourself and to be frank, I don't think he's the sort of man you would want to mess with, Mister McGrath. I understand from the local officers he has a bad reputation."

I'm wondering now if her comment is some sort of veiled warning. We sit there facing each other in silence, a silence that lasts for nearly a minute. Now, let me tell you, staring at somebody for almost a minute can be a bit daunting when you know you're hiding something from the other person.

"I'll formally ask you, Mister McGrath. Do you wish to make a complaint against Neil McMillan?"

"You mean, give you a statement or something like that?"

"A statement," she nods as if I'm an idiot that needs it explained, "yes."

"And would I need to go to court?"

"If there is sufficient evidence to corroborate your statement and I charge him with assaulting you, he will be summonsed and if he refuses to plead guilty then yes, it might mean you having to attend court to give evidence against him. Would that be a problem?"

I'm aghast and stutter, "A problem, hen! Can you imagine what my life would be like round here if I gave you a statement and you charge him! No way," I'm shaking my head and crossing my hands in front of me.

Obviously irritated, she shoves the form back into her folder and getting to her feet says to me, "I might need to speak with you again at some point, Mister McGrath. You're not planning to go away anywhere; on holiday or anything like that, are you?"

I also get to my feet and I take a deep breath and let it slowly out before I quietly reply. "I'm on my own here and living on my pension. Where would I go and who with?"

I don't intend sounding as angry as I do and it seems to take her by surprise for she blushes and nods that she understand before turning towards the door.

I follow her to the front door and fetch her coat from behind the cupboard door.

Lifting her brolly she pulls open the door and shrugging into her coat, turns and says, "You understand I've a job to do, Mister McGrath."

I nod but I'm too upset to reply and watch as she pops the brolly up against the showery rain and disappears along the path to the CID car parked behind the Escort.

I watch as she gets into the driver's door though I don't see her drive away and I close the front door.

I stand with my back against the door and a shiver runs down my spine, for the one, awful thought that runs through my head is…she knows.

I'm too upset by her visit to even contemplate any dinner and sit in the kitchen, my mind in a whirl.

I re-run her questions and the things she told me and I'm even more convinced that the police have a CCTV camera set up either at or near the phone box opposite St Convals.

One thing she did say that now strikes me as strange for she said 'if there was sufficient evidence to corroborate your statement.'

Now, I'm not at all technically minded, but I would have thought CCTV film of McMillan slapping and kicking me should surely count as 'sufficient corroboration' so why didn't she mention that?

Like I said, I have simply no idea how these things work, but the one thing I'm almost sure of now she's gone is that there can't be any sound on whatever the police are watching. If there was then she would have known what Neil McMillan said to me when he threatened me.

I think about writing down on a sheet of paper what the police might know or suspect they know, but I quickly discount that idea. That's all I would need; the polis chapping my door and finding my near confession written down for them.

No, I'll need to work out in my head the possible evidence they have. I start with what DC Hopkins more or less admitted; that the police have a camera watching the telephone box or the area around it. The main question is when did they put the camera in place? Was it before or after I killed Calum Black? If it was *before* I killed him then they'll know or guess I'm not a big black man, but if that is the case then why did the STV reporter say the police are looking for a Jamaican man? If it was *after* I killed him then they will have to rely on the guy's statement that he saw a big black man and that's why it was reported on the tele.

I'm nodding and rightly or wrongly, I'm guessing the camera must have gone in after Black's murder. I suppose Father Stephen might have an idea when it was put in place because he spoke with the police Superintendent at Pollok who more or less told him the police were collecting evidence, but was that before or after I killed Black? Unfortunately, it's hardly the thing I can go and ask the Father, is it? Then there were her questions about the Escort. It's clear the lad who saw me driving off after I killed Kylie Morrison saw a bit more than I had hoped for and I suppose the CID are checking out all the black or dark coloured Ford Escort cars in the area. Given the age of the Escort there can't be too many around these days. Owning a dark coloured Ford Escort will obviously bring them to my door, but I'm confident it won't be enough to charge me. The question is though can the lad identify *me*?

And that brings me back to the lassie in the Co-operative; Gina who works behind the till.

If she is re-interviewed, which is likely, will she remember and be able to identify the wee man who stood behind Alex Paterson?

And what was all that about, am I planning any holidays? For heavens sake, where the *heck* would I go? Is she so convinced I'm a real suspect that she's worried I might take off somewhere?

I'm unconsciously drumming my fingers on the table top and my right knee is shaking; it's a habit I have had since childhood.

It's a lot to think about, isn't it?

When the detective spoke about Scooby being a possible suspect for Paterson's murder, it never in a million years occurred to me that he would be a viable suspect or that the CID might consider he arranged for the murder to be committed. I mean come on; who thinks about this sort of thing?

I'm frowning because then I remember what she said, that Scooby might have arranged for a family member or a friend to commit the murder.

A friend…was she meaning me?

Aye, I'm almost convinced now. She suspects me, but is she alone in her suspicion or does her boss also know of her suspicion?

I suppose you might think I'm being a bit paranoid here, but let's face it. If you were to commit three murders and the police were out to catch you, would you not be a little paranoid too? Particularly if a detective visits you twice and more or less infers your best pal arranged for a friend to commit the murder…you being the friend?

You know, I'm sitting here in my kitchen and no matter what thought I give to what's happened or what is about to happen, there's no way I can change anything.

What *is* I suppose, just *is*.

I'm wondering why it's getting so dark then I realise I have forgotten to switch on the kitchen light. I get up from my chair and as I'm here anyway, I'll make myself some oven fish and chips. It's an easy and quick meal so I set the oven to heat and wander back into the living room.

It's at times like this I wish I still drank.

I tried to watch a bit of television, but my mind is elsewhere and so I give up and head to bed in the back bedroom with a book. Since the carry-on up in the field began I've more or less got used to sleeping there.

The book is a crime fiction novel about a pathologist who works in New York. It's quite graphic when describing the pathologist's dissection of a series of murder victims who are all murdered by the same man and it's only when I stop and think about it, I begin to laugh. I've been rooting for the detective catching the murderer before I realise I *should* be rooting for the murderer for after all, we're not really that much different. He's murdering the gangsters who have killed his family and I'm murdering the sods that belong to the gang who battered my pal Scooby.

Aye, there's a definite parallel there, I grin to myself.

My eyes are going together and I'm just about to drop off. I glance at the digital clock and see it's a little after one o'clock in the morning when I hear the fracas and I know right away…they're back.

Suddenly there's the sound of glass breaking and my first thought is my windows have been put in. I grab my dressing gown and make my way to the front bedroom and sneak a look through the window.

In the darkness I can see figures, maybe three or four, running across the field and hear them shouting, but I can't make out what's being shouted.

Safe in the knowledge that they're running away I make my way downstairs and into the living room, but even in the darkness I can see my windows are intact.

I can hear shouting outside and with the light still off I peek through the curtain.

There are a number of my neighbours out in the street, some in pyjamas and they're screaming after the neds who are running across the field.

I feel obligated to go out and find out what's happened and opening my door I see Billy and Irene King standing with the Campbell's, Mary Burns and her man and a half dozen other neighbours.

It's soon apparent to me that there are windows broken in several houses and includes the King's windows. Irene is crying and as I walk towards her, she turns and wraps her arms about me.

"The bastards, Jimmy! Look what the bastards have done!" she wails.

I'm a bit numb and can only give her a hug before she tears herself away to try and calm Billy down. He's being held back by big George Campbell and a couple of other guys and women for he is going ballistic and threatening to chase the neds across the field.

The sound of sirens and the hue of blue lights appear from along the road and within minutes there's at least four police cars there and eight or nine officers. I'm thinking that maybe these polis are the 'extra patrols' the area was promised.

"You're too fucking late again!" Billy King screams at them and again he has to be restrained by Irene and George Campbell who has a firm grip of him.

It doesn't help any when I hear a sergeant say to Billy, "You need to calm down or I'll arrest you."

I don't know where I get the bottle, but suddenly the humiliation of me by Neil McMillan and the probing questions by DC Hopkins jump into my head and an unaccountable rage overcomes me as standing there in my dressing gown and slippers, I find myself between the sergeant and Billy and I'm shouting, "Arrest him? Arrest him? You've got a bloody nerve! There would be no need to arrest him if *your* lot were doing your job properly!"

Well, the next thing I know is I'm grabbed by two cops, handcuffed at the back and with my head forced down, I lose a slipper as I'm bundled into the back seat of a panda car.

I don't really know much of what went on in the road between my neighbours and the police after that because I'm being driven away and taken to Pollok police office in Brockburn Road.

Ten minutes later I'm standing in front of the station sergeant, a large heavy built man with a thick moustache and ruddy face. I'm still dressed in my dressing gown and one slipper, giving him my name, my date of birth, my address and I'm being charged by the male cop with a breach of the peace. Me, who never has even been inside a police station let alone committed any crime or offence; arrested!

I am totally mortified!

Then the sergeant asks if I require a lawyer to be contacted and I shake my head. I mean, why would I need a lawyer? It's *these* buggers that will need a lawyer, I'm thinking.

"I don't suppose there's any need to search him for weapons or drugs," I hear the sergeant say, his voice dripping with sarcasm and it causes the two cops holding me to snigger.

The cop who has a hold of my left arm, a tall, heavyset brute of a woman with tight, curly hair, finally lets go of my arm and says, "Who do you want informed of your arrest, pal?"

Shocked though I am, I'm angry at her insolence and though my throat's dry, I reply in a shaky voice, "Nobody, I don't have anyone. I live alone and I'm not your pal, I'm Mister McGrath to you!"

The sergeant smirks and staring at me, says to her, "Please take *Mister* McGrath to cell number one and see that he's made comfortable."

He turns away as the female cop again grabs my arm and lifting a bunch of keys from the bar, hustles me away towards a door behind me that leads into a short passageway. I see there are six doors lying open and she shoves me into the first door on the right and I find myself in a cell. I turn to speak to her, but the door is already slamming shut and don't ask me why, but suddenly I'm afraid.

Now, I'm not claustrophobic or anything, but a panic overcomes me and I can't explain it. The overhead light is bright enough to be sore on the eyes and enclosed in a kind of wire cage. The four walls are painted a garish green colour, but defaced with graffiti, some of which is so obscene and crude I can't possibly repeat for fear of offending you. There's a raised concrete plinth about a foot off the ground and I'm guessing it's supposed to serve as a bed because it has a grey coloured blanket folded on it. On the wall at the door is a toilet seat that is concreted to the floor. The toilet seat is a dull and a scratched stainless steel thing without any kind of flushing handle and looking at I'm glad I don't immediately need to use it. The only window is set about seven feet from the floor, but the glass is glazed and reinforced and so thick I'm certain it can't be seen through. But the thing that strikes me most is how cold the cell is and already I'm beginning to shiver. My dressing gown isn't designed for this kind of cold and my bare foot is already turning blue.

After a few minutes I've no option but to wrap the blanket around me to keep warm and I'm hoping there aren't any fleas in it.

Ten minutes later, in the absence of a chair, I'm sitting on the raised plinth and even with the blanket, I'm still shivering and now both my feet are freezing.

So, that's how my night ends, me locked up in a cell at Pollok police office and worrying myself silly because I've left my front door unlocked.

When I waken I don't know what the time is, but the overhead light is still switched on and there's daylight coming through the window. I've obviously dozed off sitting in the corner on the plinth and I'm absolutely aching and when I try to stand, I almost fall over.

There's some laughter coming from outside in the passageway, then the toilet is flushed and the door is banged and opened and it's the sergeant from the night before. He's got a plastic mug of tea in one hand and a plastic plate with a roll and sausage in the other. "Here," he hands them to me, "have this before you go," then to my surprise reaches into his pocket and pulls out my lost slipper.

"This was in the panda," he says and throws it down at my feet.

"Where am I going?" I ask, wondering why he couldn't have given me the slipper earlier when I really needed it.

"You're being released as soon as the Inspector has a word with you," he tells me then closes the door behind him.

I don't fancy the roll and sausage and leave it on the plinth, but I'm gasping for a hot drink and with my hands wrapped round the mug to heat them, I sup at the tea.

It's about ten minutes later when the door is pulled open and there's an Inspector standing there who says to me, "Out you come, Mister McGrath."

I shuffle out of the cell after him and he leads me through the office to a room on the other side of the building where he sits down at a desk and tells me to sit in the chair facing him.

I can see from the wall clock that it's nearly eight in the morning. I'm guessing the Inspector can't be any older than his early thirties and at first he busies himself with some paperwork on his desk, then glances up at me and says, "Right then, Mister McGrath, to business. You were arrested last night for a breach of the peace. My officers inform me that you interfered with them in the commission of their duty when they were attempting to calm down some of your neighbours and that you swore…"

"Now, wait a minute there," I raise a hand to stop him. "For one thing, I don't use bad language and any one of my neighbours will confirm that to you," I tell him.

"That's not what my officers say," he glances down at the paperwork and then he adds, "and that you pushed a constable…"

"That's a downright lie!" I protest. "For heaven's sake, look at the size of me. I'm in my nightclothes and do I look like I'm a man that would try to tackle those lumps you call constables?"

He doesn't reply, but stares at me then he leans forward and rests his forearms on the desk and sighs.

"Look, Mister McGrath. I wasn't there last night, but I've a report here that says you were bang out of order. I've done a background check on you and you don't seem to have come to our attention previously and according to what I learned, you're known locally as a decent man. Now, if you listen to me here's what I propose. If you choose to accept my warning regarding your future behaviour, I'll ensure any charge against you will be shelved."

I'm immediately suspicious and I ask him, "What do you mean, shelved?"

He sits back like he's doing me some kind of favour and making an arch of his fingers, he tells me, "I'll ensure that on *this* occasion the charge of breach of the peace is not proceeded with, but your details will remain on record so that if you come to the attention of the police in the future, your conduct in the early hours of this morning will be brought to the attention of the Procurator Fiscal."

Aye, and lets not forget the three murders I'm thinking.

Now, I'm not stupid and I'm guessing that the arresting officers have made a mistake giving me the jail, that they thought I was some kind of hooligan but now realise that I'm just a wee man who lives alone and was simply protesting their treatment of my neighbour. They probably know fine well that if they tried to proceed with the charge they'd be laughed out of the courtroom.

So, what do I do here, I wonder? Do I refuse the offer the Inspector is making and tell him that it's no deal? Or do I accept the offer and forget my night in the cell and put it down to experience?

I'm staring back at him and my inclination is to tell him to stuff his offer and that he can take me to court. Well, that's my inclination, but the reality is I'm tired and aching and I just want to go home to bed and forget about what happened. Besides, I'm thinking I will probably need a lawyer and where will I find the money to pay for one?

It's a bit like being bullied because it's happened to me all through my working life. Management ask things of you and know that you won't refuse because you need the job and that you don't wish to piss them off; but it's not really asking. It's subtly telling you if you don't comply with their request then the first opportunity they get they will stick it to you.

Oh aye, I know the Inspector is bullying me because sitting in front of him he sees a wee, elderly dishevelled man in a dressing gown who if I push it might have the grounds for a serious complaint against his officers. Likely he knows from his computer checks that I haven't been in bother before and so he's threatening me with court in the hope I give in to the threat. I mean, how would the police defend their actions if word got out to the newspapers for instance or I get myself a sharp lawyer who would complain that a man nearly sixty years of age was taken in his dressing gown to a police station and locked up when there must be a dozen witnesses who would state that all I did was make a verbal protest to the polis. Besides, it's well known among my neighbours I'm a quiet man who doesn't drink or use foul language and I'm certainly not a fighter, so that nonsense about me swearing and pushing a cop wouldn't stand up in court.

No, it's not me who should be worried, but the Inspector who should be worried that his officers would be found out for their lies.

Sounds straight forward enough, doesn't it, but like I say, all I want to do is go home and so to my shame I nod and tell him that I accept his warning.

"Right then, we'll consider the warning heeded and the matter closed," he rubs his hands together like he's won some sort of competition and I can almost hear the relief in his voice. Then he tells me, "I'll get a car organised to get you home, Mister McGrath." He leaves me sitting in his office and a couple of minutes later I hear a voice behind me say, "Understand you need a lift, Mister McGrath."

I turn to see DC Hopkins standing in the doorway. Her blonde hair is rolled up into a bun and she's dressed in a light blue trousers suit and holding a file.

"Good morning, hen," is the only thing I can think to say to her and wonder, of all the officers in the station it had to be her.

When she leads me back through the office to a door that exits into the bright sunlight of the back yard I get some strange looks from the polis because I'm hobbling along in my slippers and dressing gown. Outside in the chilled air of the morning, I'm squinting against the sun and shiver as she holds open the passenger door of a CID car.

It's when I'm getting in I see a detective walking across the yard towards the rear door who calls out to her, "Morning, Ella. Sorry to hear about your sad news, pal."

"Thanks, Danny," she replies then gets into the driver's seat.

When she grasps the steering wheel, I notice a wedding band on the third finger of her left hand and being a nosey bugger, I'm tempted to ask what her sad news is, but it's really none of my business so I keep my mouth shut.

We're turning onto Brockburn Road before she speaks.

"I hear you were arrested last night, Jimmy, that it was the neds in the field at it again."

So I'm Jimmy again, I think and reply, "Aye, they broke a number of my neighbours windows. The police arrived, but as usual too late and one of my neighbours…"

"Mister King?"

"Aye, Billy King. He was irate and complained a bit too fiercely. I thought he was going to be arrested and I tried to complain, but the next thing I know is that *I'm* being arrested instead."

She concentrating on her driving, but she nods and says, "I read the report. I think the arresting officers were a little bit zealous," she admits.

I'm inclined to agree, but I hold my tongue and stare out of the side window. That's when I begin to wonder if the Inspector deliberately arranged for Hopkins to take me home so that she might quiz me to find out if I intend making a complaint against his officers.

With that thought in mind I break the silence and say, "I thought it might have been a panda that would take me home."

"It should have been," she gives me a tight smile, "but I've a couple of people to interview in Hapland Road, so I volunteered."

"Well, thanks anyway," I reply, though I don't really believe her.

Driving along Hapland Road, I see a couple of vans parked near to my house and some of my neighbours out in the street. One van belongs to the Council and the other is a glazier's van. The glazier is working at the privately owned homes while the Council workers are working at the rented homes.

DC Hopkins stops the CID car outside my house and the car gets a few curious stares.

"Right, Jimmy, here you are," she tells me and narrowing her eyes she gives me an odd look. "I hope that you manage to stay out of trouble in future," she says and smiles tightly.

I don't say anything, but simply nod and get out of the car. Some of the neighbours see me and as the car drives off, there's a bit of a cheer goes up and suddenly I'm surrounded by almost a dozen folk. Billy King is slapping me on the back and his wife Irene is hugging me. Big George Campbell is pumping my hand and his wife May also gives me a hug. A number of other neighbours are clapping their hands and I feel a wee bit embarrassed. One neighbour, I don't see who it is, calls out, "Good man, Jimmy, you're a decent man," and another shouts, "Well done, wee man," and they're treating me like some sort of hero which I can assure you I most certainly am not.

"Did they charge you, Jimmy?" asks Irene.

"Aye, but they dropped the charges provided I don't get into any more bother," I tell the crowd and then I add, "If you don't mind, I think I'm ready for my bed."

"Aye, we can see that," says Mary Burns and that gets a big laugh from them all.

There's a bit more back slapping and eventually I manage to get along my path and into the house, but not before I hear Irene calling out, "We kept an eye on the house while you were in the jail, Jimmy."

I give her a wave of thanks and finally, I'm home.

I'm shaking my head as I think about what Irene shouted; while I was in the jail. Bleeding heck, that makes me sound like some sort of criminal and finally, with the front door closed behind me I'm so exhausted and about to give in to the tiredness, so make my way upstairs to bed, knowing the even the sound of the workmen hammering as they replace the broken windows is unlikely to disturb me.

Pulling the quilt cover over me, I can't explain why, but for some strange reason I start to giggle.

CHAPTER SEVENTEEN

I sleep right through to almost two o'clock that afternoon and when I waken I'm still a bit sore, but with the added pain of a raging headache.

Two Paracetamol and five minutes later I'm beginning to feel a wee bit better and decide that rather than my usual shower, a hot bath might ease my aching joints and I stick the kettle on while the bath is running.

The phone rings and it is Scooby.

"How you doing," he begins and I can almost hear the laughter in his voice.

"I heard a wee story that you got the jail this morning."

I sigh and I'm shaking my head when I reply, "Who told you?"

"Who told me?" he giggles. "You're the talk of the steamy, Jimmy. Some of your neighbours were yapping about it down at the shops at the roundabout and Alice got wind of it." He hesitates then he asks, "You're all right, aren't you? I mean, it's a mistake, isn't it? You're not really going to court?"

"No, I'm not going to court, but I can tell you it was a bleeding uncomfortable mistake, Scooby. The sods locked me in a cell," I tell him and I can almost hear the whining in my own voice. I take a deep breath and trying a little bravado, I add, "Nothing I couldn't handle, though."

"Aye, right," he laughs because he's been my pal since primary school and he can see right through me and knows fine well that I must have been scared witless.

"Well, that's definitely the best laugh I've had for a while," and he continues to laugh, then says, "Of all the people that deserve the jail, Jimmy, you must be the last one that I would ever have thought of. I mean a decent wee guy like you? What the hell was the polis thinking about? My God, you would think they've got enough on their plate in this area trying to catch that madman who's murdering them teenagers."

He pauses for breath then says, "Alice told me that the sods punted in a few of your neighbour's windows. That's what she heard them talking about before they mentioned you got yourself arrested. How many houses got done?"

"Six," I tell him, then remember that the water's running. "Hang on a minute," I say and place the phone down. I run to the bathroom, turn off the tap and return to the phone.

"Six houses," I repeat.

"But they didn't do in your windows?"

"No," I shake my head. "For some reason they didn't do mine."

"I wonder why," I hear him say and it's almost as if he's thinking to himself. "Were all the houses on one side of your house?"

"No, two on one side and four on the other side if you include old Missus Baxter's house, but she's not there anymore. She's away in a care home."

"Wonder why they missed you out," he asks again.

"I have no idea," I sigh, but of course as you would expect, Scooby has sown the seed of doubt in my mind and I'm beginning to wonder if it was just good luck or deliberate. But then again, it they *deliberately* didn't break my windows, that begs the question; why not and who told them not to?

We chew the fat for another couple of minutes then Scooby makes me promise that if I'm intending any bank jobs or anything, to give him the nod first. I'm laughing as I hang up on him with the agreement that I'll pop down for a cuppa later that night and give him the craic about my arrest.

So, two minutes later I'm standing naked and about to dip my toe into the bath when the doorbell rings. Bugger it, I'm thinking, am I ever going to get this bleeding bath?

I slip my dressing gown back on and unlock the door to find two guys who are a bit scruffily dressed with two uniformed cops behind them.

"Mister McGrath, Mister James McGrath?" the older guy asks.

"Aye," I nod.

"DS McIntyre, Pollok CID. Can I come in?"

"I'm just about to jump into the bath."

"You've no choice in the matter, Mister McGrath," he says and nods to the really tall guy with him as the two of them and the cops walk past me. "We've got a drugs warrant to search these premises."

My mouth drops open in shock. A drugs warrant? What the heck, I'm thinking.

I close the door and one of the uniformed cops takes me by the elbow and directs me through to the living room where the other three are standing waiting for me.

"Let's make this easy," says the guy called McIntyre. "We've information that you are storing drugs in this house. If you cooperate, it'll go better for you in the trial, so where's the stash?"

I can hardly speak and I'm thinking; this can't be happening to me and the first thing that comes to mind is I'm innocent. There are no drugs in my house unless you count the Paracetamol and some antiseptic throat lozenges, so with my voice shaking and without thinking, I tell him, "Search away, there's nothing like that in this house."

But then with a shock I think, nothing except a murder weapon hidden in the cupboard underneath the sink that I *should* have bleeding destroyed, but forgot about!

"Look, Mister McGrath," says McIntyre with a right cheesy grin that wouldn't fool a five year old, "I don't want to have to turn your house upside down, but I assure you I'm more than happy to do that. So," he waves a hand about, "unless you want this nice wee house of yours wrecked…" then leans into my face so that our noses are almost touching, snarls, "tell me where the fucking charlie is!"

Now don't laugh because I'm not really up to speed with the drug culture and I don't really mean to upset him any further, but when I ask who this charlie is, it seems to cause a vein in his neck to burst because his face turns red with rage.

I get the impression he's about to grab me, but then the tall detective with him touches his arm and quietly says, "Mac, a word."

The two of them walk into the kitchen leaving me standing in the middle of the living room with the other two cops staring curiously at me.

A minute later, they return to the living room and the other detective who I think is called Gus or something, he says to me, "Do you have a garden shed, Mister McGrath?"

"Aye, out the back," I reply, just thankful that he didn't ask to look under the kitchen sink.

"Can you come out there with me and unlock it for me?"

"Aye, okay," I readily agree and with him and with McIntyre behind me, I go through the kitchen to the back door, grabbing the padlock key from the hook that's in the tall cupboard by the door.

I lead the way down the three steps to the hut and that's when I notice that though the padlock is still intact, there's something wrong with the hasp for it doesn't look like it's sitting properly on the door. The guy called Gus takes my arm and kind of pushes me to one side, but not roughly or anything; just to move me out of the way.

"Is it always like this?" he turns and asks me, pointing to the hasp and that's when I see small slivers of wood on the ground beneath where the hasp has been forced.

"Of course not," I reply a little more sharply than I meant to because this guy is polite and courteous, not like his ignorant pal. "There wouldn't be any need for the padlock if the hasp is broken off, would there?" I explain.

He doesn't reply, but I see him glance at the door. Then he bends down and pokes at the slivers on the ground and I see him glance up at McIntyre and there's the briefest shake of his head.

"When was the last time you were in here, Mister McGrath?"

I shake my head and I'm shrugging, but my blood runs cold for suddenly I've remembered Billy King's two heavy duty plastic carrier bags that he asked me to keep for him. God, what the *heck* is in those bags, I wonder?

"So, you don't mind us taking a wee look in the shed, do you?" asks Gus.

"Doesn't matter if he minds," growls McIntyre, "We've got a fucking warrant, haven't we?"

I don't know where it came from, but my fear of the burly McIntyre is overtaken by my dislike of him and turning towards him, I say, "You're not a very nice man, are you Mister McIntyre; using language like that in a Christian home."

I'm pleased to say his mouth falls open and I think it's all that the detective Gus can do to stop from laughing as I watch him first pull on a pair of light blue coloured plastic gloves and then push open the shed door.

The light coming through the window in the shed is enough to see things clearly. I'm peeking in through the shed door and I can see Billy's two plastic bags under the workbench, but that's not what takes Gus's attention. He's pointing to a small, clear plastic bag, like the bags you keep small quantities of food in for the fridge that is sitting smack in the middle of the workbench and knotted at the top. It looks like there's something inside, like wee grains of sand or something similar.

"Is this yours, Mister McGrath?" he asks me.

I'm puzzled and I shake my head and he lets out a breath, then turns towards McIntyre and says, "This is all wrong, Mac. I think we've been had."

McIntyre doesn't reply, but tight-lipped stares evilly at me and turning away he then stomps back up the stairs and disappears into the kitchen.

"What is it?" I ask Gus as I point to the small bag.

Gus smiles, but without humour and lifting the bag by the knot he stares at it and replies, "It's about a five hundred pound fine at court, Mister McGrath, but to be honest, I don't think it's anything you are going to have to worry about. Tell me this; is there anybody that you know who has it in for you or anybody that you have recently pissed off…I mean, upset?"

The families of my three murder victims come to mind and of course there are two cops that work out of Pollok police office, but I shake my head and simply reply, "No, why would anybody be annoyed with me?"

Funny, but I don't want to mention my recent encounter with Neil McMillan.

Gus takes out a notebook from his jacket pocket and produces a brown label that he has me sign and date.

"This is just to record you witnessing me seizing this," he tells me.

"But what is it?" I press him again.

He smiles and indicating we should return to the house, follows me back up the steps.

In the kitchen he says, "What I *think* it is though the lab will need to verify it, is a small quantity of cocaine and not the hoard the phone call that led us to your house promised." He takes a deep breath and says, "I think somebody is trying to set you up to be charged with a drugs offence, Mister McGrath."

He stares curiously at me and asks, "Have you any idea, any idea at all, who that might be?"

He's standing with his back to the sink and I'm thinking all he has to do is search the cupboard under there and he's found the baton.

I resist the temptation to stare down at the cupboard door and swallowing hard I reply, "You might have heard about the trouble we've been having round here with the gang up in the field, out in the front of the houses, I mean."

"Aye, I know something of it," he slowly drawls and now I know he's fibbing and likely he knows a lot more than he's letting on.

"Well, round about the back of one this morning my neighbours on either side of my house had their windows broken by these people, but my windows were left untouched."

He slowly nods and says, "We've just come on late shift, but yes; I read a report about it. How does that answer my question?"

"Well, I was a wee bit suspicious that my windows weren't broken and couldn't understand why that was," not thinking it necessary to tell him it was actually Scooby who had drawn my attention to it.

"Anyway, while I was outside with my neighbours I was arrested and taken to your office, but your Inspector said the charges were dropped. I think whoever it was that left that," I pointed to the bag in his hand, "must have been the person who phoned you. Does that sound plausible?"

"Well," he drawls and then smiles, "So *you're* the guy in the dressing gown and slippers who was wandering round the office this morning, eh?"

I blush and grace him with a grin.

His brow furrows and nodding, he says, "Aye, what you say does sound plausible and yes, it does seem likely. The call was anonymous and did say we had to search your garden shed, so who ever made the call I'm in no doubt knew what we would find there, though they said we'd find…"

"When you're quite finished in there, DC Dunbar," McIntyre's voice booms through from the living room.

"Coming, sarge," he calls back and then with a wink, surprises me when he says, "Oh, and by the way, Mister McGrath. You seem to be a decent wee man, so you might want to shift those bags of scrap or whatever's in them from under the bench in the shed before somebody makes a phone call about *them*."

I go to the front door and I see them walk to their cars, a CID car and a panda.

McIntyre, who's driving the CID car, roars away with a screech of tyres and is probably angry that he didn't get an arrest, but not before I see Dunbar in the passenger seat giving me a friendly wave cheerio.

I close the door and I'm thinking, bugger the bath, I'd be quicker having a shower and then I'd better see about replacing the screws that held the hasp with bolts.

It takes me just under half an hour to ensure that the garden shed door is secured and I'm doing a lot of thinking during that time. Maybe that old paranoia is kicking in again, but what I think is that the breaking of my neighbour's windows was a diversion to allow some bugger to break into my shed and plant that bag.

I get myself showered and dressed and now it's nearly five o'clock so I decide to have my dinner then I'll nip down as I promised to visit Scooby for a cuppa.

Now, don't think I'm not worried about the visit from the two detectives, because I am.

I am in no doubt that it was Neil McMillan or one of his cronies that broke in and put that drug in my garden shed; no doubt whatsoever. I mean, who else round here has easy access to the drug that the detective found and likely the value of the drug, whatever it is, wouldn't mean as much to McMillan as setting me up for a visit from the CID.

The worrying thing is that if it was McMillan who is behind it, then he not only knows my address but somebody who clearly meant me harm was round my back. It could just have easily been my house that was broken into, I'm thinking.

Why would McMillan have picked on me though? It can't have been because I didn't choose him for the football team, all those years ago. I mean, who in their right mind would carry a grudge as trivial as that for all they years?

But then again, I'm thinking that McMillan doesn't seem to be the kind of man who is in his right mind. A bleeding nutter, if that wee encounter I had with him is anything to go by.

Aye, I'm agreeing with myself. It is just the sort of thing that McMillan would do; the sort of twisted joke a bully like him would think of. I don't for one minute think it was him that broke into my shed. No, he would have had one of his flunkies' do that, I'm certain of it.

The thing I have to worry about though is if he learns that the CID didn't arrest me, what will he do next?

Before I get into the car I knock on Billy King's door, but it's Irene who answers and tells me that Billy isn't home from work yet. She sighs with a smile when she winks and tells me he's probably away for his Friday night pint.

"Oh, right, I was wondering. It's about them two bags he left in my garden shed. Can you let him know that the polis was round to check the shed…"

"The polis?" she interrupts. "Why did they want into your shed, Jimmy?"

I give her a half smile and tell her, "Somebody told them that there were drugs in the shed."

Irene is aghast and before she says anything, I say, "My shed was broken into. I'm not sure when, but I think it was when all the windows were getting panned in. Whoever it was left a wee bag of drugs on my workbench for the police to find, but fortunately the big detective that came to the house believed the drugs weren't mine."

She shakes her head and I can see she's angry. "Of course they're not yours, Jimmy, but who the fuck would do something like that to you!"

I'm almost tempted to tell her it was probably Neil McMillan, but before I can say anything she shakes her head and says, "I'll tell Billy when he comes in. It's probably that mob from up in the field, them that work for that bastard McMillan. My God, Jimmy, if Billy ever gets a hold of one of them…"

She's close to tears now and I'm almost tempted to reach out to her, but she shrugs and sniffing, says, "Right, Jimmy, I can see you're on your way out, so you just watch yourself and from now on Billy and I will be keeping an eye on you as well."

I'm touched by her concern and can only nod as she closes the door and I head towards the Escort.

Before I get in the car, I see a car draw up behind mine and it's DC Hopkins at the wheel with a man in a suit in the passenger seat.

This is getting beyond a joke, I sigh and I'm immediately suspicious and as I watch I see her speak to the passenger, then she gets out of the car and walks towards me.

"Jimmy," she smiles and for a minute, because she calls me 'Jimmy' I almost relax my guard.

"I was talking with Angus Dunbar at the office," she says, but I'm not sure who she means. "He says he was down here searching your house for drugs."

That's when I realise that Angus Dunbar must be the tall detective called Gus. I nod and am about to speak when she continues, "He thinks that some bad person is trying to fit you up."

I get the feeling that she's quietly laughing at me, but I simply shrug as though it's just another day in my boring life. Then she takes me by surprise and asks, "What do you think? Maybe Neil McMillan thinking that you know or have something to do with the murders of his pals?"

She stares at me, almost daring me to deny it and I feel my legs weakening.

I can't read her face, whether she's being serious or just joking with me, but there's that shiver again running down my spine.

I smile weakly at her, not trusting myself to speak.

After what seems an eternity, but is likely just a few seconds, I put my hands out and I shake my head as I reply, "DC Hopkins, I have no idea who put that drug into my garden shed and I have no idea why you would even think I know anything about the murders of those young people."

And do you know, even *I* don't believe me!

Before she can reply I ask her, "Why do you think it might have been Neil McMillan? Do you have some information that it was him that broke into my shed and put the stuff there and if you *have*, why aren't you arresting him then?"

She doesn't respond to my angry question, but changes tact and says, "DC Dunbar told me that you seem a decent man, that whoever is trying to set you up for the drug charge might try again, perhaps even try to hurt you, Jimmy."

Now that has also been worrying me and I think she can see it in my eyes for she leans slightly forward towards me and says in a voice so low that I have to strain a little to hear her, "If there is anything that you wish to tell me, now might be a good time. Anything at all because it might save you from being very badly hurt."

We're staring at each other and you know, her eyes are so hypnotic that I almost think that it might be a good time to unburden myself, but I catch my breath and simply reply, "I'm sorry, I have no idea what you're talking about, hen."

She continues to stare at me for a few seconds and then with a soft smile, nods and says, "Okay, Jimmy, but please remember we've had this little chat. I just don't want to see you get hurt."

I'm tempted to ask her why she thinks that I might have some knowledge of the murders, but she's a detective after all. She's not likely to give me information that might be evidence against me, is she?

I watch her walk back to her car and then drive off and a little shaky, I get into the driver's seat of the Escort, but I decide to sit for a minute to collect my thoughts.

I can't imagine why she thinks I'm involved in the murders, but it's obvious she does. The lassie strikes me as being quite bright, but if the CID has some evidence against me, why haven't I been taken to an office and interviewed?

Now, maybe I'm grasping at straws here, but it's possible that it is only Hopkins who suspects me, that she hasn't told any of her colleagues of her suspicions. I mean, is that even worth a thought? Could it be that she thinks if she arrests me she will get some kind of promotion, so is she keeping whatever information about me she has, to herself?

I shake my head to try and clear it as a jumble of thoughts, some faintly ridiculous, rush through my mind.

The truth is though I can't make head or tail of what's going on in that woman's mind. If Hopkins thinks I am the murderer, there's not a lot I can do about that and before you even think it, no; there is no way that I am going to harm that young woman, not even if it meant saving myself.

God almighty, what kind of man do you think I am?

Now, Neil McMillan, that's a completely different story.

It's just gone six o'clock when I get to Scooby's house and it's as I'm parking the Escort I remember that I still haven't cut up the bleeding baton. Bugger it; once again I'm thinking my memory is getting that bad I'll need to start writing things down.

It's Alice who opens the door and she gives me a crushing hug.

"Come away in, Jimmy," she takes my jacket from me. "Have you had any dinner?"

I assure her that I've eaten as she leads me into the living room.

Scooby is sitting in his favourite armchair, a small table to one side of him on which lies a tray with a dinner plate that has the remains of his meal on it and which Alice lifts.

"Sit down, Jimmy," she tells me, "and I'll get you a cup of tea and a biscuit."

"So, what's the craic," asks Scooby.

I sink into the comfortable couch and take deep breath and I'm about to start at the beginning when Alice pokes her head through from the kitchen and calls out, "Don't you be saying a word, Jimmy McGrath, till I'm there to listen too."

Scooby and I are grinning and so have a wee chat till Alice reappears with the tray on which are three mugs of tea and a plate of digestive. Now settled in the other armchair, I glance at them both and begin.

I tell them about being woken by the sound of breaking glass, the police arriving and me being hustled into the back of the panda. I tell them about being taken to the charge bar and hear Scooby whisper under his breath, "Bastards!"

I tell them about my night in the freezing cell, minus my slipper and the interview in the morning with the Inspector.

It's when I start to relate the visit from the CID looking for drugs that Alice stops me and says, "Jimmy! You can't sit there and tell us that they searched your house for drugs? My God, of all the people in the world…"

"Shhhsss, woman," says Scooby, waving a hand at her. "Let him finish. Go on, Jimmy," he tells me, his eyes wide with surprise.

I tell them about the detective searching the garden shed that had been broken into and finding the wee poke of whatever it was."

"Did you say they called it charlie?" asks Alice.

"Aye," I nod to her.

"That'll be cocaine then," she sniffs.

"How do you know that?" Scooby turns towards her.

"It's in the women's magazines I read," she replies with an air of authority. "It's a nickname for cocaine. All them film stars are into it, you know."

"But it wasn't yours then, Jimmy?" asks Scooby, but with a twinkle in his eye.

"No, Scooby," I sigh. "I only use heroin."

So I continue with my tale and what I don't mention is Billy King's two bags or the conversation I had with DC Ella Hopkins because as much as I trust and love Scooby and Alice as family, I don't want to sow any seed of doubt in *their* minds that I might have some information about the murders.

By the time I've finished my story, a full half hour has passed and Alice jumps up from her seat and says, "I need another cup of tea after hearing that."

She's about to walk past me, but stops and leaning down, strokes at my balding head and kisses me of the cheek.

"My God, Jimmy, but you've been through the wars these last twenty-four hours. Don't you be forgetting that we're here if you need us, okay?"

I'm a wee bit choked by her attention and I can only nod.

It's during our second cuppa that Scooby again relates the incident in the pub and Alice tells me that earlier today she saw George Paterson down at the shops with a crony, who she calls "…one of his jakey pals," buying a bottle of wine and a half dozen cans of beer and scoffs that for a man that's reputedly never worked a day in his life, he gets through some amount of alcohol a week.

Scooby tells me that young Craig the polis popped by and informed him that because of the threat to Scooby in the pub, Paterson has been officially warned that if he is seen anywhere near Lochar Crescent he will be arrested and detained for court.

Apparently Craig had said whether or not he takes the warning wasn't known, but if Paterson is seen anywhere near the house Scooby is to dial nine-nine-nine straight away.

We ponder whether or not Paterson has the nerve to attack Scooby and I'm feeling a wee bit guilty that my best pal has been put in this situation because it was me that murdered Paterson's son and I'm thinking, if Paterson *does* attack Scooby or God forbid, Alice, then the baton won't be getting cut up after all.

To be honest, it's a lot easier to sound brave that it actually is *being* brave.

I sit for another hour and a bit chewing the fat with Scooby and Alice, who tells us at that morning's Mass it was announced the funeral service for Missus Laurie is due to take place at ten o'clock on Tuesday morning. I'm a bit surprised at that and say I thought the police usually didn't permit victims to be buried so soon, but Alice just shrugs and repeats that's what was announced. The open Mass will be in St Convals and then a private ceremony for the family and close friends who will travel with the cortege to the cemetery in Barrhead.

"Do you think you'll be going to the Mass, Jimmy?" asks Alice, but I know why she's asking for the pain of Jeannie's funeral service is still with me, even after this time.

I nod for even though I only knew Missus Laurie by sight and not to speak with, I'm thinking that it is only right and fitting that the parish turn out as a mark of respect for the poor woman. I just can't imagine what her husband and her family must be going through.

I'm a bit surprised to see it's almost nine o'clock and so rising, I take my leave of Scooby and Alice, promising that I'll pop by some evening for my dinner.

Alice sees me to the door and reminds me that if I need anything all, I only have to ask and kisses me on the cheek before closing the door behind me.

Since I've arrived at Lochar Crescent, the weather has taken a bit of a bad turn and now it's raining steadily, so I turn my jacket collar up and mosey along the garden path to the car.

It's when I'm getting into the driver's seat that I catch something out of the corner of my eye and as I glance across the road towards the parkland opposite the houses, I'm guessing a distance of about forty or fifty yards away, I see what looks like two figures in the dark backing into the shadows by the bushes there. They're behind the council's six feet metal fence that borders the kind of parkland, so I don't really get a good look at them. I get into the car and slam the door closed and for good measure, lock the doors. Switching on the engine, I put on the windscreen wipers and peer into the dark before switching on the headlights, but whether it was a trick of my imagination or I did see two figures, I'm not really sure.

Still, it's rattled me a wee bit and now as I drive away I'm wondering. If there *were* two people standing there in the darkness, were they watching Scooby's house or were they watching for me? I know I sound paranoid, but you know what's being going on so if I am sounding a wee bit nervous, then I'm sure you'll understand, eh? I was going to drive straight home, but my curiosity got the better of me and being the nosey bugger I am I decide to drive past the police caravan and see if there is anything happening there.

The journey from Lochar Crescent to where the caravan is parked in Linthaugh Terrace is a short, one minute trip and as I pass by the caravan, sure enough the lights are on inside and there seems to be at least three cars parked nearby that look like CID cars. Not that I'm an expert, but don't forget I've seen a more than a couple of the detectives cars in the last few days. Of course, I don't stop but make a complete circle at the roundabout and then turn into Braidcraft Road and head towards Hapland Road.

I can't explain it, but my nerves are on edge and I'm feeling some trepidation as I approach my house. It's because I'm thinking of the two figures I thought I saw outside Scooby's house and it has really rattled me. I stop the car outside my house, but before I get out, I check along the road in front of the car and using my mirror, behind me to ensure that there's nobody about. Okay, we already know I'm not a brave man and it's now I suddenly wish I had brought the baton along with me. Don't get me wrong now; if somebody was outside the house waiting for me I wouldn't get out the car, but drive away like a bat out of hell. No, it's the thirty feet between the car and my front door that I'm worried about.

As satisfied as I can be that there's nobody lurking about in the darkness waiting to jump me, I get out of the car and my hands are shaking as I try to lock the door. Yes, I know what you're thinking, that most cars these days have remote locking by pressing a button on the key, but my Escort is a nineteen ninety-five model and is a right old thing that I bought second hand and had three previous owners, so when the remote locking did work that was a long, long time ago. That aside, the old girl has given me good service so I shouldn't really complain and unconsciously I slap the roof in apology to her.

Anyway, here's me with a dry mouth and sweaty palms and eyes dancing back and forth as I search the darkness round about me. I hurry along my path and fumble with my front door key and at last, the doors open.

I'm no sooner in and locking the door behind me when I hear my phone ringing. I switch on the hall light and hurry through to the living room. In the darkness I snatch the phone from its cradle on the wee side table in the corner.

"Hello?"

"Nice to see you got home safely, janny," says the voice and my blood runs cold.

Neil McMillan.

I'm about to ask how he knows I've just arrived home when I realise and I shiver.

I'm being watched.

"How did you get this number?" I croak at him and my throats as dry as a witch's tit.

There's a short snigger and I hear him say to someone with him, "The old bastard's never heard of the telephone directory."

My instinct is to slam the phone down, but some part of me continues to clutch the handset to my ear and even though I instinctively know I'm alone in the house, I'm afraid; very afraid.

"What is it that you want?" I can hear the tremor in my voice.

"How does it feel to be *really* scared, you little shit!" says McMillan and then laughing, he abruptly hangs up or rather, ends the call because though I'm not sure, I'm guessing it's a mobile he's phoning from because I can't believe he's in a house near me.

I'm still standing here in the darkness, my legs shaking and with the handset still clamped to my ear.

A couple seconds pass before I slowly return the handset to the cradle and then I reach out for the arm of the couch and I slump down.

I can hardly breathe.

The light from the outside streetlamp is shining through the open curtains casting a rectangle on the carpet in front of me and I realise if he and whoever he's with saw me get out of the car, then they must be outside. I force myself to my feet and stumble to the window where I snatch at the curtains and pull them closed. But still, I don't switch on the overhead light.

Taking a deep breath I take the edge of the curtain and with shaking hands, I open it a fraction and I peek outside, but though the rain has now stopped, I don't see anyone.

Now, you might be thinking that it would be wise to call the police, tell them that I'm being threatened, but therein is the problem.

For one, I don't want the police knocking at my door for any reason because the last thing I need is them sniffing around me. I'm in such an excitable and frightened state I don't know what I might say and I might end up blurting out something I shouldn't.

Besides, McMillan said he was glad I got home safely. Now you and I both know that he's threatening me by the very phone call, but the polis would likely say there's no threat if somebody is being pleased I got home safely, is there?

I could phone Scooby, but he's got enough on his plate with that drunken thug George Paterson threatening him and being warned to stay away from him.

My neighbour Billy King is just a couple of doors away and would be only to glad to have the opportunity to rattle McMillan's teeth, but I've already committed a murder to clear him of suspicion so the last thing I want to do is bring him back to the attention of the police.

Yes, I know what you're thinking. Why don't I take a few days away somewhere; a wee break in a B&B or a hotel down by the coast. Not a bad idea I agree, but if McMillan is really intent on doing me some harm it will only postpone what he has in mind, not solve my problem.

I'm trapped and I know it.

Still in the dark I rise from the couch and make my way into the kitchen for a cuppa and you know, I always seem to get my best ideas when the kettle's boiling.

I'm shaking my head for what I intend doing might sound really, really crazy, but if McMillan *is* going to hurt me or have his cronies hurt me then I think that I should consider taking out some insurance.

CHAPTER EIGHTEEN

A half hour has passed and I'm sitting in my armchair, patiently waiting. The tray with the two cups and saucers and the plate of biscuits is prepared in the kitchen, the teapot is ready and the kettle has already boiled in anticipation.

I glance at the clock and see it is ten minutes to ten and I'm thinking that maybe I was too late, but then the doorbell is rung and I take a deep breath as I get to my feet. Oh, I should mention that I've been expecting this visitor and so, nervously, I head for the front door.

At the door I compose myself and pull it open.

DC Hopkins is standing there and she's alone, for which I'm grateful for I half suspected that she might bring one of her colleagues with her.

She nods to me and says, "I understand you phoned the office looking for me, Mister McGrath."

Mister McGrath again, I'm thinking. Well, maybe not the start that I was hoping for.

"Please, come in," I return her nod and stand to one side.

She's carrying her folder and wearing a light lemon coloured raincoat over her skirted suit, but the coat's dry and I'm guessing the rain has stopped. As she steps through the door I see the CID car parked outside in front of my Escort.

She doesn't wait for my invitation, but continues through the hallway into the living room and then turns to face me.

Before she can speak, I say, "I'm glad you came, DC Hopkins. I wasn't certain if maybe you had finished duty, but the lassie at your office said she would try to contact you."

She turns her head and with her eyes indicates the couch and I say, "Oh, sorry, please, sit down."

She doesn't take off her raincoat, but unbuttons it as she sits down and curls her long legs beneath her. She places her folder on the couch beside her before she replies, "I was just finishing off a report when I got your message." She cocks her head and narrowing her eyes, asks me, "Is there something you want to tell me, Mister McGrath?"

What, is she looking for an immediate confession to murder? She's probably thinking that's why she's here, so I nod my head in response to her question and I can almost see the gleam in her eyes. "I'll just pop the kettle on," I tell her and before she can protest, I slip into the kitchen and switch it on. While I wait the minute or so for the kettle to boil again, I'm thinking as fast as I can. Now, I've already admitted I'm not the brightest bulb in the box and truth be told, I can get confused and I tend to stammer a wee bit if I'm put under any kind of verbal pressure. However, what I've also realised in the last week is that stressed though I have been, my mind has been ticking over a lot faster than normal. It's almost as if murdering those toe-rags and doing what I can to avoid the polis arresting me has activated brain cells I didn't know I had. Not that I'm overly confident. I'm not that stupid that I'm just going to roll over, if you know what I mean.

I know it sounds really daft, but I'm actually working out scenarios in my head; kind of thinking on my feet, as it were.

Now this is the real test for me, because this young woman DC Hopkins is a smart cookie; of that I'm in no doubt. I only hope that what I'm about to tell her sounds plausible and she won't cotton on that I'm lying. Well, lying in part, so stick with me here and you'll understand what I mean.

I return to the living room with the tray and set it down onto the wee side table. Believe it or not I actually have to force my hands from shaking and my stomach, not the most reliable part of my anatomy, is feeling very queasy right now.

"You really shouldn't have bothered, Mister McGrath," she sighs and glances meaningfully at her wristwatch.

"Right then," almost with reluctance, she accepts the teacup and saucer from my hand and stares at me, "why did you phone to get me here? You *do* want to speak with me?"

"It's about the man we discussed the other day, Neil McMillan." Her face doesn't change as she simply replies, "Go on."

Now is when I pass the test or not, I'm thinking and taking a deep breath, I say, "I think he's going to hurt me or have me hurt."

She doesn't reply, but continues to stare at me for a few seconds before she then asks, "Why do you think that and why would he?"

"Well," I drawl, "without going over it again, you already know about the confrontation I had with him outside St Convals, where he slapped me…"

"And kicked you on the backside," she adds straight-faced, but I'm sure there's the hint of amusement there in her voice and to be honest, that riles me a wee bit.

"Yes," I lower my voice because my face is again burning with shame, "when he kicked me on the backside."

I swallow with difficulty and taking a deep breath I say, "I know you also suspect he is the person who arranged for my garden shed to be broken into and that drug to be left there."

"I've no evidence of that," she smoothly replies.

"Well, perhaps not, but I think he's stalking me."

Her eyes narrow and I can see I've surprised her. "What makes you think that?"

I tell her about visiting Scooby earlier in the evening, though I don't mention the two figures standing in the shadows and about the phone call when I get back through my front door and that it's my opinion he must have been outside and seen me arrive home.

"Did he say who he was, give his name I mean?"

"No," I shake my head, "but I recognised his voice."

"But he didn't *threaten* you with violence?"

Again I shake my head. It had occurred to me to lie, tell her McMillan *did* threaten me, but I'm thinking the closer I stick to the truth, the easier it will be to remember the story if I'm asked to repeat everything again.

"So, why do you think McMillan is stalking you?"

"I have no idea," I carefully reply and then as I've planned, I carefully choose my words when I add, "You said earlier this evening when I was at my car that you thought McMillan might have some idea I know about his pals getting murdered. But that's a load of nonsense; I mean, how would I know anything about that?"

I put on my most innocent face and now here it is; just the two of us sitting here in my living room. Neither of us with a witness to say he said that or she said that; a totally deniable situation for us both.

As I stare at her I know I've given her the opportunity to ask me or to tell me why she thinks I have something to do with the murders, but will she take it?

She stares back at me without expression, but then slowly smiles. Not a happy or a sarcastic smile; just a smile I can't quite figure out. A smile that tells me there is a lot going on in her head and it's then I realise that she won't tell me anything. Whatever she thinks she has on me, she isn't going to give it up sitting on my couch.

And that frightens me because it only convinces me even more that she suspects I'm the killer she and her CID pals are looking for.

"So, why have you *really* got me here tonight, Jimmy?"

Jimmy. Seems I'm back to being her pal again, then.

I swallow deeply and here's what I tell her.

"Like I told you, I think that Neil McMillan is going to have me hurt. It's nothing to do with anything; it's just that he's picking on me because he knows I'm defenceless and can't fight him back. Remember, I told you that even as a wee boy he was a bully who picked on those that were weaker than him. So, here's what I'm thinking. I'd like to give you a statement about him assaulting me outside St Convals and tonight's phone call. I don't want him charged," I tell her, "but if anything does happen to me then you will have, I'm not sure what do you call it," I shake my head. "Is it probable cause? Then you can arrest him."

"Probable cause might work in New York, Jimmy, but not here in Pollok," she smiles softly, "but after you categorically told me you wouldn't give a statement against him, the best I can probably do is to bring him into the office and caution him about his future behaviour."

I lean forward in my seat. "Don't you understand? I *will* give you a statement, but only to be used if something happens to me."

She stares at me like I'm off my head and then shakes her own head. "No, Jimmy. That doesn't work in the real world. What I will do is have the uniformed officers patrolling the area made aware of his attention with you and ask them to pass by your house during their patrols."

I sigh and tell her, "Look, hen. Thanks for that but if they can't catch the buggers up in the field that are making our lives miserable round here, how are they going to catch McMillan or one of his cronies if they have a go at me?"

"And I ask again," she tries to surprise me. "Do you think he's after you because you know about the murders?"

Slippery bugger isn't she, trying to catch me out with that one.

I shake my head and reply, "How many times must I tell you, hen. I know *nothing* about the murders other than what I've read in the papers or heard on the television."

"Did you know Theresa Laurie, the woman who died?"

Now that takes me by surprise.

"No, I'm sorry to say I didn't know Missus Laurie other than to see her and her husband, either at Sunday Mass in St Convals or in the social club. I know she was a very well respected woman and her death is a great tragedy. I can't imagine what her husband and her family might be going through, right now."

I shake my head in sympathy for the Laurie family's loss. "I only heard tonight from my pal Scooby's wife Alice that the funeral service will be this coming Tuesday."

"Will you be attending the ceremony?"

"Oh, aye," I nod. "It's only right and fitting that we all pay our respects to a decent lady."

She gives me an odd look and then standing, says, "Well, Jimmy, if there's nothing else then."

I stand and as she turns towards the door I ask, "Are you any closer to finding who killed Missus Laurie?"

"Not yet, but we'll get whoever it was, rest assured on that."

"Not that it's any help, but the general opinion in the parish is that it was one of McMillan's mob," I venture.

She doesn't at first respond to that comment and I'm a bit taken aback at the look she gives me, but then she turns and is walking towards the front door that she pulls open. Walking along the path, she calls to me over her shoulder, "That's what we've heard too. Goodnight, Jimmy."

I watch her walk towards the CID car, but she doesn't turn and it's only when she's driving off that she gives me a wee wave.

I have a wee look round about in the darkness before I close the door, but can't see anyone hanging about.

Locking the door I head back into the living room to clear away the tea things. My mind's in a whirl.

Okay, I admit it, I'm a little disappointed that my plan for giving her a statement about McMillan has fallen flat and I'm no nearer to finding out why she thinks I'm the killer. At least I can rest assured that she now knows how frightened I am and God forbid if anything happens to me; well, maybe she will be able to arrest him for something. I really did think that she would have taken my statement, but I won't pretend that I know the law for after all she's the detective so I wasn't going to argue with her. If nothing else though, I'm pleased with my own little act for I'm quite confident I haven't given anything away either.

It's Saturday morning and I waken after a good night sleep, probably the best I've had for some weeks now to find that the weather has taken a nasty turn. It's dark and gloomy outside with the rain beating a tattoo on the rear bedroom window.

The clock says seven-fifty, so feeling quite fresh I get out of bed and decide to shower and dress before breakfast.

Half an hour later I'm flipping two eggs and watching the toast when the back door gets chapped.

A wee bit surprised, I turn off the gas and when I open the door I find Billy King standing there, holding one of Irene's brollies over his head.

"Sorry to bother you so early, Jimmy."

He sees me glancing at the brolly and grins, "Pink to go with my eyes after that bevy session last night," and leaves the dripping brolly on the outside doorstep as he steps into the kitchen. "The insurance money has come through so I'm going out early this morning to look at a new van. Well, second-hand I should say, so I thought after you spoke with Irene yesterday that I'd come and collect those two bags from your shed."

"Aye, no problem Billy," I reply and I fetch the padlock key from its hook.

He sniffs the air and says, "Sorry, Jimmy, I'm disturbing your breakfast."

"No problem," I hush him with a wave of my hand and hand him the key.

His eyes narrow and he says, "Irene told me about the CID searching the shed. Drugs, she said they were looking for. Who the fuck... oh, excuse me, Jimmy. Who the hell would do something like that to a decent wee man like you?"

I didn't think it worth the trouble re-telling the tale, so shrug my shoulders and let the question go unanswered.

"When they were in the shed, did the CID have a look in the bags?"

"No, they weren't interested in the bags," I reply, "though one of them did say I should get rid of the scrap or whatever was in them."
"Ah," he sighs and nods. "Well, let's just say it *is* scrap and leave it at that." He holds up the key and grins. "Anyway, I'll take them away out of your shed."
I watch Billy collect his two bags from the shed and standing at the back door I hand him his brolly and he turns to leave, but stops and says, "When I was in the pub last night down at the halfway with my mate, there was a guy there at the bar mouthing off about his son being murdered."
My eyes narrow and my first thought is George Paterson. "Was he a skinny guy in his forties with greasy looking fair hair?"
"Aye, a dirty looking bugger, but I don't know his name though. He was with a couple of other guys that looked like down and outs. Noisy bastards they were too.
The bar man had to tell the guy a couple of times to shut up or he was out of there."
Billy took a deep breath and then said, "Anyway, I passed them when I was going for a pee and I overheard this guy telling his pals that it was your mate who killed his boy."
I gulped. "You mean my mate Scooby, Scooby Toner?"
"Aye, that was the name I heard, Toner. He's your pal that lives down off Linthaugh Road, isn't he?"
"Aye, Scooby's my pal right enough," I reply with a nod, but my thoughts are elsewhere. "Did he say anything about challenging Scooby, anything else about hurting him?"
"To be honest, I was half pissed myself, Jimmy, so I didn't hear that much else. Sorry."
"No, you're alright Billy. I'm grateful for you letting me know. I'll need to tell Scooby to watch himself."
With that, Billy lifts his bags and with a cheery wave, he walks off along the back path that runs behind the houses, but not before I remember to wish him good luck with the van viewing.
I close the door and relight the gas under the eggs.

After my breakfast I sit with my tea and wonder if I should go ahead as I planned and saw the baton into wee pieces, but I shake my head. I was that sure that was what I was going to do, but this new information from Billy about that drunken sod George Paterson has set me to worrying about Scooby. That and the two figures that I saw last night and I'm more convinced than ever it was probably Paterson.

My mistake was in not asking Billy what time he saw Paterson in the pub because I don't think it was any later than half eight or nine o'clock when I saw the figures in the darkness. I reason that if Paterson *had* been in the pub at that time, it might not have been him. On that point, it probably wasn't Neil McMillan either because I'm sure he must have been watching me getting out of the car when he phoned.

No, I'm sighing; there's no way to tell who the two figures were, but my instinct, my gut, tells me it was Paterson.

Could it have been a courting couple? No, I shake my head, not with that heavy rain it wasn't.

Whoever it was, I'm convincing myself, was watching either my car or Scooby's house and it was too random they'd know my car was going to be there, so the safe bet is they were watching the house. I finish my tea and consider that maybe it was just as well I haven't destroyed the baton after all.

I check my larder and my cleaning materials and make a wee list of the shopping and things I need to buy, for you see Saturday's market day down at Govan near the underground station and I usually get my bleach and cleaning sprays down there. I like the craic from the stall holders when I'm doing my shopping and there's no problem with the parking either.

There is also a couple of charity shops in the shopping centre and one in Burleigh Street as well that I like to take a wander into. I'm at that age now it's no use me buying new stuff like shirts or trousers. I've probably got enough to do me, but if I see something that catches my eye; well, I'm like most people. I like a wee bargain now and then.

Though the Govan shopping centre isn't that big, there's a cracking butchers there where I get my meat and when I've stowed my shopping in the car I have a treat to myself. I head into the Pearce Institute café on the Govan Road for a roll and sausage, a cuppa and one of the delicious home made pastries they do and also have a read of the early edition of the 'Glasgow News' while I'm there.

So that's my day organised and glancing out of the kitchen windows as I'm washing up my dishes, I see that the rain has calmed down to a squall, so I'd better get myself wrapped up, I'm thinking.

I let the water drain away and dry my hands and twenty minutes later I'm in the car and driving down to Govan.

The car radio is on and I'm listening to the news. The main items are about the budget, but I'm only half-listening to that when the third item begins about the Pollok murders.

Unfortunately, the newscaster doesn't tell me anything new, but she does go on to report the sad death of Missus Theresa Laurie, reminding the listeners of the poor woman being struck on the head by a brick and who has since 'succumbed to her injuries at the city's Southern General Hospital.' What then startles me is the newscaster ends the item by quoting a police spokesperson who said that Missus Laurie's death is not related to the ongoing murder inquiry of the three youths in the Pollok area.

I'm stunned. Not bleeding related? How the heck they can come to that conclusion, I'm wondering. I mean, wasn't the poor woman struck on the head by a brick thrown by one of the gang; the same gang to which the three that I killed belonged?

I'm wondering why the police have not publicly connected the murders. The only conclusion I can arrive at is that they're hunting me for the three I killed and also hunting whoever threw the brick; Missus Laurie's killer. It seems kind of daft to me that they don't run the one inquiry for all the murders, but then a thought strikes me. If the police admit the four deaths *is* connected, then it might suggest to the people in Pollok that the three murders committed *after* Missus Laurie's death could be revenge killings by some sort of vigilante.

Oh aye, I'm thinking; the media would just love that.

But then it also occurs to me; what if the CID cotton on and instead decide that Alex Paterson, the first one I killed, is nothing to do with Missus Laurie's killing, but is a revenge killing for Scooby being mugged?

I get that same, icy shiver up my spine because if the CID comes to that conclusion then they will start to look at Scooby's family and friends; or is that what DC Hopkins is already doing, I wonder?

Is that why she's looking at me?

If that's where her suspicions lie then is she investigating me on her own or has she been instructed to try and get me to confess? Is that why she always seems to be hanging around me and turning up when I least expect it?

Sounding paranoid, aren't I?

Well, as I've already suggested, if I've murdered three people I think I'm entitled to be a little paranoid, aren't I?

If the CID do come to arrest me, then they must have evidence, but for the life of me I can't think what that evidence might be.

Unless Gina the Co-operative lassie has remembered and told them and described me being behind Paterson in the queue the night of his murder; or the guy who was standing with Calum Black admitting it wasn't a big, black guy he saw but a wee, skinny ex-janny with boot polish on his face or the wee lad who saw me when I drove off after killing Kylie Morrison perhaps knows me from seeing me around the area.

Why am I not sounding as worried as I should be?

I'll tell you why because no matter what thoughts race through my mind, there is absolutely *nothing* I can do about it. No, I'm better just getting on with my day and letting matters run its course.

I like Govan and the Govan people. Since the demise of the shipyard era, Govan has had its ups and downs, but the folk there just get on with life. When Jeannie and I had our wee flat in Langlands Road, the best thing about the place other than each other was the neighbours. Aye, I like the Govan folk right enough.

I park the car in the car park behind the shopping centre and attend to my shopping. In the charity shop in Burleigh Street I find a nice black tie that cost me fifty pence and will replace the old, tattered one I've got in the wardrobe. I buy it because I'm thinking of Missus Laurie's funeral that is to take place this coming Tuesday morning. I also find a pair of black, highly polished brogue shoes that fit me fine; a bargain at three pounds.

Once I've finished shopping, I dump the bags into the car and make my way across to the PI for my lunch and a read of my newspaper. Because it's Saturday, the place is busy but I get a seat at a table with a couple about my age and give them a courteous nod as I sit down.

The woman smiles and daintily pecks at her cake while her man returns my nod with his own nod.

"Hell of a day out there," he says by way of opening a conversation.

"Aye," I agree. "I had the windscreen wipers going full blast on the way down here," I reply and I'm thinking, I'm not going to get a read of my paper after all.

"Oh, you're not from Govan?"

"No, I'm living up in Pollok."

"Bad business up there the now, with all those murders," his wife butts in, shaking her blue rinse hair. "You must be double locking your doors at night, eh?"

"Well," I slowly reply and tap the 'Glasgow News' in front of me, "according to what I've heard and read in the newspapers there hasn't been a murder in anyone's house. I'm given to understand the murders have all been outdoors." I give her a grim smile, but the truth is that I don't really want to sit and discuss what's going on in Pollok. This is *supposed* to be a relaxing day for me, I inwardly sigh.

"Aye, but there was another murder about the same time too, wasn't there? That woman who got herself hit on the head. Was that not at a wee dance or something? Have the polis not got a clue who did that one too?" her man asks.

"Missus Laurie," I nod as I wolf down my roll and sausage. "Aye, you're right. She was out at a wee social night," I tell him, brushing crumbs from my shirt; however, I don't think it's worth mentioning that I was at the same social night.

His wife leans across the table and peers at me through her thick lens glasses.

"What about the other murders? Has the polis no idea who killed those three young people? Were they not murdered because one of their pals killed the woman at the dance?"

"I've no idea," I shrug my shoulders and sip at my tea.

"I mean, those poor young teenagers," she shakes her head, "murdered in the prime of their life."

I decide I've had enough of this and quite literally gulp down my tea. It briefly occurs to me to tell her that those 'poor young people' were three bad young drug dealing teenagers and deserved what they got, but I really, really don't want to get involved in this nosey wee woman's gossip. Besides, why does she think *I* should know any more than what the newspapers and the TV is reporting?

"Oh, is that the time," I make a point of glancing up at the huge wall clock. "I'd better be getting home."

I force a smile and wrap my pastry in the paper napkin as I get to my feet.

"Well, it's been nice speaking with you," I nod to them both in turn as they stare at me and then tucking my paper under my arm, I head for the exit.

Outside the main door of the PI, I'm unaccountably annoyed that my relaxing lunch has been disturbed. I know I told you that Govan folk can be neighbourly, but I should also have mentioned they can be a nosey bunch too. I think it's a hangover from the days they were all crowded together into those old tenements.

Back at the car I switch on the engine, but a thought occurs to me and slowly I reach forward and switch the engine off again.

They were just two retired people sitting at a table in a Govan café, yet even though other than what they've read or heard on the tele, they have no idea about the murders in Pollok, but they're cute enough to have concluded that the killing of Missus Laurie and the murder of the three teenagers is probably related.

So, why should the CID think differently?

No, I'm shaking my head; I don't think the CID *does* think differently.

I think what the CID is really investigating and what the media is being told they are investigating is not the same thing.

I'm almost convinced that to prevent the media stirring up a storm about a vigilante being on the warpath in Pollok, the CID is publicly treating Missus Laurie's killing and the three murders as separate investigations. In reality, they are looking for a killer who is seeking revenge for Missus Laurie's murder.

If I'm correct and I sincerely hope I am, then it's likely that they won't connect Scooby's mugging and the death of Alex Paterson to any of Scooby's family or his friends.

But why then, I wonder, is DC Hopkins so intent on focusing on me?

It takes me nearly half an hour to get home because of diversions round the Ibrox area for the football.

I've never really followed football, though I have to admit I do like to see the Celtic winning. It's ingrained in me. Like I said before, if you're brought up a Glasgow Catholic, you follow Celtic. Glasgow

Protestants usually follow the Rangers while the odds and sods have Patrick Thistle, Clyde or Queen's Park to choose from.

Back at the house I'm pacing the living room floor and wracking my brains trying to work out how I can stop George Paterson from hurting my pal Scooby.

I haven't realised the time and already it's starting to get dark which confuses me a wee bit, until I look out the window and see the clouds gathering for another night of heavy rain. Sure enough, it's not even turned five o'clock when the downpour arrives.

I pull the curtains together, but not before I have a wee look outside to ensure nobody's hanging around and then switch on the living room light.

The roll and sausage at the PI and this new threat against Scooby has killed my appetite, but I still manage to scoff the pastry with a cuppa.

There's no question about it and I make a decision.

Under no circumstances will I see Scooby or any of his family getting hurt. If Paterson truly believes that Scooby is the killer of his son and the CID start to look at Scooby or his family for Alex Paterson's murder, then if the worst comes to the very worst, I'll contact the CID and put my hands up to the murders and that will settle the issue.

The decision doesn't make me any kind of hero. No, if anything I shouldn't have put Scooby in this position in the first place.

All it will take is for me to hear is that him or that one of his family is at risk from being hurt or under suspicion for murder and I'll be up at Pollok police office like a shot.

I'm even thinking I might even make my confession to DC Hopkins. All things aside, she seems to be a nice young woman and catching me could be a tick in the box for her career.

Funny that; even though nothing has happened yet, I'm almost resigned to being arrested.

Yet one thing still bothers me. If it doesn't happen for a while, that sod George Paterson might have time to have a go at Scooby and for all his bravado, Scooby isn't fit or young enough to take on a bampot like Paterson.

So, I'm thinking to myself; if I am to be arrested, like I've told you before. Better to go as a sheep than a lamb.

So, here's my plan.

It is half past seven now and it's as dark as a coal cellar outside. I'm dressed in the navy blue polo shirt, the police trousers, heavy working boots and my maroon coloured anorak. I'm wearing the dark coloured Tammy and the baton is in the pocket of the police trousers. In my anorak pocket, now don't be laughing; I've a tin of boot polish.

I thought about driving down to Lochar Crescent, but it occurs to me if the polis, and by polis I mean DC Hopkins, is keeping an eye on me then I'll leave the light on and the car outside.

Besides, walking in the rain in this darkness I'll easily spot a police car cruising around and that should give me time to duck into a gate or hide in a hedgerow.

You'll be wondering where I'm going and why?

If, as I think, George Paterson is hiding in the bushes watching for Scooby to leave the house, then I'm going to find him first.

Now, I know I'm not a hard man and I can't punch my way out of a paper bag, but I'm remembering a book I once read that was written by a military man. I can't remember his name and I think I mentioned it before because what the author wrote was surprise is the best advantage an attacker can have over a bigger force. That kind of stuck with me, probably because I'm such a wee man and I thought if I ever found myself in the position of squaring up to a bigger bloke, I'd get a kick in first before I run away.

Well, that said I'll need to gamble on surprise and getting close enough to use the baton. Another thing I'm banking on is that if he's true to form, Paterson will likely have a drink in him, whereas I'm sober.

I know what you're thinking. It's a bit random isn't it, me hoping to find Paterson in the dark, hiding in the bushes.

The thing is I can't just sit here worrying. I need to do *something*.

I leave the house by the back door and purposefully make my way along Hapland Road to the junction at Hapland Avenue and turn down the road towards Meiklerig Crescent. I've decided if anyone sees me it will look suspicious me doddering along in the heavy rain rather than hurrying to get where I'm going.

By the time I get to Meiklerig Crescent, I've only seen two cars pass by and one of those was a private hire taxi.

Again I'm thinking, so much for the extra police patrols, but on this dark night I'm grateful for their absence.

I cross Linthaugh Road and head directly towards the thick bushes that surround Lochar Crescent. There's a high metal fence there that separates the pavement and the park area, but it's not in great repair and I soon find a gap to squeeze through. I'm guessing it's taken me less than ten minutes to get here.

My heart's thumping in my chest and I'm nervously reaching for the baton.

I'm reasonably confident that in the darkness, in the rain with me wearing dark coloured clothing, nobody can see me unless they're nearby and looking for me.

As slowly as I can, I start to make my way through the bushes, tiptoeing forward and trying to avid becoming snarled and tangled in the heavy undergrowth. I breathe through my mouth like I saw once in a war film.

I'm tense as piano wire and listening for any sound, but all I hear is some kids laughing on the road, oh, I don't know; maybe a hundred yards away.

I stop because I can also hear the faint sound of music that seems to be coming from an open, upstairs window in a house near to where Scooby lives.

I peer into the darkness at the houses across the road and by my reckoning, I must be close to where I saw the figures the other night because I can almost see Scooby's garden gate.

You'll be wondering what I intend doing if Paterson is there with a mate. Well, what I'm going to do is I'll scream like a banshee and use the baton on Paterson. I'm hoping that if I sound frightening enough, anybody with him will crap themselves and run off.

Well, that's my plan.

Rubbish, isn't it?

I can hardly breathe I'm so scared, but scared or not, I'm committed now and determined that nobody will hurt my old pal Scooby and if it means me getting a bleaching or being arrested, so be it.

I'm breathing heavily now and worried that Paterson will hear me coming.

Suddenly, I'm there, in the bushes where I'm sure I saw them standing the other night.

The place is empty; there's nobody here.

I turn and look around me in case I'm in the wrong bit, but no, I'm convinced this is the place I saw the two figures.

I don't know whether to be disappointed or relieved.

There is a very faint light penetrating the bushes from the nearby street lamp, and I see something glinting in the ground, something that is catching a bit of the street lighting.

I bend down and I see it's an empty wine bottle. I can see another empty wine bottle nearby and yes, what looks like cigarette fagends; lots of them. I also find an empty fag packet.

This convinces me that I've found where Paterson has stood because from here I've a good view of Scooby's garden path and front door. It also tells me that he's spent some time at this spot, watching Scooby's house.

I'm idly kicking at the bottles, four I've counted now, when I hear one that doesn't sound empty.

Sure enough, when I lift it I see that though the seal at the cork is broken, the wine bottle is more than half full.

Now why would Paterson leave a bottle with wine…then, with sudden realisation I know why.

He's going to return; he's coming back sometime.

I quickly glance about me and listen, but there isn't a sound other than the faint music from the open window.

I get the weirdest feeling. I can't really describe it other than to say that I'm frightened of the expected confrontation, it's like… I don't know, like I'm excited.

Does that sound utterly mad?

I take a deep breath and still listening for Paterson I push my way into the thick shrubbery behind me and I crouch down.

If he does return then I'll see him long before he'll see me and I'll still have the advantage.

The rain has slackened to a drizzle and wet though I am, I'm not too cold.

So I sit here for, I don't know because I'm not wearing my watch, but I'm guessing it's about two hours.

Paterson doesn't turn up and I watch as one by one, the lights go out in most of the houses across the road. I wait for fifteen minutes or so after the lights in Scooby's house have gone out. Then I decide enough is enough and stand up to go home.

I haven't realised how cold I have become and the cramp in my legs is awful; so bad that I stumble like an arthritic old woman through the bushes towards the gap in the metal fence where I entered the park area and bugger the noise I'm making.

I'm through the fence now and shivering with the cold, so start walking quickly and retrace my route back home.

To be honest, I'm so cold I hardly notice anything or anyone about me and the polis could have passed by and I wouldn't have seen them.

Anyway, I get safely home and in the back door and it's only when I'm taking my sodden jacket off I realise I hadn't even put the boot polish on my face.

Thankfully the central heating has been on and with a cuppa, I'm soon warmed up and well, that's the end of my night, so I'm off to bed.

CHAPTER NINETEEN

Sunday morning and I decide that I'll show my face at eleven o'clock Mass this morning. I know Scooby and Alice in particular will be pleased to see me and anyway, there's no better place to hear the local craic about what's going on and if there's any news about the murder investigations.

I make myself some breakfast and get dressed. Call me old fashioned, but even though not a lot of younger people bother these days, I still like to wear a shirt and tie on the occasion I do attend Mass.

The clouds are threatening to unleash their load, but for the minute it's dry so I stick an old tweed cap in my pocket and with a wee glance at the Escort to ensure the windows are still all there, I start to make my way round to the chapel.

The walk won't do me any harm for my old legs are a bit stiff and I'm thinking it was crouching in the cold for that length of time last night.

I see a few of the congregation heading the same way as me and greet those I know, to speak with or nod to, with a smile.

The closer I get to the chapel the more people I see and frankly, I'm a wee bit surprised by the large turnout.

Parked on the roadway among some of the parishioner's cars I see a couple of CID cars and sure enough, there are some detectives with clipboards standing in a wee group inside the front gates. They aren't speaking to anyone that I can see and I'm wondering what their game is.

It's when I'm about to pass through the gates that I see her, arm in arm with a young guy; the lassie Gina from the Co-operative.

The lassie stares straight through me and honestly, I thought I was going to have a heart attack, but she walks right past me without a second glance. So there you are. All this time she's been at the back of my mind and I've been worrying myself sick, thinking she would remember me being in the store the night I killed Alex Paterson and she hasn't even given me a second look.

Talk about relief.

I take a deep breath and follow the crowd through the gates and I turn my head away from the detectives. Then I hear my name 'Jimmy McGrath' being called and you know that sudden sinking feeling you get in your stomach? Well, mine literally dropped to my feet and then I turn round and see that it's Mary Burns, one of my neighbours calling and waving her hand at me.

"Hello, Mary," I try to smile and I can hear my voice sounding a bit shaky.

"Sorry, Jimmy, did I startle you?" she ask, concern etched on her face.

"No, you're all right."

"Ah, good," she smiles at me, but then glances towards the detectives and lowering her voice, she says, "It's just that I wanted to tell you I was speaking to Irene King and she told me that your garden shed was broken into and some drugs were planted." She takes my arm and leads me towards the grassy verge and away from the parishioners who are passing us. Leaning into me she says, "Now look, I'm not sure about telling you this, Jimmy, but the night it happened, I mean, the night when our windows were panned in and you got arrested by the polis. My man had sent me back to my bed because I'd work in the morning. Anyway, I got up to go to the toilet and thought I heard something round our back garden. It was a couple of hours after the ruckus and the joiners were out the front and things had settled down a bit, when I heard the noise."

"What, round your back garden?"

"Aye, well, that's what I thought at first, so I peeked out of the upstairs window and I saw somebody in the dark, but he wasn't at my back garden, Jimmy; he had climbed the fences I think between the gardens and was in *your* back garden. It was him climbing the fence; that was the noise I heard."

Maybe I should explain, but the fences between my neighbours and me are the standard council fencing and can't be any more than four feet tall. Of course some of them have been replaced over the years, but the fences that still stand between Mary's house and her next door neighbour Missus Baxter and my house is the original fencing.

"Did you see who it was, Mary? Did you not think to phone the police?"

She takes a deep breath as she stares at me and says, "Look, Jimmy. We'd already had our windows panned in by those bastards up in the field. I was worried if I told you or the polis what I seen then they'd come back and do something even worse. Besides, when he was in your garden I couldn't quite see him because of the curve of the building and I didn't know he was at your shed door. I could have leaned right out of the window but to be honest, Jimmy, I wasn't happy about doing that in case he saw me. You know how bad these people can be."

Now I'm not annoyed or angry with Mary because after all, wasn't it me that refused to give DC Hopkins a statement against Neil McMillan because *I'm* worried what he might do if he found out? I place my hand on her shoulder and tell her, "Listen, hen. It wouldn't make any difference and besides, the polis that arrived knew fine well that it wasn't me that had the drug in the shed. What's done is done, so don't worry about it; honestly."

I can see the relief in her face and she tries to smile, obviously happy that I'm not trying to persuade her to tell the police what she had seen.

"Thanks, Jimmy and I'm sorry that I didn't phone the police at the time, but I wasn't sure what to do. I'm just annoyed that bastard Paterson is getting away with it."

She must have seen my face turn pale for she put her hand over her mouth and whispered, "Did I not say, Jimmy? I went to the front window when I saw him going through the rear of the close to the front of the houses. He walked past my place and when I saw him under the street light, that's when I recognised him. It was George

Paterson. I'd know him anywhere that sod. He's the guy whose son got murdered. He used to drink in the bar in the Craigton Hotel when I worked there as a barmaid, until he got barred for noising up the customers and fighting. He's a right bad one is Paterson and I heard he runs errands for that evil bugger, Neil McMillan; him that's supposed to be dealing the drugs and lives down in Dormanside Road."

I try to smile, but she can see I'm upset and sounding a wee bit choked again she says, "I'm sorry, Jimmy," before hurrying off to catch up with her man who's standing at the church door, looking curiously at me while he waits for her.

"You okay there, Jimmy?" says the voice at my side.

I startle as I turn and see it is DC Hopkins and suddenly, I've a decision to make.

Do I tell her I know it was George Paterson who broke into my shed and left the wee bag of drugs or do I keep quiet and respect Mary Burns's secret?

If I *do* tell Hopkins then she'll demand to know how I knew it was Paterson and if I *don't* tell her, she'll probably dismiss my information as simply an allegation to get Paterson into more trouble.

I can see Mary at the top of the church stairs, her hand on her man's arm and she's staring at me talking to the detective.

I turn to Hopkins and I raise a hand and reply, "No, you're all right there, DC Hopkins. I was just thinking about the poor woman's funeral service on Tuesday and it reminded me of my own loss; my wife, Jeannie."

She stares curiously at me then with a tight smile she nods to me and wordlessly turns to rejoin her colleagues.

I take a deep breath and make my way with the rest of the latecomers into the church.

One of the church pass-keepers directs me to an empty seat in one the pews near to the back of the church, which by the way is mobbed, and I'm feeling guilty.

Why?

Well, I'm feeling guilty because last night I was prepared to murder George Paterson because he was a threat to my pal Scooby, but now I'm even more prepared to murder him because he's a threat to me too.

Father Stephen is one of the few priests I've known with the ability to empathise with his congregation. He doesn't stand up in the pulpit and lecture to the parishioners, but preaches with them. When he delivers his sermons it's as if he's speaking directly to each individual and there's no doubt in anyone's mind that he truly believes what he is saying.

With such a devoted and decent priest whom I'm privileged to call my friend, why then I wonder, am I such a bad person?

So I'm sitting here in God's house and of course I stand or kneel when everyone else stands or kneels, but my mind is full of thoughts of torturing George Paterson and I don't immediately realise that Father Stephen is calling the congregation to communion.

Those of you who are aware of the Catholic Mass will know that towards the end of the Mass, the congregation is invited to partake of the Eucharist or Holy Communion as it's also known, when they receive the small sliver of bread that symbolises the body of Christ. Those of age are also offered a sip of wine that symbolises the blood of Christ. Of course, it is those who have already made their confession and are at that time free from mortal sin, who receives these rites.

The last time I partook of communion and wine was at Jeannie's funeral and I think it is highly unlikely I will ever again receive these rites.

No, it won't be heaven for my soul, I'm afraid. I only hope my beloved Jeannie will understand that the weakness in me that led me to murder those three young people was in defence of others.

Well, two of them anyway.

I have no excuse for what I intend doing to George Paterson.

He's getting it just because he's such a nasty bugger.

"You okay there?" says the quiet voice beside me.

I turn to the man on my left who spoke, a younger man than me with two small children seated on the other side of him and a woman, his wife I think, who is also staring at me.

"Eh?"

"You were growling loudly," he whispers to me and then again asks, "Are you okay?"

Growling? I'm not just okay, I'm embarrassed and I nod. "Sorry, I was miles away."

He returns my nod and when he turns away I take the opportunity to slip out of my seat and walk towards the rear door.

Outside in the fresh air, I stand at the top of the steps and see that the detectives, six of them, are still waiting for the congregation to leave and I'm guessing they're again hoping to find some witnesses to the murders.

Funny though, I don't see DC Hopkins among them and she's not sitting in one of their cars either.

Behind me the congregation begin to exit the church and I stand to one side, hoping to catch sight of Scooby and Alice.

It's actually Alice who spots me first and she drags Scooby by this arm through the crowd to me. The first thing I notice is he's not using a stick.

"Back on your own two feet," I remark.

"Nothing gets past you, Sherlock, does it?" he quips in return.

"Ignore him, Jimmy," interrupts Alice. "He's just peed off because I forgot to get black pudding for his brunch this morning. So, if you haven't already eaten, maybe you can walk this old moaning faced bugger home and join us and that'll let me nip down to the Co-op to buy some."

I can hardly turn down one of Alice Toner's famous fry-ups now, can I?

We walk through the crowd to the pavement and watch Alice hurry off to the shops. Mindful of his injured leg, Scooby and I stroll along at a more leisurely pace.

"How are things?" I ask him, but I'm distracted by what I see across the road.

Standing on the far side of a large, red coloured four by four vehicle, I'm not sure what kind it is, I see DC Hopkins speaking with a young couple in their mid-thirties, a woman of about her own age and an older man.

The man seems vaguely familiar and as I'm watching, I almost barge into a woman who has stopped in front of me to speak with her pal.

"Mind yourself there, Jimmy," says Scooby, who then stares at me and asks, "Are you alright?"

"Oh, aye," I reply and force a smile.

"Who's that guy talking with the blonde lassie, Scooby; the detective lassie? I'm sure I know him."

Scooby slows down and stops to turn to see who I'm talking about and I kind of nudge him in the right direction.

"Oh, that's Martin Laurie. Do you not know him, Jimmy? It was his wife that was hit with the brick." He sighs and shaking his head, adds in a low voice. "Shame what happened to her. I don't know him well, but a decent enough man by al account. Raised a nice family and if I remember correctly, Alice told me something about…" he narrows his eyes as he tries to recall and shakes his head. "Nope, it's gone."

We start walking again and I take the chance to ask him, "Heard anything else about that guy Paterson? The one the polis warned about approaching you?"

"Not a peep. Alice was a bit nervous about the whole situation and phoned our Michael to ask if he'd come over for a couple of nights, but I told him not to be so stupid.

"He's back from Tenerife then?"

"Aye, and brought me a bottle of Sangria," he scoffs and shakes his head. "I ask you. All the whiskies in the world to choose from at a decent price and he brings me Sangria!"

I choke back a laugh because it's an open secret that Alice and the kids have been trying to wean their father off his generously poured nightcaps for a number of years now.

"So, I take it you're not worried about Paterson?" I probe a wee bit more.

"Not at all," he gives me a look that suggests he thinks I'm being daft then jokes, "If Paterson has the balls to come to my door then he'll need to get past Alice first!"

Or me, I silently promise.

Fortunately for our walk the rain has stopped and we get to his garden gate in Lochar Crescent without getting wet.

We're only in the house five minutes when Scooby pops into the loo and then Alice arrives, but it seems to me she's a bit flustered.

She heads straight for the kitchen and her face is chalk-white.

I follow her into the kitchen as she's taking off her coat and I ask her, "You alright, hen?"

She glances behind me to ensure Scooby isn't there listening and in a low voice, she tells me, "That guy George Paterson was down at the Co-operative buying his cheap bevy when I was there."

I get that old, familiar cold feeling in the pit of my stomach and I reply, "Did he say anything to you?"

In a voice that's trembling she says, "No, he didn't *say* anything, but he must know who I am, because he grinned at me and gave me the finger; bastard!" She bursts out.

Now, let me explain Alice to you.

A nicer, more God fearing woman you won't meet and for her to use *any* kind of expletive, well; there must be a *really* good reason.

We both hear the toilet flush and she quickly whispers, "Not a word to Scooby. Please, Jimmy. He'd go mental if he knew."

I nod and then familiar with their kitchen as I am, I start setting the table for our brunch while Alice turns to ignite the gas cooker.

My Jeannie wasn't a bad cook; not brilliant like, but she could whip up a nice meal. However, Scooby certainly won a watch when he married Alice. That woman could turn dog meat and weeds into a cordon bleu dish. Now, a simple fry-up brunch is what we had, but cooked to absolute perfection. At the end of it I just wanted to go through to their living room, sit in their comfortable couch, put my feet up and go to sleep.

That's what I would like to have done, but of course I'm a guest so refusing my offer to tidy up the dishes, we take our tea through to the living room and sit chatting.

Both Alice and Scooby are rightly proud of their children's achievements and the kids and grandkids are often the topic of their conversation. As I told you, Jeannie and I weren't blessed with children, but as their honorary uncle I don't mind hearing about the Toner's weans; not at all.

It was Scooby who mentions seeing Martin Laurie and is about to ask her something, but Alice interrupts him and asks if I will be going to the funeral ceremony?

I confirm I'll attend and give them a laugh when I tell them about my fifty pence black tie from the charity shop in Govan.

"Aye, you were always one with the eye for a bargain, Jimmy," sniggers Scooby.

"I heard that the burial will be private, family and close friends only and then they're going to a hotel in Paisley Road West later, for a private reception," says Alice. "However, Martin has also arranged for a purvey in the church hall after the Mass for those who attend the ceremony. Cup of tea, sausage rolls and sandwiches I expect," she tells us.

"What, no bar?" asks Scooby and earns himself a scowl from his wife.

"Right," I push myself to my feet, "now that I'm fed and watered I'll head up the road. Alice," she stands to see me to the door as I add, "that was a smashing breakfast, hen."

"Well, don't be a stranger, Jimmy McGrath and I'll expect you for your dinner during the week sometime."

"We'll make an arrangement on Tuesday at the church," I wink and wave cheerio to Scooby.

At the front door, I turn to her and knowing that Scooby won't hear me, I tell her, "If you see that guy Paterson hanging about outside, don't think about it, Alice. Ring the police right away. They already warned him so if he's near your house he'll get the jail. Okay?"

"Aye, okay," she smiles softly to me and pecks me on the cheek before closing the door behind me.

I'm about to chap the door to warn her to lock it, but I hear the key being turned and smiling, make my way along the garden path.

I glance across the road at the thick shrubbery and it occurs to me I should get home and have myself a midday nap because I'm expecting it will be a long night.

So, that's exactly what I do. I get home and settle myself comfortably in my favourite armchair and before I know it, I'm out for the count.

I must have needed the sleep because it's after four o'clock when I waken and only then because I hear a car horn sounding outside somewhere along the road and guess it's a taxi, because being Pollok it wouldn't occur to the driver to get out of his car and knock on the hire's door!

Already it's starting to get dark and I can see and hear the rain is beating off the living room window.

I don't immediately rise from my chair, but sit staring at the darkness through the window and wonder if I should go out tonight.

I ask myself, will George Paterson stand in the rain to watch Scooby's house?

In fact, will he go back at all or perhaps the police warning has worked and he won't again risk getting the jail.

I suppose the easiest thing to have done would be to have warned Scooby that I saw Paterson was watching the house and let him tell the police. But that would have meant the police coming to visit me and let's face it; the less contact I have with them right now, the better.

I admit it, I'm trying to convince myself that I shouldn't go out tonight, that my anger earlier in the day has subsided and yes, the old fear of being knocked about and beaten has returned.

Let's face it, I ask myself, who the hell do I think you are, Jimmy McGrath; Rambo?

I force my head back against the headrest and slowly let my breath out because I know that if I *don't* go and look for Paterson and something should happen to Scooby or even worse, to Alice; I would never, could never, forgive myself.

Of course, another option might be to try and catch Paterson in the street before he gets to Lochar Crescent, but that is too random. I mean, when I found Kylie Morrison walking in the street that was pure luck and I don't expect that luck to hold a second time.

No, if I'm going to get Paterson it will need to be by surprising him in the bushes when he least expects it.

And another thing and let's not forget it. There's over a half bottle of wine he's planked there and I'm as confident as I can be that drunkard that he is, he's not likely to forget about the bottle.

I glance again out into the growing darkness and the rain is still coming down.

Oh well, I rise from the armchair, time for a cuppa before I go.

I'm dressed again in my dark clothes with the baton tucked into the side pocket of the police trousers. One extra thing I'm taking with me is a pair of navy blue, woollen gloves because I remember how cold it was last night and I don't want the baton falling out of my hands when I need it most.

I check the tin of polish is in my pocket and decide that I won't apply it to my face until I know for definite that Paterson is hiding in the bushes. My forgetfulness last night was lucky because even though I wasn't stopped by the police, how would I explain a black face if they'd caught me walking home.

I mean, there's not a lot of tall, big built, Jamaican guys here in Pollok so any black face would undoubtedly make them suspicious, even if it was a wee, skinny guy like me.

I glance out of the kitchen window while I'm having a final slurp of tea and see the rain is still pelting down. The wall clock tells me it's now half past eight, so I guess I'd better be on my way and slip out of the kitchen door, locking it behind me. Still conscious that Mary Burns heard Paterson round my back, I'm careful not to make any noise that might attract her or anybody else's attention.

Being Sunday night, there's not a lot of folk walking the streets in the rain and as I make my way again to Lochar Crescent, I'm as sure as I can be that nobody sees me. That said, this is Pollok so you are never really sure who might be watching out of their window as you pass by. If they are, what they will see is a figure in dark clothes and wearing a dark coloured Tammy, huddled against the rain as I pass quickly pass by.

Yes, I see a couple of cars and even a police car that turns into Dormanside Road, but fortunately it's going in the opposite direction to me.

Walking along the darkened streets I find myself chuckling as I'm thinking maybe that car's the extra police patrols the detective on the television was talking about because I sure as heaven haven't seen any others. Must be budget cuts, I'm thinking.

Before I cross over Linthaugh Road to turn into Lochar Crescent I linger for a minute or so, checking both ways along the road. The last thing I want is to find myself stumbling into George Paterson or worse, him and a pal.

I satisfy myself that the road is clear and quickly make my way across the road to the fence where it's damaged and again squeeze through.

That's when it occurs to me that maybe this is where Paterson enters the park area and perhaps I could crown him with the baton when he's bent down. The only problem is that the fence isn't in good repair and there might be other bits of it damaged where he can gain access so there's nothing to say he gets in this way.

I stop and listen as I glance about me, but apart from the noise of the rain battering against the leaves, I don't hear anything else. That's probably why I can't hear the music from across the road either;

likely if the person who was playing it loudly last night has any sense, they'll have closed their window against the driving rain. You'll have guessed that by now, even though my anorak is supposed to be waterproof, I'm almost soaked through.

Something tells me that Paterson won't show tonight, but like I told you earlier, I can't afford to take the chance that he just might.

So here I am for the second night in a row; sitting in a damp bush watching with bated breath for Paterson to appear and as the time rolls by, it becomes clear that again it will be a no-show. I decide that I won't wait any longer than watching for Scooby's house lights to go out and when that happens I rise from my cramped position, stretch and slowly begin to make my way through the shrubbery to go home.

Am I wasting my time, you might ask, but to be honest I'm thinking instead that I'll be able to sleep a bit better tonight knowing that Scooby is okay, that Paterson hasn't harmed him.

Yes, I realise it's possible that Paterson might do something to the house during the night; maybe chuck a brick through the window like cowards do, but at least I know Scooby is in his bed and not out in the street and defenceless.

I'll give you a laugh and tell you that the only thing that had disturbed me happened about an hour into after I got there.

Crouching as I was, I heard a rustling sound behind me and thinking that somehow Paterson has got behind me, I almost evacuate my bowels. I didn't dare turn for fear of giving my position away and nerves shredded, I waited as quietly as I could. Then I heard something small, a rabbit or a fox maybe, slipping through the shrubbery.

Well, I almost laughed out loud with relief, I can tell you, but it didn't half give me a fright.

As I trudge home, I'm not so cold now and more alert than I was last night. I see a car headlights turning from Dormanside Road into Meiklerig Crescent and I back into a garden hedge, but the car turns out to be a taxi that passes by without the driver giving me a second look.

Breathing a sigh of relief I start walking again and before I know it, I'm at my back door and in the house. I switch on the kitchen light, but I'm too tired for a cuppa and after I put my wet clothes around the radiators, I make my weary way upstairs to my bed.

CHAPTER TWENTY

I waken stiff and aching and wishing I was still asleep, though to be honest I don't know why I'm still tired because I've had another good nights sleep. Maybe it's an age thing. Anyway, I'm guessing that the rain through the night has probably been the reason the neds have not been in the field.

Pulling the rear bedroom curtains apart I see that the rain has finally stopped and the grass in my garden looks lush and green. Now, I know I was a janny for a lot of years, but that doesn't mean to say that I like gardening. Truth be told I'm all for low maintenance myself and even from one storey up I can see that I've been neglecting the garden and there's a fair bit of weeding needing done as well as the grass is needing cut once it's dried out a bit.

And that reminds me. I promised Father Stephen I'd get back to working round about the church grounds once the weather has cleared, but I'm hoping that he'll give me a day or two respite to let the heavy rain soak away before I get stuck in.

In my dressing gown, I make my way downstairs and stick the kettle on to boil. I'm still yawning and even considering having another hour in bed because I'm a retired man, so what the heck am I doing up at seven-thirty in the morning?

But that's not my style because I've never been one for lying in my bed.

It's become a habit for me to peek out through the living room curtains to ensure that the Escort is still okay and the windows have not been panned in.

I'm a wee bit suspicious that after the phone call from Neil McMillan, there's been nothing since. It's kind of like expecting something *is* going to happen, but not knowing when, where or what.

Monday has never been my favourite day and what I usually did before all this palaver started was used Monday as my washing and cleaning day. Well, that was my usual routine, but I'm feeling a bit tired today so I'll defer it till I get back from the funeral service tomorrow.

After breakfast of toast and fried eggs I head for the shower and get dressed. It's when I hear a car door slam outside the house I peek through the bedroom window and see a CID car parked outside Billy King's house.

I head downstairs to brew a cuppa and then about fifteen minutes later I hear my doorbell ring.

When I open the door I see it's the big detective, DC Dunbar who is standing there with another man, a detective like him I'm thinking.

"Morning, Mister McGrath," Dunbar smiles at me and holding up his hands, says, "Don't be worrying now. No search warrant this time. Can I come in?"

I know he was a nice enough guy when he was here the last time, but I'm not too happy about being visited again and ask him, "Why?"

"It's about the murders. We're following up the initial door to door inquiries, just to ask if anyone has any new information."

I realise it might look a bit suspicious if I refuse, so I nod and stand to one side to let them through the door, then lead them into the living room.

"Please, sit down," I invite them and before I even know what I'm saying, my inbred courtesy kicks in and I'm asking if they'd like a cuppa.

"If you've coffee, yes please," replies Dunbar.

It takes me a couple of minutes to organise a tray of coffee and biscuits for them both and I carry the tray through and sit it on the wee side table.

"Help yourselves to milk and sugar," I say and that's when I realise my mouth is dry and I'm on edge.

As I've said before, I've never been a good liar and to be honest, being married to my Jeannie I never had any need to tell lies. That's why when I've had to speak to the police I always keep as close to the truth as possible and that way I won't need to rely on my very poor memory.

Dunbar opens his folder and fetches out a dog-eared form that I recognise as the one DC Hopkins used to take my details.

"Just a few questions," he says and like Hopkins did, asks me again who lives through the wall on either side of my house, what kind of car I drive and nothing that seems particularly probing. He's a pleasant young man and his manner is very easy going and unconsciously I'm beginning to relax.

That was my first mistake.

"So, what's your connection again with Neil McMillan?" he asks as he stares at me.

I'm caught out with that one and I stammer, "What do you mean my connection?"

"Well, isn't it him that you suspect broke into your shed and planted the bag of drugs there?"

I'm swallowing hard and trying to regain my composure, I reply, "I thought you were here to ask about the murders?"

"Aye, but you must know from the media reports, Mister McGrath that the three dead kids were connected to McMillan and with the anonymous phone call we received about drugs in your garden shed, so are you."

"So, what you're telling me is that you know McMillan was the one who broke into my shed and planted that stuff?"

"No," he takes a deep breath, "we *suspect* that is who did it."

"Other than *suspecting* he did it, you have nothing definite to connect me to him, have you?"

"We have his assault upon you."

"I explained that to your colleague…"

"Aye, DC Hopkins. We know about her visit to you when you phoned for her," he replies.

"Look," I spread my hands wide, "you guys must have a lot more information than I have about McMillan and his carrying on. All I can tell you is that yes, he ridiculed and embarrassed me outside St Convals on the pretext of something he thinks I did when he was at the primary school. If he's that twisted that he breaks into my garden shed to plant some drugs because of it, then that is the only *connection* as you call it that I have with him. Nothing else."

I can't help it, but my voice is rising because I'm getting angry and before I know it I'm on my feet. "Now, unless there is anything else," I bark at them.

Dunbar and his partner continue to sit, staring up at me.

"I'm sorry, Mister McGrath," Dunbar apologises with a half smile. "It wasn't my intention to upset you and of course you must realise that I have a duty to ask questions that sometimes put people's teeth on edge."

I'm still standing when I reply, "But how does trying to tie me in with McMillan help you ask me questions about the three murders?"

That is my second mistake because now I'm stupidly *inviting* him to question me about the murders. What a bleeding *idiot* I am!

He smiles and glances down at his paperwork and then to my surprise, changes his line of questioning.

"The car you own, the black coloured Ford Escort. According to the DVLA you registered as the owner of the vehicle back in two thousand and four, so you'll have had it, what, eleven years and a bit?"

"Aye," I'm sitting back down in my armchair as I reply, "that sounds about right, though as you'll know from your records, the car is a lot older than that."

"Indeed," he nods as he glances at the form. "Anyone insured to drive the car or maybe even driving it without insurance?"

"Nobody," I shake my head. "There are only two sets of keys and I have them both."

"So, you're telling me that at no time in the last two weeks, nobody else has driven the car other than you, Mister McGrath?"

If these questions are designed to scare me then he's doing a bleeding good job of it because obviously what is rushing through my mind is the wee lad who saw me after I murdered Kylie Morrison in Barnbeth Road.

"Nobody," I quietly reply with a shake of my head.

"The thing is, Mister McGrath, there isn't *too* many Ford Escorts knocking about these days and certainly not the age of your model. What is even more curious is that your car is only one of a very few that is locally registered and only one of three that is of a dark colour. Now isn't that strange?"

"Why would that be strange," I reply, but my blood is turning cold.

"It's strange because a vehicle similar to yours and dark coloured like yours was seen by a witness at the scene of the last murder. The murder of Kylie Morrison in Barnbeth Road," he slowly replies.

He stops speaking and I'm wondering if he's waiting for me to make some kind of admission, but I decide not to reply and just return his stare.

"Isn't that curious?" he adds.

"I suppose if you think it is, then it is," I say and even I'm wondering what the heck I mean by that.

He slowly takes a deep breath and then asks, "Would you be willing to attend an identification parade, Mister McGrath?"

I stare at him and force myself to look curious when I reply, "What, me or the car do you mean?"

He smiles and replies, "You, of course."

"I thought you said it was a car like mine that was seen by your witness? Why would you want me to stand in an identification parade?"

"I should have said the witness also saw the driver," he slowly adds and I realise both him and his partner is staring at me for my reaction. "The purpose of the parade is for elimination purposes, Mister McGrath. If you're *not* the man who was seen driving the car then we can eliminate you and your vehicle from the inquiry as suspects.

Even though my stomach is lurching and I'm working at stopping my teeth chattering, I hear myself reply, "So, you think I might be a suspect? Okay then, yes, no problem; when and where?"

I think I've taken him by surprise because his eyes open wide and turning to his partner, he nods at him and then says to me, "How about later this afternoon? Say, about two o'clock at Pollok office?"

I rise from my chair and nodding at them both as they also rise, I repeat, "Two o'clock. I'll be there."

He grins at me and adds, "Maybe better if on this visit you wore some regular clothes rather than a dressing gown and slippers, Mister McGrath."

I smile, but there's no humour in my smile and my nerves are on edge as I walk them to the door.

Through the side panel I see them drive off and I'm guessing that their visit to my neighbours wasn't to follow up on their door to door inquiries; that it was a lie. No, the visits must have been a blind and they were here for the sole purpose of persuading me to attend their identification parade.

Cunning sods!

So, I return to the living room and sit down. I'm a suspect after all and it seems that either it isn't just DC Hopkins who suspects me or what is more likely, she has shared her suspicions with the rest of her inquiry team.

Now, you might think that the few hours I have left before the two o'clock deadline I should be making some sort of plan.

Maybe you're thinking I should run away, get on my toes. Or perhaps you're thinking that if I do attend the parade, I get myself a lawyer or even that I don't attend the parade at all.

If I choose to avoid the parade or hire a lawyer, it will only make them more suspicious of me.

Am I frightened? Of course I am, but there is really nothing I can do about this situation.

My only regret is that I won't get the opportunity to deal with George Paterson before two o'clock.

I decide that I'll wear a suit for the visit to Pollok police office. If I'm to be arrested I might as well be smartly turned out.

I've also decided that when I'm picked out by the wee lad I'll make a full confession and include the bit about me seeing Paterson hiding in the bushes and watching Scooby's house. If the police are aware of this then hopefully they'll do something about it.

Now dressed with a small photograph of my Jeannie in my inner pocket, I'm sitting in the armchair and watching the clock on the mantelpiece. It's almost half past one and I've about thirty minutes of liberty left to me.

With a sigh, I rise to my feet and take one last look about my home. I've made the bed, done the washing and tidied the kitchen. I'll ask the police to give my house keys to Alice Toner. I know that Alice will see to things because I know that I'll not be returning here ever again.

I take a deep breath and locking the door behind me, make my way to the car.

The journey to the police office in Brockburn Road takes just a few minutes and I park and lock the car across the road, but some two hundred yards from the front door of the building.

My legs feel shaky and my feet are like lead as I trudge along the pavement.

Pulling open the front door there's a young woman wearing a white blouse and a blue jacket that smiles at me and asks if she can help me.

I don't tell her, but what I'm thinking is I'm in the lions den, hen and nobody can help me now. Instead, I reply, "My name's James McGrath. I'm here for an identification parade."

She obviously hasn't been told to expect a mass murderer and asking me to wait where I am, then appears a few seconds later from a door on my side of the foyer and tells me to follow her.

She leads me along a corridor and into a room that has several seats against three of the walls with a window high up on the outside wall. "You can wait in here, Mister McGrath and someone will be along shortly."

There are two other men sitting in the room. One is in late forties and a younger man with long hair heavily tattooed arms and who looks to be in his mid-twenties. The younger man is dressed in a short sleeved shirt and trousers and drumming his hands on his knees. Turning to me as I sit down he says to me, "Suspect or stand-in?"

I don't really have a clue what he's talking about and then he adds, "Are you here for the parade, pal?"

I nod and he asks again, "Suspect or stand-in?"

The older guy obviously sees the confusion in my face and sighing, explains, "We're here for the ID parade because we've got cars that the polis are interested in for the murders. What he's asking is, are you a stand-in for the parade or do you own a car like the one the cops are looking for and they think you're a suspect?"

Honest, you could have knocked me over with a feather.

"What's a stand-in?" I ask.

The young guy looks at me like I'm a doddery old idiot and by the way, he's probably correct and then replies, "A stand-in is one of the guys they pull off the street to make up the numbers, pop. They get paid for it, about a tenner or something. Isn't that right," he turns to the other guy.

"Aye, I think so," sighs the older guy who glances at his watch and sighs. "Wish to God they'd hurry up. I've the wean to collect from the nursery at half three."

We sit in silence for another five minutes or so then a detective arrives and on a clipboard he's holding, he takes a note of our details; names, addresses and asks if any of us are to be represented by a lawyer. Like me, the other two don't have a lawyer with them, though the younger guy smirks and asks, "Will I need one?"

The detective replies, "Only if you're picked out for the murder, son," and that puts the young guys gas at a low peep.

The detective then tells us his name, Detective Inspector something or other, I can't really recall because my head is up my proverbial, and then he explains to us that he will run the identification parade and asks if we have any questions?

Other than the older guy asking if he'll be finished for half three and being assured we will be, we don't have any questions.

You might find it a bit hard to believe and especially after my concern about coming here today, but I'm starting to be a wee bit hopeful. Could it be, I'm asking myself, that the CID don't suspect me in particular, but really are just chancing their arm and checking all the local drivers of cars like mine in the hope the wee lad will pick out the killer of Kylie Morrison?

Then paranoia sets in again and I'm back to thinking it's just another ruse to make me relax and then they'll catch me off guard and make me confess. I even sneakily give the other two guys in the room the once-over and I wonder if they're part of the plan to get me.

The door opens and a young and very pretty uniformed constable tells us to follow her.

She leads us to a narrow room further along the same corridor and ushers us in.

There is already six or seven men, I'm not sure exactly how many, standing in a line in the room facing a mirrored wall and they give the three of us some curious stares as we enter.

The detective who is running the parade speaks to us from behind the mirrored wall and he says, "If you gentlemen wish to take a place in the line, any place that suits you and as quick as you like, please."

I look at the other two and they shuffle into positions in the row of men and I do the same. I'm not sure, but I think I'm in position number three, but this is confirmed when the detective calls out my number as 'Number Three' and the other two as positions number five and eight.

We stand like that for about three or four minutes and already I'm feeling faint from the heat of the overhead lights. Well, that and nervous exhaustion I suppose.

Then I hear the detective call out, "Witness number one, please."

Of course, all I can see is the reflection of the men standing in a row. I look ghastly, pale and older than my sixty years.

I hear a door open and close on the other side of the mirrored wall and then the detective is telling someone, the witness I suppose, that he can look at the row of men, ask them to move, walk, talk or do anything within reason and if he sees the man he described in his statement to call out that man's number. That's the first time I realise there is numbers placed at our feet and glancing down I see an upside down number three.

I almost faint when the detective sharply calls out, "Number three. Head up, please!" I snap my head backwards and wait.

Then I hear a door opening and closing and the detective calls out, "Thank you gentlemen. If the stand-ins please exit the room to the door on their left and the other three please remain where you are." The men who are the stand-in's shuffle off through the door and I'm stood waiting with the other two.

A minute later, the detective who is running the parade enters by the door on my right with the uniformed constable behind him and says, "Thanks for your time, gentlemen. There's no need to detain you any longer. If we need anything further from you, we'll be in touch." He nods to the officer behind him and adds, "This young lady will show you out and thanks again."

With that he turns on his heel and disappears through the door.

I'm so shocked I can hardly move.

I came here today thinking I was going to be identified and arrested for at least one murder and now I'm being let go.

I work hard at not shaking and my legs feel so rubbery I'm wondering how they can hold me upright. I begin to stumble after the policewoman and the other two when the young woman says to me, "Mister McGrath, are you okay, sir"

The guy who is in his forties takes my arm and says to her, "I think he needs a seat, hen and maybe a glass of water." He turns to stare at me and adds, "Are you okay, old yin?"

But I don't hear him too clearly for his voice begins to fade as suddenly I seem unable to stand and I crash to the floor.

When I come to I'm lying on a leather bed thing in what seems to be a doctor's room. The young policewoman is sitting beside me, holding my hand and a glass of water in her other hand and my heart feels like it's going twenty to the dozen. Mind you, having a pretty young woman holding your hand does tend to make your heart race that wee bit faster. She asks me how I'm feeling and tells me I was out for just a few minutes.

My head hurts and my throat is really dry and with the lassie holding the glass I bend my head forward to sip at the water, aware my tie has been loosened and that I'm dripping some of the water onto my shirt front.

The door opens and a man comes into the room. His face is vaguely familiar and when he bends down to peer at me the police woman rises from her chair and steps back and it's then I realise the man is the detective I saw on the television who is in charge of the murder inquiries.

"Mister McGrath, how are you feeling there? I'm DCI John McManus. Can I call you Jimmy?" he smiles at me.

I nod because I don't trust myself to speak and besides that, his breath smells rotten and I'm guessing he's had tuna or some kind of fish for his lunch.

"You took a wee bad turn coming out of the parade room and bumped your noggin on the deck when you fell."

That would account for the throbbing head, I'm thinking. He's speaking a little louder than he needs to because like most people, he probably thinks us older folk are all half deaf.

"We've called the police casualty surgeon and he'll be here anytime," he tells me.

"There's no need for that," I croak and try to rise, but the room begins to spin again and gently though firmly, he puts a hand on my shoulder to prevent me from rising.

"No, just rest there the now, Jimmy. I'd like him to have a wee look at you. We can't have somebody visiting a police station at our request then collapse on us without getting them checked out and besides, you've taken that blow to the head too," he says.

The door is knocked and a young guy wearing a bright blue bow tie...aye, that's right; a bow tie, comes into the room.

"Afternoon, Doc," McManus greets him and explains, "Mister McGrath here took a wee bad turn."

"What, and there's me thinking it was another case of police brutality," replies the doctor with a wide grin, but the joke falls flat and with a tight smile, McManus turns to me and says, "Nice meeting you, Mister McGrath and I hope you feel better soon," then leaves the room.

The doctor places his bag onto a nearby table and turning towards the young policewoman, smiles, "If you please, Lorna."

The lassie takes the hint and follows the detective out of the room. "Now then," he smiles softly at me and says, "What ails you, my good man?"

The doctor takes just a few minutes to check my pulse, listen to my chest and heart, run his fingers across my bruised brow and do whatever it is that tells them there's nothing really wrong with me that getting the CID off my back won't cure.
But of course I'm jesting about the CID.
After he's completed his examination and confirming I don't take any kind of prescribed medication, he chastises me for not having a full breakfast...you see, I've lied and said I only had a cuppa...and recommends I get down the road and eat a hearty late lunch.
"Can I drive?" I ask him.
He steps as far back from me as the room will allow and holding his hand up, asks me, "How many fingers do you see?"
I stare and say, "Three."
"Aye, you're fine, Mister McGrath," he grins at me, "though I'd really prefer you didn't drive for say, at least twenty-four hours; not after having that bump to your forehead. Other than that you might look like you're sixty," then he narrows his eyes and adds, "but it seems to me with that pulse rate and your heart beating like a drum in your chest you're as fit as any man your age. Am I right?"
He seems to be a nice man so I return his grin and agree, "Aye, doctor, you're right."
He pulls open the door and summoning the young policewoman back into the room, is packing his equipment back into his case when he tells her, "Mister McGrath is fine, Lorna, so if you'd kindly inform the DCI, I see no medical reason to detain him any further. I do recommend though that he doesn't drive for twenty-four hours so you might like to arrange a lift home for him, if you please."
The policewoman smiles coyly at the doctor and I'm guessing there's a wee spark there between those two.
"If you follow me, please Mister McGrath," she says and with a further smile at the doctor, slowly leads me to the foyer at the front door and asks me to take a seat.
I say slowly because to be honest, I still don't trust my legs.
Well, as you will imagine, I'm sitting here on this plastic bum-numbing chair and my head is a jumble of thoughts.

For one I didn't expect to be getting back out of here and it causes me to think, could it be that DC Hopkins aside, the CID don't really suspect me as their killer?

If the witness who viewed the identification parade is as I think the wee lad who saw me in Barnbeth Road, he clearly was unable to identify me after all. I mean, what other witness could they have?

I'm beginning to get a little excited here for I'm also remembering that at Mass yesterday, Gina the Co-operative lassie looked straight at me too, but didn't seem to recognise me. So, could it be that my chances of evading arrest are increasing?

I'm so excited I can hardly breathe and just when I think my luck is getting so much better, the door opens and there standing with her hands on her hips is DC Hopkins.

"Well, well, Jimmy. Got away with it, eh?"

I stare at her and I can feel my face pale, but before I can reply she grins and tells me, "The boss says I've to run you back down the road and ensure you get home safely and says he doesn't want anything else to happen to you that the polis might be blamed for."

I ask about my car, how will I get it home and tell her that it's parked along the road, but she replies, "I think it will be all right there for one night, don't you?" and that settles that issue.

"Right," she sharply says, "I'm parked out at the front, so if you're ready I'll just grab my coat and handbag and meet your outside."

I'm still reeling from her comment that I 'got away with it' and can only nod at her as I stand.

In the fresh air, I'm feeling a wee bit better, though still got a pounding headache.

When a couple of minutes later she joins me at the front door, I find my voice and quietly ask her, "What do you mean? I got away with it?"

"A joke, Jimmy," she smiles at me and points to where the CID car is parked. "I was only joking."

She walks over to the CID car and holds open the passenger door, but I'm still staggered by her comment. It's completely deflated me and I'm not that excited now, but even more convinced that DC Hopkins thinks I'm the killer.

I get into the passenger seat of the CID car and we drive to Hapland Road in almost complete silence.

It's when she stops outside my door she says to me, "Will you be fit for tomorrow, then?"

"Tomorrow," I glance uncertainly at her.

"Aye, the funeral service…" she hesitates and then slowly adds, "…for Missus Laurie."

"Oh, sore head or not I'll be there to pay my respects," I reply as I nod and open the car door.

"What, not inviting me in for a cuppa?" she asks.

Now, at any other time my natural courtesy would be to say yes, but I pause then tell her, "Sorry, no. If you don't mind," and I point to my forehead, "I'm feeling a wee bit dazed and think I'll go for a lie-down."

He brow creases and she says, "You sure you're okay, Jimmy? Don't you want me to maybe contact your friend Mister Toner and tell him you've had a fall?"

"No, no, not at all," I hastily reply. "Scooby's got enough on his plate without worrying about me," I tell her.

"Oh, aye, the threat from George Paterson," she replies and then she's giving me that stare again; you know, the stare that says, 'I know what you did, Jimmy McGrath.'

What *is* it that this young woman knows or thinks she knows about me?

I return her stare then I smile.

"Have you, I mean the police, any further information about George Paterson; is he really intending to hurt my pal?"

"No, I don't think so," she replies with a shake of her head. "If what I hear about Paterson is true, he's all mouth and no bottle, but it has been circulated among the inquiry team that if Paterson is seen anywhere near your friend's home then he's to be arrested. There's no evidence that your friend killed his son, Jimmy," she shakes her head and frowning at me, leans across the seats to place her hand on my right arm. She stares meaningfully at me as she adds, "And there's certainly no reason why Paterson should be arrested, Jimmy, or for anything to happen to him."

I might be sixty and not very well educated, but I recognise a veiled a warning when I hear one and slowly nodding, I mutter back, "I agree, DC Hopkins. If Paterson doesn't go after Scooby, then you're right; there's no reason at all."

With that, I get out of the car and close the door then watch as she drives off.

"And not even a goodbye wave," I murmur to myself.

In the house I'm sitting having a cuppa and I still can't believe my good luck.

It's just gone four o'clock and I'm as excited as a wean at Christmas, but unlike a wean, my excitement is because it seems that I've got my life back and I'm not going to the jail like I thought I was; well, at least not yet.

Then again, I can't dismiss DC Hopkins suspicions either, can I? My head where I battered it off the floor in the police station is beginning to ache and when I look in the bathroom mirror, I can see it's staring to bruise too, so I help myself to a couple of Paracetamol and wash them down with a full glass of water that undoubtedly will mean at least four toilet visits.

There's that age thing again.

The phone goes and it's Scooby.

"Just thought I'd give you wee ring to confirm if you're okay for tomorrow," he says.

"Aye, I am," I reply, but don't think it's worth getting into a conversation over the phone about the identification parade or me taking a fainting fit.

After a bit of chit-chat, Scooby tells me him and Alice is staying in for the night because she's a couple of soaps to catch up with on the tele and he intends getting an early night anyway. After he hangs up I think it's about time I got my old black suit out and ironed for Missus Laurie's funeral tomorrow morning. You might not realise it, but most men of a certain age have what they call their funeral suit. The thing is when you do reach that certain age you find that you are increasingly attending funerals, so it's handy to have a dark suit, white shirt and black tie on standby.

I had just set up the ironing board in front of the television because I like to watch the TV when I'm doing my ironing, when the front doorbell rung.

Glancing at the clock, I'm wondering who's calling at five o'clock at night. Pulling the door open, I see it's my neighbour Mary Burns and she's looking a bit agitated.

"Jimmy, can I come and speak with you for a minute?"

"Aye, of course hen; come away in," I tell her and stand to one side to let her pass me. I'm about to lead her into the living room, but she stops me when she says, "No, the hallway here's okay."

"What is it, Mary? Is anything wrong?"

She's got her arms wrapped about her and biting at her lower lip and I can see she's really upset.

"Jimmy, that guy I told you about; that George Paterson. I was closing my curtains about half an hour ago and I seen him walking past our houses. I'm sure it was him," she's nodding her head.

A cold hand grips my bowels and I suggest, "Maybe he was just passing by on his way home or something."

"No," she vigorously shakes her head. "He slowed up when he was passing your house and I seen him looking in your window. Did you not see him?"

"No, I didn't."

"I'm sorry to tell you this, Jimmy; bringing this worry to your door."

I force a smile and reply, "You're okay, Mary. I'm glad you told me. I'll make sure my doors are locked tonight and if the worst comes to the worst, I've got the phone handy in case I need the polis."

"Are you sure you will you be alright on your own? I mean, you're not a young man anymore, Jimmy."

No, I think to myself; I'm a decrepit old git who's afraid of his own shadow. But that's not what I tell her, because what I say is, "Don't you be worrying about me, hen. You get yourself home and I'll see you in the morning. If Paterson's got any sense, he'll stay away from here because at the first sign of him, I'm definitely phoning the police, okay?"

I usher Mary back through the door and watch till she's safely in her own garden path and see her wave to me that she's going in her front door.

Closing my door, I lock it and when I'm back in the living room, I start my ironing. My mind's wandering though and while I had considered that it might be another wasteful night in the bushes outside Scooby's house, Mary's information has changed my mind. It sounds to me like it's another of McMillan's scare tactics and Paterson obviously knows my address seeing that he's already broken into my garden shed. I'm guessing that he has no real grudge against me other than maybe because he knows I'm Scooby's pal. In fact, I'm certain he doesn't know me at all unless he remembers me from sitting with Scooby in the pub that day when he was arrested. No, it's more likely he's acting on the instruction of Neil McMillan who probably told Paterson to walk past my house in the daylight, hoping I'd see Paterson and that would worry or frighten me.

Well, I didn't see Paterson, but McMillan's plan worked.

I *am* worried and frightened.

The thing is it's easy to be brave when you're in the safety of your own home, but like it or not, it seems Paterson has now forced my hand and I give an involuntary shudder for it seems that now I have no choice; I'm going out tonight after all, to Lochar Crescent.

CHAPTER TWENTY-ONE

I have a light dinner of a baked potato and tuna with mayonnaise because my stomach is still turning over and I don't want to chance anything too heavy.

Again it's getting dark earlier and by the time I have eaten and washed up, it's time to draw the curtains and switch the lights on. My head's beginning to throb a bit from my fall and when I again examine it in the bathroom mirror I can see that the bruising is turning a yellowy blue colour. I touch it with the tip of my fingers and can feel the swelling of blood, but I have a jar of some of Jeannie's Arnica cream that she swore by for cuts and bruises and I dab a liberal amount over the bump. I also take another two Paracetamol for the headache.

The clothes I wore last night are dry now so I change into them and ensure I have everything; the boot polish, the baton and I'm also bringing a plastic carrier bag with me in case I get the baton bloodstained.

You might wonder how I'm feeling; well, the truth is I don't really think Paterson will arrive tonight and this is a waste of time, but like I already told you, I just can't take the chance he won't show up.

Oh, do you mean how do I feel about the possibility that my plan for using the baton might not work out, that Paterson or if Paterson's with a mate, that either himself or the two of them might give me a kicking instead?

Well, I know I've been lucky so far…lucky? My God, I can't have been more lucky that if I'd won the lottery. Three murders and an identification parade where the witness didn't pick me out is a lot more than just lucky. It's downright incredible!

I'm shaking my head because I know that by going out tonight I'm pushing my luck to the extreme.

But as I said, I've no real choice, have I?

I peek through the living room curtains, but though the rain is off for the minute, the road is glistening wet and reflecting the overhead street lights. I can see somebody at Billy King's new van and as I watch I realise it is Billy himself. He steps away from the van and he must have clicked a button or something because the van's indicator lights flash and the van's horn sounds, but just for a few seconds before Billy switches them off again.

Obviously after having his last van torched, he's fitted this new van with an alarm system.

I watch him go into his garden path then lose sight of him.

Nothing else moves in the road and I think as it has gone eight o'clock, it's about the right time to leave through the kitchen door. I pull on my woollen Tammy and just as I did the last two nights, leave a light and the television on in the living room so if anyone comes they'll think I'm in, but I'm just not answering the door. Well, that's the plan anyway.

I sneak down the path behind the houses and I'm mindful of not making a noise because I'm thinking that my neighbour Mary Burns might be half listening if she thinks George Paterson might try to break into my shed again.

At the end of the common path I make my way into Hapland Avenue and start briskly walking towards Lochar Crescent. Just my luck that it starts to rain so I turn the anorak collar up, but then think maybe the rain is a good thing; maybe it will keep Paterson away.

It's as I'm crossing the Linthaugh Road I see the blue flashing light and hear the siren coming down the road towards me and I almost panic. I'm preparing my bandy wee legs to make a run for it when I see that it's not the police, but an ambulance.

Talk about relieved!

I almost *relieved* myself in my underpants!

Anyway, that wee scare over, I make my way towards the same gap in the fence and start to quietly sneak through the shrubbery; well, as quietly as the jaggy and clinging bushes will allow, I mean.

I get to the place where I've sat for the last two nights and see that Scooby's lights are on and…

I hear a cough from close by; a hacking, smokers cough.

I tense up and realising my hands are shaking, I stuff them into my anorak pocket and slowly crouch down.

I can hear somebody coming through the bushes towards me, but they're not like me; they're not trying to be quiet.

It sounds like two men who are talking in low voices.

Is it the polis, I'm wondering? Have they realised what I'm up to? No, it can't be. They would send their dogs in, not come through the bushes themselves and another thing; they'd probably use torches too.

They're getting closer and I force my body not to shake. I hear one of the voices say, "Fucking bushes!" then somebody replies, but I can't quite make out what's been said.

I'm now sure it's George Paterson and he's got somebody with him. I'm crouching and trying to make myself as small as possible and I'm wondering if I should make a run for it, but how far will I get in the thick shrubbery and besides, what if they chase me? Where in the park could I run to?

But that's not why I'm here, I force myself to remember. I'm not here to run *from* Paterson. I'm here to use the baton on him.

The voices become darkened figures as they approach the place where I think they've previously stood and to my relief, they stop just there, about ten feet away from me.

"Where's that bottle?" I hear one figure mutter and I know from his voice that it's Paterson. They're not being quiet at all and I realise they don't suspect that there might be anyone else here in the bushes with them.

The other figure bends down and I hear what sounds like him falling against a bush for he cries out loudly, "Aw, shite! Fuck this, Geo, I'm not standing here in the rain in the hope that guy comes out his house. I'm out of here!"

"Give it ten minutes, for fucks sake!" Paterson replies and I see what looks like his silhouette raising the bottle to his lips.

"Well, no more than ten minutes then," the other guy reluctantly responds and then says, "Give me a mouthful of that," then he too raises the bottle to his lips.

I'm hardly breathing, I'm that scared.

The other guy then laughs, but not with humour and I hear him ask, "Why don't we just punt the bastards windows in?"

"No!" Paterson forcefully replies. "He killed my Alex. I want to wait till he leaves his house and get him and put the boot in! He's fucking getting it!"

"You'll not get near him," the other guy's slurred voice replies. "The polis warned you off, you stupid bastard! Why don't you get him when he's on his own during the day?"

"And how am I supposed to know where he'll be?" responds Paterson, his own slurred voice dripping with sarcasm.

"How the fuck do I know that? But what I do know is that we'll not get him at this time of night standing in the pissing rain in these fucking bushes!" barks his pal.

"He's got to come out sometime," snarls Paterson and that's when I realise that they're both really drunk; not steaming, falling about drunk, but certainly drunk.

Now, you're wondering that knowing this why don't I take advantage of them being drunk and wade right in and batter the two of them about their evil heads?

Well, simply put, I was too scared; too scared to even remember to use the boot polish I had in my pocket, too scared to even think about tackling them and too bleeding scared to even move.

I just sit here like a frightened wean and it doesn't help that I really, *really* need to pee.

Of course, I tell myself that if I *did* attack them I wouldn't be able to properly swing the baton because of the thick shrubbery, but we both know that's just my excuse for being a coward.

I'm that busy castigating myself that I hardly notice they're both moving away from my position. I can hear Paterson effing and blinding as he follows the other guy to the gap in the fence where they must have entered the park.

I'm straining to listen for them, but after a few minutes I don't hear anything other than the sound of traffic that is travelling several hundred yards away on the Corkerhill Road.

I breathe a sigh of relief and my whole body is shaking.

Once again the night has been a waste of time.

Well, not really a waste of time because now I know for certain that Paterson does intend hurting Scooby.

I stand up and still shaking, my whole body aches from the tension of crouching while I listened to them.

I wait for, I don't know; about ten minutes I think it is before I make my way to the gap in the fence.

Before I poke my head through though, I have a good, long look to make sure they're gone and not waiting for me.

At last I'm satisfied they're away and I squeeze through the gap.

No, I'm not proud of myself. Three days I waited for the opportunity to batter Paterson on the head and when I do get the chance, I completely funk it.

God, I wish I was a braver man.

With one eye open for any sign of them, I start to walk back towards the house and only hope that nothing happens to Scooby before I find the guts to deal with Paterson.

Safely back in the house I'm completely deflated. I don't *really* need to know your opinion of me because nothing could make me feel any worse than I do right now.

I sit for, I dunno, maybe half an hour nursing a cuppa before I wearily go to bed.

The bedside clock in the back bedroom says eleven o'clock and whether the gang arrive tonight or not, I don't really care.

Tuesday morning and it is still raining. Not heavily, but enough to warrant a raincoat and a brolly.

Surprisingly, I slept like a log and waken reasonably fresh; feeling a bit guilty of course, but that's just my conscience telling me I'm a useless bugger.

I wish I was more of a man.

It's Missus Laurie's funeral ceremony this morning and I've arranged to meet Scooby and Alice on the pavement opposite the church gates

I get dressed, but I've no appetite and so other than a cuppa, I leave the house with an empty stomach.

There are a few people walking on Hapland Road towards the church, most with their heads bowed against the rain or tucked under a brolly.

I get there to find that Scooby and Alice have already arrived there and waiting for me. With Alice between us taking our arms, we cross the road and enter the church where Father Stephen is patiently waiting for the arrival of the cortege.

I'm not really surprised to find that the church is almost full with the front three or four pews left empty for attending family members. Scooby, Alice and I find seats about half way down the aisle and squeeze past a couple of stout women, whose snooty attitude would make you think they owned the bleeding pews.

I don't recognise the women and I'm thinking they're, what is it the radio reporters call them again? Oh, aye, rubber-necks; people who have attended the ceremony simply to do their nosey. I glance about me and sure enough, while I recognise quite a lot of the parishioners and believe me, I don't know them all, there's a lot that just don't seem to be local.

Alice nudges me with her elbow and I follow her stare to the centre aisle where I see a number of people wearing black making their way down to the front pews.

Curiously, I see DC Hopkins who is also wearing a black, skirted suit and small, black hat, among them and when I whisper to Alice, "She's a detective."

Alice nods that she's seen Hopkins and whispers back, "She's probably one of them family polis. You know the police officer that's assigned to the family and who supports them during a murder. You see them sitting with the family at the table when it's a news conference on the tele."

I nod because I know what Alice is talking about. "I think they're called family liaison officers."

"That's them," she whispers.

A few minutes later she again she digs me in the ribs and I see a frail man, Missus Laurie's husband Martin, being helped along the centre aisle by two younger men who I take to be his sons.

Once he has passed by and is at the front pew, like a ripple the congregation all stand as we become aware that preceded by Father Stephen and two mass servers, the coffin is carried into the church.

I won't go into details about the ceremony because like I told you a lot earlier, it still hurts because it reminds me of my Jeannie's own funeral service.

Before I know it, an hour has passed and we're standing while the coffin is carried from the church and followed by the family.

Unsupported this time, Mister Laurie bears himself well, though a number of the family, both male and female shed tears as they follow on.

I see DC Hopkins supporting an elderly woman who walks with a stick and I wonder what training the detective must have received for such a challenging job.

After the family have left the church, the congregation begin to filter out through the main and side doors and with Scooby and Alice, I decide that after all I will go to the purvey in the church hall.

The place is mobbed and there's a bit of a slow meander through the double doors as the pass-keepers help people crowd into the hall, but at last we're in and we find a table that is already almost fully seated.

Alice heads off to fetch Scooby and me a cup of tea and a few minutes later, arrives back with a tray upon which rests three cups and saucers and two paper plates of sausage rolls and sandwiches.

Suddenly I realise I'm ravenous and I've swallowed a sausage roll and three egg sandwiches before I realise that Scooby and Alice are staring at me.

"Not had your breakfast then, Jimmy," Alice shakes her head at me.

"Eh, no," I shamefacedly admit and then I grin because Scooby's grinning too and his grin is infectious.

"You'll be coming back with us then for some lunch," says Alice in her quiet way that that I've learned not to argue with.

"And maybe a dram too," adds Scooby, knowing fine well I don't touch whisky these days.

"Aye, that'll be right," Alice quietly rebukes him as she sips at her tea.

I see the hall is full and I recognise most of the people, so obviously there is nothing in here now to interest the nosey rubberneckers, as I call them.

Alice is well known in the church social circle and she's nodding and chatting to several people at our table and the one next to us. It's during her chat that I hear someone tell her that the police are no nearer finding the bugger that threw the brick and killed Missus Laurie. But then a fat, baldy man with a tattoo on his neck, who I've never seen before and is sat at the next table, taps his forefinger against the side of his nose and interrupts with a faint air of superiority, "The polis will get him, never fear about that. These bastards, excuse my language missus, have got no loyalty to each other and somebody will grass him up, you can bank on that."

I know he's only guessing, but he puts it out like he's got some sort of inside knowledge about the police inquiry. Personally, I think he's just a blowhard.

But then he says, "They think these murders of the teenage bastards, excuse my language again, missus, is some sort of revenge for Theresa Laurie being killed."

I can't help myself and before I realise it, my teeth are bared and I'm asking him, "How do you know that? I mean, who told you this or are you just making it up, you fat git!"

Suddenly, there's a deathly silence surrounding me. The fat man's face has gone crimson and I'm aware of Alice's restraining hand on my arm.

"Who the fuck…" he starts to reply and is rising off his seat when Scooby interrupts and says, "I think we should all calm down here. Come on now, this is a wake. Let's not be having any trouble, eh?"

The fat man is almost fully rose from his seat and to my shocked surprise so am I.

So there we are, two elderly idiots squaring up to each other in a church hall at a murdered woman's wake. Honestly, it's typical of Glasgow weddings and funerals. There's always somebody spoiling for a fight, but never in a thousand years would I ever suspected it would be me.

The next thing I know Scooby is standing up between us and with Alice at his side, is trying to calm things down while a couple of guys with the fat man are thankfully holding him back.

Now I'm asking myself, why did I provoke this between me and the fat man? The only thing I can think of is that I'm still so ashamed of my cowardice last night that I need to lash out at somebody, even if it means me taking a hiding, because let's face it; a fighter I most definitely am not!

Anyway, my stupidity cools a lot quicker than the fat man's rage and humbled now by Alice's anger at me, I sit down.

A minute later the fat man also sits down and with some reluctance on his part, is persuaded to shake my hand and forget about the near fistfight we almost had.

I say fistfight, but we both know that he would likely have battered me senseless.

For the next five minutes or so that we're sitting there, we politely ignore each other then Scooby nods to Alice and with the two of them, I leave the hall and walk with them to the front doors.

While we're walking away from the hall, to their credit neither Scooby nor Alice makes any reference to the near fight I had in the hall though I'm certain they must have been wondering what got into me. I think maybe they've decided that I'm a bit stressed, that the funeral reminded me of Jeannie's ceremony and they're letting it go at that.

The rain's taking a break and it's as we're crossing from Hapland Road into Linthaugh Road that we see George Paterson and two cronies, each carrying a plastic carrier bag, walking in Linthaugh Terrace from the roundabout past the police caravan. Fortunately, there is a uniformed cop and two detectives standing outside the caravan talking who watch them as they pass by, so Paterson can't shout any abuse towards us, but with his back to the police officers, he sees Scooby and makes a cutting motion across his own throat. The message is clear. He's out to get my pal.

Alice is enraged and right there and then wants to challenge Paterson; verbally of course, not physically. However, with Scooby on one side and me on the other we hustle her away towards Lochar Crescent, with Scooby telling her, "Just ignore the idiot, hen. He's only doing that to impress his pals."

Waking along Linthaugh Road, I sneak a couple of glances behind us, but Paterson must have cut into Hapland Road, for there's no sign of him.

It's almost one o'clock and now, sat in the Toner's kitchen waiting for an Alice Toner fry-up, Scooby grins and in a falsetto voice that I presume is supposed to parody me, says, "Or are you just making it up, you fat git?" then laughs uproariously.

Even Alice smiles as she turns from the cooker and with a fish slice in her hand, waves it at me and asks, "What the hell were you thinking, Jimmy McGrath? I've never in all the years we've known each other heard you raise your voice to another human being. What got into you?"

Now, I could have said it was a late response to my shameful cowardice from last night when I was supposed to be protecting your husband from that bugger George Paterson, but instead I weakly grin and shrug my shoulders.

"The emotion of the moment," says Scooby, now the wise sage. "It was the funeral service. You were probably wrapped up in your thoughts about Jeannie's funeral and then that stupid git opened his mouth, trying to tie in Theresa Laurie's murder with the murders of they three tearaways; it probably just got to you, Jimmy."

"Aye, you're probably right," I nod, grateful for his intervention.

Alice lays a steaming hot plate full of food in front of me and for the next five minutes as I tuck in, everything else goes on the back burner.

After Alice again refuses my offer to help her clear the table and wash up, I'm sitting in the living room with Scooby chewing the fat when Alice brings us a coffee each.

"It wasn't a bad send-off, the number of people at the church I mean," says Scooby.

"Aye, but quite a lot of folk there I didn't recognise," comments Alice.

"I thought they were what the radio traffic lassie calls rubbernecker's, you know, the morons that stop to look at accident's. That kind of people, you know?"

"What, just there to do their nosey, like?"

I nod and Alice purses her lips. "Takes all sorts," she wryly comments with a shake of her head.

Then the elephant in the room gets raised.

"What about that nutcase, Paterson? Should we phone the police about him?" asks Alice and it's clear to me from the expression on her face that she's worried.

"I wouldn't bother about him," scoffs Scooby with a shake of his head. "The guy's just a nutter..."

"Aye," she quickly interrupts and sits meaningfully forward in her chair, "but a nutter that might try to hurt you! I really think you should phone the police and tell them what he did."

He stares at her through narrow eyes. "But he didn't really *do* anything, Alice. All he did was..."

"Pretend to cut your throat!"

"No, he didn't," Scooby shakes his head. "He pretended to cut his *own* throat. How the hell would I explain that to the polis as a threat to me? Tell me?"

She sits back, her arms folded in indignation.

I agree with her, but hold my tongue. I don't think it is for me to volunteer my opinion unless I'm asked.

But of course, then I'm asked.

"What do you think, Jimmy?" she says.

I take a deep breath and hating myself for agreeing with Scooby, tell her, "He's right. From what you told me, Paterson has been warned off approaching you and clearly, he didn't do that today. In fact, if you think about it he's got three police officers that were standing outside their murder caravan when he passed them by who would confirm he *didn't* approach you. As for the throat cutting thing, yes; we *know* that was meant to intimidate Scooby, but try proving that in a court. All he would say was he was scratching his neck or something like that."

"And by the way, I am *not* intimidated by that clown," grunted Scooby.

Alice knew she was losing the argument and sighing, said, "Well, can we at least tell that nice young officer, eh…"

"Craig Wallace," I suggest.

"Aye, him; so can't we at least tell *him* about today?"

Scooby looks at me and I give him the slightest of nods and he replies, "I'll give him a phone and let him know. Will that settle your mind, hen?"

Alice gives a weary nod and that ends that conversation, but not before I realise how upset she is and it worries me.

Of course, this is the ideal time for me to tell them about Paterson watching their house, but cowardly me just doesn't have the bottle to own up because I know it would only lead to questions that I am not prepared to answer; not to anyone, let alone my best friends.

Admit to them that their lifetime pal Jimmy is a murderer?

My God, they'd never again speak to me and that I promise you is worse than keeping them in the dark.

I finish my coffee and stand to go when Alice jumps to her feet and tries to persuade me to phone for a taxi. I'm about to laugh because really, even though it's still raining a wee bit, I'm only ten minutes walk away before I realise she's worried about me being out there with Paterson on the loose.

I persuade her that I'll be all right, that it's still light outside and besides, as far as I know, I cheerfully lie to her face, Paterson doesn't even know me.

Still, her warning is enough to give me the heebie-jeebies and I as step out from their house, my eyes are everywhere.

Fortunately, there's no sign of Paterson, but it occurs to me that he might be across the road watching from the bushes so instead of turning left and taking the shortest route home, I turn right. Outside the garden gate I turn to wave and I see Alice is puzzled so I call out, "I need to walk off that big lunch, hen."

She nods, but I can see she's still suspicious and then she shouts after me, "Phone me to let me know you're home safe, okay?"

I wave in acknowledgement then quickly hurry along the road.

I'm in Hapland Road now and about to pass by St Convals gates when a big, black coloured Co-op funeral car stops at the gates and I see that it's carrying Father Stephen who is returning from the funeral.

The driver hurries out with a brolly, but Father Stephen waves him away then seeing me, calls out, "Jimmy. Have you got a minute?"

So here's the two of us standing in the rain and he's asking me if I'm all right, is there anything wrong?

I'm puzzled and I ask why when he says to me, "One of the mourners, a young lassie; I think she's a detective. She was asking if I know you. Of course I know Jimmy McGrath, I told her.

Everybody in the parish knows Jimmy. A decent wee man if ever there was one."

I feel my blood run cold and ask, "Was her name Hopkins, DC Hopkins?"

He shakes his head and replies, "Sorry, I didn't get her name. She's blonde, a nice looking lassie, maybe in her early thirties, a bit taller than you. Is she a friend, then?"

"No, not really," I hear myself reply and then he tells me, "She seems to be interested in you, what kind of man you are. Your comings and going like. Jimmy, is there something I should know?" then he smiles. "I mean, if you can't trust your parish priest…"

"No, it's nothing like that Father," I hurriedly assure him. "DC Hopkins is one of the inquiry officers investigating the murders of they three…" I'm about to say wee shites, but I catch myself and instead, say "…unfortunate teenagers. She's spoken to me about my car, but I attended at her office and stood in an identification parade with a number of other car owners and I was cleared from their inquiry."

Well, I *hope* I was cleared, I'm thinking now.

He seems puzzled and says, "She's one of the murder inquiry team you say? Oh, really? I thought…" but he's interrupted by a pass keeper who calls out from the vestibule, "Father Stephen, that's us cleared away and we're about to lock up here."

"Okay, I'll be right with you," then turns to me and smiling, says, "Sorry to have kept you back in this foul weather, Jimmy. If that polis woman asks me again about you, I'll tell her I heard you ran away to Australia."

I smile, but without humour as I watch him jog into the vestibule and I'm thinking that apparently these days, you no longer need a criminal conviction to get into Australia.

I start walking again, but with a shiver running down my spine for unless I'm mistaken, then that as far as DC Hopkins is concerned I'm still her number one suspect.

It seems the heavy meal I enjoyed at the Toner's is working its magic and relaxed me so much that not even my worries about DC Hopkins can prevent me from dozing in my favourite armchair. Burping, I again taste the fry-up and decide it's time I wash my face and brush my teeth.

The rain's stopped beating against the windows and it seems to me there with the clouds lying so low, there will be no let up this evening. However, regardless of what the weather is going to be, after that encounter with George Paterson today it's made me even more determined to get him before he gets Scooby.

If only this time I have the nerve to follow this through, I'm thinking.

I decide to go out a bit earlier than before because last night I was only in the park literally minutes before Paterson turned up with his pal and tonight there is no way I want him to be in there waiting for me.

Conscious of the time, I hurriedly dress in the old, police trousers and heavy boots and grabbing the baton from its hiding place under the sink, stuff it into the special pocket. Then it's on with my anorak and I grab the woollen Tammy from the radiator and I'm actually racing, though I don't realise it because I'm pulling the Tammy down onto my head and cringing when I pull it against my bruise. It's only when I'm walking in Hapland Avenue that I realise I've been in that much of a hurry to get out of the house that I've forgotten not just the tin of black boot polish, but a plastic bag to carry the baton in if I should get bloodstained.

Bugger it I think, but I'm worried about Paterson getting into the bushes before me so I'm not going back to the house now.

I trudge along Hapland Avenue and it starts to rain again and to be honest, I'm not really thinking what I'm doing.

I should be paying more attention to what's happening round about me and if I had been, I would have not have been startled by the dark coloured car that slowly passes by me and then stops about twenty feet in front of me. I slow down and stand still as I stare at the car.

At first I'm thinking it is a Ford Escort just like mine, but though the shape is similar, it's not the same make and then I realise it's one of them foreign cars; a Japanese car I think.

The driver, a big guy I see, gets out of the car and walks round the front of it in front of the headlights and when he steps onto the pavement and faces me, my blood runs cold.

It's Neil McMillan and he's leering at me.

My legs feel weak and I know that I can't run, let alone outrun him. In the light of the street lamps I see he's smiling as he walks towards me, but not a smile that says he's pleased to see me. No, he's smiling because it's dark and I'm alone and vulnerable.

He's wearing a long, dark overcoat and dark jeans and if I thought he was big and scary when I met him outside St Convals church that day, let me tell you he is even more so in the half light of the darkened street. In fact he looks not just big, but *huge* and very, very menacing.

It occurs to me to shout for help, but I know that the steady patter of the falling rain and the high hedgerow that borders the garden beside me and the pavement will mask any sound. Besides that, I can't get any spit and my tongue is rattling in my mouth.

He's a few feet from me now with his hands on his massive hips, the rain plastering his hair to his head. He stops and standing still, grins down at me.

It's an evil grin and without any doubt in my mind, I know he's going to hurt me.

"Well, well, well, janny. I *thought* it was you when I saw your bandy wee legs. Fancy meeting you here and all by yourself, eh?"

He licks at his lower lip and turns his head back and forth as he takes a glance about us, but there's nobody in the street and then his eyes bore a hole in my forehead.

"What…what…what do you want?" I manage to gasp, but he just sniggers and with another quick glance around him, leans forward and completely takes me by surprise when he reaches out with his right hand and grabs me by the throat, his fingers tightening on my windpipe.

I'm so shocked at how quick he is that all I can think about is to reach up with both my hands to ease his grip because he's choking me and I wish to God I had gone for that last pee before I left the house. I can't help myself and I can't stop myself and release my bladder and I feel the warmth of my pee in my trousers. Mind you, I'm past worrying about humiliation and because I'm already wet, I don't think he notices.

"You fucking little scrotum!" he hisses at me. "You thought you were the bees-knees because you run the fucking primary school football team," he snarls. "A big man among the wee weans, you thought you were, eh?"

Now, it might be occurring to you that I should say something brave here, be a man as it where. Well, that's easy for you to think that, but right now, my trouser legs soaking with my own urine, the last thing I want to do is - please pardon the pun – piss this guy off.

Besides I'm starting to find it hard to breathe let alone speak because now he's half turned me and got me pushed against the unforgiving hedgerow at my back to give him more leverage. My feet are kind of lifted off the pavement and now he's using both hands to strangle me.

I'm gasping for breath and panicky because it feels as though my eyes are about to pop from my head when I remember the baton. I'm not being brave here; no, far from it. It's more of a survival instinct I think.

I force my right hand away from trying to make him relinquish his grip on my throat and grab at the trouser pocket holding the baton. With a great effort and believe me, it *was* a great effort because remember, my feet are off the ground and my legs are swinging as he strangles me. I get the baton out of the pocket and holding it in my shaking hands, I feebly swing it at him.

Feeble is the word. It kind of bounces off his arm and he turns his head to see what I'm doing, then he grins and as though I'm hearing him through a fluffy pillow, he says, "What the *fuck* have you got there, you skinny wee bastard?"

He lets his left hand go from my throat and easily snatches the baton from my hand. Snatches? God, I was seconds away from dropping it because I'm starting to feel faint from the lack of oxygen. The only advantage I have now is that as he's released one hand I can breathe a little easier, but that's short-lived because terrified, I stare at him and watch as he lifts his hand back and swings the baton above his head.

I'm in a state of terror now because I know what's coming next. Well, you'll have heard stories about how your life flashes in front of you and all that guff, well, let me assure you, guff it is. I think I hear a high pitched scream and realising it is me, I prepare to die. Above my scream I hear someone else screaming too, but it's not me and it don't *think* it's him and frankly, I don't really care who it is because it's just then Neil McMillan swings down with all his strength and murders me with my own baton.

CHAPTER TWENTY-TWO

Okay then, you'll probably realise that no, I'm not dead.

Me, I don't really know where I am and I'm afraid to open my eyes in case I am in...well, you know, where I expect to be.

"Jimmy? Jimmy? Can you open your eyes for me?"

I don't want to open my eyes. I don't want to see where I am. I don't want to...

"Jimmy!" the voice, it's a young woman's voice, is more persistent now.

I grit my teeth and try to open my eyes, but they feel gummed shut.

"Here, try this," says the voice and I feel something, a straw I think it is, being forced between my lips. That's when I realise how thirsty I am and I instinctively gulp at the water coming through the straw and I feel it dribble down my chin. I choke a bit and that sets me off coughing.

"There, there, that's better, eh?"

The voice is speaking to me like I'm a wean.

The straw is again pushed between my lips and I'm being urged to, "…take another sip, but slowly this time."

Again I choke a little and I cough. A hand is slipped behind my neck and my head is gently forced upwards.

"There, there now. Take it easy. We don't want to overdo it, do we?"

I'm a little irate and wondering whose the 'we' here, because I'm the one that's choking.

"Can you open your eyes for me, Jimmy?" the voice asks again. A young woman I think.

Maybe I'm not in hell after all and I take a deep breath and slowly do as I'm asked.

The light hurts and I squint up to see a smiling face.

The lassie, well, young woman really, is smiling down at me and she's dark haired wearing and a blue top and I'm confused.

I'm supposed to be dead.

Where the heck am I?

There's a beeping noise coming from somewhere. The woman, yes, okay, I've realised she's a nurse, the nurse stands up just out of my sight and then the beeping stops.

"Bloody machines," I hear her mutter.

She bends down again and in her hand she's holding one of them wee torches, a pencil torch I think they're called and shines it into my eyes.

I'm blinking and she's smiling.

"Well, hello there Jimmy," she says and tells me her name is Angela. Angela. Angel, I'm thinking.

I try to speak, but all I can manage is a croaking sound because my throat is sore, my head is aching and oh, I'm a bit embarrassed to admit this but my willie is uncomfortable too.

"Do you know where you are, Jimmy?" the angel asks me.

Like I say, I'm finding it hard to speak so as slowly as I can I shake my sore head.

"You're in ward sixty-four of the Southern General Hospital, Jimmy. Now," she pats my cheek, "just lie there sweetheart and I'll fetch the doctor. She'll want to know you're awake, okay?"

Aye, like I'm in any state to go anywhere, I'm thinking.

The nurse disappears from my view and I hear a door slowly swishing closed.

A couple of minutes pass and then I hear the door swish open and a young blonde lassie with a stethoscope round her neck is bending over and peering down at me.

"Aye, you're right, Angela. He seems to be consciously aware," I hear her say and then she smiles at me and asks, "Jimmy, can you understand me?"

I manage a wee smile and a slight nod of my head.

"Good. I'm going to have a wee look in your eyes with a torch," she says and I'm grateful that at least this time I'm getting a warning. The bright light causes me to flinch and the lassie, the doctor I should say, seems happy with my reaction to the light. Then I hear her tell the nurse, "Page Mister Colquhoun please, Angela."

Anyway, cutting a long story short, about ten minutes later while the other two are probing and poking at me this baldy guy about my age arrives and he's obviously the boss. Bending over me, he more or less confirms the other two's diagnosis that I'm alive. Alive and conscious, I should say.

This guy Colquhoun turns out to be a nice man and with both hands resting on the side of my bed, he leans over me and in the quietest of voices tells me that four days earlier…What! Four days? …I'd been subjected to a violent attack, that my skull was fractured and that I had to have an operation, something about bleeding on the brain. Tell me something I *don't* know I'm thinking, but of course I just weakly smile at him that I understand.

According to him I've had an operation to reduce swelling on the brain where I was struck with a weapon.

Now, we don't need to know what kind of weapon, do we?

He tells me that the operation was a success and there will be a little discomfort 'down below' because I've a catheter fitted and if the day goes well and I respond as he expects, he'll recommend that the physiotherapist has me up on my feet by tomorrow.

Before he goes, Mister Colquhoun pats me on the shoulder and tells me that I'm a lucky man and he'll be back to see me tomorrow.

So, that's you more or less up to date with what happened to me.

It's later that day, well, late afternoon actually, I'm sitting up in bed with my head swathed in bandages, the door is pushed open and in they come.

No, not somebody I'm pleased to see. It's the police; DCI McManus and another detective that I recognise as the officer who conducted the identification parade at Pollok police office.

The two of them look grim faced and I hear a nurse behind them say, "No more than ten minutes, please gentlemen," before she pulls the door closed and leaves me to their tender mercies.

"Mister McGrath," says McManus as he pulls up a chair and sits heavily down. The other detective remains standing at the foot of the bed.

This is it, then. They're going to arrest me and just like the tele, I'll have a policeman posted outside my door in case I try to shimmy down the eight storeys to the ground and run off.

Run off? With this bleeding catheter attached to my willie, I won't be going anywhere; stand on me regarding that.

"How are you feeling?" McManus asks and I notice that at least his breath smells a wee bit fresher.

I consider moaning and groaning a bit and maybe provoke a bit of sympathy, but one look at his hard face and I know that's not going to work. Instead I decide to brazen it out and reply, "As well as any man my age that has been battered on the head with a big stick."

"Ah, so you know how you came to be here?"

"Aye, things are a wee bit fuzzy, but the doctor Mister Colquhoun told me I had been assaulted."

I catch McManus briefly glance at his pal when he replies, "Do you recall anything at all about the circumstances of the assault that was perpetrated upon you?"

I've already decided to play that old chestnut, the loss of memory so I shake my head and tell him "Honestly, no. I'm really, really trying, but no. I can't recall anything."

Does he believe me? I don't know for his face is too hard to read. He sighs and asks me, "What were you doing out at that time of night in the rain and where were you going?"

Now, I've just told him that I can't recall anything, so is this a trick question?

"Where was I?"

"Walking in Hapland Avenue about eight o'clock on Tuesday night. Three nights ago you were walking in the road when you met with someone. A fight ensued and you came off worse. You suffered a life threatening injury and it was only the skill of the surgeon, Mister Colquhoun, who saved you. Doesn't anything come back to you at all?"

"Sorry," I'm shaking my head. "I don't remember. Hapland Avenue? I was probably going to visit my pal, Scooby…I mean, Michael Toner. He lives in Lochar Crescent." I screw my eyes as though I'm really trying to remember and then I add, "I didn't have my motor. It was still up in Brockburn Road near to the polis station. But that's about it. Sorry."

I must have seemed to be pretty credible for he shakes his head and sighs.

The other detective says, "Maybe you'd better just tell him, boss. We have enough evidence anyway."

Here we go. I'm about to be charged. Well, if they give me the opportunity, I'm just going to tell them everything and even about Neil McMillan trying to kill me.

I brace myself for the bad news when McManus says, "We've arrested a man called Neil McMillan for attempting to murder you, Mister McGrath," then half smiles and then adds, "Can I call you Jimmy?"

I nod and my stomach lurches, because there's something about his change of attitude that takes me by surprise.

"I gather that McMillan is known to you, Jimmy, and he's had it in for you for some time now. Is that correct?"

"Aye, he is known to me and that's correct." I slowly reply. "He's threatened me and then my garden shed was broken into and …"

But I get no further, for McManus is himself nodding and then tells me, "We know about that. Your neighbour Mary Burns heard about you being assaulted and came to us with a wee story about a man called George Paterson. Apparently she saw him round your back the night your garden shed was broken into and the drugs were left there to implicate you. Missus Burns has given us a statement and you might be pleased to know Paterson was arrested and has confessed. As well as that, we discovered Paterson's fingerprints on the inside of the plastic bag so given that he has a number of former convictions for the Misuse of Drugs Act, he's going to be with us for quite a wee while. He also admitted he was instructed to do this by his boss, Neil McMillan. In addition, our Forensic people have matched the drugs found in your shed to an extremely large batch of cocaine that we recovered in a safe house in the Mosspark area that is owned and leased by McMillan. In plea of mitigation, the tenant of that house has admitted she was threatened to hold the drugs for McMillan, but the court will decide whether that's true or not."

My stomach lurches again and "You mean he might get out if the court doesn't believe the woman?"

McManus gives me a tight smile and replies, "Let's talk about the murders of Alex Paterson, Calum Black and Kylie Morrison. You of course know who I mean, Jimmy?"

I slowly nod.

"Well, stop me if I'm going too fast for you here, Jimmy. Let's begin by saying that our investigation that commenced with the murder of Alex Paterson quickly established that McMillan was running a tightly knit group of teenagers in the area, most of whom were involved in the importation and distribution of Class A and class B drugs in the Pollok and surrounding area."

"I'm sorry, but I don't know what you mean by Class A and Class B drugs."

He tightly smiles and takes a deep breath before he replies, "Suffice to say they're not drugs you get prescribed down at the chemists, eh? Anyway, our Drug Squad were well aware of McMillan's involvement in the trade, but were unable to make any headway in bringing him to court. The main problem was he had such a tight control over the youths in the area that he used them to both collect and deliver the drugs as well as intimidating the local populace. He made them too afraid to speak out against him. Do you follow?"

I slowly nod that I understand, slowly because my head is again pounding.

"He shrewdly conducted this campaign of harassment against not just your street, but other streets in the area so that while everyone likely knew he was responsible, you and your neighbours would be too terrified to speak out against him."

"That's true," I tell him.

"Indeed. Anyway, he also had to control his own gang and he did this by randomly meting out violence when he believed this was justified. Any slight discretion by any of the gang resulted in at least a kicking or at worst…"

He sat back in his chair and stared straight at me.

"When Alex Paterson was murdered, we thought at first it was a random attack. We even considered it was some kind of revenge attack for the murder of poor Missus Laurie who was hit by the brick. I understand you were in the hall that night?"

"I was," I confirm to him and I hear the tremor in my voice.

"A sad night for all," he again sighs. "At the time, I considered a number of options as to why Paterson was murdered." He stops and again stares at me. "That was just after your own friend Mister Toner was assaulted, wasn't it?"

"Aye, it was about then I think."

"Well, it seems that Paterson was one of the persons who assaulted Mister Toner and we even considered that perhaps him or a family member or friend might have been responsible," then surprises me by adding, "but we soon discounted that theory."

Where is he going with this story I'm wondering and I feel my breathing becoming a little more rapid.

"Would you like a drink of water?" asks the other detective.

Gratefully, I nod and accepting the paper cup he brings to me from the sink in the room, I can't stop my hand from shaking.

I'm holding it with both hands to keep it steady and sipping at it when the nurse pokes her head round the door, but before she even speaks, I'm raising a hand and telling her, "I'm fine nurse, honest. The officer needs to tell me something."

She pulls an unhappy face and with obvious reluctance, closes the door behind her.

Now, I'm thinking, why the *heck* didn't I take the opportunity to get them the hell out of here?

"Good man," McManus tightly smiles at me. "Now, where was I? Oh, aye. I'm in the incident room at Pollok and I'm considering a surveillance operation against the main figure in the drug inquiry, but I'm assured by the divisional surveillance team leader," and it's obvious from his face, he wasn't happy with what he was told, "that the Pollok area is unsuitable for close surveillance. However, there then occurs another murder, that of Calum Black. Now, we were led to believe that it was a tall, well built black man who murdered Black, but we quickly discounted that…"

Here we go, I'm thinking.

"…and believe that some sort of makeup had been applied to the culprits face to disguise him."

He pauses for breath and continues, "Our inquiries then discover that Black, like Paterson who was also an associate of McMillan, was deeply in debt and owed a substantial amount of money for drugs that he and his father had obtained from McMillan." He stopped to draw breath and gave a quick glance to the other detective before continuing. "Then as you will be aware of course, there is the third murder of Kylie Morrison, yet another close associate of McMillan. In fact later intelligence has indicated that last year, Morrison's sister bore McMillan's child."

That will be the fifteen year old, I'm thinking. Bloody pervert! The lassie can only have been fourteen when he…he…doesn't even bear thinking about!

"Our inquiries into the Morrison family have discovered that Kylie was attempting to extort money from McMillan to keep the family's mouths shut about his siring a child with her underage sister, Charlene."

He grinned at me. "Sounds a bit like a television soap, doesn't it, Jimmy?"

I can only numbly nod at him.

"Well, in the midst of this I had obtained a warrant to use CCTV cameras in certain crucial area that over a period of time, provided me with enough intelligence to identify and evidence the goings on with McMillan's gang regarding their drug dealing activities and I'm pleased to say that over the last few days, drug squad and CID officers are rounding up a significant number of the gang who will in due course appear in court to answer a plethora of charges relating to these activities. Needless to say, a fair number of them have turned Queens Evidence and provided us with statements that firmly and categorically place Neil McMillan at the hub of this spider's web."

He stares at me and then say, "Now, about the three murders."

This is it and I prepare myself.

"It wasn't till last Monday, the day before you were attacked, that I was able to obtain authorisation for a foot and vehicular surveillance of McMillan and his vehicle."

He sees my eyes narrow and asks, "Are you still with me here, Jimmy? I'm not going too fast for you, am I?"

I shake my head and then I ask, "You say his vehicle. Is it like my Escort? A dark coloured car?"

"Aye," he nods to me, his eyes continuing to bore into mine. "A navy blue coloured Mitsubishi Lancer. It's an older car, Jimmy; why, do you remember seeing it?"

I shake my head and hope he doesn't realise I'm holding out on him as I say, "Just some kind of fleeting memory of a car."

Like I told you before, keep it near to the truth and keep it simple. That way it's easy for me to recall what I've said.

"Good, good. Hopefully it will come back to you. Anyway, the surveillance team followed him on Monday and then again on Tuesday and it was on Tuesday night when they saw him turn into Hapland Avenue and stop the car near to a man; that man was you, Jimmy. As the team scrambled to get into a position to see what was happening, they thought it was some kind of handover of drugs. The weather was raining and it was pretty dark, but they watched McMillan approach you and then in the confusion, they see him with you pressed against a hedge and he seems to be assaulting you. Then as they run at him, they see him lift a weapon, a homemade baton as it turns out and strike you on the head with it."

He sits back, his narrative almost complete and takes a deep breath. "I'm sorry Jimmy…"

Here it comes, I'm thinking.

"…they didn't stop him in time and he almost killed you using the same baton he murdered the other three with."

Time stands still.

Did I hear him correctly?

Did he say, "…that *he* murdered the other three with?"

McManus must see the shock on my face and mistakes it for anger or annoyance or whatever, for he then adds, "We let you down, Jimmy. You might have been killed right in front of a full police surveillance team. I can only offer you my *deepest* apology and let me assure you, heads *will* roll for this."

At first I'm too afraid to speak in case this is some sort of joke, but then I find my voice and I ask him, "He killed the other three?"

"Oh aye," McManus nods. "Of course, he's denying it," and softly laughing, tells me, "He's alleging the weapon belongs to you."

"Belongs to me?"

I must have sounded pretty surprised when I said that, for McManus shakes his head and it seems obvious he didn't believe McMillan.

"We've got him in possession of it, trying to murder you with it, his previous acrimony and threats towards you and an incident that was recorded by our CCTV cameras outside St Convals church where he, ah…"

"Kicked me on the arse," I helpfully interrupt.

"Yes, indeed. That evidence plus we have the statement of Paterson who confesses that McMillan evinced ill-will towards you and his statement includes McMillan's instruction your shed be broken into and drugs planted to liable you to prosecution. As for the weapon itself, we've matched it to the wounds of the three victims so there's no doubt it *is* the weapon he used. Alex Paterson apparently had a fall out with him some days before he was murdered, Calum Black owed him a substantial amount of drug money and of course the girl Morrison was trying to screw him for cash because of his unlawful sex with her younger sister. All three had in their own way incurred his hatred and for that they paid the ultimate price. According to statements from his former gang members, McMillan made it no secret he would murder anyone who stepped out of line."

He forces a smile in an attempt at humour and tells me, "You were lucky your skull is a wee bit thicker."

"He clearly had it in for you, Mister McGrath," interjects the other detective.

I'm still stunned that they think the baton belongs to McMillan.

"So, is he being…"

"Charged with the three murders? Oh aye, Jimmy. He's already been to court and remanded till time of trial, though to be honest with you, I don't see us getting any kind of plea. Not for a charge of three murders. He's kicking up blue murder and insisting he's innocent, but the evidence against him is, frankly, overwhelming."

He sighs and as if apologising, tells me, "There *is* the likelihood you might have to give evidence about the attempt on your life, but don't be worrying about it. We've plenty of police witnesses who saw you being attacked so if your memory of the incident fails you…"

He leaves the rest unsaid and I decide there and then that maybe it will be a good time when I go to court to conveniently forget that night and I'll need to practice shrugging my shoulders in front of the wardrobe mirror. Besides, it what Mister Colquhoun told me is correct, I should have a cracking scar on my head to point to.

"What about Missus Laurie, the woman that got killed by the gang? Have you charged somebody with her murder yet?"

McManus sighs and shrugs his shoulders. "We're still trying to solve that one, Jimmy, but those of the gang who know are so far keeping their mouths shut and the only thing we do know with any certainty is that it wasn't McMillan who was responsible. Well, I should say not *personally* responsible, but he certainly was the driving force behind the gang's violence. Whether or not the Crown Office will be able to justify a charge against him, I can't say with any certainty. I'm of the opinion that in the dark the gang member who threw the brick that killed her wasn't seen by any of his pals and for obvious reasons, he or she is keeping their mouth shut."

I could go on about the rest of their visit, but my minds in a whirl and they obviously think they've worn me out, for I can see the concern on their faces at how pale I am, so much so that before they go McManus calls for a nurse to check on me.

So basically, the story is that I murder three wee shites and Neil McMillan, who failed to murder me, gets done for the murders. Added to that the bonus is Scooby is now safe and Paterson's in the jail.

With luck like this I'll need to get the nurse to put me a lottery ticket on tonight.

The rest of the afternoon passes quickly.

I get an evening visit from Scooby and Alice who insist that when I'm discharged, which by the way won't be for at least another week till the operational wound in my noggin mends, I'm to stay with them till I'm back on my feet.

I don't argue because Alice is weeping throughout the visit and keeps leaning across to kiss my cheek and stroke my bandaged head and I don't want to upset her anymore than she already is.

Through her tears, she tells me that during the period I was unconscious, Father Stephen had been down visiting me and she was to let me know that he'd be back tomorrow morning and that prayers were being said daily for me at each Mass.

According to Scooby, I'm the talk of Pollok and that there are a fair number of pints being put behind the bar for me at Howden's and he'll be happy to help me drink them.

They're away about half an hour when the auxiliary nurse, do they still get called that these days I wonder, comes round with the tea trolley and a slice of toast.

I'm still a bit dazed and not because of the injury; I'm finding it hard to relax after the news DCI McManus broke earlier.

I've just finished the tea when the door gets knocked and I get another visitor.

DC Hopkins, dressed in a charcoal grey trousers suit with a lighter grey coloured blouse beneath the jacket, her blonde hair plaited and hanging over her left shoulder, says, "Can I come in, Jimmy?"

Right away I'm wary. Don't get me wrong, I don't thing what McManus told me is a trick or anything. I believed him when he told me that McMillan is in the jail for the murders.

But let's face it; you know that I'd already decided DC Hopkins is more than just a pretty face. She's a sharp cookie is this lassie.

I push myself into a better sitting position and I invite her to sit down.

She draws a chair up to the side of the bed and grimacing, tells me, "I told the nurse that I needed to urgently speak with you regarding your statement. A wee white lie, so don't be telling on me, eh? Oh, and I forgot to bring grapes."

Now I *think* she's joking about the grapes, but the one thing I've learned about Ella Hopkins is that I can't let my guard down, not for one second.

"I'm pleased to see you, I think," I warily tell her, but she just smiles; it's one of them what they call beguiling smiles and I'm sure has caused many men to let their guard down with her.

"I understand the DCI and the DI called in earlier today to speak with you," she says.

"Aye, they told me about Neil McMillan."

She nods and glancing around her, says, "Nice room. I gather you'll be here for about a week?"

"At least a week, so they say," I shrug. "Can I ask you; is this an official visit? Are you really here to take a statement or something?"

She stares at me and sitting comfortably back in her chair, slowly shakes her head. "No, this is a personal visit, Jimmy; just to have a wee chat between me and you."

There's a short silence and then she says to me, "Can I share something with you about me, Jimmy, something that will remain between us?"

I slowly nod and underneath the sheets, I'm shaking because there's that old feeling back again. This lassie scares me. No, not physically; it's her manner and besides, I'm still certain that she knows I'm the murderer.

"I'd like to tell you a story, Jimmy. Please, let me finish it and honestly, there's no need for you to even make any comment. Just let me finish my story and then you and I can come to an agreement." She takes a breath and slowly exhales through pursed lips. "My brother Ian and I were orphaned when I was ten and he was twelve. It was a stupid and wasteful accident that took my parents from us when the boat they were sailing on Loch Lomond one weekend overturned and they hadn't bothered with lifejackets. No health and safety in those days unfortunately and they drowned. Of course, at that age it would have been simple for the family to have us taken into care by the local council, but my mum's older sister wouldn't hear of it and even though they had their own four kids, they took us in."

She drew a deep breath and stared at me as I sat there listening. "Things were a bit tight for a working class couple with four kids, so you can imagine they got even tighter with another two kids to feed and clothe. But my auntie," she smiled as if at some distant memory. "She managed to cope and I never once heard her complain. Her husband, my uncle worked every hour God sent as a welder in the shipyard in Govan. Birthdays and Christmas," she shakes her head, "we never wanted for a single thing. I shared a room with my two cousins and Ian was in with the boys. It was a three bedroom mid-terraced house in Pollok, Jimmy; much like your own house and actually not too far from where you live. As time went on, we six kids all grew up and while the others stayed local with their jobs or got married, I had itchy feet and I joined the RAF when I was nineteen and became a military policewoman. When my six year enlistment was finished it seemed a natural transition to join the civilian police and that's what I did. So here I am today, thirty-three years of age and a detective; a happily married wife and mother with my own wee girl. Now, with my RAF police service and my civilian police service, I think it's fair of me to say I've seen and done quite a bit; I've experienced policing in the war theatres of Iraq and Afghanistan," she smiles humourlessly and adds, "as well as some of the less salubrious areas of Glasgow. What I've learned and seen has changed me a bit and some of what I've learned has taught me that the law and justice is *not* the same thing. Does that sound strange to you, Jimmy?"

I'm staring back at her and really, I don't know how to answer this. What the heck is she getting at, I wonder?

She draws another deep breath and holding up her hand, says, "Don't bother answering that. It's just an observation, so let me finish my story. While I was away serving in the RAF, my auntie Terry worried herself sick about me being in these war zones. She'd write to me weekly, send me shoeboxes full of goodies and light a candle every Sunday at Mass asking God to keep me safe. Well," she shrugs and smiles, "it seems to have worked for here I am, sharing a bit of my life story with you, Jimmy."

I'm about to speak, but she holds up her hand to stop me and says, "Ah, ah, Jimmy. Let me finish. Anyway, my wee auntie Terry lit her candles to keep me safe, but unfortunately nobody lit any candle for her. So, there she is one Saturday night with my uncle Marty, dancing away with her friends in the church hall when a brick comes through the window and hits her on the head and sadly, she later dies from her injury."

My God, I swallow with difficulty! Her auntie Terry is Theresa Laurie! I never would have guessed! It all makes sense now; the detective in the yard at the police office with his condolence and her presence with the family at the funeral ceremony.

Her eyes are bright with unshed tears and blinking them away, she stares at me, her voice now beginning to quake.

"Like I said, Jimmy, the law and justice is not the same thing. The *bastard* from the gang that killed my wee auntie Terry might not get caught by us, but three of them are dead and their boss is in the jail and unlikely to get back out again anytime soon."

Now she's staring hard at me, her voice unconsciously rising as she angrily adds, "Those *shits* in that gang frightened a community and the police couldn't do a bloody thing about it! They pedalled their drugs and terrorised people in their own homes with impunity and a complete disregard for a law and police service that couldn't do a thing to stop them! Well," she calms a little, "then something changed and I have my suspicions that it was a local man, a wee decent man, who took it upon himself to do something about the gang who were threatening his friend and his community."

She's slowly shaking her head as she stares at me, then holds up her hand and says, "Don't you dare speak, Jimmy McGrath. It's only a suspicion based on nothing other than my own intuition and it's not evidence. If it *were* evidence, Jimmy, I would probably be legally bound as a police officer to report it, but how can I report a feeling? How can I tell my boss I *think* he might have arrested the wrong man for the murders of three members his own gang, a gang that is responsible for so much heartache in the community as well as the death of my auntie Terry?"

She stops and I see a lump in her throat and her shoulders slump as a tear trickles down her cheek.

"I loved my wee auntie Terry. She never had a bad word to say about anyone and my uncle Marty will be lost without her. Already I'm watching him waste away without her."

She shakes her head as if to clear it and then abruptly stands up.

"I'm glad he didn't kill you, Jimmy, and that Neil McMillan will get at his sentencing what he *definitely* deserves. I'm glad that you're going to be okay, but I will be really, *really* upset if I hear that anybody else in the Pollok area gets hurt again because I hope that the problems that plagued the area are now mainly gone. You *are* a decent wee man Jimmy McGrath and I would prefer that you stay that way. Do we understand each other?"

I force a smile and tell her, "Yes, Ella. We understand each other," and I nod as if to confirm that her warning is absolutely clear.

She returns my nod with her own smile and then without a backward glance, opens the door and leaves the room.

They say that confession is good for the soul.

I can't confirm that because even if I ever again attend at Mass, I will not be making my confession anytime soon.

No, my confession to a good man like Father Stephen would place an unfair burden on him and so I must carry the knowledge of what I have done with me.

Well, not exactly me alone.
Each night before I go to bed I have a little two minute chat with my Jeannie and I ask her, can I be forgiven?
Then of course, you too know so my question is, would *you* forgive me?

Needless to say, this story is a work of fiction. As readers of my previous books may already know, I am an amateur writer and therefore accept that all grammar and punctuation errors are mine alone. I hope that any such errors do not detract from the story.
If you have enjoyed the story, you may wish to visit my website at:
www.glasgowcrimefiction.co.uk

I also welcome feedback and can be contacted at:
george.donald.books@hotmail.co.uk